罗尔德·达尔短篇故事品读及汉译探索（第1卷）

An Interpretation of Short Stories by Roald Dahl and Their Chinese Translations (Volume 1)

于本凤　王永胜　著
YU Ben-feng, WANG Yong-sheng

哈爾濱工業大學出版社

内容简介

本书系对英国作家罗尔德·达尔"非儿童类"短篇故事(小说)进行研究所著系列图书中的第1卷,包括11部短篇小说。这些小说长短不一、难易各异,按照不同的主题分成四章加以编排,分别为"愿赌服输""莫惹娇妻""战争创伤"和"战场硝烟"。每章收录至少两篇作品,包括原作导读、原作释读和翻译探索。

本书适合英语专业的大学本科生及研究生阅读、研究、翻译之用(不少小说也可供高中生阅读、学习),也适合广大的文学爱好者阅读,更适合搞英汉翻译或外国文学研究的学者、教师、学生等阅读、参考。

图书在版编目(CIP)数据

罗尔德·达尔短篇故事品读及汉译探索.第1卷/于本凤,王永胜著.—哈尔滨:哈尔滨工业大学出版社,2014.4
ISBN 978-7-5603-4541-3

Ⅰ.①罗… Ⅱ.①于… ②王… Ⅲ.①短篇小说-小说研究-英国-现代 ②短篇小说-文学翻译-英国-现代 Ⅳ.①I561.074

中国版本图书馆CIP数据核字(2013)第300135号

责任编辑 田新华
封面设计 思 华 高永利
出版发行 哈尔滨工业大学出版社
社 址 哈尔滨市南岗区复华四道街10号 邮编150006
传 真 0451-86414749
网 址 http://hitpress.hit.edu.cn
印 刷 哈尔滨市工大节能印刷厂
开 本 880mm×1230mm 1/32 印张11 字数380千字
版 次 2014年4月第1版 2014年4月第1次印刷
书 号 ISBN 978-7-5603-4541-3
定 价 38.00元

前言

对于罗尔德·达尔,中国读者耳熟能详的恐怕是他的一些儿童文学作品,国内外对他称呼最多的莫过于"儿童文学作家"。他的儿童文学作品的确十分畅销,几乎家喻户晓。可以说,在所有儿童文学作家中,罗尔德·达尔是最为成功、最为知名的作家之一。达尔的书深受全世界小朋友的喜爱,其中包括《詹姆斯与大仙桃》(*James and the Giant Peach*)、《查利与巧克力工厂》(*Charlie and the Chocolate Factory*)、《魔法手指》(*The Magic Finger*)、《查利与大玻璃升降机》(*Charlie and the Great Glass Elevator*)、《了不起的狐狸爸爸》(*Fantastic Mr. Fox*)、《特威特夫妇》(*The Twits*)、《女巫》(*The Witches*)、《好心眼儿的巨人》(*The BFG*,1983 年获"惠特布雷德奖"——Whitbread Award)以及《玛蒂尔达》(*Matilda*)等。

然而,作为英国儿童文学作家的罗尔德·达尔还写过其他类型的文学作品,特别是那些"非儿童类"(个别篇章具有"儿童类"文学作品特点,但由于是罗尔德·达尔早期作品,也被收录进来,作为研究的对象)的短篇小说(也可以说"成人类"短篇小说,即为成年人写的文学作品。当然,这些作品中有些具有"成人"色彩——含有色情内容,但达尔"成人"作品中的色情内容大多是比较"隐晦"的。这样的"成人"作品,基本收录在他的《迷情乱性》——Switch Bitch 一书中)也同样精彩。其实,这些"非儿童类"短篇故事(小说)绝大多数是达尔转笔写儿童文学作品之前完成的。这些作品受到西方 19 世纪现实主义文学的影响,多数采用现实主义的创作手法。同时,他也从美国短篇小说家欧·亨利(O. Henry)那里汲取了一定的营养。就达尔作品本身对人物和景物的描写来看,可以说,他是"20 世纪英国变形精神世界的一位工笔画家"(陈钰,1985)。同他的儿童文学作品一样,他早期这些"非儿童类"作品也具有结尾出奇、结局令人意想不到等特点,但是,他此类短篇小说这方面的特点尤其突出。这类作品充满奇思妙想,人物刻画细腻入微,其中不乏道貌岸然者、悲观主义者、心理变态者。此类作品也不乏荒谬、贪婪、邪恶、虚伪的成分,其中的人物大都在"机关用尽"之时,一不小心就"栽了跟头",或者在"聪明绝顶"之际,反而被自己的"聪明"所误。

罗尔德·达尔的父母是挪威人,达尔本人1916年出生在英国格拉摩根郡的兰达夫(Llandaff, Glamorgan,格拉摩根原来是英国南威尔士的一个郡——笔者注),并在雷普顿公学(Repton School)接受教育。第二次世界大战爆发,他应征入伍,加入英国皇家空军,驻扎在内罗毕。后来,加入驻利比亚的一个战斗机中队,受了重伤。之后,又作为一名战斗机飞行员到希腊和叙利亚参加战斗。1942年,达尔作为英国大使馆的空军助理专员去了华盛顿。华盛顿成为他人生的转折点,因为在那里他开始了自己的创作生涯。随后,他被调到情报部。战争结束的时候,他成为英国皇家空军中校。他的第一批短篇小说共有12篇,都是根据他战争期间的经历写成。这12篇作品首先发表在美国的一些主流杂志上,后来编撰成书出版,书名为《向你飞跃》(*Over to You*)。

罗尔德·达尔所有受到高度赞誉的作品都被译成多种文字,成为全世界的畅销书。安格利亚电视台(Anglia Television)将他的一些短篇小说改编成电视系列剧,冠以标题《出乎意料的故事集》(*Tales of the Unexpected*)。他的作品还包括两本自传——《男孩时代》(*Boy*)和《独闯天下》(*Going Solo*),还有赢得很多赞誉的小说《我的叔叔奥斯瓦尔德》(*My Uncle Oswald*),以及《罗尔德·达尔的鬼怪故事集》(*Roald Dahl's Book of Ghost Stories*)。最后一本是他自己编辑的。在生命的最后一年,他收集了一些奇闻轶事,并跟妻子弗利西蒂(Felicity)一道,整理了一些烹饪食谱,汇编成一本书。这本书1996年由企鹅出版集团出版,书名为《罗尔德·达尔的烹饪书》(*Roald Dahl's Cookbook*)①。

---

① Roald Dahl. *The Best of Roald Dahl*[M]. England: Penguin Books Ltd., 2006。

罗尔德·达尔于1990年11月去世。《泰晤士报》(*The Times*)称其为“我们这一代人中,最为有影响力的作家之一,也是拥有极其广泛读者群的作家之一”,并在写给他的讣告中写道:“孩子喜欢他写的故事,把他当成自己心目中最喜爱的人……他的作品将成为未来的经典之作”。据报道,在2000年英国的“世界图书日”(*World Book Day*)投票中,罗尔德·达尔当选为“读者最喜爱的作家”(Favourite Author)①。

对于20世纪的英国作家罗尔德·达尔及其作品,《爱尔兰时报》(Irish Times)的一篇评论,可谓一语中的:“罗尔德·达尔是我所认识的为数不多的作家之一,可以准确无误地说,其作品令人沉醉、上瘾。他的作品始终贯穿着一条主线,这条主线令人毛骨悚然,充满恶意和凶险,但却更加行之有效,因为其来源是一些不起眼的、几乎微不足道的日常事物。结果,最为错综复杂的黑色幽默便应运而生了”②。

罗尔德·达尔在20世纪中叶之所以蜚声世界,就是因为他所创作的这些“非儿童类”的短篇小说(当然,个别篇章具有“儿童类”文学作品特点)。但是,当时中国翻译出版业不是很发达,对他的作品译介的也不是很多。就算是有所译介,也是零星的“散兵作战”状态,不成体系。在全球化浪潮滚滚而来的今天,研究罗尔德·达尔的这部分作品,并系统地加以翻译,就如同打开尘封已久的大门,门内的景色依然会令当代中国读者惊喜不已。对于广大的英语学习者和文学爱好者来说,阅读达尔的这部分作品将会带来迥然不同的人生体验。其实,罗尔德·达尔这部分短篇小说的实质和绝妙,可以从英美主流媒体的评价窥见一斑:

“Roald Dahl is the prince of storytellers.” —*Daily Mail*

“罗尔德·达尔是位讲故事的王子。” ——(英国)《每日邮报》

---

① Roald Dahl. *The Collected Short Stories of Roald Dahl*[M]. England: Penguin Books Ltd., 1992。

② 著者译自 Roald Dahl (1916—1990) “*The Best of Roald Dahl*” (《罗尔德·达尔小说精品集》)一书的封底(back cover)。此书由英国“Penguin Books Ltd.”出版公司于2006年出版发行。

"The absolute master of the twist-in-the-tale" —*The Observer*

"绝对的大师,其故事的结局出人意料。"

——(英国)《观察家报》

"These stories pack their punch." —*The Observer*

"这些故事蓄满了惊人之力。" ——(英国)《观察家报》

"An unforgettable read, don't miss it." —*Sunday Times*

"一次难忘的阅读体验,不可错过。"

——(英国)《星期日泰晤士报》

"One of the most widely read and influential writers of our generation" —*The Times*

"我们这一代人中,(罗尔德·达尔是)最为有影响力的作家之一,也是拥有极其广泛读者群的作家之一。"——(英国)《泰晤士报》

"Dahl is too good a storyteller to become predictable, so you never know whether the tyrant or the tyrannized will win in the end."

—*Daily Telegraph*

"达尔的故事讲得太精彩了,结局简直令人无法预测。因此,你永远都无法得知,最后的赢家是残暴的人,还是受到残暴对待的人。"

——(英国)《每日电讯报》

"Dahl has the mastery of plot and characters possessed by great writers of the past, along with a wildness and wryness of his own. One of his trademarks is writing beautifully about the ugly, even the horrible."

—*The Los Angeles Times*

"达尔拥有以往伟大作家的资质——善于营造情节、精于刻画人物,但达尔也拥有自己荒诞不经的一面,以及自己的一套挖苦讥讽的手段。其中的一个标志就是他对丑陋之人的精妙刻画,更有甚者是对恐怖之人的精妙刻画。" ——(美国)《洛杉矶时报》

“An ingenious imagination, a fascination with odd and ordinary detail, and a lust for its thorough exploitation are the... strengths of Dahl's storytelling.” —*The New York Times Book Review*

“达尔写作的影响力在于其独特的想象力，在于其对稀奇古怪和平淡无奇的细节的着迷程度，在于其对细节完完全全加以利用的欲望。”

——(美国)《纽约时报·书评》

“The mind of Roald Dahl is quintessentially nasty and wicked.”

—*The Washington Post*

“罗尔德·达尔的思维具有典型的特点，那就是肮脏和邪恶。”

——(美国)《华盛顿邮报》

在此前提下，研究并翻译罗尔德·达尔的“非儿童类”短篇小说，将具有一定的学术价值和社会价值，会为中国文学的百花园增添一个品种，会为文学翻译者提供一个可供参考的文本。

在历时三年多对罗尔德·达尔“非儿童类”(个别篇章具有“儿童类”文学作品特点，但由于是罗尔德·达尔早期作品，也被收录进来，作为研究的对象)短篇故事(小说)进行研究和翻译的过程中，共收集到长短不一的此类作品60篇，并站在一定的角度，根据个人的理解，细加编排，精心安排，详加注释，分册编辑，最终通过翻译，引介给中国读者。

本书在对罗尔德·达尔短篇小说的翻译探索中，采取了严谨的翻译态度，形成了以下基本的翻译思路：

(1)人名、地名按照一定的标准进行“异化”式翻译(极个别人名作了“归化”式处理)，主要依据《世界人名翻译大辞典》(新华社译名室编，中国对外翻译出版公司1993年第一版，2007年第二版)以及《世界地名翻译大辞典》(周定国主编，中国出版社集团、中国对外翻译出版社公司2008年第一版)等，个别的人名、地名的翻译兼顾了流行的译法。

(2)绝大多数非国际化的度量衡单位，特别是英制的度量衡单位,采用"同化"或"归化"的处理方法,以便汉语言思维者能形象化加以理解。

(3)每一篇的题目都采用汉语四字格来处理,以求汉语的工整,发挥汉译的四字格表达的优势,但同时最大限度地兼顾原文题目的字面意义。

(4)就汉译本整体而言,尽量杜绝"翻译腔",以保持汉语语言的纯洁性和规范性。

(5)尽量完美再现原文的风格,虽然做到这一点并不是轻而易举的事情。原文有些风格,在翻译中只能退其次而求之——基本上采用"归化"处理手法,照顾了汉语的通畅性。比如,原文中很多非标准的英语表达汉译时就没有在"风格"上充分得以体现,这也是以后有待继续探讨的一个翻译问题。

当然,"金无足赤,人无完人",匆忙且蹒跚的步履必将会迈步"不和谐"的步伐。在对罗尔德·达尔的"非儿童类"短篇故事(小说)进行研究、翻译并成书的过程中,不当、甚至错误之处在所难免,还望读者不吝赐教,多多批评,特别是多做文学翻译方面的批评。

需要特别声明的是,本系列书中所引的罗尔德·达尔原著内容以及所做的翻译探索,旨在学术研究,不做商业用途。

于本凤　王永胜

2014年1月于渤海大学所在地

——古城锦州

目 录

第一章 愿赌服输

赌,乃人之天性;赌,乃残酷无情;赌,乃有败有胜;赌,更多的是让人痴醉狂疯。还是汉语中的四个字说得好:愿赌服输。

“愿赌服输”这个四字词语出自“《春秋》第3卷,原文‘怀公怒,欲杀之,术急曰,赌者必有输,何故迁怒与人’,后作‘愿赌服输’”①。

愿赌服输,不管你的赌注是一根小手指,还是全部的家当;愿赌服输,不管你赌的是名贵的凯迪拉克、客船航行的里程,还是训练有素的赛犬;愿赌服输,不管你是“南方来客”,还是“费西先生”,还是什么三教九流,终将“赌海沉溺”。

突然之间,曾经的一首中文流行歌曲浮现在脑海,其中几句歌词可谓精彩:

这次到底谁赢谁输?
原来我拿幸福当成了赌注。
输了你,我输了全部。
谁叫我拿幸福当成了赌注?

① 参见“百度百科”相关词条,网址:http://baike.baidu.com

输了你,我愿赌服输[①]。

那么,就让我们走进罗尔德·达尔三篇小说里的世界,去细心体会"愿赌服输"的精彩吧。

第一节 《南方来客》*Man from the South*

罗尔德·达尔的《南方来客》(*Man from the South*)首次发表在《科利尔》杂志(*Collier's*,也有人译作《柯里尔》《科里尔》或《柯莱尔斯》)1948年9月4日出版的那一期上,题目叫《收藏品》(*Collector's Item*)。后来,这个故事以"*Man from the South*"为题,收录到《罗尔德·达尔小说精品集》(*The Best of Roald Dahl*)、《出乎意料的故事集》(*Tales of the Unexpected*)、《罗尔德·达尔短篇故事集锦》(*The Collected Short Stories of Roald Dahl*)、《如你之人》(*Someone like You*)等书中,也被改编成电影《非常赌注》(*The Bet*)以及电视系列剧——分别是1960年1月3日播映的《阿尔弗雷德·希区柯克出品短剧选》(*Alfred Hitchcock Presents*)中第168集(Episode 168),以及1979年3月24日播映的《出乎意料的故事集》(*Tales of the Unexpected*)第1部中的第1集(Episode 1.1)[②],可见其影响力之大。

顺便提一下,达尔似乎有更换小说标题的习惯,当初发表是这个题目,后来再发表又变成另一个题目,但换"汤"不换"药";或者说,

---

① 百代唱片公司1999年7月1日出版发行的那英个人专辑《干脆》中的一首歌曲《愿赌服输》。参见"百度百科"相关词条,网址:http://baike. baidu. com

② 以上信息以及本节以下部分资料取自克里斯廷·霍华德(Kristine Howard)创建并维护的网站"Roald Dahl Fans. com"(罗尔德·达尔粉丝网),网址为:http://www. roalddahlfans. com/,由著者翻译整理。以后各章的此部分信息,若没特殊标明,其出处则同此注

发表在这个地方是一个题目，发表到另一个地方却变成了另一个题目。当然，标题的最终确定的确是一件十分困难的事情，涉及诸多因素，这本来就是无可厚非的事情，有点类似文学作品翻译中对标题的处理。

一、原作导读

《南方来客》这篇小说，跟达尔的其他很多小说一样，故事的叙述者"我"身份不明确，或者说，叙述者处于"无名"的"隐性"状态，但是，纵观全文可以这样去设想：故事的叙述者"我"就是作家罗尔德·达尔本人，就是达尔本人的"化身"。

在牙买加一座宾馆的游泳池旁边，叙述者"我"正仰卧在躺椅里休息呢。这时，"我"注意到一位个头矮小、有点上了年纪的男子沿着游泳池边缘向"我"走来。他头戴一顶大大的、奶油色的巴拿马平顶草帽。一番交谈之后，他跟"我"坐到了一起。听口音，他是南美人，算是一位南方来客了。没过多大工夫，一个美国男孩和一个英国女孩也加入到我们行列中来，跟我们坐到了一块儿。美国男孩给我们每人递上一支香烟，并吹嘘说自己的打火机一打就着——哪怕是在这样的风刮得很厉害的天气里。于是，这位南方来客就问男孩是否愿意就此打个赌。南方人说，要是男孩连续十次将火机打着，就把自己那辆崭新的"凯迪拉克"给男孩，但是，男孩要是输掉的话，他就将男孩左手的小手指砍下来。

经过一番苦苦的思考之后，男孩子最终同意跟他赌一把。于是，"我"跟着他们，包括那个女孩，一起到了南方人所住的房间。南方人有条不紊地做着赌前各项准备工作。他将男孩子的手绑到桌子上，只允许小手指伸出来，他自己则拿着一把砍刀站在男孩子身边，做好了随时要砍掉小手指的准备。

男孩子用另一只手连续八次成功地将火机打着之后，房间的门突然打开，一名妇女说着西班牙语闯了进来。她喊叫着，将南方人推倒在床，同时向其他人道歉，说她不应该丢下他不管。她还说，在家乡的时候，他赢过 47 根手指了，但最终，她将他的一切都赢到自己的手中,但是赢的过程漫长而艰辛。

小说的最后,叙述者"我"要离开的时候,看了看那个女人的一只手,那只手上只剩下一根手指和一只大拇指了——"I can see it now, that hand of hers; it had only one finger on it, and a thumb"。

二、原作释读

下面是罗尔德·达尔这篇小说的原文,难度适中,但麻烦之处是对小说中主人公那口非标准英语的理解。写到关键时刻,达尔及时收笔,故事悬念顿生,耐人寻味。

Man from the South[①]

It was getting on towards six o'clock so I thought I'd buy myself a beer and go out and sit in a deck-chair[②] by the swimming pool and have a little evening sun.

I went to the bar and got the beer and carried it outside and wandered down the garden towards the pool.

It was a fine garden with lawns and beds[③] of azaleas[④] and tall coconut palms[⑤], and the wind was blowing strongly through the tops of

---

① 本部小说原文出自"*Roald Dahl. The Best of Roald Dahl*[M]. England: Penguin Books Ltd., 2006."

② deck chair or deck-chair: *Noun* a folding chair for use outdoors; a wooden frame supports a length of canvas 帆布躺椅;甲板折椅;折叠帆布长椅

③ bed: Noun a plot of ground in which plants are growing 苗圃;花坛

④ azalea: *Noun* any of numerous ornamental shrubs grown for their showy flowers of various colors 杜鹃花

⑤ coconut palm: *Noun* tall palm tree bearing coconuts as fruits widely planted throughout the tropics 椰子树;椰树

the palm trees[1], making the leaves hiss[2] and crackle[3] as though they were on fire. I could see the clusters of big brown nuts hanging down underneath the leaves.

There were plenty of deck-chairs around the swimming pool and there were white tables and huge brightly coloured umbrellas and sunburned men and women sitting around in bathing suits. In the pool itself there were three or four girls and about a dozen boys, all splashing[4] about and making a lot of noise and throwing a large rubber ball at one another.

I stood watching them. The girls were English girls from the hotel. The boys I didn't know about, but they sounded American, and I thought they were probably naval cadets[5] who'd come ashore from the US naval training vessel which had arrived in harbour that morning.

I went over and sat down under a yellow umbrella where there were four empty seats, and I poured my beer and settled back[6] comfortably with a cigarette.

It was very pleasant sitting there in the sunshine with beer and

---

① palm tree: *Noun* any plant of the family Palmae having an unbranched trunk crowned by large pinnate or palmate leaves 棕榈树

② hiss: *Noun* a fricative sound (especially as an expression of disapproval) 嘶嘶声;(表示反对或嘲笑的)嘘嘘声(e. g. The speaker was received with a mixture of applause and hisses. 那演说者同时得到喝彩声和嘘声。)

③ crackle: *Noun* the sharp sound of snapping noises 轻微的爆裂声;噼啪声

④ splash: *Verb* cause (a liquid) to spatter about, especially with force 使(液体)溅起(e. g. The children love splashing water over each other. 儿童喜欢互相泼水。)

⑤ cadet: *Noun* a military trainee (as at a military academy) 陆军或海军学校学员

⑥ settle back: sit back 仰坐

cigarette. It was pleasant to sit and watch the bathers splashing about in the green water.

The American sailors were getting on nicely with the English girls. They'd reached the stage where they were diving under the water and tipping them up by their legs[①].

Just then I noticed a small, oldish man walking briskly[②] around the edge of the pool. He was immaculately[③] dressed in a white suit and he walked very quickly with little bouncing strides, pushing himself high up on to his toes with each step. He had on a large creamy Panama hat[④], and he came bouncing along the side of the pool, looking at the people and the chairs.

He stopped beside me and smiled, showing two rows of very small, uneven teeth, slightly tarnished. I smiled back.

"Excuse pleess[⑤], but may I sit here?"

"Certainly," I said. "Go ahead."

He bobbed around to the back of the chair and inspected it for safety, then he sat down and crossed his legs. His white buckskin[⑥] shoes had little holes punched all over them for ventilation.

---

① to tip someone up by their legs 抓住他人的腿抬起来(将他人扔倒)(e. g. A youth sprinted past, tipping over her glass. 一个年轻人冲过去,把她的玻璃杯撞翻了。)

② brisk: *Adjective* quick and energetic;轻快的;活泼的;伶俐的(e. g. The actress is walking at a brisk pace. 那位女演员正以轻快的步伐走着。)

③ immaculately: *Adverb* in an immaculate manner 干净地;无瑕疵地

④ Panama hat: *Noun* a stiff straw hat with a flat crown 巴拿马(式);平顶的草帽

⑤ pleess:"please"的非标准发音形式

⑥ buckskin: *Noun* a soft yellowish suede leather originally from deerskin but now usually from sheepskin 鹿皮;硝好的羊皮

"A fine evening," he said. "They are all evenings fine here in Jamaica[①]." I couldn't tell if the accent were Italian or Spanish, but I felt fairly sure he was some sort of a South American. And old too, when you saw him close. Probably around sixty-eight or seventy.

"Yes," I said. "It is wonderful here, isn't it."

"And who, might I ask, are all dese[②]? Dese is no hotel people." He was pointing at the bathers in the pool.

"I think they're American sailors," I told him. "They're Americans who are learning to be sailors."

"Of course dey[③] are Americans. Who else in de[④] world is going to make as much noise as dat[⑤]? You are not American no?"

"No," I said. "I am not."

Suddenly one of the American cadets was standing in front of us. He was dripping wet from the pool and one of the English girls was standing there with him.

"Are these chairs taken?" he said.

"No," I answered.

"Mind if I sit down?"

"Go ahead."

"Thanks," he said. He had a towel in his hand and when he sat down he unrolled it and produced a pack of cigarettes and a lighter. He offered the cigarettes to the girl and she refused; then he offered them to

---

① Jamaica: *Noun* a country on the island of Jamaica; became independent of England in 1962; much poverty; the major industry is tourism 牙买加(1962年从英国独立出来,十分贫穷,以旅游业为主。)

② dese:"these"的非标准发音形式

③ dey:"they"的非标准发音形式

④ de:"the"的非标准发音形式

⑤ dat:"that"的非标准发音形式

me and I took one. The little man said, "Tank[①] you, no, but I tink[②] I have a cigar." He pulled out a crocodile case and got himself a cigar, then he produced a knife which had a small scissors in it and he snipped the end off the cigar.

"Here, let me give you a light." The American boy held up his lighter.

"Dat will not work in dis[③] wind."

"Sure it'll work. It always works." The little man removed his unlighted cigar from his mouth, cocked his head on one side and looked at the boy.

"All-ways[④]?" he said slowly.

"Sure, it never fails. Not with me anyway."

The little man's head was still cocked over on one side and he was still watching the boy. "Well, well. So you say dis famous lighter it never fails. Iss[⑤] dat you say?"

"Sure," the boy said. "That's right." He was about nineteen or twenty with a long freckled face and a rather sharp birdlike nose. His chest was not very sunburned and there were freckles there too, and a few wisps[⑥] of pale-reddish hair. He was holding the lighter in his right hand, ready to flip the wheel. "It never fails," he said, smiling now because he was purposely exaggerating his little boast. "I promise you it never fails."

---

① tank:"thank"的非标准发音形式

② tink:"think"的非标准发音形式

③ dis:"this"的非标准发音形式

④ all-ways:"always"的非标准发音形式

⑤ iss:"is"的非标准发音形式

⑥ wisp: *Noun* a small tuft or lock 一缕;一绺(e. g. Wisps of smoke rose into the air. 缕缕轻烟袅袅升起。)

"One momint[1], pleess." "The hand that held the cigar came up high, palm outward, as though it were stopping traffic. "Now juss[2] one momint." He had a curiously soft, toneless voice and he kept looking at the boy all the time.

"Shall we not perhaps make a little bet on dat?" He smiled at the boy. "Shall we not make a little bet on whether your lighter lights?"

"Sure, I'll bet," the boy said. "Why not?"

"You like to bet?"

"Sure, I'll always bet."

The man paused and examined his cigar, and I must say I didn't much like the way he was behaving. It seemed he was already trying to make something out of this, and to embarrass the boy, and at the same time I had the feeling he was relishing[3] a private little secret all his own.

He looked up again at the boy and said slowly, "I like to bet, too. Why we don't have a good bet on dis ting? A good big bet."

"Now wait a minute," the boy said. "I can't do that. But I'll bet you a quarter. I'll even bet you a dollar, or whatever it is over here—some shillings, I guess."

The little man waved his hand again. "Listen to me. Now we have some fun. We make a bet. Den[4] we go up to my room here in de hotel where iss no wind and I bet you you cannot light dis famous lighter of yours ten times running without missing once."

---

① momint:"moment"的非标准发音形式

② juss:"just"的非标准发音形式

③ relish: *Verb* "Relish" is a word that normally refers to enjoying a simple pleasure, to enjoy without really doing anything about it. So if he's relishing a little secret all his own, it means that he's enjoying his little secret all to himself, and nobody else knows. 享受;从……获得乐趣

④ den:"then"的非标准发音形式

"I'll bet I can," the boy said.

"All right. Good. We make a bet, yes?"

"Sure, I'll bet you a buck."

"No, no I make you a very good bet. I am rich man and I am sporting man also. Listen to me. Outside de hotel iss my car. Iss very fine car. American car from your country. Cadillac①— "Hey, now. Wait a minute." The boy leaned back in his deck-chair and he laughed. "I can't put up that sort of property. This is crazy."

"Not crazy at all. You strike lighter successfully ten times running and Cadillac is yours. You like to have dis Cadillac, yes?"

"Sure, I'd like to have a Cadillac." The boy was still grinning.

"All right. Fine. We make a bet and I put up my Cadillac."

"And what do I put up?" The little man carefully removed the red band from his still unlighted cigar. "I never ask you, my friend, to bet something you cannot afford. You understand?"

"Then what do I bet?"

"I make it very easy for you, yes?"

"Okay. You make it easy."

"Some small ting② you can afford to give away, and if you did happen to lose it you would not feel too bad. Right?"

"Such as what?"

"Such as, perhaps, de little finger on your left hand."

"My what?" The boy stopped grinning.

"Yes. Why not? You win, you take de car. You looss③, I take de finger."

---

① Cadillac:一个著名汽车的品牌,通常译作"凯迪拉克",也有人译作"卡迪拉克"。本书采用的是前一个翻译。

② ting:"thing"的非标准发音形式

③ looss:"lose"的非标准发音形式

"I don't get it. How d'you mean, you take the finger?"

"I chop it off."

"Jumping jeepers! That's a crazy bet. I think I'll just make it a dollar."

The little man leaned back, spread out his hands palms upwards and gave a tiny contemptuous shrug of the shoulders, "Well, well, well," he said. "I do not understand. You say it lights but you will not bet. Den we forget it, yes?"

The boy sat quite still, staring at the bathers in the pool. Then he remembered suddenly he hadn't lighted his cigarette. He put it between his lips, cupped his hands around the lighter and flipped the wheel. The wick lighted and burned with a small, steady, yellow flame and the way he held his hands the wind didn't get to it at all. "Could I have a light, too?" I said.

"God, I'm sorry, I forgot you didn't have one."

I held out my hand for the lighter, but he stood up and came over to do it for me.

"Thank you," I said, and he returned to his seat.

"You having a good time?" I asked.

"Fine," he answered. "It's pretty nice here."

There was a silence then, and I could see that the little man had succeeded in disturbing the boy with his absurd proposal. He was sitting there very still, and it was obvious that a small tension was beginning to build up inside him. Then he started shifting about in his seat, and rubbing his chest, and stroking the back of his neck, and finally he placed both hands on his knees and began tap-tapping with his fingers against the knee-caps[①]. Soon he was tapping with one of his feet as well.

"Now just let me check up on this bet of yours," he said at last. "You say we go up to your room and if I make this lighter light ten times running I win a Cadillac. If it misses just once then I forfeit the little finger of my left hand. Is that right?"

"Certainly. Dat is de bet. But I tink you are afraid."

"What do we do if I lose? Do I have to hold my finger out while you chop it off?"

"Oh, no! Dat would be no good. And you might be tempted to refuse to hold it out. What I should do I should tie one of your hands to de table before we started and I should stand dere[②] with a knife ready to go chop de momint your lighter missed."

"What year is the Cadillac?" the boy asked.

"Excuse. I not understand."

"What year—how old is the Cadillac?"

"Ah! How old? Yes. It is last year. Quite new car. But I see you are not betting man. Americans never are."

The boy paused for just a moment and he glanced first at the English girl, then at me. "Yes," he said sharply. "I'll bet you."

"Good!" The little man clapped his hands together quietly, once. "Fine," he said. "We do it now. And you, sir," he turned to me, "you would perhaps be good enough to, what you call it, to—to referee." He had pale, almost colourless eyes with tiny bright black pupils.

"Well," I said. "I think it's a crazy bet. I don't think I like it very much."

---

① knee-cap: *Noun* the convex bone in front of the knee joint; the patella 膝盖骨

② dere:"there"的非标准发音形式

"Nor do I," said the English girl. It was the first time she'd spoken. "I think it's a stupid, ridiculous bet."

"Are you serious about cutting off this boy's finger if he loses?" I said.

"Certainly I am. Also about giving him Cadillac if he win. Come now. We go to my room."

He stood up. "You like to put on some clothes first?" he said.

"No," the boy answered. "I'll come like this." Then he turned to me. "I'd consider it a favour if you'd come along and referee."

"All right," I said. "I'll come along, but I don't like the bet."

"You come too," he said to the girl. "You come and watch."

The little man led the way back through the garden to the hotel. He was animated now, and excited, and that seemed to make him bounce up higher than ever on his toes as he walked along.

"I live in annex[①]," he said. "You like to see car first? Iss just here."

He took us to where we could see the front driveway[②] of the hotel and he stopped and pointed to a sleek pale - green Cadillac parked close by.

"Dere she iss. De green one. You like?"

"Say, that's a nice car," the boy said.

"All right. Now we go up and see if you can win her."

We followed him into the annex and up one flight of stairs. He unlocked his door and we all trooped into what was a large pleasant double bedroom. There was a woman's dressing - gown lying across the bottom of one of the beds.

---

① annex: *Noun* an addition that extends a main building 裙房；附属建筑物

② driveway: *Noun* a road leading up to a private house 车库通向马路的道路；私家车道（e. g. They parked in the driveway. 他们将车停在私家车道上。）

"First," he said, "we'ave[①] a little Martini[②]."

The drinks were on a small table in the far corner, all ready to be mixed, and there was a shaker and ice and plenty of glasses. He began to make the Martini, but meanwhile he'd rung the bell and now there was a knock on the door and a coloured maid came in.

"Ah!" he said, putting down the bottle of gin, taking a wallet from his pocket and pulling out a pound note. "You will do something for me now, pleess." He gave the maid the pound.

"You keep dat," he said. "And now we are going to play a little game in here and I want you to go off and find for me two—no tree[③] tings. I want some nails, I want a hammer, and I want a chopping knife, a butcher's chopping knife which you can borrow from de kitchen. You can get, yes?"

"A chopping knife!" The maid opened her eyes wide and clasped her hands in front of her. "You mean a real chopping knife?"

"Yes, yes, of course. Come on now, pleess. You can find dose[④] tings surely for me."

"Yes, sir, I'll try, sir. Surely I'll try to get them." And she went.

The little man handed round the Martinis. We stood there and sipped them, the boy with the long freckled face and the pointed nose, bare-bodied except for a pair of faded brown bathing shorts; the English girl, a large-boned fair-haired girl wearing a pale blue bathing suit, who watched the boy over the top of her glass all the time; the little man with the colourless eyes standing there in his immaculate white suit drinking

---

① 'ave = have

② Martini: *Noun* a type of vermouth produced in Italy(意大利产)马提尼酒,也有人译作"马丁尼酒",本书采用前一个翻译。

③ tree:"three"的非标准发音形式

④ dose:"those"的非标准发音形式

his Martini and looking at the girl in her pale blue bathing dress. I didn't know what to make of it all. The man seemed serious about the bet and he seemed serious about the business of cutting off the finger. But hell, what if the boy lost? Then we'd have to rush him to the hospital in the Cadillac that he hadn't won That would be a fine thing. Now wouldn't that be a really fine thing? It would be a damn silly unnecessary thing so far as I could see.

"Don't you think this is rather a silly bet?" I said. "I think it's a fine bet," the boy answered. He had already downed one large Martini.

"I think it's a stupid, ridiculous bet," the girl said. "What'll happen if you lose?"

"It won't matter. Come to think of it, I can't remember ever in my life having had any use for the little finger on my left hand. Here he is." The boy took hold of the finger. "Here he is and he hasn't ever done a thing for me yet. So why shouldn't I bet him? I think it's a fine bet."

The little man smiled and picked up the shaker① and refilled our glasses.

"Before we begin," he said, "I will present to de—to de referee de key of de car." He produced a car key from his pocket and gave it to me. "De papers," he said, "de owning papers and insurance are in de pocket of de car."

Then the coloured maid came in again. In one hand she carried a small chopper, the kind used by butchers for chopping meat bones, and in the other a hammer and a bag of nails.

"Good! You get dem② all. Tank you, tank you. Now you can go." He waited until the maid had closed the door, then he put the

① shaker: *Noun* [with modifier] a container used for mixing ingredients by shaking 摇动器(e. g. a cocktail shaker 鸡尾酒摇壶)

② dem:"them"的非标准发音形式

implements on one of the beds and said, "Now we prepare ourselves, yes?" And to the boy, "Help me, pleess, with dis table. We carry it out a little."

It was the usual kind of hotel writing desk, just a plain rectangular table about four feet by three with a blotting pad, ink, pens and paper. They carried it out into the room away from the wall, and removed the writing things.

"And now," he said, "a chair." He picked up a chair and placed it beside the table. He was very brisk and very animated, like a person organizing games at a children's party. "And now de nails. I must put in de nails." He fetched the nails and he began to hammer them into the top of the table.

We stood there, the boy, the girl, and I, holding Martinis in our hands, watching the little man at work. We watched him hammer two nails into the table, about six inches apart. He didn't hammer them right home; he allowed a small part of each one to stick up. Then he tested them for firmness with his fingers.

Anyone would think the son of a bitch had done this before, I told myself. He never hesitates. Table, nails, hammer, kitchen chopper. He knows exactly what he needs and how to arrange it.

"And now," he said, "all we want is some string." He found some string. "All right, at last we are ready. Will you pleess to sit here at de table?" he said to the boy.

The boy put his glass away and sat down.

"Now place de left hand between dese two nails. De nails are only so I can tie your hand in place. All right, good. Now I tie your hand secure to de table—so."

He wound the string around the boy's wrist, then several times around the wide part of the hand, then he fastened it tight to the nails. He made a good job of it and when he'd finished there wasn't any question about the boy being able to draw his hand away. But he could move his fingers. "Now pleess, clench de fist, all except for de little finger. You must leave de little finger sticking out, lying on de table."

"*Ex*-cellent! *Ex*-cellent! Now we are ready. Wid① your right hand you manipulate de lighter. But one momint, pleess."

He skipped over to the bed and picked up the chopper. He came back and stood beside the table with the chopper in his hand.

"We are all ready?" he said. "Mister referee, you must say to begin."

The English girl was standing there in her pale blue bathing costume right behind the boy's chair. She was just standing there, not saying anything. The boy was sitting quite still holding the lighter in his right hand, looking at the chopper. The little man was looking at me.

"Are you ready?" I asked the boy.

"I'm ready."

"And you?" to the little man.

"Quite ready," he said and he lifted the chopper up in the air and held it there about two feet above the boy's finger, ready to chop. The boy watched it, but didn't flinch② and his mouth didn't move at all. He merely raised his eyebrows and frowned.

"All right," I said. "Go ahead."

The boy said, "Will you please count aloud the number of times I light it."

"Yes," I said. "I'll do that."

With his thumb he raised the top of the lighter, and again with the thumb he gave the wheel a sharp flick. The flint sparked and the wick

---

① wid: "with"的非标准发音形式

② flinch: *Verb* draw back, as with fear or pain(因危险和痛苦)退缩;畏惧(e. g. She flinched at the acidity in his voice. 他尖刻的话音令她畏缩。)

caught fire and burned with a small yellow flame.

"One!" I called.

He didn't blow the flame out; he closed the top of the lighter on it and he waited for perhaps five seconds before opening it again.

He flicked the wheel very strongly and once more there was a small flame burning on the wick.

"Two!"

No one else said anything. The boy kept his eyes on the lighter. The little man held the chopper up in the air and he too was watching the lighter.

"Three!"

"Four!"

"Five!"

"Six!"

"Seven!" Obviously it was one of those lighters that worked. The flint gave a big spark and the wick was the right length. I watched the thumb snapping the top down on to the flame. Then a pause. Then the thumb raising the top once more. This was an all-thumb operation. The thumb did everything. I took a breath, ready to say eight. The thumb flicked the wheel. The flint sparked. The little flame appeared.

"Eight!" I said, and as I said it the door opened. We all turned and we saw a woman standing in the doorway, a small, black-haired woman, rather old, who stood there for about two seconds then rushed forward, shouting, "Carlos! Carlos!" She grabbed his wrist, took the chopper from him, threw it on the bed, took hold of the little man by the lapels[①] of his white suit and began shaking him very vigorously, talking

---

① lapel: *Noun* lap at the front of a coat; continuation of the coat collar(西服上衣或夹克的)翻领

to him fast and loud and fiercely all the time in some Spanish-sounding language. She shook him so fast you couldn't see him any more. He became a faint, misty, quickly moving outline, like the spokes① of a turning wheel.

Then she slowed down and the little man came into view again and she hauled him across the room and pushed him backwards on to one of the beds. He sat on the edge of it blinking his eyes and testing his head to see if it would still turn on his neck.

"I am sorry," the woman said. "I am so terribly sorry that this should happen." She spoke almost perfect English.

"It is too bad," she went on. "I suppose it is really my fault. For ten minutes I leave him alone to go and have my hair washed and I come back and he is at it again." She looked sorry and deeply concerned.

The boy was untying his hand from the table. The English girl and I stood there and said nothing.

"He is a menace," the woman said. "Down where we live at home he has taken altogether forty-seven fingers from different people, and has lost eleven cars. In the end they threatened to have him put away somewhere. That's why I brought him up here."

"We were only having a little bet," mumbled the little man from the bed.

"I suppose he bet you a car," the woman said. "Yes," the boy answered. "A Cadillac."

"He has no car. It's mine. And that makes it worse," she said, "that he should bet you when he has nothing to bet with. I am ashamed and very sorry about it all." She seemed an awfully nice woman.

---

① spoke: *Noun* each of the bars or wire rods connecting the centre of a wheel to its outer edge 辐条;轮辐

"Well," I said, "then here's the key of your car." I put it on the table.

"We were only having a little bet," mumbled the little man.

"He hasn't anything left to bet with," the woman said. "He hasn't a thing in the world. Not a thing. As a matter of fact I myself won it all from him a long while ago. It took time, a lot of time, and it was hard work, but I won it all in the end." She looked up at the boy and she smiled, a slow sad smile, and she came over and put out a hand to take the key from the table.

I can see it now, that hand of hers; it had only one finger on it, and a thumb.

三、翻译探索

就像对本篇的阅读和理解一样,翻译的麻烦之处也在于主人公那口非标准的英语,做到风格上的对等,并非易事。下面的译文只是在某些方面做出了相应的调整,很多地方没有做到风格上的完全再现,有待进一步的探索。若无特殊说明,"翻译探索"中的译文均为著者所译。

南方来客

将近六点了,我寻思着为自己买一瓶啤酒,然后到外面去,坐到游泳池边的折叠帆布躺椅上,享受一下夕阳的余晖。

我到酒吧买了啤酒,拿到外边,溜达着穿过花园向游泳池走去。

花园很不错,种了好几坛杜鹃花。里面有草坪,还有高高的椰子树。强风从棕榈树顶上吹过,叶子随风摆动,发出"嘶啦啦""噼啪啪"的声音,仿佛要着火似的。一抬头,我就看到一串串大大的椰子果悬吊在叶子下面。

游泳池周围有很多帆布躺椅、白色桌子、颜色鲜艳的六个太阳伞,还有皮肤晒得黝黑的男男女女。他们身穿泳衣,坐在那儿。泳池里,三四个女孩子和十二三个男孩子吵吵闹闹地把一只大橡皮球抛来抛去，弄得水花四溅。

我站在那儿看着。女孩是宾馆里的，都是英国人。男孩子嘛，我不认识，但口音听起来像美国人。我猜想，他们或许是海军学校的水手学员，刚从靠岸的美国海军训练舰下来。那艘训练舰是当天早晨到达的。

我走了过去，坐到一把黄色的太阳伞下，因为那里有四个空位子。我倒了杯啤酒，点了支烟，坐了下去，感到很是惬意。

坐在那儿享受着阳光，喝着啤酒，抽着烟，我感觉快活无比。坐在那儿，看着男男女女在绿汪汪的池子里玩得水花四溅，我感到惬意开心。

美国水手跟英国女孩玩得不亦乐乎，很是融洽。他们已经玩到了这样的地步：潜到水下，扯着腿，把人拽倒在水里。

就在那时，我注意到一个个子矮小、有点上了年纪的男子，沿着游泳池边缘敏捷地行走。他穿了一件白色的衣服，一点污渍也没有。他走得很快，每迈一步，他就稍微向上弹起一点，那是每迈一步，大脚趾就用力把他抬高的缘故。他头戴一顶大大的、奶油色的巴拿马平顶草帽。他沿着池边一路弹跳着走来。边走边看着那里的人和椅子。

他在我旁边停下来，笑了笑，露出两排小小的、高矮不齐的牙齿，但牙齿稍微有点发灰。我回应他一个微笑。

“情[①]原谅，坐这儿可以吗？”他英语说得不很标准。

“当然，”我回答。“请便。”

他回身看看椅子的后面，检查一下是否牢靠，然后叉腿坐了下来。他脚蹬一双鹿皮鞋，鞋面打满了通风用的小孔。

“傍晚不错，”他说。“在牙买加这儿，所有傍晚都不错的。”我说不清他操的是意大利口音还是西班牙口音，但我感到相当有把握的

① 由于小说中说话者的发音不标准，为体现出原文的风格来，这里采取了一个权宜之计：将“请”字有意译成“情”。周全与否，有待探索。

是,他是美国南方某地的人,而且待他走近一看,年纪也不小了,约有六十八,或许有七十了。

“没错,”我回应道。“这儿很棒的,谁说不是呢?”

“那么,我可以问问,这伙儿是啥人呢?这伙儿人是非宾馆的。”一边说着不很标准的英语,一边指着泳池里的那些人。

“我想,他们是美国水手吧,”我回答。“他们是美国人,正在学习,准备当水手。”

“当然是美国人啦。世界上还有谁能像那啥那样吵吵闹闹呢?你不是美国人,俺说中没有?”

“是的,”我回答。“我不是美国人。”

猛然间,一个美国水手学员站到我们面前,身上湿漉漉地淌着从泳池里带上来的水,还有一个英国女孩跟他一起站在那儿。

“这些椅子有人吗?”他问。

“没有人,”我回答。

“可以坐吗?”

“请便。”

“谢谢,”他说。他手里拿了条毛巾。坐下后,把毛巾摊开,从中拿出一盒烟和一只打火机。他把烟递给那女孩,女孩没要;又递给我,我抽出一支。小个子男子说:“谢你,不要。不过,我有雪茄烟。”他随即打开一只鳄鱼皮包,为自己拿出一支雪茄,然后又拿出一把刀,刀上带一把小剪子,他打开刀上的小剪子,剪掉了雪茄烟的尾部。

“来,我给你点上吧,”美国男孩举起了打火机。

“那啥啊,这风大啊,点不着的。”

“肯定行,能点着。没有点不着的。”

小个子男子把未点火的雪茄从嘴里取下,头歪向一边,看着这个男孩子。

“没有……点不着的?”他慢慢地反问。

“肯定行,一打就着。起码,我没有失过手。”

小个子男子的头仍歪向一边,仍居高临下地看着男孩子。“喔,喔。这么说,你这是名牌打火机啦,一打就着。是你说的吗?”

“当然，”男孩回答。“是我说的。”他约摸有十九到二十岁的样子，一张长脸长满了雀斑，鼻子尖尖的，像鸟的尖嘴；胸部晒得不是很黑，也有些雀斑，还长了几缕灰中稍微带点红色的毛发。他右手握住火机，准备“啪”地一下转动轮子把火打着。“一打就着，”他边说，边微笑着，因为此时他是在有意“吹”大他那小小的“牛皮”，继续说：“我保证，我这火机一打就着。”

“情等一分钟。”他握雪茄的手高高抬起，掌心向外，摆出一副好像要来往车辆停住的架势。“现在，就一分钟。”他很好奇，声音也轻了许多，调子很平，发音不准，但始终盯着那男孩子看。

“或许，我们是否就那啥打个小赌呢？”他微笑地看着男孩。“就你的火机能不能打着火，我们小赌一把咋样？”

“太好了，我赌，”男孩应道。“干吗不赌呢？”

“你喜欢赌？”

“当然，我总赌。”

这个男子停顿了一下，看了看自己的雪茄烟。我必须承认，我不喜欢他的所作所为，似乎他想从赌博中捞点什么似的，似乎也想难为难为这个男孩子。同时，我感觉他正因为自己内心那点小算计而暗自得意呢。

他又抬头看了看男孩子，慢慢地说：“我也喜欢赌。我们为什么不就此好好赌一把？好好大赌一把。”

“现在，等一等，”男孩说。“我大赌不了。只是，我可以跟你赌二十五分硬币，甚至一元钱，或者任何我身上有的。我想，也可以赌些先令。”

小个子男子又挥了挥手。“听我说，现在我们来点有意思的。我们赌一把。我们到宾馆我的房间，没有风。我打赌，你无法把你这啥名牌火机打十次，而没有一次不失误的。”

“我打赌，我做得到，”男孩子说。

“那好吧。不错。我们赌一把，好吗？”

“当然。我跟你赌一块钱。”

“不，不。我跟你好好赌一把。我是有钱人，我也是一个好赌之人。听我说,这宾馆外面有我一辆车,很好的一辆车。美国车,你国家的,叫'凯迪拉克'来着……"

"嘿,现在等一下啊。"男孩子在椅子上向后一躺,大笑道:"我拿不出那样豪华的赌注。这有些疯狂啊。"

"一点也不疯狂。你十次都成功,把火机打着,凯迪拉克就归你了。你喜欢拥有这辆凯迪拉克,是吧?"

"当然,我想拥有一辆凯迪拉克。"男孩子还是张嘴笑着。

"好的,太好了。我们赌一把,我押上我的凯迪拉克。"

"那么,我押什么呢?"

小个子男子小心地把红色包装条从他那根还没有点着的雪茄烟上取下。"我的朋友,我从不要求你赌你支付不起的东西。你明白吗?"

"那我拿什么赌呢?"

"对你,这一把,我可以简单赌一下,可以吗?"

"好的。简单一赌。"

"赌某种你能给得起的小东西吧。要是碰巧输掉了,你也不觉得太可惜。行否?"

"具体说说。"

"比如,或许你左手那小手指啥的。"

"我那什么?"男孩子不再那么笑了。

"没错,何乐不为呢?你赢了,车你开走。你输了,手指我带走。"

"我不明白。手指你带走,是什么意思呢?"

"我把它剁下来。"

"我的老天爷啊!赌得忒疯狂啦。我想,我还是赌一元钱吧。"

小个子男子向后一仰,摊开双手,掌心朝上,双肩一耸,略微显示出一种鄙视的神情。"嘿,嘿,嘿,"他说。"这我就不明白了。你说火机准能打着,但却不愿意打赌。那啥,算了吧,可否?"

男孩子一动不动地坐着,盯着泳池里的人。接着,他突然想起,自己的烟还没有点呢。他嘴叼着烟,双手捂住打火机,"啪"地一转轮子,火机的芯捻就着了。黄色的火焰不是很高,但很稳,因为手把那火机挡得刚刚好，风根本吹不到。

“我能点一下火吗？”我问。

“哎呀，不好意思。我忘记你没有火机了。”

我伸手要拿火机，但他却站起来，走过来为我点上了。

“谢谢，”我说。他又回到座位上。

“你玩得好吗？”我问道。

“很好，”他回答。“这里真不错。”

紧接着，一阵沉默。我看得出，小个子男子的提议尽管荒谬，却很奏效，因为那个男孩子开始不安起来。他坐在那儿，一动也不动。很显然，他内心在微微地翻腾着，而且翻腾得愈来愈厉害。然后，他就开始在座位上换了一个姿势又一个姿势，手在胸前揉搓着，还拍了拍后脖颈。最后，双手放到膝盖上，手指开始不断地轻敲膝盖。很快，他的一只脚也开始敲打起来了。

“现在，我来把你说的赌注核实一遍啊，”他最终开口说话了。“你说，我们去你房间。如果我把火机打着十次，我就赢，凯迪拉克归我。如果哪怕有一次打不着，我就输掉我左手的小手指。是这样吗？”

“当然是的。那啥，就这样赌。可是，我看你害怕了。”

“要是我输了，我们怎样进行？我就伸出手指让你剁掉吗？”

“噢，不是那样的。那样不好。因为你会企图拒绝伸出手来。所以，在开始前，我要把你的一只手绑到那桌子上，我拿一把刀就站在那儿，时刻准备在你打不着火而输掉的时候，一刀剁下去。这就是我要做的。”

“凯迪拉克是哪一年的？”男孩问。

“抱歉，我——不懂。”

“哪一年……凯迪拉克开了多少年了？”

“啊，多少年啊？懂了。去年的。相当新的。但，我看得出，你不是打赌之人。美国人从来就不打赌的。”

男孩子顿了一小会儿，先看了看那个英国女孩，又看了看我。“好吧，”他尖声说道。“我跟你赌。”

“好样的！”小个子男子两手合到一起，拍了一下，但没有发出声响。“很不错,”他说。“我们现在就赌。你嘛,先生,”他转向我说,“或许,你可以充当——叫什么来着——裁判。”他的双眼暗淡,几乎没有什么颜色,瞳孔小得很,黑中透着亮光。

“噢,”我说。“我想,这赌得太疯狂了。我想,我很不喜欢这样赌。”

“我也不喜欢,”英国女孩说。这是她第一次开口说话。“我想,这赌打得很愚蠢、很荒谬。”

“要是这个男孩子输了,你要剁掉他的手指,此话当真?”我问。

“肯定当真的。他赢,我也给他凯迪拉克。来吧,到我的房间。”他站了起来。“你想先穿点衣服吗?”他问。

“不穿了,”男孩回答。“就这样来吧。”然后,男孩转向我说:“要是你一起来当裁判的话,我会很感激的。”

“好吧,”我说。“我来,但我不喜欢这样的赌法。”

“你也来吧,”他对女孩说。“你来看看。”

小个子男子带路,又经过花园,来到宾馆。他现在更活跃了,也很兴奋,走起路来大脚趾把他整个人弹起得比刚才更高了。

“我住在宾馆的裙房,”他说。“你们想先看看车吗?就在这儿。”

他带我们走到能看到宾馆前面停车道的地方,停了下来,手指向一辆光亮的、暗绿色的、紧靠车道停放的凯迪拉克。

“就是它啦,绿色的那个。你喜欢否?”

“哇,很不错的车,”男孩说道。

“好吧。现在我们上楼,看看你能否赢到手。”

我们跟随他来到了裙房,爬上一段楼梯。他开了房门,我们几个走了进去。里面是个双人间,屋子很大、很舒适,有一件女子的睡袍横放在其中一张床的床脚。

“我们,”他说,“先喝点马提尼酒吧。”

远处角落里的一张小桌上摆放着各种酒,随时准备调制。桌上还放了一个调酒用的摇匀器,还有冰块和很多玻璃杯。他开始调马提尼酒了,但与此同时又按了下铃。有人随即敲门,一个黑人女佣走了进来。

“啊,”他说。放下手中那瓶杜松子酒,从衣兜里掏出一个钱夹,抽出一张一英镑的钞票。“现在,你帮我做点事儿,拜托了。”说完,他把钞票塞给女佣。

“钱,你拿着,”他说。“现在,我们要在这儿玩一个小游戏,我要你出去为我弄那两样——不,三样东西:几枚钉子,一把锤子,还有一把砍刀,就是可以从那啥厨房借到的、屠夫砍东西用的那种刀。弄到这些东西,有困难吗?”

“一把砍刀!”女佣两只眼睛睁得大大的,双手紧紧扣在胸前。“你的意思是说,弄一把真的砍刀吗?”

“是的,当然。现在快去吧,拜托了。你肯定能为我弄到那啥些东西的。”

“是的,先生。我试试,先生。我肯定会设法弄到的。”她说完,就出去了。

小个子男子给每人递了一杯马提尼酒。我们就站在那儿,小口喝起酒来。长了一张长雀斑脸和尖鼻子的男孩子,除了一条褪了色的游泳短裤外,什么也没穿;长了一副大骨架、一头秀发的英国女孩穿了一件灰蓝色的泳装,始终透过杯沿看着那个男孩;眼睛没有颜色的小个子男子穿了件一尘不染的白衬衫站在那里,一边喝着马提尼酒,一边看着穿灰蓝色泳装的女孩。我却不知道如何是好。那男子似乎很把这一赌当回事儿,也似乎对剁手指这件事很当回事。可是,老天啊,男孩输掉可怎么办啊?那样的话,我们就必须用那辆他没有赢到手的凯迪拉克载他匆忙赶去医院,这也不算是很糟糕的事。那么,难道这真的是不很糟糕的事情吗?就我来看,这将会是一件倒霉的、愚蠢的事情,而且根本没有必要发生。

“难道你认为这赌打得不是相当的愚蠢吗?”我问。

“我想,这赌打得很好,”男孩回答。他已经喝下了一大杯马提尼酒。

“我想,这赌打得很愚蠢、很荒谬,”女孩说道。“要是你输了,如何是好?”

“不打紧的。想想啊,我从不记得一生中用我左手的小手指干过什么。就这只。”男孩握住那只指头。“就这只,从来没有为我做过什么事,哪怕是一件事。所以嘛,为什么不拿它来赌一赌呢?我想,这赌打得很好。”

小个子男子微微一笑,端起摇匀器,把我们的杯子又满上了。

“开始前,”他说,“我将把那啥……车钥匙……给裁判。”他从兜里掏出一把车钥匙,交给我。“那啥证件,”他说,“持车证件和保险都放在车的那啥匣子里。”

就在这时,黑人女佣又走了进来。一只手拿着一把小砍刀——就是屠夫砍带肉的骨头用的那种刀,另一只手拿了一把锤子和一袋钉子。

“很好。你都弄到了,谢你啦。现在你可以走了。”他一直等到女佣出去把门关好,才把所有的用具放到一张床上,说道:“现在,我们各自准备,可以吗?”他对男孩说:“情帮把手,把这张桌子挪一下,搬出来一点。”

这是一张很普通的、宾馆用的写字桌,一张很简朴的长方形桌子,约有一米二长、九十厘米宽,桌子上有吸墨垫、墨水、钢笔和纸。他们把桌子搬离墙壁,往屋子里靠,并把上面的写字用具拿开。

“那么,现在,”他说,“来把椅子。”他拿起一把椅子,放到桌旁。他动作敏捷,人也很活跃,就像儿童聚会上组织游戏活动的人。“现在拿钉子,我必须把钉子钉到那啥上去。”他取来钉子,开始用锤子在桌面钉了起来。

我们三个人——那男孩、女孩还有我——站在那儿,手里握着马提尼酒,看着那个小个子男子干这干那。我们看到他把两枚钉子钉到桌子上,相距约十五厘米。他没有把钉子全部钉进去,而是每枚留出一小部分在外头,然后用手指扳了扳,看牢不牢固。

我自己寻思着:谁都看得出来,这个婊子养的以前干过这事儿。他没有一点儿犹豫的意思,桌子啦、钉子啦、锤子啦、厨房用的砍刀啦,每样都丝毫不差。他知道自己需要什么,也知道如何安排这些东西。

“那么,现在,”他说,“我们只差一些线了。”他找到了线。“妥了,总算准备好了。情你坐到这儿,桌子旁边,”他对男孩子说道。

“现在,你把你那啥左手放到两枚钉子之间。只有靠那啥钉子把你的手固定到位啦。好了,很好。现在,我要把你的手牢牢固定到桌子上……是这样的。"

他把线绕着男孩的手腕缠了一下,然后又在男孩手部宽的部位缠了好几下,最后把线系到钉子上。这事他干得很麻利。干完后,一看就知道:男孩要想把手抽回去是完全不可能的,但手指还是可以动来动去的。

"现在情握紧拳头,但小手指不要收进去。你必须把小手指露出来,放到桌子上。"

"好——极啦!好——极啦!现在算是准备好了。用你的右手摆弄那啥打火机,但情稍等一分钟。"

他一下子蹦到床前,拿起那把砍刀,转身回到桌旁,手里握紧砍刀。

"我们大家都准备好了吧?"他问。"裁判先生,你必须喊开始,才能开始的。"

英国女孩穿着灰蓝色泳装,站在那儿,就站在男孩坐的那把椅子后面。她只是站在那儿,一言不发。男孩坐在椅子上,一动不动的,右手举着火机,眼睛看着那把砍刀。这时,小个子男子看了看我。

"你准备好了吗?"我问那男孩。

"准备好了。"

"你呢?"我问小个子男子。

"早就好了,"他说。然后把砍刀举起来,停在男孩手指上方约六十厘米的地方,随时准备一刀剁下去。男孩子看着刀,但并没有退缩,只是一言不发,抬起眼睛,皱着眉头。

"可以了,"我说。"开始。"

男孩说:"我点着的次数,你能数大声点吗?"

"好的,"我说。"可以的。"

他用大拇指把火机盖扳开,又用大拇指"啪"地使劲一拨轮子。只见火石发出火花,碰上芯捻,燃起小小的黄色火焰。

"一!"我大声数。

他并没有把火焰吹灭,而是把机盖合上灭火。等了约五秒钟,又打开盖子。

他又一次使劲拨动轮子,小小的黄色火焰随即在芯捻上燃起。

"二!"

谁都没有说话。男孩死死盯着火机,而小个子男子举着砍刀停在半空中,也盯着火机不放。

"三!"

"四!"

"五!"

"六!"

"七!"很显然,这个打火机算是好用的一个了:火石擦出的火花够大,芯捻长度也正合适。我看着他的大拇指"嘭"地合上盖子,压住了火焰。然后,又停了一下。紧接着,大拇指又把盖子弹起。这些都是拇指操作的,一切都是拇指完成的。我喘了口气,准备数"八"。他拇指拨动轮子,火石发出火花,小小火焰又出来了。

"八!"我喊道。刚喊完,门就开了。我们大家都转过身,看见一个女人站在门口。这个女人个子矮小,一头黑发,年纪不小了。她在门口那儿站立还没超过两秒钟,就向屋里冲来,喊道:"卡洛斯!卡洛斯!"她抓住他的手腕,夺下砍刀,扔到床上;又抓起小个子男子白色衣服的两个领角使劲摇晃着,始终操着一口听起来像某种西班牙语的口音咆哮着,语速很快、声音很大。她摇晃他时,速度太快了,快得就看不到他的样子了。他变成了一个轮廓,模模糊糊、朦朦胧胧的,而且越转越快,就像车轮旋转时轮辐所呈现出的令人眩晕的轮廓。

接着,她摇晃的速度渐渐慢了下来,小个子男子又清晰可见了。她拽着他穿过屋子,推推搡搡地致使他仰倒在其中一张床上。他起身坐到床边,眨了眨眼,目的是测试一下,看看项上人头是否仍在。

"我很抱歉,"那女子说道。"竟发生这样的事,我十分抱歉。"这时,她英语说得几乎无可挑剔了。

"太糟糕了,"她继续说。"我想,错误完全在我。我去洗头,让他单独呆了一会,才十分钟。这不,我回来一看,他又重操旧业了。"她看起来怀着歉疚又流露出深深的关切。

男孩子把手从桌子上解开。英国女孩和我站在那儿,什么也没说。

"他这个人到处惹麻烦,"女人说。"在我们老家那儿,他从不同人身上总共剁掉了四十七根手指,而他自己已经输掉了十一辆小汽车。最后,那些人威胁要把他送到某某地方关押起来。因此,我把他带到这里来了。"

"我们只是小小赌一把,"小个子男子在床那边嘟嘟囔囔地说。

"我猜,他跟你赌的是一辆车吧,"女子说道。

"是的,"男孩回答。"一辆凯迪拉克。"

"他哪有车啊,那是我的。这就更糟的,"她说,"糟就糟在,他一无所有、没有什么可赌时,竟然还跟你打赌。对此,我颇感耻辱,也很抱歉。"这个女人看起来相当不错。

"噢,"我说,"那么,这是你车的钥匙。"我把钥匙放到桌子上。

"我们只是小小赌一把,"小个子男子嘟嘟囔囔地说。

"他没有任何东西可赌,"女人说道。"他一无所有,身无分文。事实上,很早以前我从他那儿把所有东西都赢了过来。这过程很漫长,需要很多时间,也付出很多辛苦,但最终我都赢了过来。"她抬头看了看男孩子,慢慢地开始微笑,笑容中透着一丝伤感。她走过来,伸出一只手,拿起钥匙。

此时,我看到了她的那只手,上面只剩下一根手指,还有一个大拇指。

第二节 《赌海沉溺》*Dip in the Pool*

罗尔德·达尔的《赌海沉溺》(*Dip in the Pool*)首次发表在《纽约客》杂志(*The New Yorker*,也有人译作《纽约人》)1952 年 1 月 19 日出版的那一期上。后来,这篇故事收录到《罗尔德·达尔小说精品集》(*The Best of Roald Dahl*)、《出乎意料的故事集》(*Tales of the Unexpected*)、《罗尔德·达尔短篇故事集锦》(*The Collected Short Stories of Roald Dahl*)、《如你之人》(*Someone like You*)等书中,也被改编成电视系列剧——分别是 1958 年 6 月 1 日播映的《阿尔弗雷德·

希区柯克出品短剧选》(*Alfred Hitchcock Presents*)中的第113集(Episode 113),以及1979年5月12日播映的《出乎意料的故事集》(*Tales of the Unexpected*)第一部中的第8集(Episode 1.8),其影响力也是很大的。

一、原作导读

这部小说充满了微妙的色彩,这一点从小说的标题就可以窥见一斑。有意思的是,本故事的主人公博迪博尔先生(Mr. Botibol)跟达尔另一部短篇小说《音乐"大师"》(*Mr. Botibol*)中的主人公博迪博尔先生有着一样的名字。这从一个侧面说明,作家罗尔德·达尔对"素材"善于加以充分的利用,从他许多其他作品中也不难发现他的这一特点。

博迪博尔先生乘坐一艘客轮在大海上航行。他的心思放在客轮上常规的赌局上面:每天晚上,船长就会估算一下未来24小时轮船会航行的距离,然后将一组可能的航行距离数字公布给乘客,让乘客来"竞拍",哪位乘客要是猜中了第二天的航行距离数字就会赢得参加竞拍的人押上的那笔钱。

博迪博尔先生注意到,大海突然之间变得波涛汹涌起来,这当然会令船的航行速度减慢,船长估算的数字就会出现偏差。于是,他对赢得这场赌局变得信心十足起来,拿出了毕生的积蓄押到了"小点数"数字上。具体来说,在这部小说中,"小点数"就是指每一个低于五百零五的数字。

但是,事与愿违。第二天早晨醒来的时候,博迪博尔先生吃惊地发现大海风平浪静,客轮平稳行驶,就要把昨日耽搁的时间弥补回来了。这可怎么办呢?绝望之中,他得出了一个结论,认为唯一挽救的措施就是从甲板上跳下大海,让船上的人对他施救,从而减慢航行速度,才能得到那笔钱。对此,他做了精心的策划:穿上轻便的衣服,以便游起来轻松;要确保有人看见他"落水",以便向船长报告。而且,要尽可能游得离船远一些,好让船完全掉头对他施救。

来到甲板上以后,博迪博尔先生发现上面除了一位上了年纪的妇女之外，空空如也。跟老妇人进行了一番简短的交谈之后，他放心了：老妇人既不聋，也不瞎。于是，没多久，他纵身跃下，呼喊着"救命！救命！……"老妇人见状，迷茫了片刻，随后轻松起来，看着大海中的那个小人一上一下跳跃着，越来越远、越来越远……

故事结束的时候，一位骨感十足、棱角分明、戴了一副角质架眼镜的女子来到甲板上呼喊这位老妇人，埋怨老妇人不该私自出来瞎溜达，要老妇人跟她回去。老妇人笑了，笑得温文尔雅、令人信任。老妇人抓住刚上来那个女子的手，让她领着，穿过甲板往回走。

老妇人边往回走，边嘟嘟囔囔地说：

"多么好的一个人啊，"她说。"他向我挥手了。"（"Such a nice man，" she said. "He waved to me."）

二、原作释读

通读达尔的"非儿童类"短篇故事，发现达尔对于"赌"是"津津乐道"的，这也许是人之天性使然。本篇就是描写英式赌博中精彩的一篇。当然，有关"赌"的英文也就构成了理解本篇故事的一大障碍。

Dip in the Pool[①]

On the morning of the third day，the sea calmed. Even the most delicate passengers—those who had not been seen around the ship since sailing time—emerged from their cabins and crept on to the sun deck[②] where the deck steward gave them chairs and tucked rugs around their legs and left them lying in rows，their faces upturned to the pale，almost heatless January sun.

It had been moderately rough the first two days，and this sudden

---

① 本部小说原文出自"Roald Dahl. *The Best of Roald Dahl*[M]. England：Penguin Books Ltd.，2006"。

② sun deck：*Noun* an unroofed deck（客船上的）运动甲板；遮阳甲板

calm and the sense of comfort that it brought created a more genial① atmosphere over the whole ship. By the time evening came, the passengers, with twelve hours of good weather behind them, were beginning to feel confident, and at eight o'clock that night the main dining - room was filled with people eating and drinking with the assured, complacent air of seasoned sailors.

The meal was not half over when the passengers became aware, by the slight friction between their bodies and the seats of their chairs, that the big ship had actually started rolling again. It was very gentle at first, just a slow, lazy leaning to one side, then to the other, but it was enough to cause a subtle, immediate change of mood over the whole room. A few of the passengers glanced up from their food, hesitating, waiting, almost listening for the next roll, smiling nervously, little secret glimmers of apprehension in their eyes. Some were completely unruffled②, some were openly smug③, a number of the smug ones making jokes about food and weather in order to torture the few who were beginning to suffer. The movement of the ship then became rapidly more and more violent, and only five or six minutes after the first roll had been noticed, she was swinging heavily from side to side, the passengers bracing themselves in their chairs, leaning against the pull as in a car cornering.

At last the really bad roll came, and Mr. William Botibol, sitting at

---

① genial: *Adjective* diffusing warmth and friendliness 和蔼的;温暖的(e.g. a big, genial man of 45 一个身材高大,和蔼可亲的45岁男子)

② unruffled: *Adjective* free from emotional agitation or nervous tension 镇定的;平静的

③ smug: *Adjective* marked by excessive complacency or self-satisfaction 自满的;沾沾自喜的(e.g. He was feeling smug after his win. 他获胜以后很是得意。)

the purser's[①] table, saw his plate of poached turbot[②] with hollandaise[③] sauce sliding suddenly away from under his fork. There was a flutter of excitement, everybody reaching for plates and wineglasses. Mrs. Renshaw, seated at the purser's right, gave a little scream and clutched that gentleman's arm.

"Going to be a dirty night," the purser said, looking at Mrs. Renshaw. "I think it's blowing up for a very dirty night." There was just the faintest suggestion of relish in the way the purser said this.

A steward came hurrying up and sprinkled water on the table cloth between the plates. The excitement subsided. Most of the passengers continued with their meal. A small number, including Mrs. Renshaw, got carefully to their feet and threaded their ways with a kind of concealed haste between the tables and through the doorway.

"Well," the purser said, "there she goes." He glanced around with approval at the remainder of his flock who were sitting quiet, looking complacent, their faces reflecting openly that extraordinary pride that travellers seem to take in being recognized as 'good sailors'.

When the eating was finished and the coffee had been served, Mr. Botibol, who had been unusually grave and thoughtful since the rolling started, suddenly stood up and carried his cup of coffee around to Mrs. Renshaw's vacant place, next to the purser. He seated himself in the chair, then immediately leaned over and began to whisper urgently in the purser's ear. "Excuse me," he said, "but could you tell me something, please?"

---

① purser: *Noun* an officer aboard a ship who keeps accounts and attends to the passengers' welfare(轮船、班机等)事务长;(尤指客轮上的)乘务长

② turbot: *Noun* flesh of a large European flatfish 大菱鲆;比目鱼

③ hollandaise: *Mass Noun* a creamy sauce of melted butter, egg yolks, and vinegar, served especially with fish 蛋黄奶油酸辣酱

The purser, small and fat and red, bent forward to listen. "What's the trouble, Mr. Botibol?"

"What I want to know is this." The man's face was anxious and the purser was watching it. "What I want to know is will the captain already have made his estimate on the day's run—you know, for the auction pool? I mean before it began to get rough like this?"

The purser, who had prepared himself to receive a personal confidence, smiled and leaned back in his seat to relax his full belly. "I should say so—yes," he answered. He didn't bother to whisper his reply, although automatically he lowered his voice, as one does when answering a whisperer.

"About how long ago do you think he did it?"

"Some time this afternoon. He usually does it in the afternoon."

"About what time?"

"Oh, I don't know. Around four o'clock I should guess."

"Now tell me another thing. How does the captain decide which number it shall be? Does he take a lot of trouble over that?"

The purser looked at the anxious frowning face of Mr. Botibol and he smiled, knowing quite well what the man was driving at. "Well, you see, the captain has a little conference with the navigating officer, and they study the weather and a lot of other things, and then they make their estimate."

Mr. Botibol nodded, pondering this answer for a moment. Then he said, "Do you think the captain knew there was bad weather coming today?"

"I couldn't tell you," the purser replied. He was looking into the small black eyes of the other man, seeing the two single little specks of excitement dancing in their centres. "I really couldn't tell you, Mr. Botibol. I wouldn't know."

"If this gets any worse it might be worth buying some of the low numbers. What do you think?" The whispering was more urgent, more anxious now.

"Perhaps it will," the purser said. "I doubt whether the old man allowed for a really rough night. It was pretty calm this afternoon when he made his estimate."

The others at the table had become silent and were trying to hear, watching the purser with that intent, half-cocked, listening look that you can see also at the race track when they are trying to overhear a trainer talking about his chance: the slightly open lips, the upstretched eyebrows, the head forward and cocked a little to one side—that desperately straining, half-hypnotized, listening look that comes to all of them when they are hearing something straight from the horse's mouth.

"Now suppose you were allowed to buy a number, which one would you choose today?" Mr. Botibol whispered.

"I don't know what the range is yet," the purser patiently answered. "They don't announce the range till the auction starts after dinner. And I'm really not very good at it anyway. I'm only the purser, you know."

At that point Mr. Botibol stood up. "Excuse me, all," he said, and he walked carefully away over the swaying floor between the other tables, and twice he had to catch hold of the back of a chair to steady himself against the ship's roll.

"The sun deck, please," he said to the elevator man.

The wind caught him full in the face as he stepped out on to the open deck. He staggered and grabbed hold of the rail and held on tight with both hands, and he stood there looking out over the darkening sea where the great waves were welling up high and white horses[1] were riding against the wind with plumes of spray behind them as they went.

"Pretty bad out there, wasn't it, sir?" the elevator man said on the way down.

Mr. Botibol was combing his hair back into place with a small red comb. "Do you think we've slackened speed at all on account of the weather?" he asked.

"Oh, my word yes, sir. We slackened off considerable since this started. You got to slacken off speed in weather like this or you'll be throwing the passengers all over the ship."

Down in the smoking-room people were already gathering for the auction. They were grouping themselves politely around the various tables, the men a little stiff in their dinner jackets, a little pink and overshaved and stiff beside their cool white – armed women. Mr. Botibol took a chair close to the auctioneer's table. He crossed his legs, folded his arms, and settled himself in his seat with the rather desperate air of a man who has made a tremendous decision and refuses to be frightened.

The pool[2], he was telling himself, would probably be around seven thousand dollars. That was almost exactly what it had been the last two days with the numbers selling for between three and four hundred apiece. Being a British ship they did it in pounds, but he liked to do his thinking in his own currency. Seven thousand dollars was plenty of money. My goodness, yes! And what he would do, he would get them to pay him in hundred-dollar bills and he would take it ashore in the inside pocket of his jacket. No problem there. And right away, yes right away, he would

---

① white horse: *Noun* a wave that is blown by the wind so its crest is broken and appears white 波峰;浪尖

② pool: *Noun* the collective amount of players' stakes in gambling or sweepstakes; a kitty 集体赌注;抽头

buy a Lincoln convertible. He would pick it up on the way from the ship and drive it home just for the pleasure of seeing Ethel's face when she came out the front door and looked at it. Wouldn't that be something, to see Ethel's face when he glided up to the door in a brand-new pale-green Lincoln convertible! Hello, Ethel, honey, he would say, speaking very casual. I just thought I'd get you a little present. I saw it in the window as I went by, so I thought of you and how you were always wanting one. You like it, honey? He would say. You like the colour? And then he would watch her face.

The auctioneer was standing up behind his table now. "Ladies and gentlemen!" he shouted. "The captain has estimated the day's run ending midday tomorrow, at five hundred and fifteen miles. As usual we will take the ten numbers on either side of it to make up the range. That makes it five hundred and five to five hundred and twenty-five. And of course for those who think the true figure will be still farther away, there'll be 'low field' and 'high field' sold separately as well. Now, we'll draw the first numbers out of the hat... here we are... five hundred and twelve?"

The room became quiet. The people sat still in their chairs, all eyes watching the auctioneer. There was a certain tension in the air, and as the bids got higher, the tension grew. This wasn't a game or a joke; you could be sure of that by the way one man would look across at another who had raised his bid—smiling perhaps, but only the lips smiling, the eyes bright and absolutely cold. Number five hundred and twelve was knocked down for one hundred and ten pounds. The next three or four numbers fetched roughly the same amount.

The ship was rolling heavily, and each time she went over, the wooden panelling[1] on the walls creaked as if it were going to split. The passengers held on to the arms of their chairs, concentrating upon the auction.

"Low field!" the auctioneer called out. "The next number is low field."

Mr. Botibol sat up very straight and tense. He would wait, he had decided, until the others had finished bidding, then he would jump in and make the last bid. He had figured that there must be at least five hundred dollars in his account at the bank at home, probably nearer six. That was about two hundred pounds—over two hundred. This ticket wouldn't fetch more than that.

"As you all know," the auctioneer was saying, "low field covers every number below the smallest number in the range, in this case every number below five hundred and five. So, if you think this ship is going to cover less than five hundred and five miles in the twenty-four hours ending at noon tomorrow, you better get in and buy this number. So what am I bid?"

It went clear up to one hundred and thirty pounds. Others beside Mr. Botibol seemed to have noticed that the weather was rough. One hundred and forty... fifty... There it stopped. The auctioneer raised his hammer. "Going at one hundred and fifty..."

"Sixty!" Mr. Botibol called, and every face in the room turned and looked at him.

"Seventy!"

"Eighty!" Mr. Botibol called.

"Ninety!"

"Two hundred!" Mr. Botibol called. He wasn't stopping now—not

① paneling: *Noun* a panel or section of panels in a wall or door 镶板木料

for anyone.

There was a pause.

"Any advance on two hundred pounds?"

Sit still, he told himself. Sit absolutely still and don't look up. It's unlucky to look up. Hold your breath. No one's going to bid you up so long as you hold your breath.

"Going for two hundred pounds..." The auctioneer had a pink bald head and there were little beads of sweat sparkling on top of it. "Going..." Mr. Botibol held his breath. "Going... Gone!" The man banged the hammer on the table. Mr. Botibol wrote out a cheque and handed it to the auctioneer's assistant, then he settled back in his chair to wait for the finish. He did not want to go to bed before he knew how much there was in the pool.

They added it up after the last number had been sold and it came to twenty-one hundred-odd pounds. That was around six thousand dollars. Ninety per cent to go to the winner, ten per cent to seamen's charities. Ninety per cent of six thousand was five thousand four hundred. Well—that was enough. He could buy the Lincoln convertible and there would be something left over, too. With this gratifying thought he went off, happy and excited, to his cabin.

When Mr. Botibol awoke the next morning he lay quite still for several minutes with his eyes shut, listening for the sound of the gale, waiting for the roll of the ship. There was no sound of any gale and the ship was not rolling. He jumped up and peered out of the porthole. The sea—Oh Jesus God—was smooth as glass, the great ship was moving through it fast, obviously making up for time lost during the night. Mr. Botibol turned away and sat slowly down on the edge of his bunk. A fine electricity of fear was beginning to prickle under the skin of his stomach. He hadn't a hope now. One of the higher numbers was certain to win it after this.

"Oh, my God," he said aloud. "What shall I do?"

What, for example, would Ethel say? It was simply not possible to tell her he had spent almost all of their two years' savings on a ticket in the ships pool. Nor was it possible to keep the matter secret. To do that he would have to tell her to stop drawing cheques. And what about the monthly instalments[①] on the television set and the Encyclopaedia Britannica? Already he could see the anger and contempt in the woman's eyes, the blue becoming grey and the eyes themselves narrowing as they always did when there was anger in them.

"Oh, my God. What shall I do?"

There was no point in pretending that he had the slightest chance now—not unless the goddam ship started to go backwards. They'd have to put her in reverse and go full speed astern and keep right on going if he was to have any chance of winning it now. Well, maybe he should ask the captain to do just that. Offer him ten per cent of the profits. Offer him more if he wanted it. Mr. Botibol started to giggle. Then very suddenly he stopped, his eyes and mouth both opening wide in a kind of shocked surprise. For it was at this moment that the idea came. It hit him hard and quick, and he jumped up from the bed, terribly excited, ran over to the porthole and looked out again. Well, he thought, why not? Why ever not? The sea was calm and he wouldn't have any trouble keeping afloat until they picked him up. He had a vague feeling that someone had done this thing before, but that didn't prevent him from doing it again. The ship would have to stop and lower a boat, and the boat would have to go back maybe half a mile to get him, and then it would have to return to the ship, the whole thing. An hour was about

---

① instalment or installment: *Noun* a payment of part of a debt usually paid at regular intervals 分期付款;分期交付

thirty miles. It would knock thirty miles off the day's run. That would do it. 'Low field' would be sure to win it then. Just so long as he made certain someone saw him falling over; but that would be simple to arrange. And he'd better wear light clothes, something easy to swim in. Sports clothes, that was it. He would dress as though he were going up to play some deck tennis just a shirt and a pair of shorts and tennis-shoes. And leave his watch behind. What was the time? Nine-fifteen. The sooner the better, then. Do it now and get it over with. Have to do it soon, because the time limit was midday.

Mr. Botibol was both frightened and excited when he stepped out on to the sun deck in his sports clothes. His small body was wide at the hips, tapering upward to extremely narrow sloping shoulders, so that it resembled, in shape at any rate, a bollard①. His white skinny legs were covered with black hairs, and he came cautiously out on deck, treading softly in his tennis shoes. Nervously he looked around him. There was only one other person in sight, an elderly woman with very thick ankles and immense buttocks who was leaning over the rail staring at the sea. She was wearing a coat of Persian lamb and the collar was turned up so Mr. Botibol couldn't see her face.

He stood still, examining her carefully from a distance. Yes, he told himself, she would probably do. She would probably give the alarm just as quickly as anyone else. But wait one minute, take your time, William Botibol, take your time. Remember what you told yourself a few minutes ago in the cabin when you were changing? You remember that?

The thought of leaping off a ship into the ocean a thousand miles from the nearest land had made Mr. Botibol—a cautious man at the best

---

① bollard: *Noun* a short, thick post on the deck of a ship or a quayside, to which a ship's rope may be secured（码头或船上的）系缆桩;系船柱

of times—unusually advertent①. He was by no means satisfied yet that this woman he saw before him was absolutely certain to give the alarm when he made his jump. In his opinion there were two possible reasons why she might fail him. Firstly, she might be deaf and blind. It was not very probable, but on the other hand it might be so, and why take a chance? All he had to do was check it by talking to her for a moment beforehand. Secondly—and this will demonstrate how suspicious the mind of a man can become when it is working through self-preservation and fear—secondly, it had occurred to him that the woman might herself be the owner of one of the high numbers in the pool and as such would have a sound financial reason for not wishing to stop the ship. Mr. Botibol recalled that people had killed their fellows for far less than six thousand dollars. It was happening every day in the newspapers. So why take a chance on that either? Check on it first. Be sure of your facts. Find out about it by a little polite conversation. Then, provided that the woman appeared also to be a pleasant, kindly human being, the thing was a cinch② and he could leap overboard with a light heart.

Mr. Botibol advanced casually towards the woman and took up a position beside her, leaning on the rail. "Hullo," he said pleasantly.

She turned and smiled at him, a surprisingly lovely, almost a beautiful smile, although the face itself was very plain. "Hullo," she answered him.

Check, Mr. Botibol told himself, on the first question. She is neither blind nor deaf. "Tell me," he said, coming straight to the point, "what did you think of the auction last night?"

"Auction?" she said, frowning. "Auction? What auction?"

---

① advertent: *Adjective* giving attention 注意的;留意的

② cinch: *Noun* any undertaking that is easy to do 容易做的事情;必然发生的事

"You know, that silly old thing they have in the lounge after dinner, selling numbers on the ship's daily run. I just wondered what you thought about it."

She shook her head, and again she smiled, a sweet and pleasant smile that had in it perhaps the trace of an apology. "I'm very lazy," she said. "I always go to bed early. I have my dinner in bed. It's so restful to have dinner in bed."

Mr. Botibol smiled back at her and began to edge away. "Got to go and get my exercise now," he said. "Never miss my exercise in the morning. It was nice seeing you. Very nice seeing you..." He retreated about ten paces, and the woman let him go without looking around.

Everything was now in order. The sea was calm, he was lightly dressed for swimming, there were almost certainly no man-eating sharks in this part of the Atlantic, and there was this pleasant kindly old woman to give the alarm. It was a question now only of whether the ship would be delayed long enough to swing the balance in his favour. Almost certainly it would. In any event, he could do a little to help in that direction himself. He could make a few difficulties about getting hauled up into the lifeboat. Swim around a bit, back away from them surreptitiously① as they tried to come up close to fish him out. Every minute, every second gained would help him win. He began to move forward again to the rail, but now a new fear assailed② him. Would he get caught in the propeller? He had heard about that happening to persons falling off the sides of big ships. But then, he wasn't going to

---

① surreptitiously: *Adverb* in a surreptitious manner 秘密地(e. g. He was watching her surreptitiously as she waited in the hotel lobby. 她在宾馆的大厅等候时,他偷偷摸摸地观察着她。)

② assail: *Verb* attack someone physically or emotionally 攻击;猛击;痛打(e. g. The police were assailed with rocks. 警察遭到石块的猛烈攻击。)

fall, he was going to jump, and that was a very different thing. Provided he jumped out far enough he would be sure to clear the propeller.

Mr. Botibol advanced slowly to a position at the rail about twenty yards away from the woman. She wasn't looking at him now. So much the better. He didn't want her watching him as he jumped off. So long as no one was watching he would be able to say afterwards that he had slipped and fallen by accident. He peered over the side of the ship. It was a long, long drop. Come to think of it now, he might easily hurt himself badly if he hit the water flat. Wasn't there someone who once split his stomach open that way, doing a belly flop from the high dive? He must jump straight and land feet first. Go in like a knife. Yes, sir. The water seemed cold and deep and grey and it made him shiver to look at it. But it was now or never. Be a man, William Botibol, be a man. All right then now... here goes.

He climbed up on to the wide wooden toprail[①], stood there poised, balancing for three terrifying seconds, then he leaped—he leaped up and out as far as he could go and at the same time he shouted "*Help*!" "*Help*! *Help*!" he shouted as he fell. Then he hit the water and went under.

When the first shout for help sounded, the woman who was leaning on the rail started up and gave a little jump of surprise. She looked around quickly and saw sailing past her through the air this small man dressed in white shorts and tennis shoes, spread-eagled[②] and shouting as he went. For a moment she looked as though she weren't quite sure what she ought to do: throw a lifebelt, run away and give the alarm, or simply

---

① toprail: *Noun* rail on the top level 上横梁

② spread-eagle: *Verb* stretch out completely 作横"一"字形;手脚伸展;横跨(e. g. They spread-eagled him across the floor. 他们将他的四肢伸展开来,让他横躺在地板上。)

turn and yell. She drew back a pace from the rail and swung half around facing up to the bridge, and for this brief moment she remained motionless, tense, undecided. Then almost at once she seemed to relax, and she leaned forward far over the rail, staring at the water where it was turbulent in the ship's wake①. Soon a tiny round black head appeared in the foam, an arm raised above it, once, twice, vigorously waving, and a small faraway voice was heard calling something that was difficult to understand. The woman leaned still farther over the rail, trying to keep the little bobbing② black speck in sight, but soon, so very soon, it was such a long way away that she couldn't even be sure it was there at all.

After a while another woman came out on deck. This one was bony and angular③, and she wore horn-rimmed spectacles. She spotted the first woman and walked over to her, treading the deck in the deliberate, military fashion of all spinsters④.

"So *there* you are," she said.

The woman with the fat ankles turned and looked at her, but said nothing.

"I've been searching for you," the bony one continued. "Searching all over."

---

① wake: *Noun* the wave that spreads behind a boat as it moves forward 伴流;尾流;航迹(e. g. The motorboat's wake capsized the canoe. 机动船的尾流将独木舟掀翻了。)

② bob: *Verb* move up and down repeatedly 使上下(或来回)快速摆动(e. g. I could see his ginger head bobbing about. 我可以看到他姜黄色的脑袋在上下移动。)

③ angular: *Adjective* (of a person or part of their body) lean and having a prominent bone structure(人、身体部分)瘦骨嶙峋的

④ spinster: *Noun* an elderly unmarried woman; (synonym) old maid 未婚女人;老处女

"It's very odd," the woman with the fat ankles said. "A man dived overboard just now, with his clothes on."

"Nonsense!"

"Oh yes. He said he wanted to get some exercise and he dived in and didn't even bother to take his clothes off."

"You better come down now," the bony woman said. Her mouth had suddenly become firm, her whole face sharp and alert, and she spoke less kindly than before. "And don't you ever go wandering about on deck alone like this again. You know quite well you're meant to wait for me."

"Yes, Maggie," the woman with the fat ankles answered, and again she smiled, a tender, trusting smile, and she took the hand of the other one and allowed herself to be led away across the deck.

"Such a nice man," she said. "He waved to me."

三、翻译探索

本篇译文在标题的处理上,颇费周折。达尔原作标题具有双关性,具有一定的指代作用。对于赌博方面表达的处理,也是本篇故事翻译的棘手之处。

赌海沉溺

第三天的早晨,海面平静下来。即使那些最为娇气的乘客,也就是那些自起航以来一直没有露面的乘客,也从客舱里出来,登上客船的露天阳光甲板。在那里,甲板服务员为他们分发躺椅,用毯子为他们裹住腿,安排他们成排地躺着,脸朝上,冲着那轮苍白的、几乎不怎么温暖的太阳。当时正是一月份。

前两天的航程里,大海时而汹涌澎湃,时而平缓宁静。这突如其来的风平浪静,以及随之而来的惬意的感觉,更增添了整艘船亲切、祥和的气氛。夜晚降临时,乘客们感到信心十足:即将度过的十二小时会天气晴好、风平浪静。晚上八点的时候,客船的主餐厅挤满了人，他们吃的吃，喝的喝，脸上显露出老练水手才有的那种确信、得意的神情。

东西还没有吃到一半，乘客们就意识到，这艘大船又开始摇晃了，因为他们的身体开始跟座位发生轻微的摩擦。刚开始只是轻柔地晃动着，慢慢地、懒洋洋地晃向一边，再晃向另一边，但却足以让整个餐厅里人的情绪立即产生微妙的变化。其中有几个乘客一边吃着东西，一边抬起头观望，犹豫地等待着，几乎是在听下一波晃荡的动静；他们微笑着，却有点紧张兮兮；他们眼里微微闪动着小小的、不为人知的恐惧的光芒。他们中有些人完全是波澜不惊，有些人则毫不掩饰地幸灾乐祸。这些幸灾乐祸的人里面，有不少人竟然就吃的东西和天气开起了玩笑，目的就是折磨那几个由于摇晃而担惊受怕的人。船的摇晃突然变得越来越猛烈。从感觉到第一波晃动的时候起，过了才五六分钟，船体就十分剧烈地从船舷一边晃荡向另一边了。乘客牢牢地在座位上支撑着，对抗着摇晃产生的作用力，就像坐在转弯的小汽车里那样。

最后，真正糟糕透顶的摇晃终于开始了。此时，威廉·博迪博尔先生和乘务长坐在一张桌子旁。他看到，他叉子底下的盘子突然间滑走了，盘子里盛的是清蒸比目鱼，上面还浇了一层蛋黄奶油酸辣酱。顿时，一阵兴奋的声音响起，大家都伸手把住盘子和酒杯。坐在乘务长右边的伦肖夫人短短地尖叫一声，一下子抓紧了这位男士的胳膊。

"要度过一个脏兮兮的夜晚了，"乘务长看着伦肖夫人说道。"我想，大风会把这个夜晚吹得很脏。"从他说这话的方式来看，只能看出他有那么一点点开心的神态。

一个乘务员匆忙上来，端的水喷溅到盘子之间的桌布上。大家兴奋之情逐渐退去，但多数乘客继续用餐。包括伦肖夫人在内的那么几个乘客，小心翼翼地站起，在桌子间歪歪扭扭地往前走。他们走的时候，心里确实着急，但表面上却装作不紧不慢的样子走到了门口。

"噢，"乘务长说道，"她走啦。"他向四围看了看，对周围还没离开的那伙人投以赞许的目光。那伙人静悄悄地坐在那儿,一副副得意的样子,脸上明显流露出来的自豪感可非同一般——得到认可,成为一名“老练水手”,是任何一个游客都引以为荣的事情。

就餐完毕,咖啡端了上来。自船体晃荡时起,博迪博尔先生一直严肃有加、若有所思。突然,他站了起来,端着咖啡绕道走到伦肖夫人空座处,挨着乘务长,坐了下来。他刚一落座,身体就立即向后一倚,赶忙凑到乘务长耳边,小声说:“打扰了。不过,您能告诉我点事儿吗?”

乘务长个子矮矮的、身体胖胖的、脸部红红的。他身体向前倾斜,以便耳朵凑近听听。“有什么麻烦事吗,博迪博尔先生?”

“我想知道的是这事儿。”博迪博尔先生脸上露出焦虑的表情,而乘务长正看着他那张焦虑的脸。“我想知道的是,船长是否已经估算了今天的航程。你是知道的,主要是为拍卖而做的估算。我的意思是说,在没开始像这样波涛汹涌之前,是否已经估算了呢?”

乘务长凑近耳朵,本来认为会听到什么私人间的知心话,可一听到这话就微微一笑,身体随即在座位上向后一靠,放松一下他那紧绷绷的肚子。“我应该这样说:是的,”他回答。回答的时候,他自动压低声音,但并不是有意要低声耳语的,这就像有人对你低声耳语,你也低声耳语回应是一样的。

“你认为,大约是多长时间以前,他做的估算?”

“今天下午某个时候吧。他一般在下午做估算。”

“大约什么时间呢?”

“哎呀,我不知道。我估摸着,大约是四点。”

“现在,再告诉我件事儿吧。船长如何确定是哪一个数字呢?他是不是费尽周折才估算出来的呢?”

看着博迪博尔先生那张焦虑不安的、眉头紧蹙的脸,乘务长微微一笑,表示他清楚地知道这个伙计指的是什么。“噢,要知道,船长要跟航海长开一个小会,会上他们共同研究天气状况,还有很多其他因素,然后再做出估算。”

博迪博尔先生点了点头,琢磨一阵儿这个回答,随后说道:“你认为,船长知道今天会有恶劣天气吗?”

“这个我无法告诉你,”乘务长回应,盯着这伙计的小小的黑眼睛,只看到两点小小的、兴奋的火星在他眼球中心跳跃。“博迪博尔先生,我真的无法告诉你。我无从知道。”

“如果天气情况继续恶化下去,你认为,小点数是否值得一买呢?”现在,这伙计的耳语声变得更急切、更焦虑。

“或许值得吧,”乘务长回答。“我怀疑的是,这个老伙计是否考虑到,今晚真会波涛汹涌的。今天下午他估算的时候还是风平浪静的。”

同桌的其他人一言不发,尽力听着他俩说话,看着乘务长聆听时的神态:头半偏着,表情专注。这种情形在赛马场上也能看到:赌马人尽力侧耳细听驯马师谈论其马胜算的几率。驯马师有时嘴唇轻微张开,有时眉毛向上挑起,有时头向前伸去并向一边稍微一歪;赌马人仔细聆听的时候,神经紧绷、半信半疑,特别是当场亲耳听到某些话的时候。

“现在,设想让你买一个点数,你今天会选什么样的呢?”博迪博尔先生悄声问道。

“我还不知道点数范围有多大,”乘务长耐心地回答。“晚饭后竞拍才开始,到时候就会公布点数范围。无论如何,我真的不擅长这个。要知道,我只是个乘务长。”

就在那当儿,博迪博尔先生站了起来。“各位,我失陪一会儿,”说完,他就小心地踩着桌子之间那摇晃的地板走开。走的时候,有那么两次,他不得不抓住椅子的后背来抵消船体晃荡的力量,自己才能站稳一些。

“拜托,到露天阳光甲板,”他对电梯操作工说。

一踏上露天甲板,风“呼”的一声径直吹在他的脸上。他身体一个趔趄,随即双手猛地抓住栏杆,紧紧把住不放。他站在那儿,向外张望,看着远处逐渐黑下来的大海。只见海面上阵阵大浪高高竖起,浪尖被风卷着,向前奔腾,随即跌落下去,摔出无数浪花泡沫。

“先生,外面这儿天气十分恶劣,对吧?”电梯操作工要下去的时候说道。

博迪博尔先生用一把红色的小梳子将头发向后梳理成原来的样子。“由于天气的原因,你认为,我们的速度会迟缓下来吗?”他问道。

“噢,先生,要我说,会的。这种天气一开始出现,我们的速度就慢多了。像这样的天气,速度不慢下来的话,所有乘客在船上都会东倒西歪的啦。”

在下面的吸烟室里,人们已经聚集起来,等待竞拍开始。他们围着各式餐桌,分成一组一组的,彼此客客气气。做丈夫的穿着半正式的就餐晚礼服,显得有点拘谨,脸微微泛红,胡子剃得太狠,一动不动地站立着。他们胳膊白白的太太就在旁边,显得镇定自若。博迪博尔先生在靠近拍卖人的桌子旁坐下。他坐在座位上,双腿交叉,胳膊叉起,犹如做出重大决定后,孤注一掷的架势,可谓天不怕地不怕了。

他暗自思忖:赌金或许有七千美元左右吧。这个数目跟前两天竞拍所卖出的钱数差不多——每人出价在三百到四百之间。由于这是艘英国船,所以他们用英镑结算,可是他喜欢用自己国家的钱币来衡量。七千美元可不是一笔小数目啊。我的天,想想啊。他要做的就是,必须让他们给他支付一百美元大钞,他也好塞进上衣的内兜带上岸。应该是稳操胜券的。马上,对,就是马上,他要买一辆林肯牌活动顶篷式汽车。他会在回家途中把车买下,下船就开回家,目的就是想从埃塞尔的表情中获得快感:她从前门出来,一下子看到这辆车。他开着崭新的、暗绿色的林肯车——顶棚还可以折叠起来——慢慢滑行到家门前,然后再看看埃塞尔脸上的表情,那感觉是何等的了不起啊!他就会喊道:嗨,埃塞尔,我的心肝宝贝儿!可语气却要显得若无其事,会这样说:我想,我要为你买个小礼物。经过的时候,在橱窗里看到这辆车,于是马上就想到了你,想到你一直是多么想拥有这样的车。喜欢吗,心肝宝贝儿?喜欢这种颜色吗?然后,他就会看着她的脸。

他身后桌子旁的那个拍卖人站了起来。“女士们,先生们!”他大声说。“船长已经估算出今天的航程,截止明天中午,具体数值是五百一十五英里。按照常规,竞拍的航程的范围就是这个数字通过减十、加十获得,也就是在五百零五和五百二十五之间。当然啦,要是有谁认为真正的航程数离这个范围更远的话,也可以单独买'小点数'和'大点数'。现在,我们随意抽取第一个数字……看看,有了……五百一十二,有买的吗?"

屋子里静悄悄的。大家坐在椅子上,一动不动,所有的目光都投向这个拍卖人。空气中散发着某种紧张的气氛。随着价码出得越来越高,气氛也越来越紧张,因为这不是开玩笑,也不是玩游戏。这一点,从现场的情形就看得出来:一有人抬高价码,就有人看过去,看的时候或许会露出微笑。就算是微笑,也就是双唇微微那么一动,眼睛亮亮的,发出的绝对是冷光。

五百一十二这个数字最后在一百一十英镑这个价码上一锤定音。接下来的三四个数字的价码跟这个也差不多。

船摇晃得很厉害,而且每一次晃荡,墙上的木制镶嵌材料就会"嘎吱"作响,好像要裂开似的。乘客们则紧握椅子扶手,注意力都放到竞拍上面了。

"小点数!"拍卖人叫了出来。"下一个数字是:小点数。"

博迪博尔先生坐在那儿,腰板笔直、紧张异常。他已经决定,要等下去,一直等到其他人都出完价码。然后,他再一下子插进来,最后拍板定案。他早就算计过,他家在银行账户里至少有五百美元,或许差不多将近六百美元,相当于二百英镑——甚至超过二百,而这个数字的价码是不会超过这个钱数的。

"你们大家是知道的,"竞拍人说道,"小点数是低于本次航程范围的任何一个数字的,具体来说,就是每一个低于五百零五的数字都算。所以啊,如果你认为本船在二十四小时内的航程,截止到明天中午,要是低于五百零五英里的话,最好赶快行动,买下这个数字。所以嘛,我该叫出多大的价码呢?"

出价径直攀升到一百三十英镑。博迪博尔先生旁边的那些人似乎已经注意到天气的恶劣、风浪的猛烈了。一百四十……五十……这时,出价停住了,拍卖人举起了锤子。

"就要定在一百五十……"

"六十,"博迪博尔先生叫道,屋子里每一张脸都转了过来,看着他。

“七十!”

“八十!”博迪博尔先生喊道。

“九十!”

“二百!”博迪博尔先生又叫道。现在,任何人只要再加码,他都不会停止,也会再加的。

暂停了一会儿。

“二百英镑,还有加的吗?”

他对自己说,坐稳,要坐得绝对的稳,不要抬头看;屏住呼吸,只要你屏住呼吸,没有谁会再跟你竞价了。

“就要定在二百英镑……”拍卖人是个秃头,头皮粉嘟嘟的,头顶上一粒粒细小的汗珠闪着光亮。“要……”博迪博尔先生屏住了呼吸。“要……成交!”这名男子“嘭”的一声,锤子落下。博迪博尔先生开了张支票,递给拍卖人的助手。然后,他在椅子上向后一仰,等着竞拍结束。他要等到最后。等到赌金总数算出来,才能回去睡觉。

最后一个数字成交后,他们加了加,赌金总数为二千一百多英镑,约合六千美元。其中的百分之九十归赢家,百分之十用来救济船员。六千的百分之九十就是五千四啊。哇,足矣。买完林肯牌活动顶篷式汽车,钱还会有剩余的。带着这个心满意足的想法,他回到自己的客舱,开心得不得了,兴奋得不得了。

第二天早晨醒来的时候,博迪博尔先生静静地在床上躺了几分钟,眼睛没有睁开,耳朵却听着大风的呼啸,等待着船体的摇晃。可是,没有任何的呼啸声,船体一点也没摇晃。他猛地蹦了起来,隔着舷窗向外窥探。这个大海——噢,苍天大地啊——平缓如镜,大船正穿越大海快速前进。很显然,要把昨夜耽搁的时间补回来。博迪博尔先生转回身体,慢慢地坐到铺位的边缘。胃部皮肤下面,一股纤细的恐惧电流开始刺来,阵阵疼痛。他现在没有什么希望了。现在起,大点数中的某个数字会成为赢家。

“噢,我的天啊,”他大声说道。“我该怎么办呢?”

比如,埃塞尔会说他什么呢?轻描淡写地告诉她,他把他们两年的积蓄几乎都作为客船上的赌金,换回一张票据吗?是不可能这么说的。这件事也不可能秘而不宣，纸包不住火的。要保密，就得告诉她以后不要再开支票了。要是不开支票，那么，买电视，还有《大不列颠百科全书》每月的分期付款怎么支付？他已经看到这个女人眼里流露出的愤怒和蔑视，蓝眼球变成了灰眼球，眼睛也变窄了。她只要一生气，两只眼睛就会变窄。

"噢，我的天啊！我该怎么办呢？"

现在，丝毫赢的机会都没有，自欺欺人也没有一点意义，除非这条该死的船再倒回去。现在，他要是有赢的机会的话，他们就得调转方向，全速向后航行，不停歇地航行。那么，或许他就应该去要求船长那样做，把赢钱的百分之十给船长，嫌少的话，再多给点。想到这儿，博迪博尔先生咯咯笑了起来。接着，突然间他不笑了，眼睛睁得大大的，嘴巴张得大大的，显露出某种巨大的吃惊之情。因为就在那一刹那，一个想法涌上心头。这个想法来得很猛烈，也来得很迅速。他"腾"的一下从床上跳起来，显得异常兴奋。他跑向舷窗，又向外窥探。他想：哇，为什么不试试呢？不试试怎么知道？海面风平浪静，在上面漂浮一会，直到有人把他救起，不应该有什么大不了的。他朦朦胧胧地感觉，以前有人这么做过。做过也不要紧，他可以再做一次的。那样的话，大船就得停下，放下一只小船，小船就得向后行驶约半英里的距离来搭救他。然后，小船再回到大船那儿，被吊回甲板上。整个过程下来，至少得一个小时，一小时大约行驶三十英里。那么，这一天的航程无形中就扣掉了三十英里。这行得通。到那时，"小点数"就一定能赢了。只不过，要确保有人看见他落水，但这设计、安排起来很容易的。他要穿轻型的衣服，游起来轻松。运动装如何？对，就运动装。他的穿着要让人看起来就好像到甲板上打网球。那么，就穿一件衬衫、一条短裤和一双网球鞋吧，手表就不要戴了。对了，几点了？九点十五了，越快行动越好。现在就行动，做完就万事大吉。必须快点行动，因为时间期限是今天中午。

一身运动装的博迪博尔先生踏上露天阳光甲板的时候，既恐惧又兴奋。他身材矮小，臀部却很宽。臀部向上至双肩逐渐变得相当的细窄，双肩耷拉下来。那体型，不管按照什么比率算，极像系船缆的柱子。他两腿白白的、瘦瘦的,上面长了些黑毛。他小心谨慎地跨上甲板,穿网球鞋的双脚轻轻迈步,紧张兮兮地四处观瞧。甲板上除了他,还有一个人,一个上了年纪的妇女,长了一副厚厚的踝关节,屁股硕大。她正倚在栏杆上,看着大海,目不转睛。她身穿一件波斯羔羊皮外衣,衣领向上高高竖起。因此,博迪博尔先生看不到她的脸。

他站着不动,从远处仔细地审视着她。他对自己说,不错,她或许可以。她或许跟任何其他人一样,会很快尖叫起来,发出警报。可是,且慢,别着急。威廉·博迪博尔,别急。还记得几分钟前在客船里换衣服时你对自己说了什么吗?你记得吗?

此时,一想到要跳下大船,纵身跃入离最近的陆地一千英里远的大海,博迪博尔先生——这位在最佳时刻总会谨小慎微的男子——格外谨慎起来。他无论如何也不能确定:当他纵身一跃时,眼前他看到的这位女子就绝对肯定会尖叫,发出警报。在他看来,她做不到或许有两点原因:首先,她或许听不见、看不见。这点倒不是很可能。但是,反过来想想,或许就是如此,那为什么还要冒险呢?所以,他首先要做的就是,事先跟她谈一会,以便检验;其次嘛——这其次的一点最能暴露一个人的自我保护机制和恐惧机制发挥作用时,这个人的多疑性会达到一个什么程度——其次,他突然想到,这位女子本人或许在竞拍中买的是大点数,因此出于钱方面的考虑,她不希望船停下来,这也是合情合理的。博迪博尔先生想起来,为了区区六千美元,人们杀害了自己的同胞,这事儿报纸上每天都有报道。所以啊,为什么还要因为这一点而冒险呢?先检验一下,弄清事实吧。就跟她稍微谈谈,检验一下,要彬彬有礼地谈。接下来,要是这个妇女看起来也是一个令人愉悦、心地善良的人,事情就好办了,他也就能轻松、愉悦地跳下去了。

博迪博尔先生若无其事地向这个妇女走去,在她旁边的一个位置站住,身体倚靠着栏杆。“嗨,你好,”他说道,语气很是愉快。

她转身,冲他笑了笑。尽管她那张脸本身普通得很,可那笑容却优雅美丽、活泼可爱,叫人意想不到。“嗨,你好,”她回应道。

博迪博尔先生对自己说,第一个问题,检验通过,她既不聋也不瞎。

“跟我说说，”他开门见山，直击主题。“你觉得昨晚的竞拍如何？”

“竞拍？”她问，眉头紧皱。“竞拍？什么竞拍？”

“要知道，那是老一套的蠢玩意儿，也就是晚饭后在那个大厅里进行的，出售客船每日航程的数字。我就是想了解一下，你对那，是怎么个看法。”

她摇摇头，又笑了笑，笑容甜甜的，很令人愉快，笑容里或许还带有那么一点点的歉意。“我这个人很懒的，”她说。“我总是早早就睡下。晚饭是在床上吃的，那样感觉很舒适，优哉游哉的。”

博迪博尔先生冲她一笑，作为回应。随即，他缓缓迈步，走开了。“现在，要去锻炼了，”他说。“早晨锻炼，从未间断。见到你，很高兴……”他向后退了大约十步远。那个妇女也没转过身来，任由他走开。

目前，一切准备就绪。海面风平浪静，他也轻装上阵，做好了游泳的准备，大西洋的这一部分几乎可以肯定没有什么食人鲨鱼，更何况还有那个令人愉悦、心地善良的妇女会尖叫，发出警报。现在剩下的唯一的问题是，大船救他所耽搁的时间是否会长到能扭转平衡，转而对他有利。几乎可以肯定的是：会的。任何情况下，他本人都能稍微做点什么，以有助于向这个方向发展。救生船把他向上拉起的时候，他可以制造点难题出来；他们尽力靠近，打捞他的时候，他可以暗自迂回游一下，以退后离他们远一些。挣一秒是一秒，得一分是一分，都有助于他最后获胜。他又开始向前，走向栏杆，可现在，一种新的恐惧感开始纠结。他会不会被绞进螺旋桨里啊？他听说过，这样的事儿发生过，有人从大船的侧面落入海里，被绞进去过。那么，他不想落下去，而是要跳下去，那就大不相同了。只要他跳得足够远，就不会被螺旋桨绞进去的。

博迪博尔先生慢慢走到靠近栏杆的一个位置，离那个妇女不到二十米远。她现在没有看他，那样再好不过，他跳下去的时候不想让她看到。只要跳的时候没人看到，事后他就能够说，他是一失足，意外掉下去的。他瞥了一眼船的侧面，发现要落很长、很长的距离才能入水。现在想想吧，如果他身体横着，扁平落向海面，就会轻而易举地把自己伤得很重。以前不是有人这样落入水中,从很高的地方落下,肚子“啪”地拍打水面,胃部被劈开过吗?他一定要笔直跳下,脚先入水,就像一把刀插入水中。对,就这样,好样的。海水似乎寒冷刺骨、深不可测、灰暗阴沉,光看那么一眼,他就浑身哆嗦。就是现在啦,不跳就血本无归。做个男子汉,勇敢些吧。威廉·博迪博尔,做个男子汉。那么,好的……就现在……开始……

他向上爬,爬到了栏杆最上层的横梁——很宽,是木头做的。他站在那儿,摆出姿势,保持着平衡,约有三秒钟,那真是恐怖的三秒钟啊。接着,他起跳了——尽力向上方,向船外跳去,同时喊道:“救命!”“救命!救命!”他在落下的同时喊道。随后,他碰到海面,落入水下。

第一声“救命”响起的时候,一直倚着栏杆的那个妇女一激灵,抬起头来,轻轻跳起,很是吃惊。她飞快向周围观瞧,看见这个小个子男子如白帆在空中飘移,因为他穿的短裤和网球鞋是白色的,手脚伸展如雄鹰展翅,边飘边喊。一时间,她懵了,看起来好像不确定应该怎么做:扔救生带,跑去报警,或者干脆转身狂喊?她向后退了一步,离开栏杆,一半身体扭转过来,面对着驾驶台。就在这短短的时间里,她一动不动、紧张异常、不知所措。接着,几乎是一瞬间,她似乎松弛下来,脚也没有迈到栏杆跟前,身体就向前,斜倚在栏杆上方,眼睛盯着海面,海水在大船驶过后翻着漩涡和浪花。很快,浪花的泡沫中出现一个小小的、圆圆的黑脑袋,脑袋上方伸出一只胳膊,一下、两下,用力挥舞着;远远地传来弱小的声音,很难听懂喊的是什么。这个妇女俯身栏杆上方,又向前靠了靠,尽量不让那个上下跳动的黑色小点点从视线里消失。可是,很快,没用多久,由于距离太远,她甚至不敢确定,那个黑点是否存在。

过了一会,另一个妇女来到甲板上。这个女的骨感十足、棱角分明,戴了一副角质架眼镜。她看到那个先上来的妇女,走了过去。像所有未婚老女人一样,她迈起步来从容不迫,一副军人的派头。

“啊,原来你在这儿,”她说道。

那个踝关节厚厚的妇女转过身来,看着她,但什么也没说。

“我一直在找你呢，”骨感十足的妇女继续说。“都找遍了。”

“太奇怪了，”厚厚的踝关节说道。“刚刚一个男的从上面跳下去，还穿着衣服。”

“现在你最好跟我下去，”骨感十足的妇女说。她的嘴一下子坚挺起来，整张脸鲜明起来，有所警觉了。她说起话来，也不像先前那样心平气和了。“不要像这样一个人独自在甲板上游荡了。你很清楚，我让你等我的。”

“是的，玛吉，”踝关节厚厚的妇女回答。她又笑了，笑得温文尔雅、令人信任。她抓住刚上来的那个妇女的手，让她领着，穿过甲板。

“多么好的一个人啊，”她说。“他向我挥手了。”

第三节 《费西先生》*Mr. Feasey*

《费西先生》(Mr. Feasey)是罗尔德·达尔乡村故事“克劳德的狗(*Claud's Dog*)”系列中的一篇，首次收录在1953年出版发行的《如你之人》(*Someone like You*)一书中。后来，这篇故事收录到《罗尔德·达尔小说精品集》(*The Best of Roald Dahl*)、《奥妙生活》(*Ah, Sweet Mystery of Life*)、《罗尔德·达尔短篇故事集锦》(*The Collected Short Stories of Roald Dahl*)等书中。

一、原作导读

这篇小说的叙述者不像本书所讨论的类似《南方来客》小说里的叙述者那样“隐姓埋名”。正好相反，本篇的叙述者是“显性”的，名字叫戈登。这个名字也贯穿于达尔“克劳德的狗”乡村系列故事之中。

话说有一天，戈登跟他的朋友克劳德兴奋异常，因为这一天，他们俩要去实施共同谋划已久的人生中最重大的计划——带上他们秘密训练好的赛犬杰基去灰狗赛道赌上一大把。克劳德熟悉灰狗赛幕前幕后的一切，因此他敢肯定，他们的这条狗赢定了。

早在四个月以前，克劳德买下一条狗，那条狗跟杰基简直是一个模子里出来的,成为冒名顶替杰基的不二之选,但那却是一条根本就跑不快的狗。当时,每隔一周的星期六下午,戈登就关闭加油站,开车跟克劳德一起把这条冒名顶替的狗送到牛津的一条破旧的赛道参加比赛,一共去了八次,每次都带着他们用以作弊的那条狗跟费西先生一同入场,好让费西先生看清楚。那条狗每次跑起来,就像螃蟹在爬,成绩一路下滑到了谷底,成了下三烂货色。

费西先生是他们最终要去大赌一把的那个赛道的主人,也是横在他们和作弊赢得比赛之间的一个障碍,因为费西先生能力非凡,具有惊人的记忆力,从一千米以外就能够觉察出哪条狗是冒名顶替的。

现在,重大的时刻到来了,他们要换下冒名顶替的狗,让杰基闪亮登场,赢得头彩。但是不幸的是,到达那个赛道时,费西先生却将他们拒之门外,不让杰基入场。万般无奈之下,克劳德先拿出一英镑跟费西先生赌,赌杰基这次不会跑到最后一名。这一举动倒是激起了费西的兴趣,开始仔细对杰基查看起来,发现杰基跟他们以前牵来的狗没有什么两样,就收下了赌金,允许杰基上场参加第一轮比赛了。

于是,他们分头展开行动。克劳德牵着杰基做参赛的准备,同时贿赂了那个驱动假兔的家伙;戈登则依次沿着那一排赌注经纪人给杰基下注。若一切如愿,他们能赢得两千英镑的赌金。比赛开始,杰基轻松获胜,费西先生则恼羞成怒,禁止他们以后参加比赛。

第一轮比赛完后,克劳德牵着杰基回到停车处等候,戈登去收赌金。但是,第一位赌注经纪人并不买账,声称戈登押的不是杰基。尽管下注的细节都记录在案,但这位经纪人就是不让戈登看。其他几位经纪人也都如法炮制,都不买账,惹得戈登大骂出口,扫兴而归。

回停车场的路上,戈登——叙述者"我"——"看见克劳德站在篷车边,拎着手提箱正等着我回去呢"(... caught sight of Claud standing by the van, waiting for me with the suitcase in his hand)。

二、原作释读

多数中国人并不了解赛狗比赛,这方面的英文也构成理解本篇小说原文的一道障碍。但是,这不会影响我们对罗尔德·达尔这篇小说扣人心弦情节的理解和欣赏。

Mr. Feasey[①]

We were both up early when the big day came.

I wandered into the kitchen for a shave, but Claud got dressed right away and went outside to arrange about[②] the straw. The kitchen was a front room and through the window I could see the sun just coming up behind the line of trees on top of the ridge[③] the other side of the valley.

Each time Claud came past the window with an armload of straw I noticed over the rim of the mirror the intent, breathless expression on his face, the great round bullet-head thrusting forward and the forehead wrinkled into deep corrugations[④] right up to the hairline. I'd only seen this look on him once before and that was the evening he'd asked Glance to marry him. Today he was so excited he even walked funny, treading softly as though the concrete around the filling-station were a shade[⑤] too hot for the soles of his feet; and he kept packing more and more straw into the back of the van to make it comfortable for Jackie.

Then he came into the kitchen to get breakfast, and I watched him put the pot of soup on the stove and begin stirring it. He had a long metal spoon and he kept on stirring and stirring all the time it was coming to the

---

① 本部小说原文出自"Roald Dahl. *The Best of Roald Dahl*[M]. England: Penguin Books Ltd., 2006"。

② arrange about: make arrangement for 为……做准备(安排)

③ ridge: *Noun* a long narrow hilltop, mountain range, or watershed 山脊;山脉,岭;分水岭

④ corrugate: *Verb* to wrinkle, shrivel(使)起皱;(使)起褶

corrugation: Noun wrinkles or folds 皱纹;皱折

⑤ a shade: a little 有点;略微

boil, and about every half minute he leaned forward and stuck his nose into that sickly-sweet steam of cooking horse-flesh. Then he started putting extras into it three peeled onions, a few young carrots, a cupful of stinging-nettle① tops②, a teaspoon of Valentines Meat Juice③, twelve drops of cod-liver oil—and everything he touched was handled very gently with the ends of his big fat fingers as though it might have been a little fragment of Venetian glass④. He took some minced horsemeat from the icebox, measured one handful into Jackie's bowl, three into the other, and when the soup was ready he shared it out between the two, pouring it over the meat.

It was the same ceremony I'd seen performed each morning for the past five months, but never with such intense and breathless concentration as this. There was no talk, not even a glance my way, and when he turned and went out again to fetch the dogs, even the back of his neck and the shoulders seemed to be whispering, "Oh, Jesus, don't let anything go wrong, and especially don't let me do anything wrong

---

① stinging nettle: *Noun* a Eurasian nettle covered in minute hairs that inject irritants when they are touched. These include histamine, which causes itching, and acetylcholine, which causes a burning sensation 大荨麻

② top: (usu. tops) the leaves, stems, and shoots of a plant, especially those of a vegetable grown for its root(植物,尤指直根作物的)叶;茎;梢

③ Valentine's Meat Juice: Brought into production in Richmond, VA, in 1871, Valentine's Meat-Juice became popular with orthodox physicians and was advertised in professional publications, including the British Medical Journal. Its inventor, Mann S. Valentine, told of its origins in his "A Brief History of the Production of Valentine's Meat Juice", together with "Testimonials of the Medical Profession" (1874). 瓦伦丁肉汁

④ Venetian glass: *Noun* another term for Murano glass 彩色装饰玻璃

注:Murano glass: [*Mass Noun*] decorative glassware of a type associated with the island of Murano near Venice 威尼斯附近摩拉诺岛式的摩拉诺装饰玻璃制品

today."

I heard him talking softly to the dogs in the pen[1] as he put the leashes on them, and when he brought them around into the kitchen, they came in prancing[2] and pulling to get at the breakfast, treading up and down with their front feet and waving their enormous tails from side to side, like whips.

"All right," Claud said, speaking at last. "Which is it?"

Most mornings he'd offer to bet me a pack of cigarettes, but there were bigger things at stake today and I knew all he wanted for the moment was a little extra reassurance.

He watched me as I walked once around the two beautiful, identical, tall, velvety-black dogs, and he moved aside, holding the leashes at arms' length to give me a better view.

"Jackie!" I said, trying the old trick that never worked. "Hey, Jackie!" Two identical heads with identical expressions flicked around to look at me, four bright, identical, deep-yellow eyes stared into mine. There'd been a time when I fancied the eyes of one were slightly darker yellow than those of the other. There'd also been a time when I thought I could recognize Jackie because of a deeper brisket[3] and a shade more muscle on the hindquarters. But it wasn't so.

"Come on," Claud said. He was hoping that today of all days I would make a bad guess.

"This one," I said. "This is Jackie."

---

① pen: *Noun* a small enclosure in which sheep, pigs, cattle, or other domestic animals are kept(羊、猪、牛等家畜的)圈;栏;棚

② prance: *Verb* [no obj., with adverbial of direction] (of a horse) move with high springy steps(马)腾跃;腾跳

③ brisket: *Noun* [*Mass Noun*] meat cut from the breast of an animal, typically a cow 动物的胸肉(尤指母牛的)

"Which?"

"This one on the left."

"There!" he cried, his whole face suddenly beaming. "You're wrong again!"

"I don't think I'm wrong."

"You're about as wrong as you could possibly be. And now listen, Gordon, and I'll tell you something. All these last weeks, every morning while you've been trying to pick him out—you know what?"

"What?"

"I've been keeping count. And the result is you haven't been right even *one-half* the time! You'd have done better tossing a coin!"

What he meant was that if I (who saw them every day and side by side) couldn't do it, why the hell should we be frightened of Mr. Feasey? Claud knew Mr. Feasey was famous for spotting ringers[1], but he knew also that it could be very difficult to tell the difference between two dogs when there wasn't any.

He put the bowls of food on the floor, giving Jackie the one with the least meat because he was running today. When he stood back to watch them eat, the shadow of deep concern was back again on his face and the large pale eyes were staring at Jackie with the same rapt and melting look of love that up till recently had been reserved only for Glance.

"You see, Gordon," he said. "It's just what I've always told you. For the last hundred years there's been all manner of ringers, some good and some bad, but in the whole history of dog-racing there's never been a ringer like this."

"I hope you're right," I said, and my mind began travelling back to

① ringer: *Noun* (informal) an athlete or horse fraudulently substituted for another in a competition or event(非正式)(体育比赛)冒名顶替的运动员(或马)

that freezing afternoon just before Christmas, four months ago, when Claud had asked to borrow the van and had driven away in the direction of Aylesbury[①] without saying where he was going. I had assumed he was off to see Glance, but late in the afternoon he had returned bringing with him this dog he said he'd bought off a man for thirty five shillings.

"Is he fast?" I had said. We were standing out by the pumps and Claud was holding the dog on a leash and looking at him, and a few snowflakes were falling and settling on the dog's back. The motor of the van was still running.

"Fast!" Claud had said. "He's just about the slowest dog you ever saw in your whole life!"

"Then what you buy him for?"

"Well," he had said, the big bovine[②] face secret and cunning, "it occurred to me that maybe he might possibly look a little bit like Jackie. What d'you think?"

"I suppose he does a bit, now you come to mention it."

He had handed me the leash and I had taken the new dog inside to dry him off while Claud had gone round to the pen to fetch his beloved. And when he returned and we put the two of them together for the first time, I can remember him stepping back and saying, "Oh, Jesus!" and standing dead still in front of them like he was seeing a phantom[③]. Then he became very quick and quiet. He got down on his knees and began comparing them carefully point by point, and it was almost like the room was getting warmer and warmer the way I could feel his excitement

---

① Aylesbury: a town in south central England, the county town of Buckinghamshire; pop. 50,000 (1985) 埃尔兹伯里(英格兰中南部城市,白金汉郡首府,1985 年人口 50,000。)

② bovine: *Adjective* of, relating to, or affecting cattle 牛的;关于牛的

③ phantom: *Noun* a ghost 幽灵;鬼魂

growing every second through this long silent examination in which even the toenails and the dewclaws[①], eighteen on each dog, were matched alongside one another for colour.

"Look," he said at last, standing up. "Walk them up and down the room a few times, will you?" And then he had stayed there for quite five or six minutes leaning against the stove with his eyes half closed and his head on one side, watching them and frowning and chewing his lips. After that, as though he didn't believe what he had seen the first time, he had gone down again on his knees to recheck everything once more; but suddenly, in the middle of it, he had jumped up and looked at me, his face fixed and tense, with a curious whiteness around the nostrils and the eyes. "All right," he had said, a little tremor in his voice. 'You know what?

"We're home. We're rich."

And then the secret conferences between us in the kitchen, the detailed planning, the selection of the most suitable track, and finally every other Saturday, eight times in all, locking up my filling-station (losing a whole afternoon's custom) and driving the ringer all the way up to Oxford to a scruffy[②] little track out in the fields near Headingley[③] where the big money was played but which was actually nothing except a line of old posts and cord to mark the course, an upturned bicycle for

① dewclaw: *Noun* a rudimentary inner toe present in some dogs(某些狗的)残留趾(狗等脚上不与地面接触的无机能趾)

② scruffy: *Adjective* shabby and untidy or dirty 破旧的;不整洁的

③ Headingley: Headingley is a suburb of Leeds in West Yorkshire, England. It is approximately two miles out of the city centre, to the north west along the A660 road. Headingley is notable for being the location of the Beckett Park campus for Leeds Metropolitan University and Headingley Stadium 黑丁利(英格兰西约克郡利兹市的一个郊区。)

pulling the dummy hare[①], and at the far end, in the distance, six traps and the starter. We had driven this ringer up there eight times over a period of sixteen weeks and entered him with Mr. Feasey and stood around on the edge of the crowd in freezing raining cold, waiting for his name to go up on the blackboard in chalk. The Black Panther we called him. And when his time came, Claud would always lead him down to the traps and I would stand at the finish to catch him and keep him clear of the fighters, the gipsy dogs that the gipsies so often slipped in specially to tear another one to pieces at the end of a race.

But you know, there was something rather sad about taking this dog all the way up there so many times and letting him run and watching him and hoping and praying that whatever happened he would always come last. Of course the praying wasn't necessary and we never really had a moment's worry because the old fellow simply couldn't gallop and that's all there was to it. He ran exactly like a crab. The only time he didn't come last was when a big fawn[②] dog by the name of Amber Flash put his boot in a hole and broke a hock[③] and finished on three legs. But even then ours only just beat him. So this way we got him right down to bottom

---

① dummy hare: (also as "electric hare") a dummy hare propelled around the track in greyhound racing(跑狗比赛中的用电力驱动在跑道上奔跑的)电兔;假兔

② fawn: [*Mass Noun*] a light yellowish-brown colour 浅黄褐色

③ hock: *Noun* the joint in a quadruped's hind leg between the knee and the fetlock, the angle of which points backwards(四足动物的)跗关节;后踝

grade with the scrubbers[①], and the last time we were there all the bookies[②] were laying[③] him twenty or thirty to one and calling his name and begging people to back him.

Now at last, on this sunny April day, it was Jackie's turn to go instead. Claud said we mustn't run the ringer any more or Mr. Feasey might begin to get tired of him and throw him out altogether, he was so slow. Claud said this was the exact psychological time to have it off, and that Jackie would win it anything between thirty and fifty lengths.

He had raised Jackie from a pup and the dog was only fifteen months now, but he was a good fast runner. He'd never raced yet; but we knew he was fast from clocking him round the little private schooling track at Uxbridge where Claud had taken him every Sunday since he was seven months old—except once when he was having some inoculations[④], Claud said he probably wasn't fast enough to win top grade at Mr. Feasey's, but where we'd got him now, in bottom grade with the scrubbers, he could fall over and get up again and still win it twenty well, anyway ten or fifteen lengths, Claud said.

So all I had to do this morning was go to the bank in the village and draw out fifty pounds for myself and fifty for Claud which I would lend

---

① scrubber: Originally an English derogatory term for a coarse, sexually amenable or promiscuous woman, or a woman of loose morals, in common enough use around Leinster in its original context. In latter times it's used as a generalised derogatory term for anything or anyone of low value, limited ability or of no importance (footballer, greyhound, golfer, race-horse, driver, etc.)(本书中译作)下三烂货色(尤只在体育比赛中处于劣势者)

② bookie: *Noun* [俚](赛马等的)赌注登记者

③ lay: *Verb*[with obj.]stake (an amount of money) in a wager(用钱)下注

④ inoculate: *Verb* [with obj.]treat (a person or animal) with a vaccine to produce immunity against a disease 给(人、动物)接种疫苗

him as an advance against wages, and then at twelve o'clock lock up the filling – station and hang the notice on one of the pumps saying GONE FOR THE DAY. Claud would shut the ringer in the pen at the back and put Jackie in the van and off we'd go. I won't say I was as excited as Claud, but there again, I didn't have all sorts of important things depending on it either, like buying a house and being able to get married. Nor was I almost born in a kennel[①] with greyhounds like he was, walking about thinking of absolutely nothing else all day except perhaps Glance in the evenings. Personally, I had my own career as a filling station owner to keep me busy, not to mention second – hand cars, but if Claud wanted to fool around with dogs that was all right with me, especially a thing like today—if it came off. As a matter of fact, I don't mind admitting that every time I thought about the money we were putting on and the money we might win, my stomach gave a little lurch.

The dogs had finished their breakfast now and Claud took them out for a short walk across the field opposite while I got dressed and fried the eggs. Afterwards, I went to the bank and drew out the money (all in ones), and the rest of the morning seemed to go very quickly serving customers.

At twelve sharp I locked up and hung the notice on the pump. Claud came around from the back leading Jackie and carrying a large suitcase made of reddish-brown cardboard.

"Suitcase?"

"For the money," Claud answered. "You said yourself no man can carry two thousand pounds in his pockets."

It was a lovely yellow spring day with the buds bursting all along the

---

① kennel: *Noun* a small shelter for a dog 狗屋;狗窝
(figurative) a small or sordid dwelling(喻)陋室

hedges and the sun shining through the new pale green leaves on the big beech tree across the road. Jackie looked wonderful, with two big hard muscles the size of melons bulging on his hindquarters, his coat glistening like black velvet. While Claud was putting the suitcase in the van, the dog did a little prancing jig[1] on his toes to show how fit he was, then he looked up at me and grinned, just like he knew he was off to the races to win two thousand pounds and a heap of glory. This Jackie had the widest most human – smiling grin I ever saw. Not only did he lift his upper lip, but he actually stretched the corners of his mouth so you could see every tooth in his head except perhaps one or two of the molars[2] right at the back; and every time I saw him do it I found myself waiting to hear him start laughing out loud as well.

We got in the van and off we went. I was doing the driving. Claud was beside me and Jackie was standing up on the straw in the rear looking over our shoulders through the windshield. Claud kept turning round and trying to make him lie down so he wouldn't get thrown whenever we went round the sharp corners, but the dog was too excited to do anything except grin back at him and wave his enormous tail.

"You got the money, Gordon?" Claud was chain-smoking cigarettes and quite unable to sit still.

"Yes."

"Mine as well?"

"I got a hundred and five altogether. Five for the winder like you said, so he won't stop the hare and make it a no – race."

"Good," Claud said, rubbing his hands together hard as though he

---

① jig: *Verb* [with adverbial] move up and down with a quick jerky motion 上下急动;蹦蹦跳跳

② molar (also as "molar tooth"): *Noun* a grinding tooth at the back of a mammal's mouth 臼齿;磨牙

were freezing cold. "Good good good."

We drove through the little narrow High Street of Great Missenden and caught a glimpse of old Rummins going into The Nag's Head for his morning pint, then outside the village we turned left and climbed over the ridge of the Chilterns towards Princes Risborough, and from there it would only be twenty-odd miles to Oxford.

And now a silence and a kind of tension began to come over us both. We sat very quiet, not speaking at all, each nursing his own fears and excitements, containing his anxiety. And Claud kept smoking his cigarettes and throwing them half finished out the window. Usually, on these trips, he talked his head off all the way there and back, all the things he'd done with dogs in his life, the jobs he'd pulled, the places he'd been, the money he'd won; and all the things other people had done with dogs, the thievery[①], the cruelty, the unbelievable trickery and cunning of owners at the flapping tracks[②]. But today I don't think he was trusting himself to speak very much. At this point, for that matter, nor was I. I was sitting there watching the road and trying to keep my mind off the immediate future by thinking back on all that stuff Claud had told me about this curious greyhound racing racket.

I swear there wasn't a man alive who knew more about it than Claud did, and ever since we'd got the ringer and decided to pull this job, he'd taken it upon himself to give me an education in the business. By now, in theory at any rate, I suppose I knew nearly as much as him.

It had started during the very first strategy conference we'd had in the kitchen. I can remember it was the day after the ringer arrived and

---

① thievery: *Noun* [*Mass Noun*] the action of stealing another person's property 偷窃;行窃

② flapping track: Flapping track is British slang for an unlicensed greyhound track.（英国俚语）无许可证的赛狗场地

we were sitting there watching for customers through the window, and Claud was explaining to me all about what we'd have to do, and I was trying to follow him as best I could until finally there came one question I had to ask.

"What I don't see," I had said, "is why you use the ringer at all. Wouldn't it be safer if we use Jackie all the time and simply stop him the first half dozen races so he comes last? Then when we're good and ready, we can let him go. Same result in the end, wouldn't it be, if we do it right? And no danger of being caught."

Well, as I say, that did it. Claud looked up at me quickly and he said, "Hey! None of that! I'd just like you to know, 'stopping's' something I never do. What's come over you, Gordon?" He seemed genuinely pained and shocked by what I had said.

"I don't see anything wrong with it."

"Now, listen to me, Gordon. Stopping a good dog breaks his heart. A good dog knows he's fast, and seeing all the others out there in front and not being able to catch them—it breaks his heart, I tell you. And what's more, you wouldn't be making suggestions like that if you knew some of the tricks them fellers[①] do to stop their dogs at the flapping tracks."

"Such as what, for example?" I had asked.

"Such as anything in the world almost, so long as it makes the dog go slower. And it takes a lot of stopping, a good greyhound does. Full of guts and so mad keen[②] you can't even let them watch a race, they'll tear the leash right out of your hand rearing to go. Many's the time I've seen one with a broken leg insisting on finishing the race."

---

① feller: *Noun* non-standard spelling of fellow, used in representing speech in various dialects(非规范)同 fellow(用于多种方言)

② mad keen: (informal) extremely enthusiastic(非正式)极其狂热的

He had paused then, looking at me thoughtfully with those large pale eyes, serious as hell and obviously thinking deep. "Maybe," he had said, "if we're going to do this job properly I'd better tell you a thing or two so's you'll know what we're up against."

"Go ahead and tell me," I had said. "I'd like to know."

For a moment he stared in silence out the window. "The main thing you got to remember," he had said darkly, "is that all these fellers going to the flapping tracks with dogs—they're artful. They're more artful than you could possibly imagine." Again he paused, marshalling his thoughts.

"Now take for example the different ways of stopping a dog. The first, the commonest, is strapping."

"Strapping?"

"Yes. Strapping 'em up. That's commonest. Pulling the muzzle-strap tight around their necks so they can't hardly breathe, see. A clever man knows just which hole on the strap to use and just how many lengths it'll take off his dog in a race. Usually a couple of notches is good for five or six lengths. Do it up real tight and he'll come last. I've known plenty of dogs collapse and die from being strapped up tight on a hot day. Strangulated[①], absolutely strangulated, and a very nasty thing it was too. Then again, some of 'em just tie two of the toes together with black cotton. Dog never runs well like that. Unbalances him."

"That doesn't sound too bad."

"Then there's others that put a piece of fresh-chewed gum up under their tails, right up close where the tail joins the body. And there's nothing funny about that," he had said, indignant. "The tail of a

① strangulate: [as adj. strangulated] sounding as though the speaker's throat is constricted 使哽咽;闷住

running dog goes up and down ever so slightly and the gum on the tail keeps sticking to the hairs on the backside①, just where it's tenderest. No dog likes that, you know. Then there's sleeping pills. That's used a lot nowadays. They do it by weight, exactly like a doctor, and they measure the powder according to whether they want to slow him up five or ten or fifteen lengths. Those are just a few of the ordinary ways," he had said. "Actually they're nothing. Absolutely nothing, compared with some of the other things that's done to hold a dog back in a race, especially by the gipsies. There's things the gipsies do that are almost too disgusting to mention, such as when they're just putting the dog in the trap, things you wouldn't hardly do to your worst enemies."

And when he had told me about those which were, indeed, terrible things because they had to do with physical injury, quickly, painfully inflicted—then he had gone or, to tell me what they did when they wanted the dog to win. "There's just as terrible things done to make 'em go fast as to make 'em go slow," he had said softly, his face veiled and secret. "And perhaps the commonest of all is wintergreen. Whenever you see a dog going around with no hair on his back or little bald patches all over him that's wintergreen②. Just before the race they rub it hard into

---

① backside: *Noun* each of a series of holes for the tongu anus (非正式)(人的)屁股;肛门

② wintergreen: (also as "oil of wintergreen") [*Mass Noun*] a pungent oil containing methyl salicylate, now obtained from this birch tree or made synthetically, used medicinally and as a flavouring 冬青油;水杨酸甲酯

the skin. Sometimes it's Sloan's[①] Liniment[②], but mostly it's wintergreen. Stings terrible. Stings so bad that all the old dog wants to do is run, run, run as fast as he possibly can to get away from the pain.

"Then there's special drugs they give with the needle. Mind you, that's the modern method and most of the spivs[③] at the track are too ignorant to use it. It's the fellers coming down from London in the big cars with stadium dogs they've borrowed for the day by bribing the trainer—they're the ones who use the needle."

I could remember him sitting there at the kitchen table with a cigarette dangling from his mouth and dropping his eyelids to keep out the smoke and looking at me through his wrinkled, nearly closed eyes, and saying, "What you've got to remember, Gordon, is this. There's nothing they won't do to make a dog win if they want him to. On the other hand, no dog can run faster than he's built, no matter what they do to him. So if we can get Jackie down into bottom grade, then we're home. No dog in bottom grade can get near him, not even with wintergreen and needles. Not even with ginger."

"Ginger?"

---

① Sloane: Sir Hans (1660 - 1753), Irish physician and naturalist. He endowed the Chelsea Physic Garden, and his books and specimens formed the basis of the British Museum Library and the Natural History Museum in London 汉斯·斯隆爵士(1660 - 1753),爱尔兰医生、博物学家;他捐赠了切尔西药类植物园,他的藏书和实验标本奠定了伦敦大英博物馆图书馆和自然历史博物馆的基础.

② liniment: *Noun* [*mass noun*] an embrocation for rubbing on the body to relieve pain, especially one made with oil(止痛用)搽剂,擦剂对于"Sloan's Liniment"这个表达,本书译作"斯隆擦剂"

③ spiv: *Noun* (Brit. informal) a man, typically characterized by flashy dress, who makes a living by disreputable dealings(英国英语的非正式表达)(多指衣冠楚楚的)靠从事肮脏交易谋生的人

"Certainly. That's a common one, ginger is. What they do, they take a piece of raw ginger about the size of a walnut, and about five minutes before the off they slip it into the dog."

"You mean in his mouth? He eats it?"

"No," he had said. "Not in his mouth."

And so it had gone on. During each of the eight long trips we had subsequently made to the track with the ringer I had heard more and more about this charming sport—more, especially, about the methods of stopping them and making them go (even the names of the drugs and the quantities to use). I heard about 'The rat treatment' (for non - chasers, to make them chase the dummy hare), where a rat is placed in a can which is then tied around the dog's neck. There's a small hole in the lid of the can just large enough for the rat to poke its head out and nip the dog. But the dog can't get at the rat, and so naturally he goes half crazy running around and being bitten in the neck, and the more he shakes the can the more the rat bites him. Finally, someone releases the rat, and the dog, who up to then was a nice docile tail - wagging animal who wouldn't hurt a mouse, pounces on it in a rage and tears it to pieces. Do this a few times, Claud had said—"mind you, I don't hold with it myself"—and the dog becomes a real killer who will chase anything, even the dummy hare.

We were over the Chilterns now and running down out of the beech-woods into the flat elm[①]-and oak-tree country south of Oxford. Claud sat quietly beside me, nursing his nervousness and smoking cigarettes, and every two or three minutes he would turn round to see if Jackie was all right. The dog was at last lying down, and each time Claud turned

---

① elm (also as "elm tree"): *Noun* a tall deciduous tree which typically has rough serrated leaves and propagates from root suckers 榆树

round, he whispered something to him softly, and the dog acknowledged his words with a faint movement of the tail that made the straw rustle.

Soon we would be coming into Thame, the broad High Street where they penned the pigs and cows and sheep on market day, and where the Fair came once a year with the swings and roundabouts[1] and bumping cars and gipsy caravans right there in the street in the middle of the town. Claud was born in Thame, and we'd never driven through it yet without him mentioning the fact.

"Well," he said as the first houses came into sight, "here's Thame. I was born and bred in Thame, you know, Gordon."

"You told me."

"Lots of funny things we used to do around here when we was nippers[2]," he said, slightly nostalgic.

"I'm sure."

He paused, and I think more to relieve the tension building up inside him than anything else, he began talking about the years of his youth.

"There was a boy next door," he said. "Gilbert Gomm his name was. Little sharp ferrety[3] face and one leg a bit shorter'n the other. Shocking things him and me used to do together. You know one thing we done, Gordon?"

"What?"

"We'd go into the kitchen Saturday nights when mum and dad were

---

① swings and roundabouts (BrE, informal): used when you want to say that gaining one thing usually means losing another thing 有得有失的事

② nipper: *Noun* (informal) a child, especially a small boy(非正式)小孩(尤指小男孩)

③ ferrety: *Adjective* of or like a domesticated polecat used chiefly for catching rabbits 雪貂似的

at the pub, and we'd disconnect the pipe from the gas – ring and bubble the gas into a milk bottle full of water. Then we'd sit down and drink it out of teacups."

"Was that so good?"

"Good! It was absolutely disgusting! But we'd put lashings[①] of sugar in and then it didn't taste so bad."

"Why did you drink it?"

Claud turned and looked at me, incredulous. "You mean you never drunk 'Snakes Water'!"

"Can't say I have."

"I thought everyone done that when they was kids! It intoxicates you, just like wine only worse, depending on how long you let the gas bubble through. We used to get reeling[②] drunk together there in the kitchen Saturday nights and it was marvellous. Until one night Dad comes home early and catches us. I'll never forget that night as long as I live. There was me holding the milk bottle, and the gas bubbling through it lovely, and Gilbert kneeling on the floor ready to turn off the tap the moment I give the word, and in walks Dad."

"What did he say?"

"Oh, Christ, Gordon, that was terrible. He didn't say one word, but he stands there by the door and he starts feeling for his belt, undoing the buckle very slow and pulling the belt slow out of his trousers, looking at me all the time. Great big feller he was, with great big hands like coal hammers and a black moustache and them little purple veins running all over his cheeks. Then he comes over quick and grabs me by the coat and

---

① lashings: *Plural Noun* (Brit. informal) a copious amount of something, especially food or drink(英,非正式,尤指饮食)很多;大量

② reeling: *Adjective* losing one's balance and staggering or lurching violently 眩晕的

lets me have it, hard as he can, using the end with the buckle on it and honest to God, Gordon, I thought he was going to kill me. But in the end he stops and then he puts on the belt again, slow and careful, buckling it up and tuckling in the flap and belching with the beer he'd drunk. And then he walks out again back to the pub, still without saying a word. Worst hiding① I ever had in my life."

"How old were you then?"

"Round about eight, I should think," Claud said.

As we drew closer to Oxford, he became silent again. He kept twisting his neck to see if Jackie was all right, to touch him, to stroke his head, and once he turned around and knelt on the seat to gather more straw around the dog, murmuring something about a draught. We drove around the fringe of Oxford and into a network of narrow open country roads, and after a while we turned into a small bumpy lane and along this we began to overtake a thin stream of men and women all walking and cycling in the same direction. Some of the men were leading greyhounds. There was a large saloon car in front of us and through the rear window we could see a dog sitting on the back seat between two men.

"They come from all over," Claud said darkly. "That one there's probably come up special from London. Probably slipped him out from one of the big stadium kennels just for the afternoon.

That could be a Derby② dog probably for all we know."

"Hope he's not running against Jackie."

"Don't worry," Claud said. "All new dogs automatically go in top grade. That's one rule Mr. Feasey's very particular about."

---

① hiding: *Noun* (informal) a physical beating(非正式)痛打

② Derby: *Noun* a city in the Midlands of England, on the River Derwent; pop. 214,000 (1991) 德比(英格兰中部地区一城市,在德文特河畔,1991 年人口 214,000。)

There was an open gate leading into a field, and Mr. Feasey's wife came forward to take our admission money before we drove in.

"He'd have her winding the bloody pedals too if she had the strength; Claud said. "Old Feasey don't employ more people than he has to."

I drove across the field and parked at the end of a line of cars along the top hedge. We both got out and Claud went quickly round the back to fetch Jackie. I stood beside the car, waiting. It was a very large field with a steepish slope on it and we were at the top of the slope, looking down. In the distance I could see the six starting traps and the wooden posts marking the track which ran along the bottom of the field and turned sharp at right angles and came on up the hill towards the crowd, to the finish. Thirty yards beyond the finishing line stood the upturned bicycle for driving the hare. Because it is portable, this is the standard machine for hare - driving used at all flapping tracks. It comprises a flimsy[①] wooden platform about eight feet high, supported on four poles knocked into the ground. On top of the platform there is fixed, upside down with wheels in the air, an ordinary old bicycle. The rear wheel is to the front, facing down the track, and from it the tyre has been removed, leaving a concave[②] metal rim. One end of the cord that pulls the hare is attached to this rim, and the winder (or hare driver), by straddling the bicycle at the back and turning the pedals with his hands, revolves the wheel and winds in the cord around the rim. This pulls the dummy hare towards him at any speed he likes up to forty miles an hour. After each race someone takes the dummy hare (with cord attached) all the way down to the

---

① flimsy: *Adjective* comparatively light and insubstantial; easily damaged 轻而不牢固的;脆弱的;易损坏的

② concave: *Adjective* having an outline or surface that curves inwards like the interior of a circle or sphere (轮廓,表面)凹的

starting traps again, thus unwinding the cord on the wheel, ready for a fresh start. From his high platform, the winder can watch the race and regulate the speed of the hare to keep it just ahead of the leading dog. He can also stop the hare any time he wants to make it a ' no race ' (if the wrong dog looks like winning) by suddenly turning the pedals backwards and getting the cord tangled up in the hub① of the wheel. The other way of doing it is to slow down the hare suddenly, for perhaps one second, and that makes the lead dog automatically check a little so that the others catch up with him. He is an important man, the winder.

I could see Mr. Feasey's winder already standing atop his platform, a powerful - looking man in a blue sweater, leaning on the bicycle and looking down at the crowd through the smoke of his cigarette.

There is a curious law in England which permits race meetings of this kind to be held only seven times a year over one piece of ground. That is why all Mr. Feasey's equipment was movable, and after the seventh meeting he would simply transfer to the next field. The law didn't bother him at all.

There was already a good crowd and the bookmarkers② were erecting their stands in a line over to the right. Claud had Jackie out of the van now and was leading him over to a group of people clustered around a small stocky man dressed in riding-breeches—Mr. Feasey himself. Each person in the group had a dog on a leash and Mr. Feasey kept writing names in a notebook that he held folded in his left hand. I sauntered over to watch.

---

① hub: *Noun* the central part of a wheel, rotating on or with the axle, and from which the spokes radiate 毂

② bookmaker: *Noun* a person whose job is to take bets, especially on horse races, calculate odds, and pay out winnings; the manager of a betting shop(赛马等)赌注登记经纪人

"Which you got there?" Mr. Feasey said, pencil poised above the notebook.

"Midnight," a man said who was holding a black dog.

Mr. Feasey stepped back a pace and looked most carefully at the dog.

"Midnight. Right. I got him down."

"Jane," the next man said.

"Let me look. Jane. . . Jane. . . yes, all right."

"Soldier." This dog was led by a tall man with long teeth who wore a dark-blue, double-breasted lounge suit①, shiny with wear, and when he said 'Soldier' he began slowly to scratch the seat of his trousers with the hand that wasn't holding the leash.

Mr. Feasey bent down to examine the dog. The other man looked up at the sky.

"Take him away," Mr. Feasey said.

The man looked down quick and stopped scratching.

"Go on, take him away."

"Listen, Mr. Feasey," the man said, lisping slightly through his long teeth. "Now don't talk so bloody silly, *please*."

"Go on and beat it, Larry, and stop wasting my time. You know as well as I do the Soldier's got two white toes on his off② fore③."

"Now look, Mr. Feasey," the man said. "You ain't even seen

---

① lounge suit: *Noun* (Brit.) a man's suit consisting of a matching jacket and trousers, worn during the day, especially in the workplace(英国英语)(男式)夹克套装(尤指工作服)

② off: *Adjective* located on the side of a vehicle that is normally furthest from the kerb; offside (车马等)右侧的

③ fore: *Noun* the front part of something, especially a ship 前部;前桅;(马等的)前腿

Soldier for six months at least."

"Come on now, Larry, and beat it. I haven't got time arguing with you." Mr. Feasey didn't appear the least angry. "Next," he said.

I saw Claud step forward leading Jackie. The large bovine face was fixed and wooden, the eyes staring at something about a yard above Mr. Feasey's head, and he was holding the leash so tight his knuckles were like a row of little white onions. I knew just how he was feeling. I felt the same way myself at that moment, and it was even worse when Mr. Feasey suddenly started laughing.

"Hey!" he cried. "Here's the Black Panther. Here's the champion."

"That's right, Mr. Feasey," Claud said.

"Well, I'll 'tell you," Mr. Feasey said, still grinning. "You can take him right back home where he come from. I don't want him."

"But look here, Mr. Feasey..."

"Six or eight times at least I've run him for you now and that's enough. Look—why don't you shoot him and have done with it?"

"Now, listen, Mr. Feasey, please. Just once more and I'll never ask you again."

"Not even once! I got more dogs than I can handle here today. There's no room for crabs like that." I thought Claud was going to cry.

"Now honest, Mr. Feasey," he said. "I been up at six every morning this past two weeks giving him roadwork and massage and buying him beefsteaks, and believe me he's a different dog absolutely than what he was last time he run."

The words 'different dog' caused Mr. Feasey to jump like he'd been pricked with a hatpin. "What's that!" he cried. "Different dog!"

I'll say this for Claud, he kept his head. "See here, Mr. Feasey," he said. "I'll thank you not to go implying things to me. You know very well I didn't mean that."

"All right, all right. But just the same, you can take him away. There's no sense running dogs as slow as him. Take him home now, will you please, and don't hold up the whole meeting."

I was watching Claud. Claud was watching Mr. Feasey. Mr. Feasey was looking round for the next dog to enter up. Under his brown tweedy[①] jacket he wore a yellow pullover[②], and this streak of yellow on his breast and his thin gaitered[③] legs and the way he jerked his head from side to side made him seem like some sort of a little perky[④] bird—a goldfinch[⑤], perhaps.

Claud took a step forward. His face was beginning to purple slightly with the outrage of it all and I could see his Adam's apple moving up and down as he swallowed.

"I'll tell you what I'll do, Mr. Feasey. I'm so absolutely sure this dog's improved I'll bet you a quid[⑥] he don't finish last. There you are."

Mr. Feasey turned slowly around and looked at Claud. "You crackers?" he asked. "I'll bet you a quid, there you are, just to prove what I'm saying."

---

① tweedy: *Noun* (of a garment) made of tweed cloth(衣服)用粗花呢制的

② pullover: *Noun* a knitted garment put on over the head and covering the top half of the body 套衫;套头毛衣

③ gaiter: *Noun* a garment similar to leggings, worn to cover or protect the ankle and lower leg 绑腿(这里的"gaitered"用作形容词)

④ perky: *Adjective* cheerful and lively 得意扬扬的;神气的(e. g. She certainly looked less than her usual perky self. 她看起来确实不如往常那样生龙活虎。)

⑤ goldfinch: *Noun* a brightly coloured finch with yellow feathers in the plumage 红额金翅(雀);黄雀;金翅黄雀

⑥ quid: *Noun* (Brit. informal) one pound sterling(英国英语的非正式表达)一英镑

It was a dangerous move, certain to cause suspicion, but Claud knew it was the only thing left to do. There was silence while Mr. Feasey bent down and examined the dog. I could see the way his eyes were moving slowly over the animal's whole body, part by part. There was something to admire in the man's thoroughness, and in his memory; something to fear also in this self – confident little rogue① who held in his head the shape and colour and markings of perhaps several hundred different but very similar dogs. He never needed more than one little clue—a small scar, a splay② toe, a trifle in at the hocks, a less pronounced wheelback, a slightly darker brindle③—Mr. Feasey always remembered.

So I watched him now as he bent down over Jackie. His face was pink and fleshy, the mouth small and tight as though it couldn't stretch enough to make a smile, and the eyes were like two little cameras focused sharply on the dog.

"Well," he said, straightening up. "It's the same dog, anyway."

"I should hope so too!" Claud cried. "Just what sort of a fellow you think I am, Mr. Feasey?"

"I think you're crackers, that's what I think. But it's a nice easy way to make a quid. I suppose you forgot how Amber Flash nearly beat him on three legs last meeting?"

"This one wasn't fit then," Claud said. "He hadn't had beefsteak and massage and roadwork like I've been giving him lately. But look Mr. Feasey, you're not to go sticking him in top grade just to win the bet.

---

① rogue: *Noun* a dishonest or unprincipled man 无赖;流氓;恶棍

② splay: *Adjective* [usu. in combination] turned outward or widened 向外张开的

③ brindle: *Noun* [*Mass Noun*] a brownish or tawny colour of animal fur, with streaks of other colour(动物毛皮)带其他颜色斑纹的浅棕色(或黄褐色)

This is a bottom grade dog, Mr. Feasey. You know that."

Mr. Feasey laughed. The small button mouth opened into a tiny circle and he laughed and looked at the crowd who laughed with him. "Listen," he said, laying a hairy hand on Claud's shoulder. "I know my dogs. I don't have to do any fiddling[①] around to win this quid. He goes in bottom."

"Right," Claud said. "That's a bet." He walked away with Jackie and I joined him.

"Jesus, Gordon, that was a near one!"

"Shook me."

"But we're in now," Claud said. He had that breathless look on his face again and he was walking about quick and funny, like the ground was burning his feet.

People were still coming through the gate into the field and there were easily three hundred of them now. Now a very nice crowd. Sharpnosed men and women with dirty faces and bad teeth and quick shifty eyes. The dregs[②] of the big town. Oozing out like sewage[③] from a cracked pipe and trickling along the road through the gate and making a smelly little pond of sewage at the top end of the field. They were all there, all the spivs, and the gipsies and the touts[④] and the dregs and the

---

① fiddle: *Noun* (informal, chiefly Brit.) an act of defrauding, cheating, or falsifying(非正式,主英)欺骗;欺诈;伪造;骗局

② dregs: *Noun* the remnants of a liquid left in a container, together with any sediment 沉淀物;残渣;渣滓(e. g. Dregs settled at the bottom of the container. 渣滓沉淀在容器的底部。)

③ sewage: *Noun* [mass Noun] waste water and excrement conveyed in sewers 污水;污物

④ tout: (US) a person who offers racing tips for a share of any resulting winnings(美)赛马内部消息提供者

sewage and the scraping and the scum from the cracked drainpipes of the big town. Some with dogs, some without. Dogs led about on pieces of string, miserable dogs with hanging heads, thin mangy[1] dogs with sores on their quarters (from sleeping on board), sad old dogs with grey muzzles, doped dogs, dogs stuffed with porridge to stop them winning, dogs walking stiff-legged—one especially, a white one. "Claud, why is that white one walking so stiff - legged?"

"Which one?"

"That one over there."

"Ah. Yes, I see. Very probably because he's been hung."

"Hung?"

"Yes, hung. Suspended in a harness for twenty - four hours with his legs dangling."

"Good God, but why?"

"To make him run slow, of course. Some people don't hold with dope or stuffing or strapping up. So they hang 'em."

"I see."

"Either that," Claud said, "or they sandpaper them. Rub their pads with rough sandpaper and take the skin off so it hurts when they run."

"Yes, I see."

And then the fitter, brighter-looking dogs, the better-fed ones who get horsemeat every day, not pig-swill or rusk[2] and cabbage water, their coats shinier, their tails moving, pulling at their leads, undoped, unstuffed, awaiting perhaps a more unpleasant fate, the muzzle-strap to be tightened an extra four notches. *But make sure he can breathe now*,

---

① Mangy: (also as "mangey") having mange 患疥癣的;生癞疮的

② rusk: *Noun* a light, dry biscuit or piece of rebaked bread, especially one prepared for use as baby food (尤指用作婴儿食品的)脆饼干;面包干

Jock. Don't choke him completely. Don't let's have him collapse in the middle of the race. Just-so he wheezes[1] *a bit, see. Go on tightening it up an extra notch at a time until you can hear him wheezing. You'll see his mouth open and he'll start breathing heavy. Then it's just right, but not if his eyeballs is bulging. Watch out for that, will you? Okay?*

Okay.

"Let's get away from the crowd, Gordon. It don't do Jackie no good getting excited by all these other dogs."

We walked up the slope to where the cars were parked, then back and forth in front of the line of cars, keeping the dog on the move. Inside some of the cars I could see men sitting with their dogs, and the men scowled[2] at us through the windows as we went by.

"Watch out now, Gordon. We don't want any trouble."

"No, all right."

These were the best dogs of all, the secret ones kept in the cars and taken out quick just to be entered up (under some invented name) and put back again quick and held there till the last minute, then straight down to the traps and back again into the cars after the race so no nosy bastard gets too close a look. The trainer at the big stadium said so. *All right, he said. You can have him, but for Christsake don't let anybody recognize him. There's thousands of people know this dog, so you've got to be careful, see. And it'll cost you fifty pound.*

Very fast dogs these, but it doesn't much matter how fast they are they probably get the needle anyway, just to make sure. One and a half

---

① wheeze: *Verb* [no obj.] (of a person) breathe with a whistling or rattling sound in the chest, as a result of obstruction in the air passages(人)喘;喘息

② scowl: *Verb* [no obj.] frown in an angry or bad-tempered way(发怒)皱眉

c. c. s. of ether, subcutaneous[1], done in the car, injected very slow. That'll put ten lengths on any dog. Or sometimes it's caffein[2] in oil, or camphor[3]. That makes them go too. The men in the big cars know all about that. And some of them know about whisky. But that's intravenous[4]. Not so easy when it's intravenous. Might miss the vein. All you got to do is miss the vein and it don't work and where are you then? So it's ether, or it's caffein, or it's camphor. *Don't give her too much of that stuff now, Jock. What does she weigh? Fifty-eight pounds. All right then, you know what the man told us. Wait a minute now. I got it written down on a piece of paper. Here it is. Point I of a c. c. per 10 pounds bodyweight equals 5 lengths over 300 yards. Wait a minute now while I work it out. Oh Christ, you better guess it. Just guess it, Jock. It'll be all right you'll find. Shouldn't be any trouble anyway because I picked the others in the race myself. Cost me a tenner[5] to old Feasey. A bloody tenner I gave him, my dear Mr. Feasey, I says, that's for your birthday and because I love you.*

Thank you ever so much, Mr. Feasey says. Thank you, my good and trusted friend.

---

① subcutaneous: *Adjective* (Anatomy & Medicine) situated or applied under the skin(剖,医)皮下的;皮下用的

② caffeine: *Noun* [*mass noun*] an alkaloid compound which is found especially in tea and coffee plants and is a stimulant of the central nervous system 咖啡因;茶精(一种兴奋剂)

③ camphor: *Noun* [Mass Noun] a white volatile crystalline substance with an aromatic smell and bitter taste, occurring in certain essential oils 樟脑

④ intravenous: *Adjective* existing or taking place within, or administered into, a vein or veins 静脉内的;静脉内发生的;静脉的

⑤ tenner: *Noun* (Brit. informal) a ten-pound note(英国英语的非正式表达)十英镑钞票;十英镑

And for stopping them, for the men in the big cars, it's chlorbutal①. That's beauty, chlorbutal, because you can give it the night before, especially to someone else's dog. Or Pethidine②. Pethidine and hyoscine③ mixed, whatever that may be.

"Lot of fine old English sporting gentry here," Claud said.

"Certainly are."

"Watch your pockets, Gordon. You got that money hidden away?"

We walked around the back of the line of cars—between the cars and the hedge—and I saw Jackie stiffen and begin to pull forward on the leash, advancing with a stiff crouching tread. About thirty yards away there were two men. One was holding a large fawn greyhound, the dog stiff and tense like Jackie. The other was holding a sack in his hands.

"Watch," Claud whispered, "they're giving him a kill."

Out of the sack on to the grass tumbled a small white rabbit, fluffy white, young, tame. It righted itself and sat still, crouching in the hunched up way rabbits crouch, its nose close to the ground. A frightened rabbit. Out of the sack so suddenly on to the grass with such a bump. Into the bright light. The dog was going mad with excitement, now, jumping up against the leash, pawing the ground, throwing himself forward, whining④. The rabbit saw the dog. It drew in its head and

---

① chlorbutal: 疑为"chlorbutol"误拼形式。

chlorbutol: 氯丁醇,三氯叔丁醇。英文别名:chlorobutanol。

② pethidine: *Noun* [*Mass Noun*] (Medicine) a synthetic compound used as a painkilling drug, especially for women in labour(医)盐酸哌替啶

③ hyoscine: *Noun* [*Mass Noun*] (Chemistry) a poisonous plant alkaloid used as an anti-emetic in motion sickness and as a preoperative medication for examination of the eye(化)东莨菪碱

④ whine: *Verb* [no obj.] give or make a long, high-pitched complaining cry or sound 发出哀叫(哀叹,哀鸣)声

stayed still, paralysed with fear. The man transferred his hold to the dog's collar, and the dog twisted and jumped and tried to get free. The other man pushed the rabbit with his foot but it was too terrified to move. He pushed it again, flicking it forward with his toe like a football, and the rabbit rolled over several times, righted itself and began to hop over the grass away from the dog. The other man released the dog which pounced with one huge pounce upon the rabbit, and then came the squeals[1], not very loud but shrill and anguished and lasting rather a long time.

"There you are," Claud said. "That's a kill."

"Not sure I like it very much."

"I told you before, Gordon. Most of 'em does it. Keens the dog up before a race."

"I still don't like it."

"Nor me. But they all do it. Even in the big stadiums the trainers do it. Proper barbary I call it."

We strolled away and below us on the slope of the hill the crowd was thickening and the bookies' stands with the names written on them in red and gold and blue were all erected now in a long line back of the crowd, each bookie already stationed on an upturned box beside his stand, a pack of numbered cards in one hand, a piece of chalk in the other, his clerk behind him with book and pencil. Then we saw Mr. Feasey walking over to a blackboard that was nailed to a post stuck in the ground.

"He's chalking up the first race," Claud said. "Come on, quick!"

We walked rapidly down the hill and joined the crowd. Mr. Feasey was writing the runners on the blackboard, copying names from his soft-covered notebook, and a little hush of suspense fell upon the crowd as

① squeal: *Noun* a long, high-pitched cry or noise 长而尖的叫声(或声响)

they watched.

1. SALLY
2. THREE QUID
3. SNAILBOX LADY
4. BLACK PANTHER
5. WHISKY
6. ROCKIT

"He's in it!" Claud whispered. "First race! Trap four! Now, listen, Gordon! Give me a fiver[①] quick to show the winder." Claud could hardly speak from excitement. That patch of whiteness had returned around his nose and eyes, and when I handed him a five pound note, his whole arm was shaking as he took it. The man who was going to wind the bicycle pedals was still standing on top of the wooden platform in his blue jersey, smoking. Claud went over and stood below him, looking up.

"See this fiver," he said, talking softly, holding it folded small in the palm of his hand.

The man glanced at it without moving his head.

"Just so long as you wind her true this race, see. No stopping and no slowing down and run her fast. Right?"

The man didn't move but there was a slight, almost imperceptible lifting of the eyebrows. Claud turned away.

"Now, look, Gordon. Get the money on gradual, all in little bits like I told you. Just keep going down the line putting on little bits so you

---

① fiver: *Noun* (Brit. informal) a five-pound note(英国英语的非正式表达)面值五英镑的钞票

don't kill the price, see. And I'll be walking Jackie down very slow, as slow as I dare, to give you plenty of time. Right?"

"Right."

"And don't forget to be standing ready to catch him at the end of the race. Get him clear away from all them others when they start fighting for the hare. Grab a hold of him tight and don't let go till I come running up with the collar and lead. That Whisky's a gipsy dog and he'll tear the leg off anything as gets in his way."

"Right," I said. "Here we go."

I saw Claud lead Jackie over to the finishing post and collect a yellow jacket with "4" written on it large. Also a muzzle. The other five runners were there too, the owners fussing around them, putting on their numbered jackets, adjusting their muzzles. Mr. Feasey was officiating①, hopping about in his tight riding-breeches like an anxious perky bird, and once I saw him say something to Claud and laugh. Claud ignored him. Soon they would all start to lead the dogs down the track, the long walk down the hill and across to the far corner of the field to the starting-traps. It would take them ten minutes to walk it. I've got at least ten minutes, I told myself, and then I began to push my way through the crowd standing six or seven deep in front of the line of bookies.

"Even money Whisky! Even money Whisky! Five to two Sally! Even money Whisky! Four to one Snailbox! Come on now! Hurry up, hurry up. Which is it?"

On every board all down the line the Black Panther was chalked up at twenty-five to one. I edged forward to the nearest book.

"Three pounds Black Panther," I said, holding out the money.

---

① officiate: *Verb* [no obj.] act as an official in charge of something, especially a sporting event 经办(尤指经办体育比赛项目)掌管;经管;负责

The man on the box had an inflamed magenta face and traces of some white substance around the corners of his mouth. He snatched the money and dropped it in his satchel①. "Seventy-five pounds to three Black Panther," he said. "Number forty-two." He handed me a ticket and his clerk recorded the bet. I stepped back and wrote rapidly on the back of the ticket 75 to 3, then slipped it into the inside pocket of my jacket with the money.

So long as I continued to spread the cash out thin like this, it ought to be all right. And anyway, on Claud's instructions, I'd made a point of betting a few pounds on the ringer every time he'd run so as not to arouse any suspicion when the real day arrived. Therefore, with some confidence, I went all the way down the line staking three pounds with each book. I didn't hurry, but I didn't waste any time either, and after each bet I wrote the amount on the back of the card before slipping it into my pocket. There were seventeen bookies. I had seventeen tickets and had laid out fifty-one pounds without disturbing the price one point. Forty-nine pounds left to get on. I glanced quickly down the hill. One owner and his dog had already reached the traps. The others were only twenty or thirty yards away. Except for Claud. Claud and Jackie were only half way there. I could see Claud in his old khaki greatcoat sauntering slowly along with Jackie pulling ahead keenly on the leash, and once I saw him stop completely and bend down pretending to pick something up. When he went on again he seemed to have developed a limp so as to go slower still. I hurried back to the other end of the line to start again.

"Three pounds Black Panther."

---

① satchel: *Noun* a bag carried on the shoulder by a long strap and closed by a flap, used especially for school books(有长背带和翻盖的)书包;小背包

The bookmaker, the one with the magenta face and the white substance around the mouth, glanced up sharply, remembering the last time, and in one swift almost graceful movement of the arm he licked his fingers and wiped the figure twenty-five neatly off the board. His wet fingers left a small dark patch opposite Black Panther's name.

"All right, you got one more seventy-five to three; he said. "But that's the lot." Then he raised his voice and shouted, "Fifteen to one Black Panther! Fifteens the Panther!"

All down the line the twenty-fives were wiped out and it was fifteen to one the Panther now. I took it quick, but by the time I was through the bookies had had enough and they weren't quoting him any more. They'd only taken six pounds each, but they stood to lose a hundred and fifty, and for them—small-time[①] bookies at a little country flapping-track—that was quite enough for one race, thank you very much. I felt pleased the way I'd managed it. Lots of tickets now. I took them out of my pockets and counted them and they were like a thin pack of cards in my hand. Thirty-three tickets in all. And what did we stand to win? Let me see... something over two thousand pounds. Claud had said he'd win it thirty lengths. Where was Claud now?

Far away down the hill I could see the khaki greatcoat standing by the traps and the big black dog alongside. All the other dogs were already in and the owners were beginning to walk away. Claud was bending down, coaxing Jackie into number four, and then he was closing the door and turning away and beginning to run up the hill towards the crowd, the greatcoat flapping around him. He kept looking back over his shoulder as he ran.

---

① small-time: *Adjective* (informal) unimportant; minor(非正式)次要的;无关紧要的

Beside the traps the starter stood, and his hand was up waving a handkerchief. At the other end of the track, beyond the winning - post, quite close to where I stood, the man in the blue jersey was straddling the upturned bicycle on top of the wooden platform and he saw the signal and waved back and began to turn the pedals with his hands. Then a tiny white dot in the distance—the artificial hare that was in reality a football with a piece of white rabbit-skin tacked on to it—began to move away from the traps, accelerating fast. The traps went up and the dogs flew out. They flew out in a single dark lump, all together, as though it were one wide dog instead of six, and almost at once I saw Jackie drawing away from the field. I knew it was Jackie because of the colour. There weren't any other black dogs in the race. It was Jackie, all right. Don't move, I told myself. Don't move a muscle or an eyelid or a toe or a finger-tip. Stand quite still and don't move. Watch him going. Come on Jackson, boy! No, don't shout. It's unlucky to shout. And don't move. Be all over in twenty seconds. Round the sharp bend now and coming up the hill and he must be fifteen or twenty lengths clear. Easy twenty lengths. Don't count the lengths, it's unlucky. And don't move. Don't move your head. Watch him out of your eye-corners. Watch that Jackson go! He's really laying down to it now up that hill. He's won it now! He can't lose it now.

When I got over to him he was fighting the rabbit - skin and trying to pick it up in his mouth, but his muzzle wouldn't allow it, and the other dogs were pounding up behind him and suddenly they were all on top of him grabbing for the rabbit and I got hold of him round the neck and dragged him clear like Claud had said and knelt down on the grass and held him tight with both arms round his body. The other catchers were having a time all trying to grab their own dogs.

Then Claud was beside me, blowing heavily, unable to speak from blowing and excitement, removing Jackie's muzzle, putting on the collar and lead, and Mr. Feasey was there too standing with hands on hips, the button mouth pursed up tight like a mushroom, the two little cameras staring at Jackie all over again.

"So that's the game, is it?" he said.

Claud was bending over the dog and acting like he hadn't heard

"I don't want you here no more after this, you understand that?"

Claud went on fiddling with Jackie's collar.

I heard someone behind us saying, "That flat-faced bastard swung it properly on old Feasey this time." Someone else laughed. Mr. Feasey walked away. Claud straightened up and went over with Jackie to the hare driver in the blue jersey who had dismounted from his platform.

"Cigarette," Claud said, offering the pack.

The man took one, also the five pound note that was folded up small in Claud's fingers.

"Thanks," Claud said. "Thanks very much."

"Don't mention," the man said. Then Claud turned to me. "You get it all on, Gordon?" He was jumping up and down and rubbing his hands and patting Jackie, and his lips trembled as he spoke.

"Yes. Half at twenty-fives, half at fifteens."

"Oh Christ, Gordon, that's marvellous. Wait here till I get the suitcase."

"You take Jackie," I said, "and go and sit in the car. I'll see you later."

There was nobody around the bookies now. I was the only one with anything to collect, and I walked slowly with a sort of dancing stride and a wonderful bursting feeling in my chest, towards the first one in the line, the man with the magenta face and the white substance on his mouth. I stood in front of him and I took all the time I wanted going through my pack of tickets to find the two that were his. The name was Syd Pratchett. It was written up large across his board in gold letters on a scarlet field—SYD PRATCHETT. THE BEST ODDS IN THE MIDLANDS. PROMPT SETTLEMENT.

I handed him the first ticket and said, "Seventy - eight pounds to come." It sounded so good I said it again, making a delicious little song of it. "Seventy-eight pounds to come on this one." I didn't mean to gloat[①] over Mr. Pratchett. As a matter of fact, I was beginning to like him quite a lot. I even felt sorry for him having to fork out so much money. I hoped his wife and kids wouldn't suffer.

"Number forty-two," Mr. Pratchett said, turning to his clerk who held the big book. "Forty-two wants seventy-eight pounds." There was a pause while the clerk ran his finger down the column of recorded bets. He did this twice, then he looked up at the boss and began to shake his head.

"No," he said. "Don't pay. That ticket backed Snailbox Lady."

Mr. Pratchett, standing on his box, leaned over and peered down at the book. He seemed to be disturbed by what the clerk had said, and there was a look of genuine concern on the huge magenta face.

The clerk is a fool, I thought, and any moment now Mr. Pratchett's going to tell him so.

But when Mr. Pratchett turned back to me, the eyes had become narrow and hostile. "Now, look Charley," he said softly. "Don't let's have any of that. You know very well you bet Snailbox. What's the idea?"

"I bet Black Panther," I said. "Two separate bets of three pounds each at twenty-five to one. Here's the second ticket."

This time he didn't even bother to check it with the book. "You bet

---

① gloat: *Verb* [no obj.] contemplate or dwell on one's own success or another's misfortune with smugness or malignant pleasure 沾沾自喜;幸灾乐祸

Snailbox, Charley," he said. "I remember you coming round." With that, he turned away from me and started wiping the names of the last race runners off his board with a wet rag. Behind him, the clerk had closed the book and was lighting himself a cigarette. I stood watching them, and I could feel the sweat beginning to break through the skin all over my body.

"Let me see the book."

Mr. Pratchett blew his nose in the wet rag and dropped it to the ground. "Look," he said, "why don't you go away and stop annoying me?"

The point was this: a bookmaker's ticket, unlike a totalisator ticket①, never has anything written on it regarding the nature of your bet. This is normal practice, the same at every racetrack in the country, whether it's the Silver Ring at Newmarket②, the Royal Enclosure at Ascot③, or a tiny country flapping – track near Oxford. All you receive is a card bearing the bookie's name and a serial number. The wager④ is (or should be) recorded by the bookie's clerk in his book alongside the number of the ticket, but apart from that there is no evidence at all of how you betted.

"Go on," Mr. Pratchett was saying. "Hop it."

---

① 在《罗尔德·达尔短篇故事集锦》(The Collected Short Stories of Roald Dahl)中,此处为"totalisator ticket"(马票),而在《罗尔德·达尔小说精品集》(The Best of Roald Dahl),此处为"parimutuel ticket"(马票)。

② Newmarket: *Noun* a town in eastern England, in Suffolk; pop. 16,130 (1981). It is a noted horse-racing centre and headquarters of the Jockey Club. 纽马基特(英格兰东部一城镇,位于萨福克郡,1981 年人口 16,130,是著名的赛马中心和赛马总会总部所在地。)

③ Ascot: 英国爱斯科赛马场;爱斯科赛马会

④ wager: *Noun* more formal term for "bet"(非正式)赌注

I stepped back a pace and glanced down the long line of bookmakers. None of them was looking my way. Each was standing motionless on his little wooden box beside his wooden placard, staring straight ahead into the crowd. I went up to the next one and presented a ticket.

"I had three pounds on Black Panther at twenty-five to one," I said firmly. "Seventy-eight pounds to come."

This man, who had a soft inflamed face, went through exactly the same routine as Mr. Pratchett, questioning his clerk, peering at the book, and giving me the same answers.

"Whatever's the matter with you?" he said quietly, speaking to me as though I were eight years old. "Trying such a silly thing as that."

This time I stepped well back. "You dirty thieving bastards!" I cried. "The whole lot of you!"

Automatically, as though they were puppets, all the heads down the line flicked round and looked at me. The expressions didn't alter. It was just the heads that moved, all seventeen of them, and seventeen pairs of cold glassy[①] eyes looked down at me. There was not the faintest flicker of interest in any of them.

"Somebody spoke," they seemed to be saying. "We didn't hear it. It's a nice day today."

The crowd, sensing excitement, was beginning to move in around me. I ran back to Mr. Pratchett, right up close to him and poked him in the stomach with my finger. "You're a thief! A lousy little thief!" I shouted.

The extraordinary thing was, Mr. Pratchett didn't seem to resent this

---

① glassy: *Adjective* (of a person's eyes or expression) showing no interest or animation; dull and glazed(人的眼睛,表情)漠然的;无生气的;迟钝的;凝滞的

at all.

"Well, I never," he said. "Look who's talking."

Then suddenly the big face broke into a wide, frog-like grin, and he looked over at the crowd and shouted. "Look who's talking!"

All at once everybody started to laugh. Down the line the bookies were coming to life and turning to each other and laughing and pointing at me and shouting, "Look who's talking! Look who's talking!" The crowd began to take up the cry as well, and I stood there on the grass alongside Mr. Pratchett with this wad① of tickets as thick as a pack of cards in my hand, listening to them and feeling slightly hysterical. Over the heads of the people I could see Mr. Feasey beside his blackboard, already chalking up the runners for the next race; and then beyond him, far away up the top of the field, I caught sight of Claud standing by the van, waiting for me with the suitcase in his hand.

It was time to go home.

三、翻译探索

除了在上一节提到的赛狗方面的表达，本篇的翻译中还涉及很多医学和化学方面的名称，均需一一查证，认真处理。个别表达也许是达尔本人笔误，查无结果，只能处理成近似的表达。

费西先生

时来运转的那一天终于到来。那天早晨，我们俩都早早起床。

我溜溜达达走进厨房刮脸，而克劳德则立马穿好衣服，到外边去准备稻草。厨房位于房子的前部，透过窗户，我看到太阳刚刚从一排树木的后方升起，那排树木生长在山谷另一面的山脊顶部。

① wad: *Noun* a bundle of paper, banknotes, or documents 一捆纸；一沓钞票或文件

克劳德每次抱起一大抱稻草经过厨房窗前的时候,我都能通过镜子的边缘注意到他的神态:表情专注,气喘吁吁,大大的、子弹头形的圆脑袋向前探伸,前额皱起一道道深深的皱纹,皱纹一直到发际线才消失。他的这副模样我以前只看到过一次,那是他向克拉丽丝求婚的一天晚上。今天,他兴奋异常,走起路来甚至都显得可笑荒唐:脚轻轻抬起,轻轻落下,感觉就像加油站周边的混凝土地面有点过热、会烫坏他的鞋底似的。他将稻草抱来一捆又一捆,堆到篷车的后部,好让杰基在那儿待得舒服一些。

接着,他走进厨房,开始做早餐。我看到他将一锅汤放到炉灶上,拿起一把长长的金属勺,开始搅动起来。那把勺子在汤里就这么一直地搅啊,搅啊,一直搅到沸腾才停下来。其间,大约每隔半分钟,他就倾斜身体靠上前,将鼻子伸进蒸汽里嗅一嗅,锅里煮的是马肉汤,散发出甜丝丝的味道,令人反胃。然后,他又额外向锅里加了一些食材:三头去了皮的洋葱、几根小胡萝卜、一杯大荨麻碎叶、一茶匙瓦伦丁肉汁、十二滴鱼肝油。他那几个大大的、胖胖的手指尖每触摸到一样东西,都轻拿轻放,好像每一样东西都是彩色装饰玻璃上碎裂时留下的一小块碎片。他从冰柜里取出一些切碎的马肉,抓出一把撒进杰基的碗里,抓出三把放进另一只碗里。汤煮好后,他就分别往这两只碗里倒,将汤浇到肉上面。

过去的五个月里,每天早晨我都能看到这样相同的一幕上演,但是,哪一天他都没有像今天这样神情专注,甚至有喘不过气来的感觉。他一声不吭,甚至连瞅也没有瞅我一眼。接着,转身走出去,呼唤那两条狗。此时,就连他的后脖颈和双肩都似乎低声在说:"噢,老天,什么差错都别出。今天,千万不要让我做错任何事。"

在狗棚里,他一边给狗套皮带,我一边听到他跟那两条狗轻声说着什么。把它们归拢到一起牵进厨房的时候,它们欢快地跳跃起来,扯着皮带奔向早餐。只见两条狗的前腿蹦上跳下,大大的尾巴左右摇晃,就像鞭子一样。

"好啦,"克劳德最终说道。"哪一条是杰基?"

大多数情况下,每天早晨他都会提出要跟我赌一盒香烟,但是今天，他要押更大的注。我知道，此时此刻，他所要得到的就是一点点额外的信心保证。

克劳德两眼盯着我，我则绕着那两条长得一模一样的大狗转了一圈，他随即撤到一边，手拉着皮带站开一臂之远，好让我看得更清楚一些。这两条狗都是高高的，很漂亮，都长着一身天鹅绒般的柔软的黑毛。

“杰基！”我喊道。其实，我这是故伎重演，从未奏效。“嗨，杰基！”这时，那两只一模一样的脑袋，都一下子转了过来，用一模一样的表情看着我——四只眼睛盯着我的两只眼睛，那四只眼睛都很明亮，一模一样，颜色深黄。曾经有过那么一次，我寻思着，其中一条的两只眼睛比另一条两只眼睛的黄色稍微深那么一点儿；也曾经有过那么一次，我认为，我能够辨认出哪一条是杰基，原因是杰基胸部肌肉更厚实一些，后腿部肌肉稍微多一点儿，但却不是那么一回事。

“快啊，”克劳德催促。不管以前猜对与否，他还是希望今天我会猜错。

“这一条，”我说。“这一条是杰基。”

“哪一条？”

“就是左边的这一条。”

“看看你！”他大叫，瞬间笑逐颜开。“你又猜错啦！”

“我想，我没猜错。”

“你错得几乎一塌糊涂、登峰造极。现在听着，戈登，我跟你说道说道。过去的几周时间里，每天早晨你辨认杰基的时候，你知道吗？”

“知道什么？”

“我一直帮你数着呢。结果是，你对的次数没有超过一半啊！要是投掷硬币决定的话，你对的会更多。”

他的意思就是，我每天都跟这两条狗近距离接触，还辨别不好谁是谁呢。那么，我们还有什么理由对费西先生诚惶诚恐呢？克劳德清楚，在识别哪条狗是冒名顶替这方面，费西先生是出了名的行家里手。但是，他也清楚，在两条狗身上找不到任何区别的情况下，很难辨别出哪条是哪条。

他将碗都放到地上,给杰基的那只碗,里面的肉最少,因为杰基今天要跑赛。他退后看着它们吃食的时候,脸上又浮现出疑虑重重的表情。他那双大大的、灰白的眼睛直勾勾地盯着杰基,神情痴迷,充满了爱意。但是,截止到最近,他的这种眼神只对克拉丽丝表露过。

“戈登啊,要知道,”他说。“我反复给你讲过,在过去的数百年时间里,冒名顶替的情况各种各样,有的天衣无缝,有的糟糕笨拙,但是,在整个赛狗历史上,还从来没有过像这样冒名顶替的。”

“我希望你说的没错,”我说。随后,我的记忆开始了穿越之旅,回到了四个月以前,回到了圣诞节之前那个冰冷的午后。当时,克劳德向我借了篷车,朝埃尔兹伯里方向驶去,但并没有说要去什么地方。我当时猜想,他去看克拉丽丝了。但是,那天下午晚些时候,他带着这条狗回来了,说是给了一名男子一些好处,花了三十五先令买下的。

“它跑得快吗?”当时我这样问道。我们就站在外面加油泵的旁边,克劳德看着自己手里牵着的狗,几片雪花飘落下来,落到狗背上,篷车的马达还没有熄火。

“还快呢!”克劳德说。“在你的一生中,他就是你见过的最慢的狗啦!”

“那样的话,你买他干吗?”

“这个嘛,”他说。同时,那张愚钝的大脸上露出一副神秘兮兮、奸诈狡猾的表情。“我突然想到,它看起来或许有那么一点点像杰基。你认为呢?”

“既然你这么说,我觉得它还真的有那么一点像。”

他将拴狗的皮带递给我,我就把这条新买的狗牵进了屋,将它的毛擦干,而克劳德则去狗棚牵他的最爱——杰基。牵回来的时候,我们就第一次将两条狗放到了一起。我现在还记得,当时他向后一退说:“噢,老天啊!”他站在两条狗的前面,整个人瞬间就僵住了,仿佛看到幽灵一般,紧接着只见他动作敏捷,一声不吭,蹲下身去,开始仔仔细细、一点一点地比较起来,默默地比较了很长的时间。其间,他甚至将两条狗的趾甲和已经退化的悬蹄——每只狗身上有十八个这样的无机能趾,也一个一个精心做了比对,看看颜色是否相配。我感觉到,每过一秒钟,他的喜悦、兴奋之情就有所增加,就像整个屋子感觉越来越热一样。

“看呐,”他最终站了起来,说道。“你带着它们在屋子里溜几圈,可以吗?”他靠着炉子,就那样待了足足五六分钟的时间,脑袋歪向一侧,眼睛半睁半闭地看着这两条狗,同时还皱起眉头,咬着嘴唇。之后,他好像是不大相信第一次亲眼所见似的,又蹲下身来,把刚才所做的比对又重新做了一遍。但是,就在重新比对到一半的时候,他突然间跳了起来,看着我,表情僵硬而紧张,两个鼻孔的边缘和眼睛的周围都变成了白色,很是令人奇怪。“好了,”他说道,声音有点颤抖。“你知道吗?我们赢定啦,我们有钱啦。”

接下来,我们俩就在厨房不断地碰头、密谋,制定出详细的计划,商量如何选出最佳的赛道。然后,每隔一周的星期六下午,我就关闭加油站,开车把这条冒名顶替的狗载到牛津市。这样做一共有八次,每次都会让我损失整整一个下午的生意。一到牛津,就奔向黑丁利附近荒郊野外的一条破旧的赛道,那儿可是赛狗赌大钱的地方,但实际上,除了一行破柱子、一条用以标记场地的带子,以及用以拖动赛道上假兔子的一辆倒置的自行车之外,那儿几乎一无所有。那里远处的一端,可以看到六个放狗的隔栏,还有发令员。在那十六周的时间里,我们俩开车载着这条冒名顶替的狗去那儿,一共去了八次。每次都带着它跟费西先生一同入场,冒着雨、顶着严寒站在人群的边缘,等待着有人用粉笔将它的名字写到黑板上——我们俩称它为“黑豹”。每次它的名字一出现,克劳德就总是将它牵下去,走到隔栏那儿,而我则站在终点线那儿,等着将它抓住,好让它远离好斗分子——那些吉卜赛犬。吉卜赛人经常心怀不轨地让这些狗参加比赛,意欲在比赛结束的时候将另外一条狗撕成碎片。

这么多次一路辛苦奔波,把这条狗载到那儿去,看着它赛跑,同时希望并祈祷它无论如何都要跑在最后一名。你可要知道,每每此时,某种伤感之情就油然而生。当然,祈祷是根本不需要的,我们永远也不会真正担心的,因为这位老伙计根本飞奔不起来,它跑起来简直就像螃蟹在爬,这是明摆着的事实。有一次,一条名叫“闪亮琥珀”的浅黄褐色的大狗在跑赛中一条腿踏进坑里,折断了跗关节,用三条腿跑完全程,得了最后一名。这一次,黑豹没有跑到最后一名,也是唯一的一次,但即使这样,它也是勉勉强强领先于最后一名闪亮琥珀的。就这样,它的成绩一路下滑到了谷底,成了下三烂货色。我们最后一次去那儿的时候,所有的赌注经纪人不是将它的下注赔率标为二十比一,就是三十比一,还不断喊着它的名字,乞求人们支持它。

事到如今,在这个阳光明媚的四月里的一天,终于该轮到杰基上场、取代它了。克劳德说,让这个冒名顶替者再上场,是万万使不得的。否则,费西先生会对它腻烦透顶,将其彻底踢出赛局,因为它跑得实在是太慢了。克劳德还说,从心理学角度来说,这是让杰基顶替的最佳时机。在三十至五十个身长的距离内,杰基会稳操胜券。

克劳德开始饲养杰基的时候,杰基还是一条小狗,虽然现在只有十五个月大,但已经是跑赛高手了。杰基从未参加过比赛,但我们俩清楚,它跑得够快,因为在阿克斯布里奇的那条私人小赛道上训练它时,给它掐算过时间。它还是七个月大的时候,克劳德每周日都带它去那个私人赛道训练,仅有一次例外,那次是给它注射某种疫苗来着。克劳德说,在费西先生的赛道上,杰基的速度或许不足以高居榜首,但就我们现在给它训练的程度来看,在榜底下三烂的货色中,它就是意外摔倒、再爬起来继续奔跑的话,仍然能以二十个身长的优势获胜。再退一步说,也能以十个身长的优势,甚至十五个身长的优势获胜。

所以,今天上午我只需去村里的银行一趟,从我的账户取出五十英镑给我自己,再取出五十英镑借给克劳德当赌金用。接着,在中午十二点的时候,我就会关闭加油站,在其中一个加油泵上贴一个通知,写上“今日外出不营业”的字样。克劳德则会把冒名顶替者关到后面的狗棚里,再把杰基装上篷车,我们就会这样出发的。我要说的是,我并不像克劳德那样兴奋异常,可话又说回来了,我也没有指望用赛狗赢的钱做什么重大的事情,比如说买房子啦,结婚啦,等等。

我也不是像克劳德那样，天生就喜欢灰狗，整天四处奔走之时，除了灰狗，别的什么都不想，或许例外的是，晚上会想想克拉丽丝。我个人认为，我有我自己的事业，就是开了个加油站，整天忙里忙外的，更别提还经营些二手车什么的。但是，要是克劳德让我跟他一起摆弄摆弄狗，我也会欣然前往，特别是像今天所做的这件事情，做成了，当然更好。事实上，毋庸讳言，每次一想到我们押上去的钱，以及或许能赢回来的钱，我的内心就有些静水微澜。

现在，两只狗都吃完了早餐，克劳德将它们牵出去，到对面的田野里溜达一小会儿，我则穿好衣服，开始煎鸡蛋。之后，我去了银行，把钱取了出来，齐刷刷地都是一英镑的纸币。然后，照顾加油的客户，这个上午其余的时光似乎很快就过去了。

十二点整，我在油泵上贴好了通知，加油站就关门了。克劳德牵着杰基从后面绕出来，提着一只大大的手提箱，是用棕色的硬纸板做的，上面稍微带点儿红色调。

"干什么用?"

"装钱，"克劳德回答。"你自己说过的，谁的衣兜也装不下两千镑啊。"

今天是春季里的一天，阳光明媚，天气很好，周围都是泥土的黄色基调，但是，植物沿着树篱钻出了嫩芽。阳光穿过高大的山毛榉树刚刚萌发出来的暗绿色的叶子，在马路上投下斑驳的阴影。杰基看起来棒极了，后腿部位鼓起两大块硬邦邦的肌肉，如甜瓜般大小；它的皮毛闪闪发亮，宛如黑亮的天鹅绒。克劳德把手提箱往篷车里放的时候，这条狗踮起腿，轻微上下腾跃一下，以显示一下赛前准备的充分程度。然后，它抬头看了看我，露齿一笑，就好像知道要出发去参加比赛、赢回两千英镑、一大堆荣耀似的。这条叫杰基的狗刚才露齿的一笑，是我见到过的嘴咧得最宽的、最类似人做出的露齿一笑。它这一笑，不仅抬起了上嘴唇，几乎还拉长了两只嘴角。这样的话，除了最里面的一两颗臼齿，你几乎可以看到它的每一颗牙齿。每次看到它的这幅笑模样，我甚至迫不及待地想听到它发出"哈哈哈"的大笑声。

我们上了篷车,随即出发。车由我来开,克劳德坐在旁边,杰基则站在后部的稻草上,从我们俩的肩膀上方,透过挡风玻璃,向外看去。每次车急转弯的时候,克劳德就回过头去,尽力让它躺下来,以免被甩出去。但是,这条狗兴奋得很,只是一味地冲着克劳德露齿笑,或是摇动着大尾巴,除此之外,什么都做不了。

“你的钱带了吗,戈登?”克劳德一根接一根地抽着烟,根本无法坐安稳。

“带了。”

“我的也带了吗?”

“我总共带了一百零五镑。就像你吩咐的那样,其中的五镑给驱赶假兔子那个人,以免这个人故意停下,致使比赛为零。”

“不错,”克劳德边说,边把两只手放到一起使劲搓了起来,好像冷得要命似的。“不错不错不错。”

我们驶过大米森登的那条狭小的海伊大街时,瞥见老拉敏斯走进纳格斯黑德去取早晨喝的那半升牛奶。接着,我们驶出村子向左拐,爬上奇尔特恩斯山脊,驶向普林塞斯里斯伯勒。至此,离牛津就只剩三十多公里了。

现在,我们两个人都不说话,都有某种紧张感。我们俩都默不作声,谁都没有说话,各有各的恐惧之感和兴奋之情,各自控制着自己的焦虑和不安。克劳德一个劲儿地抽烟,抽到一半就把烟从车窗撇了出去。要是在往常,不管是在去的路上,还是回的路上,他都会一路滔滔不绝,说个不停,一会儿说他一生中所驯养的狗,一会儿说他在赛狗中做的手脚,一会儿说他去过的地方,一会儿说他赢到的钱;再过一会儿,他又说其他人驯养的狗,以及在无许可证的赛道上,这些狗的主人的窃取行为和残忍行为,还有令人难以置信的欺骗手段和奸诈头脑。然而,此时此刻,就事论事地说,我也是跟他一样的状态。我坐在那儿紧盯着路面,尽量不去想马上要面临的局面,但思绪却回到了克劳德给我讲过的那件事儿上,就是灰狗赛场上那种古怪的非法骗钱伎俩。

在这方面,我敢发誓,活着的人当中,没有一个比克劳德更轻车熟路的。我们自从有了这条冒名顶替的狗、决定要在比赛中做手脚的时候起，他就自告奋勇，给我实施这方面的教育。到现在为止，不管是在理论的哪一个层面上，我想我了解的几乎跟他旗鼓相当了。

我们俩在厨房里举行的第一次战略分析会上，这方面的教育就已经开始了。我记得，当时是买到冒名顶替的那条狗之后的那一天，我们俩坐在厨房里透过窗户看着外面的顾客，克劳德就向我解释我们要做的一切，我尽量跟着他的思路去领会。听着听着，我终于忍不住问了一个问题。

“我不明白的是，”我当时说，“为什么要用这条狗冒名顶替呢？我们始终用杰基来比赛，在前六场比赛中，直接让它停下，这样它就会跑到最后一名，这样做难道不是更稳妥吗？然后，我们一切准备就绪，时机一成熟，就让它一跑到底。要是我们处理得当，产生的结果是一样的，难道不是更稳妥吗？而且，这样做一点被逮着的危险都没有。”

正如我言，那样做的确会有效，但克劳德却飞快地抬起头，看了我一眼说：“嗨！门儿都没有！我只想让你知道，我永远不会让狗‘停’下。戈登啊，你脑袋犯了什么迷糊病吗？”我说的话似乎真的刺痛了他，令他震惊不已。

“我看不出，我刚才说的有什么错啊。”

“现在，戈登，听我说。让一条好狗半途停下，会使它心碎。好狗知道它自己跑得快，看到赛道上其他狗在前方奔跑，而自己却追不上，我对你说，它会伤透心。更何况，要是你了解到在无许可证的赛道上，那些家伙让狗停下来所用的一些伎俩的话，你就不会提那样的建议了。”

“举例说说，可以吗？”我问道。

“例如，只要能使狗的速度慢下来，几乎所有的招数都能使出来，就怕你想不出来。因此，不管多么好的灰狗，都会多次被迫停下来。这样的狗浑身是胆，狂热无比，要是带它们进来看比赛，它们会一下将你手中的皮带扯得紧紧的，后腿直立起来，意欲奔跑。有很多次，我看到腿断的狗，硬是坚持跑完比赛。”

当时他停了一下,用他那两只大大的、灰色的眼睛仔仔细细地打量着我,显得严肃无比,很明显是在深深地思考。“我们俩,”他说,“如果要把这事儿做得恰到好处,我最好再教你一两招,好让你知道什么事儿我们不该去做。”

“好吧,教教我,”我说。“洗耳恭听。”

他盯着窗外看了一会,默不作声。“你要记住的一件主要的事情就是,”他神秘兮兮地说,“这些家伙没有一个会牵着狗靠近无许可证的赛道——他们很会耍手腕的。他们的聪明劲儿就怕你想不到。”他又停了下来,梳理一下思绪。

“现在,详细跟你说说让狗停下所用的各种不同的方法吧。第一种是最为常见的,就是绑紧。”

“绑紧?”

“没错,将狗绑紧,最为常见的方法啊。将口套紧紧绑到脖子上,使其几乎无法呼吸,明白吧。一个聪明的人很清楚,绑带该扣到哪一个扣眼上,也很清楚,怎样才能让狗少跑多少个身长的距离。通常情况是,绑带紧到两三个扣眼,就足以让狗少跑五六个身长的距离。绑得紧紧的,它就会跑到最后一名。就我所知,大热天比赛,很多狗就是因为绑得太紧,最后倒地而亡。被勒死的,绝对是被勒死的,这种行为很恶劣。接下来,还有恶劣的行为,就是有些人直接用黑棉花将其中两个脚趾缠到一块儿。那样一缠,狗根本没法跑快,掌握不了平衡的。”

“但那样做,听起来不是太糟糕啊。”

“接着,还有一些人将一块刚咀嚼完的口香糖粘到狗尾巴底下,就粘到尾巴跟身体相连的最底下的部位。这样做,根本没有什么好笑的,”他说道,一副愤愤不平的样子。“狗跑起来的时候,尾巴会非常轻微地上下动弹,但是,那儿粘的口香糖会一直将屁股那儿的毛粘住,而那部位确实是一个最纤弱、最易痛的地方。你知道,没有哪条狗喜欢这样的。接下来,还有安眠药可用,当今这种方法大量使用。这些家伙就像医生一样,按照狗的体重用药。药粉的用量多少,要看你想让狗慢下五个、十个,或者是十五个身长的距离。上述那些方法都普通得很，”他说。“事实上，那些方法也没有什么大不了的。跟其他一些人使用过的、让狗在比赛中落后的方法比起来，那些方法简直是小巫见大巫，特别是跟吉卜赛人使用的方法比较起来。吉卜赛人使用的一些方法很是令人恶心，几乎难以启齿。比如，他们直接让狗落入陷阱。就算是对付你最势不两立的敌人，恐怕你也不会用这种方法。”

他给我讲的那些事情确实很恐怖，做那些事就是让狗遭受身体伤害、遭受痛苦，目的就是让狗慢下来。然后，他继续给我讲，要是想让狗比赛获胜的话，那些家伙会做些什么。

“让狗跑快所采取的手段，跟让狗慢下来所采取的手段，一样骇人听闻，”他轻声说，脸上像是罩了一层面纱，显得神秘兮兮的。“或许，最司空见惯的一种就是使用冬青油。不管是什么时候，只要你看见哪条狗背上没毛的话，或者身上有一小块、一小块的秃斑的话，那都是冬青油干的好事。比赛之前，他们将它使劲揉搓到狗的皮肤里。有的时候，他们还会涂抹斯隆擦剂，但多数情况下涂的是冬青油，灼痛得要命啊，把那些老狗痛得什么也不想干，只想拼命地跑啊，跑啊，跑啊，速度快得不能再快了，就是想摆脱疼痛感。”

“接下来，还会给狗注射特殊的药物。需要提醒你的是，这种注射的方法还很现代，赛场上那些衣冠楚楚的无耻之徒大多都没有这种聪明的头脑，根本不会用这种方法。从大城市伦敦来的那些家伙，开着大车，带着正规比赛狗，狗是他们贿赂驯养员借来用一天的，给这样的狗用的就是注射法。”

我记得，他当时坐在厨房的案桌上，嘴里松垮地叼着一支香烟，耷拉着眼皮，怕烟呛到眼睛里。他透过满是皱纹的、几乎要闭上的眼睛看着我，说道：“戈登，你必须记住，要是想让狗赢的话，没有什么事这帮家伙做不出来。再者说，不管他们怎么折腾，狗的体格在那儿摆着，更快的速度是跑不出来的。所以说，要是我们能把杰基的成绩降到谷底，我们就赢定啦。成绩降到谷底的狗，哪一条都赶不上杰基，即使使用冬青油和注射法也赶不上，就算是把姜用上了，也赶不上。”

“姜？”

“当然啦,是姜,也很常见的。他们是这样做的,取来胡桃大小的一块生姜,开跑前五分钟,将其塞进狗身体。”

“你的意思是说,塞进狗嘴,让他吃下去吗?”

“不,”他说。“不是塞到嘴里。”

我受的教育就这样继续下去。随后,我们俩八次长途跋涉,载着冒名顶替的狗去那个赛道。每一次旅途中,我都能听到关于这种迷人比赛的一些事情,受到的教育也就越来越多。特别值得一提的是,越来越多地听到如何让狗停下来,以及怎么让狗跑快的各种方法,甚至还了解到注射剂的名称以及用量。其间,我听他说过“老鼠疗法”。比赛中,参赛狗追逐的是假兔子,就是把一只老鼠放进一个罐子里,把罐子绑到狗脖子上,但罐子的顶盖要留一个小洞,洞口大小要足够老鼠伸出脑袋咬到狗。可问题是,狗咬不到老鼠。这样的话,狗就自然而然地、近乎疯狂地绕圈儿跑,意欲甩掉罐子,因为老鼠咬它的脖子,而它咬不到老鼠。它越用力甩罐子,老鼠咬得就越厉害。最后,有人将老鼠放出来。直到这个时候,这条被咬的狗,尽管还是一条被驯化的、好心肠的、摇着尾巴的、不忍心伤害小老鼠的狗,也会猛地扑上去,怒不可遏地将其撕成碎片。“多用几次这种疗法,狗就变成了真正的杀手,逮什么追什么,就连假兔子也不在话下。”克劳德当时说。“提醒你一下,我本人可不赞成这种做法。”

现在,我们驶过了奇尔特恩斯山,驶出了下山坡的那片山毛榉树林,驶到了牛津市南端开阔平坦的乡村,满目尽是榆树和橡树。克劳德坐在我旁边,一声不响,抽着烟来控制自己紧张的情绪,而且每隔一两分钟就回头看看杰基是否安好。这条狗最终还是躺下了。克劳德每次回头看它一次,它就轻声跟它嘀咕点什么。每嘀咕一次,它就轻微摇晃尾巴,表示领会。每次摇晃尾巴,稻草就跟尾巴摩擦,发出“刷”的声响。

我们很快就驶入泰姆镇,这里有宽阔的海伊大街。每逢赶集的日子,街上就会围起一圈、一圈的猪、奶牛和绵羊。这里每年举行一次商品交易会,交易中人们有得也有失。届时,镇中心区的大街就会挤满轰隆作响的汽车和吉卜赛人的马拉篷车。克劳德就是在泰姆镇出生的，每次驶过这个城镇，他都要提到这一点。

“瞧啊，”第一排房子映入眼帘的时候，他这样说道，“这儿就是泰姆镇。戈登，要知道，我生在这里，长在这里。”

“你告诉过我。”

“我们这里这些小男孩，在这周围做过许许多多有趣儿的事情呢，”他说，稍微带点怀旧的意味。

“我敢肯定是这样的。”

他暂停一下。我想，他这是纯粹想舒缓一下体内沉积下来的紧张情绪。然后，他谈起自己在这里的年轻时光。

“隔壁有一个小男孩，”他说。“名字叫吉尔伯特·戈姆，一张雪貂一般的小脸棱角分明，一条腿比另一条腿稍微短一点。我们经常在一起做些令人瞠目结舌的事儿。戈登，你知道是什么事儿吗？”

“什么事儿？”

“每星期六晚上趁爸爸妈妈去酒馆的功夫，我们就溜进厨房，将煤气管从小煤气炉上卸下来，然后再将管子伸进灌满水的奶瓶里，煤气就冒起泡泡来。于是，我们坐下来，将奶瓶里的水倒入茶杯喝了起来。”

“那玩意味道能那么好喝吗？”

“好什么好！那味道绝对恶心！但是，我们往里面多放些糖，味道就不那么糟糕了。”

“你们为什么要喝那种东西？”

克劳德转过头来，看着我，有些不大相信我的话。“你是说，你从来都没有喝过‘蛇水’吗？”

“我怎么能喝过那种东西呀。”

“我以为小时候大家都喝过呢！这东西令你麻醉兴奋，就像酒一样，但比酒更厉害，厉害程度有多大，还要看你让煤气透过水冒泡泡时间的长短。每周六晚上溜进厨房，我们经常是醉得晕乎乎的，那感觉美妙极了。但是，有一次爸爸回来得早一些，把我们逮了个正着。那一次啊，只要我有口气儿在，就永远忘不了。当时，我手握奶瓶，可爱的煤气正透过瓶子里的水，冒着泡泡，而吉尔伯特则跪在地板上，按照我的吩咐正准备关掉阀门。就在此时,爸爸推门而入。"

"他当时怎么说的?"

"噢,天哪,戈登,当时糟透了。他一句话也没说,只是站在门口摸裤带,慢慢地解开带扣,慢慢地将其从裤子上抽出来,眼睛却一直盯着我。他块头很大,一双大手就像采煤用的大锤,八字胡黑黑的,整个脸颊爬满了细小的紫色血管。接下来,他冲上来,一把抓住我的衣服,就猛劲抽打,使出浑身力气用皮带上带有搭钩的那一头抽打我。戈登,我对天发誓,我想,他是想要我的命啊。最终,他还是停了下来,把裤带系上,慢慢地、仔细得系好,搭钩扣上,衣襟拽下。然后,打了一个嗝,肚子里啤酒的味道就释放出来了。随即,他仍然一言不发,走出房门,又回到那个酒馆。这是我一生中所遭受的最严厉的痛打。"

"当时你多大?"

"约摸八岁,我想,"克劳德回答。

这时,我们离牛津更近了,克劳德又沉默起来。他不断地把脖子扭过去,看看杰基是否安好,还摸摸它,轻轻抚弄它的头。有那么一次,克劳德转过身,整个人跪到车座位上,为的是将更多的稻草聚拢到这条狗的周围,还小声嘟囔着不要被风吹着之类的话语。我们绕着牛津的外围驶入窄窄的乡村公路网。没过多大功夫,就驶上一条坑坑洼洼的小路,我们超过了路上稀稀拉拉的人群,人群中有男、有女。这些人跟我们是一个方向的,除了步行,就是骑车。有些男人手里还牵着灰狗。我们前面行驶着一辆大大的豪华轿车,透过后车窗看去,可以看到后排座上两名男子之间蹲着一条狗。

"哪儿来的狗都有,"克劳德神秘地说。"前面的那一条或许是特地从伦敦弄来的,或许是从其中一个正规的驯养场弄出来的,就是为了参加今天下午的比赛。就我们所知,那条可能就是德比赛狗呢。"

"希望它不要跟杰基对阵。"

"用不着担心,"克劳德说。"所有新参赛的狗都会自动进入最高积分等级,这也是费西先生特别讲究的一个规则。"

一扇开放式大门直通一片田地。费西太太迎上前来，收取入场费，然后让我们开进去。

“要是她力气足够，费西先生也会让她转动脚蹬子来驱动假兔子的，”克劳德说。“老费西一个人都不会多雇佣的。”

我开车穿过田地，停在沿着顶层树篱摆放的那排小汽车的后部，随即下车。克劳德绕到车后去牵杰基，我站在车旁等待着。这是一片很大的田地，坡度稍微有点陡，我们站的位置是坡顶。向下看去，我看到远处有六个起跑隔栏，还有标记跑道的木桩，跑道沿着田地底部延伸，然后一个直角急转弯，拐向人群方向，最后到达终点。终点线以外不到三十米的地方有一辆倒置的自行车，用来驱动假兔子。由于携带方便，自行车就成为所有无许可证赛道使用的标准驱兔设备，就是搭一个轻便的但不很牢靠的木制平台，高度接近两米五，由四根打入地面的柱子支撑。平台的上面固定了一辆倒置的自行车，是一辆普通的旧自行车，两只轮子朝天，后轮朝前，轮子下面能看见赛场，但是轮胎已经拆掉，只剩下凹形的金属圈，拖动假兔子用的带子的一端就系到这只圈上。绞盘手，也就是那个驱赶假兔子的人，骑跨在车后部，用双手转动脚蹬子，使后轮转动起来，将带子缠绕到圈上。这样，他愿意多快，就可以多快地将假兔子向他这边拽来，最快时速可达六十四公里。每次比赛结束后，有人就会将拴着带子的假兔子沿着赛场拉回到起跑隔栏那儿，顺势也就将轮子上缠绕的带子舒展开，随时准备重新开始。绞盘手从高高的平台上能够观察到整个比赛情况，随时调整假兔子的速度，使其跑在领先的那只狗的前方。他随时可以让假兔子停下，使比赛为“零”，但前提是，他看到不该赢的狗似乎要赢。具体做法就是，突然向后转动脚蹬子，带子就在轮毂上纠缠到一块儿。另一种做法就是突然放慢假兔子的速度，或许就放慢一秒钟的时间，这样，领先的狗就会弄不清状况而自动地稍微暂停一下。结果，其他狗就追赶上来、赶上它。所以说，这个绞盘手可是一位关键人物。

我看到，费西先生的绞盘手已经站在平台顶部了。他看起来是一个强健有力的男子，身穿一件蓝色的毛线衫，倚在自行车上，抽着烟,透过烟雾俯视着下方的人群。

英国有一项很奇怪的法律条文,此类赛会一年在同一块场地上只能举行七次。费西先生的所有的设备都是可移动的,原因就在于此。第七次赛会过后,他就径直转移到下一个场地,法律根本拿他没办法。

人群规模已经不小了,赌注经纪人已经在右侧支起一排站台。现在,克劳德已经把杰基牵下篷车,正要牵往一群人那儿,那群人聚拢在一个身体粗壮、穿着马裤的小个子男子周围。他不是别人,正是费西先生。这群人中,每一位都用皮带牵着一条狗。费西先生左手举着一个笔记本,不停地在上面写下这些狗的名字。我溜溜达达走过去看热闹。

"哪一条是你的?"费西先生将铅笔悬停在笔记本上边问道。

"午夜,"一名牵着条大黑狗的男子应声答道。

费西先生后退一步,极为细心地看了看那条狗。

"午夜,好了,我记下来了。"

"简,"下一名男子说。

"让我看看。简……简……是的,没问题。"

"战士。"牵这条狗的是一名高个男子,露出长长的牙齿,身穿暗蓝色的双排扣夹克套装,由于穿得久而磨得锃亮。说"战士"的同时,他开始用没有握皮带的那只手慢慢地抓挠裤子的后裆下部。

费西先生弯下腰察看这条狗,另一名男子则抬头看了看天空。

"把他牵走,"费西先生说。

这名男子不再抓挠,立即低头看去。

"快点,把他牵走。"

"听着,费西先生,"这名一嘴长牙的男子说话时,声音稍微有点咬舌头的感觉。"现在,不要说如此愚蠢的话,拜托了。"

"走开,拉里,快点。不要浪费我的时间。你我都清楚,战士前腿的右侧是有两只白色脚趾的。"

"费西先生,现在看看吧,"这名男子说道。"你至少有六个月没有看到战士了。"

“拉里，得拉吧，现在赶紧走开。我没有时间跟你理论。”费西先生看起来一点也没有生气的意思。“下一位，”他说。

我看见克劳德牵着杰基，向前跨出一步。他那张大大的脸很是呆滞，一动不动，表情木然，两只眼睛盯着费西先生头顶上方不到一米处的某个什么东西。他的手攥住皮带，攥得紧紧的，指关节看起来就像是一排白色的洋葱头。我了解他的感受。与此同时，我自己的感受跟他的没有两样。费西先生突然之间放声大笑时，这种感受甚至更糟。

“嗨！”他叫道。“这是黑豹嘛，就是那个冠军啊。”

“说的没错，费西先生，”克劳德回应。

“噢，我对你讲啊，”费西先生说，仍然露出牙齿笑着。“你可以立马将他带走，哪来带哪儿去。我不愿意让它参赛。”

“可是，费西先生，听我说……”

“现在，我同意它为你跑了就算不到八次，也有六次了吧，够可以的啦。你看啊，为什么对它不开一枪，一了百了呢？”

“现在，费西先生，听我说啊，拜托了。就再跑一次，然后我永远不再求你了。”

“一次也不多给！今天的狗多得很，我都忙不过来了。没有位置给他啦，简直像螃蟹在爬。”

我琢磨着，克劳德当时就差要哭出来了。

“费西先生，现在说实话，”他说。“过去的两个礼拜，我每天早晨六点起床，给它做路上赛跑训练，给它按摩，还给它买牛排吃。相信我吧，跟它上次跑赛状态比起来，它现在已经改头换面，与以前那条狗是绝对不一样的。”

听到“改头换面”这四个字，费西先生吓得一激灵，就好像被帽针猛地刺了一下似的。“这话什么意思？”他喊道。“改头换面？！”

我要给克劳德说的是，头脑要冷静啊。“听我说啊，费西先生，”他说。“你对我说话直来直去、快言快语，我很感激。你很清楚，我不是那个意思。”

“好吧，好吧。即便如此，我还是那句话，把它牵走。像它那样慢腾腾的狗参加跑赛,没有任何意义。拜托,你把它牵家去吧,不要耽搁了整个赛事。”

我看着克劳德,克劳德看着费西先生,费西先生则看着四周,等着登记下一条狗。他那件粗花呢制的夹克衫里面穿的是一件黄色的套衫。套衫的那一缕黄色在胸前露出,再加上他那两条绑起来的细腿,还有头快速地从一边转向另一边的样子,都令他看起来像一只趾高气扬的小鸟——或许像一只金翅黄雀吧。

克劳德向前跨出一步。盛怒之下,他的脸开始轻微地发紫。咽吐沫的时候,他的喉结一上一下动弹着。

“费西先生,我要跟你说说我的做法。我有十足的把握认为,这条狗已经今非昔比。我跟你赌一镑,赌它不会跑到最后一名。钱在这儿,给你。”

费西先生慢慢转过身来,看着克劳德。“你要作弊吗?”他问。

“给你一镑,我跟你赌,就是为了证明我说的话没错。”

这一步走得很危险,一定会引起怀疑的,但是,克劳德清楚,唯一能走的就是这一步了。费西先生弯腰察看这条狗时,周围一阵沉默。我看到,他的眼睛缓缓地在这只动物身上移动,一部分、一部分地察看起来。这名男子身上有些令人钦佩、赞赏的地方:做事细致周到,记事准确无误。这个自信心十足的小个子家伙身上也有些令人担惊受怕的地方——记忆力惊人:好几百条不同的狗,尽管十分相似,但他却能记住其外形、颜色和各种标记。一条小小的线索就足以让费西先生记住狗之间的差别,而且他会始终记住不忘,比如一个小小的疤痕、一个向外张开的脚趾、跗关节部位一处细微的地方、样子不起眼的轮形背部,以及稍微暗一点儿的杂色斑点等。

因此,现在他俯身杰基上方察看的时候,我就看着他:他的脸呈粉红色,圆圆胖胖的;嘴很小,闭得紧紧的,就好像无法拉伸、从而微笑似的;两只眼睛就像两架小小的相机,清晰地把焦点聚到这条狗身上。

“哦,”他挺直身体说。“不管怎么说,狗还是一样的狗。”

“我也希望如你所言啊!”克劳德大声说道。“费西先生,你把我想成一种什么类型的人呢?"

"我想你是在作弊,我就只是这么想的,但是,能轻轻松松赢得一镑,还是很不错的。上一次赛会上,它多么勉强才赢了靠三条腿跑完的闪亮琥珀啊。我想,你忘记了吧?"

"这条狗当时状况不住,"克劳德说。"近来,我一直给它做路上训练,给它按摩,还给它牛排吃,但当时却没有这些待遇。听我说啊,费西先生,你可不能为了赢那一镑而将它置于榜首行列,这可是一条位于成绩榜底部的狗啊。费西先生,这一点你是清楚的。"

费西先生哈哈大笑起来。此时,他那张如纽扣一般紧扣的小嘴张开了,张成一个微小的圆环形状。他一边笑,一边看着周围的人群,人群也随着他一同大笑起来。"听着,"他说着,一只毛茸茸的手搭到克劳德的肩上。"我了解这些狗,这一镑我不想赢得不光彩。它就到榜底比好啦。"

"妥了,"克劳德说。"赌了。"他随即牵着杰基走开,我也一同跟他走开。

"我的天啊,戈登,真是好险啊!"

"真惊险。"

"可是现在,我们登记上去了,"克劳德说。他的脸上又浮现出那种喘不过气来的表情,走起路来速度很快,样子很好笑,就像地面烫着他的脚似的。

仍然有人通过大门向场地里面走来,现在少说也有三百多了。这群男男女女人都是一些不很体面之人:他们鼻子尖尖,脸部脏兮兮,牙齿坏掉,眼睛快速移来移去;他们是大城镇里来的沉渣,就好像从破裂的下水管道里汩汩冒出来的污秽物一样,一路流淌而来,穿过大门,流淌到场地顶部把头的位置,形成一个污水小池塘,散发出难闻的臭气。他们这些衣冠楚楚的无耻之徒都涌到那儿去了,有吉卜赛人,有刺探内幕的,有沉渣,有污秽物,有拣剩的,还有大城镇破裂的下水管里冒出来的浮渣。他们之中,有的牵着狗,有的没有牵。狗都是用皮带牵来的:有的狗可怜兮兮,耷拉着脑袋;有的狗又脏又瘦,腿部还有溃疡,是在车上睡觉睡的;有的狗上了年纪,愁眉苦脸的,还带着灰色的口套;有的狗身体里灌注东西了,就是给它们填满麦片粥,好让它们比赛中停下,不让其获胜;还有的狗走起路来腿很僵直,特别是那条白色的狗。“克劳德,那条白狗走起路来怎么那样僵直呢?”

“哪儿?”

“就那边的那条。”

“哦,是的,看见了。那或许是被吊起来的缘故。”

“吊起来?”

“是啊,吊起来。用一套器具将狗吊起来,一吊就是二十四小时,四条腿悬空呆着。”

“我的老天爷啊,可那是为了什么啊?”

“目的当然是不让它跑得快起来。有的人不赞同灌注、填充、设陷阱,所以他们就将狗吊起来。”

“我明白啦。”

“要是不吊的话,”克劳德说,“他们就用砂纸对狗进行打磨,用粗糙的砂纸打磨其脚趾肉垫,把肉垫表皮打磨掉,这样,一跑起来就疼痛。”

“是的,我明白啦。”

紧接着看到的,是一些更健康、喂养得更好、看起来更欢快的狗,这些狗每天吃的都是马肉,而不是猪食、面包干之类,也不喝卷心菜汁什么的;这些狗的皮毛更加闪亮,尾巴摇地都能碰到牵着它们的皮带;这些狗未被灌注、填充,但是,等待它们的或许是更加不幸的命运:将其口套再多绑紧四个孔眼。*问题是,乔克,绑紧后,要确保这条狗现在能正常呼吸,不能让它窒息,不能让它跑到一半就瘫倒在地,让它有点气喘吁吁的程度最好,明白吧。依次继续再绑紧一个孔眼,听到它有点气喘吁吁就停。此时,你要是看到它张开嘴,呼吸开始加重,绑得就正合适,但要确保它的眼球没有凸出。你注意看着点,好吗?好不好啊?*

“*好的。*”

“戈登,我们俩不要在人群里挤来挤去啦,这样对杰基一点好处都没有，看到其他的狗，它会兴奋不已。"

我们走上山坡，走到停车的地方，然后就在这一排车的前面来回走动，好让它处于活跃状态。在一些车的里面，我能够看到，有人带着狗坐着，有人透过车窗，对我们的走来走去，怒目而视。

"现在，当心点啊，戈登。我们可不能惹出什么麻烦来。"

"好的，不能。"

车里边待着的都是一些最优秀的狗，需要保密的。快速牵出来登好记，登记的是瞎编的名字，然后再飞快牵到车里面，在里面呆到临近比赛的最后一刻，才牵出来，径直奔向隔栏参加比赛。比赛一结束，再牵回车里。所以，不管是什么样的追根问底的家伙都休想靠得太近、看个仔细。大型正规场馆的驯养员就是这么吩咐的。他当时会这么说，*好吧，你可以把它牵走，但看在老天的分上，不要让任何人认出它来。有成千上万的人认识这条狗，所以你要当心，明白吧。还有，你要付五十英镑。*

这些都是速度很快的狗，但是，不管它们速度有多快，它们或许最终被人打上一针，就是为了确保万无一失。就在车里慢慢地给它打上一针，从皮下注射一针容量达半立方厘米的乙醚。这样的话，任何一条狗都会再跑上十个身长的距离。有时候，也注射可卡因，也注射融入油里的可卡因，或者注射樟脑水；也会有效果的。大个头的车里面的那些人都了解这一点，有些人还知道使用威士忌，但那需要静脉注射，不是很容易注射的，或许注射不到静脉上。注射了半天却没有注射到静脉上，起不到作用，你会怎么办呢？所以嘛，要注射，就注射可卡因，或者注射融入油里的可卡因，或者注射樟脑水。*乔克，这玩意不要给这条母狗注射过多。她的体重是多少？58 磅。那么好吧，你记得那人吩咐怎么做吧。现在，等一等，我当时写到一张纸上了。找到了。每10 磅体重用一立方厘米量中0.1 的量，就能让她多跑五个身长的距离，就超过270 米。现在，等一等，我要算一算。天啊，算不好，你最好估计着用吧，就估摸着用吧，乔克。最终你会发现，估计起来也八九不离十。怎么说，都不会出什么差错的，因为比赛中对于其他的狗的用量我自己也估计过。因此，我给了费西老先*

生好处,是一张十英镑的钞票,我给他的可是血汗钱啊。给的时候我说,亲爱的费西先生,那钱是为你祝贺生日的,因为我爱你。

"十分感谢你,"费西先生说。"谢谢你,我的朋友,我信得过的朋友。"

为了让狗在比赛中停下,大个头的车里坐着的那些人就用氯丁醇,那可是样好东西啊,因为你可以在前一天晚上给狗注射,特别是,可以给别人的狗注射。还可以注射盐酸哌替啶,也可以注射盐酸哌替啶跟东莨菪碱的混合液,就别管那些到底是什么东西啦。

"这儿有很多优雅的英国老绅士,"克劳德说。

"那当然。"

"当心你的腰包了,戈登。那笔钱你搁严实了吗?"

我们走到这排汽车的后面,来到汽车跟树篱之间。这时,我看见杰基伸直身体,拉着皮带往前拽,直挺挺的身体蹲伏着向前挪动。不到三十米远的地方有两名男子,一名牵着一条不满周岁的大灰狗,另一名两手握着一条袋子。那条狗跟杰基一样,身体直挺挺的,一副紧张的样子。

"看着啊,"克劳德小声说。"他们要让它追杀猎物。"

一只白色的小兔子从袋子里跌落到草地上,是一只驯养的、毛茸茸的白色幼兔。只见它挺直了身体,一动不动地蹲坐着,背部隆起,鼻子紧贴地面,一副担惊受怕的样子。因为它"砰"的一声,一下子从袋子里摔到草地上,阳光明亮刺眼,还没弄明白是怎么回事呢。现在,那条狗发了疯似的,兴奋不已,上蹿下跳意欲挣脱皮带,同时爪子挠地,身体往前猛冲,嘴里发出哀嚎声。兔子看到了狗,却将头缩了回去,一动不动地待着,吓得瘫在那儿了,不敢动弹。牵狗的男子将手挪到狗的脖领处,紧紧抓住,接着,这条狗就扭曲身体跳了起来,试图挣脱。另一名男子用脚碰了一下兔子,但是兔子吓得够呛,不敢移动。他又碰了碰,就像踢足球那样,用脚轻轻地一踢,兔子随即向前翻滚几下,然后挺直身体,开始在草地上蹦跳起来,离开了那条狗。于是,牵狗的那位放开狗,狗就"嗖"的一下猛扑出去,扑向兔子。一阵尖叫声响起,声音不是很大,但却很尖锐、很痛苦,持续了很长时间。

“看到了吧，”克劳德说。“那就是猎杀成功了。”

“真的不喜欢这种做法。”

“以前给你讲过的，戈登。他们多数人这样做，为的是让狗在赛前活跃起来。”

“我还是不喜欢这种做法。”

“我也不喜欢，可是，大家都这么做呀，大型正规场馆的驯养员也是这么做的。我称之为适度野蛮化。”

我们溜达着走开了。脚下的山坡上，人群越来越稠密。现在，在人群的后方，赌注经纪人的站台也都支起来了，支成长长的一排，站台上写着经纪人的名字，有的名字是红色的，有的是金色的，有的是蓝色的。每人都一只手拿着一些标有数字的卡片，另一只手拿着一支粉笔，都踩在一只倒置的箱子上，箱子放在站台的旁边。经纪人的身后站的是各自的办事员，个个都拿着铅笔和本子。接着，我们看见费西先生走到一块黑板跟前，黑板钉在一根柱子上，柱子戳入地面立着。

“他要用粉笔写下第一场比赛名单啦，”克劳德说。“来啊，快！”

我们俩飞快走下小山，融入人群之中。费西先生正在黑板上写参赛狗的名字，正从他的软皮笔记本里往黑板上抄写呢。此时，人群稍微安静下来，人们看着，心怀悬念。

1. 萨利
2. 三镑
3. 蜗牛盒女士
4. 黑豹
5. 威士忌
6. 罗基特

“它在名单上啊！”克劳德小声说。“第一场比赛啊！第四个隔栏！戈登，现在听着！快把五镑给我，我好让那个绞盘手看看。”

克劳德兴奋得几乎说不出话来,鼻子和眼睛周围区域又变成了白色。我将五镑钞票递给他的时候,他接过钱,整个胳膊也随之颤抖起来。这位绞盘手仍然站在那个木制平台的顶上,穿着件蓝色的毛线衫,抽着烟,准备转动自行车的脚蹬子。克劳德走了过去,站在他的下方,抬头向上观瞧。

“看到这张五镑的钞票了吧,”他轻轻说道,将钞票折成一小块,握在掌中。

这伙计眼睛瞥了眼钞票,头并没有转过来。

“只要你能转动脚蹬,挺过正常比赛,明白吧。不能停,不能慢下来,要快速转动。可否?”

这名男子没有动地方,但是,他的眼眉轻微地、几乎不为人察觉地向上抬起。于是,克劳德转过离开。

“现在听着,戈登。逐渐地、一点儿一点儿地将钱押上,就像我先前吩咐的那样去做。沿着那排经纪人不停地、一点儿一点儿地往上押,别停止投注,明白吧。我牵着杰基慢慢地走过去,我会尽力慢走,给你留出足够时间。可否?”

“可以。”

“也不要忘记站在终点处等着抓住杰基,其他那些狗争抢兔子时,让它离远些。要紧紧攥住它,不要松开,等着我带着脖套和皮带一路跑过去。威士忌是条吉卜赛狗,谁挡着它的路,它就能把谁的腿撕开。”

“可以,”我说。“我们开始吧。”

我看见克劳德牵着杰基走到终点线的柱子那儿,拿起一只口套,还有一件黄色夹克衫,上面写了一个大大的号码“4”。其他五条赛狗也在那儿,其主人也忙个不停,有的给狗穿上标有数字号码的夹克衫,有的给狗整理口套。费西先生在那儿主持大局,他穿着紧身马裤,跳来蹦去,就像一只焦躁不安、趾高气扬的鸟儿。有一次,我看见他跟克劳德说着什么,然后哈哈大笑,克劳德却未加理睬。很快,他们都牵着狗沿着场地走下来,走过很长一段下坡路,穿过场地,走向这片田地远处一角的出发隔栏那儿,他们会走上十分钟的。我对自己说,我至少有十分钟时间。于是,我推推搡搡挤过人群,站在跟那行赌注经纪人前方隔开有六七排人远的地方。

"同额赌注押威士忌!同额赌注押威士忌!五比二押萨利!同额赌注押威士忌!四比一押蜗牛盒!现在快点啊!快啊,快啊!这是哪一条呢?"

这一排经纪人所有的告示板上写的黑豹的赔率是二十五比一。于是,我挤到最近的一名经纪人的前面。

"三镑押黑豹,"我举起钱说道。

站在箱子上的这位男子长着一张肿胀的、品红色的脸,两只嘴角残留些许白色的东西。他一下子抓过钱,扔进小包里。"七十五镑比三押黑豹,"他说。"四十二号。"随后递给我一张票据,他的办事员记录下这个赌注。

我退后一步,飞快地在票据背面写下"75:3"的字样,然后把它连同钱一起塞进我夹克衫里面的衣兜。

只要我把钱一点点儿像这样不断往上押,一切应该相安无事。不管怎么说,按照克劳德的指示,每次我在冒名顶替的那条狗身上都故意只押几英镑。这样,真正比赛那天就会避免引起怀疑。所以嘛,我一路蛮有信心地、不慌不忙地沿着那排经纪人走下来,每个人那儿都押下三镑,但是,我也并没有浪费时间,每次下完注,就在票据后面写上数量,然后再塞进衣兜。赌注经纪人一共有十七位,一轮下来,我得到十七张票据,投出了五十一镑,但丝毫没有扰乱投注的进程。这样的话,还剩下四十九镑可以押。我飞快地朝小山下方瞥一眼,看见一条狗的主人牵着狗已经到达了隔栏处,其余的人离那儿也只有十八至二十八米的距离吧。但是,克劳德除外,他牵着杰基只走了一半的距离。我看到克劳德穿着他那件旧卡其布厚长大衣,牵着杰基慢悠悠地向前逛,杰基则一个劲儿地向前拽着皮带。有一次,我看见克劳德完全停下,弯下腰,假装捡起一个什么东西。再次开始走的时候,他似乎开始有点一瘸一拐了,速度依然很慢,走得比以前更慢了。我匆忙返回那排经纪人的另一端,重新开始投注。

"三镑押黑豹。"

听到这话,经纪人猛地抬起头来,脑袋里闪现出上一次的情景。此人正是刚才那位长着品红色脸孔、嘴边残留着白色东西的经纪人。只见他以近乎优雅的动作迅速地一挥胳膊,随后舔湿手指,利索地将告示板上二十五这个数字擦掉。他的弄湿了的手指在黑豹名字旁边留下一块小小的黑色斑点。

“好啦,你又有一个七十五比三了,”他说。“但,那是批量数。”然后,他提高嗓门喊道:“黑豹变更为十五比一! 黑豹都是十五啦!”

这一排经纪人告示板上的二十五都擦掉了,现在,黑豹的赔率变成了十五比一。我行动很快,到我投完的时候,经纪人收到的就足够了,也都不会再提起杰基了。他们每个人收到的只有六镑,但赔掉的却多达一百五十。对他们这些小小乡村里的、无许可证赛道上的不入流的赌注经纪人而言,一次比赛赔掉这么一笔钱,算是很大的数目了。十分感谢你们。对于完成这件事情所采取的方式方法,我感到心满意足。现在,我已经收到很多票据了。我将它们从衣兜里掏出来,数了一遍,一共有三十三张。将它们握在手里,如同握着一副薄薄的纸牌。我们会赢多少呢? 让我想想……约摸会超过两千英镑。克劳德说过,以三十个身长的优势,它就能赢。现在,克劳德在哪儿呢?

山下很远的地方,我看见卡其布厚长大衣站在隔栏边,身边是那条大黑狗。其他所有的狗都已经进入隔栏,狗主人也都走开了。现在,克劳德正弯腰连哄带劝地将杰基弄进四号隔栏,然后关上栏门,转身开始向山上人群方向跑去,边跑边回头,厚长大衣在他身体周围摆来摆去。

发令员站在隔栏边,一只手举起,挥舞着手绢。在赛道的另一端、终点柱以远、离我站的位置很近的地方,木制平台上的那个身穿蓝色毛线衫的男子跨坐在倒置的自行车上,看到了发令信号,他摆手回应,随后就开始用双手转动脚蹬子。紧接着,远处一个微小的白点开始从隔栏处向外移动,速度越来越快。那个小白点就是假兔子,实际上是一只足球,上面用平头针钉上一块白兔皮。隔栏打开,所有的狗一跃而出。就看见一大团黑色几乎同时一跃而出,如同一条身体宽宽的大狗一跃而出,看不出是六条狗一跃而出。几乎与此同时,我看见杰基从赛场上脱颖而出，是杰基没错，因为它的颜色独特，这场比赛没有第二条狗是黑色的。肯定是杰基啦。我告诫自己，不要动，哪怕是一块肌肉、一个眼皮、一个脚指头、一个指甲尖儿也不要动一下。要一动不动地站在那儿，看着它跑。加油，杰克逊！好小子！不，不能喊出声，喊叫是不吉利的。要一动不动站着，就二十秒的时间。现在，绕过急弯，向山上冲去。它领先没有二十个，起码也有十五个身长的距离了。就算领先二十个身长的距离，也是轻松自如的事情。不要数身长，那是不吉利的。要一动不动地站着，头也不要动一下，只要用眼角观看就可以了。看杰克逊跑的啊！它真的是技压群雄，跑到了山上。现在，它已经赢了！现在，它不可能输掉……

我赶过去的时候，它正在撕扯兔皮，想用嘴叼起来，但是带着口套，只能是白费劲。其他几条狗追赶上来，为争夺兔子突然间都压到它身上。我按照克劳德事先吩咐的那样，抓住它的脖子，将它拽得远远的。我跪在草地上，两只胳膊紧紧地按住它的身体。其他狗的主人也都忙着抓自己的狗。

紧接着，克劳德气喘吁吁地跑来。他喘得厉害，兴奋异常，说不出话来。他给杰基摘下口套，套上项圈，系上皮带。费西先生也来了，双手放到屁股上，站在那儿，嘴如同系上扣子紧闭着，嘴唇就像蘑菇一样向上翘起，两只照相机般的小眼睛又聚焦到杰基身上，上下左右打量起来。

"真是场好戏，对吗？"他说。

克劳德俯身狗的上方，那架势像是没有听到他的话。

"这场过后，我不想再看到你，明白我的话吗？"

克劳德继续摆弄杰基的项圈。

我听到身后有人说："那个紧皱眉头的扁脸家伙，这次为老费西驱动假兔子，倒挺卖力气的。"随即，另外一人大笑起来，费西先生趁机走开。克劳德直起身来，牵着杰基向穿着蓝色毛线衫的驱动假兔子的人走去，那个人已经从平台上下来了。

"抽烟，"克劳德说着，递过一盒香烟。

这名男子抽出一支，若无其事地拿走克劳德手指间夹着的、折叠得很小的那张五镑钞票。

"谢谢,"克劳德说。"非常感谢。"

"不客气,"男子说道。

然后,克劳德转向我。"戈登,都押妥了吗?"他说话时,双唇在颤抖。他上下跳动,搓着双手,拍着杰基。

"是的。一半是二十五,一半是十五。"

"噢,天哪。杰基,干得太棒了。在这儿等着,我去拿手提箱。"

"你带上杰基走,"我说,"到车里坐着。一会儿见。"

现在,经纪人周围已经空无一人,只有我有钱进账,内心情感澎湃,感觉美好无比。于是,我慢悠悠地走过去,迈着类似跳舞的步伐,走向第一个经纪人那儿,就是那个长着品红色脸孔、嘴上残留白色东西的男子。我站在他面前,愿意花多长时间,就花多长时间在我那一摞票据里翻找属于他的那两张,那两张的上面应该写着他的名字"叙德·普拉切特",因为他的名字是用金色的字母,大大地写在他那个告示板上面的一块深红色区域内:*叙德·普拉切特,英格兰中部地区声望最高的赌注经纪人,即刻兑现*。

我把第一张票据递给他,说道:"应赔付七十八镑。"此言一出,我感觉棒极了,于是,我就像哼唱一首甜美短歌一般,又说了一遍:"这张应赔付七十八镑。"我并没有打算对普拉切特先生表现出幸灾乐祸的样子。事实上,我开始相当地喜欢他了,甚至因为他要掏出这么多钱而感到歉疚。我希望,他的妻子和孩子不要因此而遭受痛苦。

"四十二号,"普拉切特先生转身冲着他的办事员说,办事员手里举着一个大账本。"四十二号赔付七十八镑。"

暂停了一会儿。办事员的手指沿着记录有赌注的纵栏,快速移动起来,来回查看了两遍,然后抬头看看老板,摇了摇头。

"不对,"他说。"不能赔付,那张票据押的是蜗牛盒女士。"

站在箱子顶上的普拉切特先生将身体倾斜过去,眼睛向下瞥了眼账本,对办事员所说的话似乎感到不安,只见他那张大大的、品红色的脸上浮现出一种真正开始焦虑的表情。

我想,那个办事员就是傻子一个,现在起,普拉切特先生随时会这样骂他的。

但是，普拉切特先生转身面向我的时候，他的双眼眯缝起来，显得敌意十足。“现在听着，查利，”他轻声对我说。“你我都不要干什么蠢事。你清楚得很，你押的是蜗牛盒。你都想些什么呢？”

“我押的是黑豹啊，”我申辩道。“分别押了两次，每次押的是三镑，赔率为二十五比一。你看，这是第二张票据。”

这次，他甚至连账本也懒得看一眼了。“查利，你押的是蜗牛盒，”他说。“我记得呢，你来下的注。”说完这话，他转过身去，开始用一块湿抹布将那张告示板上第一批赛狗的名字擦去。他身后的办事员已经合上账本，随手点燃一支香烟。我站在那儿看着他们，感到汗水不由自主地从皮肤下冒出，淌遍了全身。

“让我看看账本。”

普拉切特用湿抹布擤了一下鼻涕，然后将其扔到地上。“听着，”他说，“你为什么不能走开，别再烦我了呢？”

问题的关键是，有关赌注的性质方面，赛狗赌注经纪人的票据上从来都不写的，这跟赛马赌注的票据是不一样的。这种做法很正常，在这个国家任何一条赛道上都是这样做的。不管是在纽马基特的银环赛道，还是爱斯科的皇室宫殿赛道，还是牛津附近无许可证的乡村小赛道，都是如此。押注之后，你所得到的，就是一张写有经纪人姓名的、标注了序列号的卡片。赌注连同序列号码是由经纪人的办事员记录到账本上的，也应该记录到账本上。但是，除此之外，根本没有任何证据证明当初的注是怎么押的。

“走吧，”普拉切特先生说。“快走吧。”

我退后一步，沿着那一大长排经纪人队列看去，发现他们没有一个人向我这边看。他们每个人都一动不动地站在自己那只小小的木制箱子顶上，旁边都立着一个木制告示板，都目视前方，看着人群。我走到下一个经纪人那儿，拿出一张票据。

“我押了黑豹三镑，赔率是二十五比一，”我斩钉截铁地说。“应赔付七十八英镑。”

这名男子温和的脸有些肿胀，做事的程序跟普拉切特先生如出一辙:问了下办事员,瞥了眼账本,给了我一模一样的回答。

“你这个人到底是怎么回事?”他轻声说,就好像我是一个八岁的孩子似的。“像这样愚蠢的事儿,你也干啊。”

这一次,我使劲向后退了退。“你们这帮家伙!”我大骂起来。“你们这些下流的杂种,简直就是窃贼!”

突然之间,他们这些人的脑袋齐刷刷地、自动化一般,猛地向我转来,看着我,如同木偶一般,表情都僵住了。十七人都一动不动的,只有脑袋在动。所有十七个人瞪着十七双呆滞的眼睛看着我,没有一双眼睛闪现出一丝一毫关切的神情。

“有人说话了,”他们似乎异口同声地说。“但我们什么都没听见。今天天气可真不错。”

人群感觉到要有兴奋之事发生,开始向我聚拢而来。“我跑回到普拉切特先生那儿,站到他眼皮子底下,用手指戳着他的肚子。“你是一个窃贼!一个卑鄙拙劣、腐败透顶的小偷!”我大喊起来。

出乎意料的是,普拉切特先生对此似乎一点也不恼火。“哦,我从不偷窃,”他说。“看看你,还有脸说啊。”

接着,他那张大脸突然之间向两边伸开,嘴张得跟青蛙似的,露出牙齿,笑了起来。他看向人群,喊道:“看看你,还有脸说啊!”

毫无防备之下,大家“哄”一声笑了起来。那一溜儿经纪人也复活了,彼此转身,相互看着,指着我喊道:“看看你,还有脸说啊!看看你,还有脸说啊!”人群也接茬儿喊了起来。我站在那儿的草地上,站在普拉切特先生的旁边,手里握着这一叠票据,一叠跟一副纸牌一样厚的票据。我听着他们的喊声,感觉有点要歇斯底里。透过攒动的人头,我看见费西先生站在黑板旁边,已经开始用粉笔写着下一场参赛狗的名字。再往他以远的地方看去,就在场地顶部很远的地方,我看见克劳德站在篷车边,拎着手提箱正等着我回去呢。

该回家了。

第二章　莫惹娇妻

英国戏剧家莎士比亚(William Shakespeare)在其著名喜剧《哈姆雷特》(Hamlet)中,写过这样的句子“Frailty, thy name is woman!”[①],翻译过来,意思就是“脆弱,你的本质就是女性”。莎翁将自己对自己母亲的愤怒之情,转嫁到所有女性身上,认为女性就是弱者,是脆弱的代名词。

是啊,在中国传统的文化意念中,女性柔情似水,温柔无比;女性倾国倾城,英雄一怒为红颜。然而,女性也被指责为“红颜祸水”,是“害人精”,是“狐狸精”。看来,女性本身即是一个矛盾的统一体。

家有娇妻,百依百顺,甚至“逆来顺受”;家有娇妻,温柔体贴,甚至“宛若羔羊”。但是,男人啊,你要注意了:物极必反。劝你“莫惹娇妻”,否则,在作家罗尔德·达尔的笔下,娇妻就会向你举起冰冻的羔羊腿,就会令你走向“通天之路”。

① 参见“The Phrase Finder”网站,网址:http://www.phrases.org.uk/meanings/142800.html

第一节 《宛若羔羊》*Lamb to the Slaughter*

罗尔德·达尔的《宛若羔羊》(Lamb to the Slaughter)首次发表在《哈珀》杂志(Harper's,也有人译作《哈珀斯》)1953年9月号上。后来,这篇故事收录到《罗尔德·达尔小说精品集》(The Best of Roald Dahl)、《出乎意料的故事集》(Tales of the Unexpected)、《罗尔德·达尔短篇故事集锦》(The Collected Short Stories of Roald Dahl)、《<宛若羔羊>及其他故事集》(Lamb to the Slaughter and Other Stories)等书中,也被改编成电视系列剧——分别是1958年4月13日播映的《阿尔弗雷德·希区柯克出品短剧选》(Alfred Hitchcock Presents)中的第106集(Episode 106),以及1979年4月14日播映的《出乎意料的故事集》(Tales of the Unexpected)第一部中的第四集(Episode 1.4),是颇具影响力的一部短篇小说。

一、原作导读

在这个短篇故事中,作家罗尔德·达尔塑造了一个我们既熟悉又陌生的女性形象——玛丽·马洛尼:一位等待着做警察的丈夫下班回家的温柔妻子。故事情节简单,甚至单一:玛丽等待丈夫回家以及丈夫回来后发生的事情。到了故事的最后,我们熟悉的玛丽突然变得陌生起来。虽然没有跌宕的情节,但故事本身合情合理、毫无破绽、一气呵成。

小说的女主人公玛丽·马洛尼是一个忠心耿耿、百依百顺的妻子,也是一个怀有身孕、即将做母亲的人。丈夫帕特里克是个警察——这多少为后来的案件打下了颇具讽刺意义的伏笔。

玛丽每天晚上都满怀喜悦的心情等待着丈夫下班回家,丈夫帕特里克在警察局当差。故事发生的这天晚上也不例外,她照等不误,但是丈夫回来后,她却发现丈夫的话语中透露出某种不详的预兆……一阵眩晕的感觉袭来,但她佯装没有听见他说的是什么,走进厨房继续忙活着要做晚饭，并从冰箱的冷冻室里拽出了一只冻得硬邦邦的羔羊腿。还处在麻木情感之中的玛丽不知不觉地就拎起羔羊腿走进了起居室，冷不防从后面将其砸向丈夫帕特里克的脑袋。

她放眼看去的时候，竟然发现丈夫帕特里克躺倒在地，不幸身亡。于是，她慢慢地回过神来，很快意识到自己闯下了大祸，后果十分严重。但是，她不想让自己还未出生的孩子由于她自己的罪行而遭受痛苦，于是，她就开始快速盘算起来，制造自己不在犯罪现场的证据。

她将羔羊腿放到一个浅盘中，推入了烤炉。然后若无其事地去街角的杂货店，对店老板说自己要为"帕特里克准备晚饭"，要买点东西回去吃。回到家中，发现帕特里克躺倒在地，她尖叫起来，随即拨通警察局的电话，也就是丈夫上班的那个警察局，对警察局的警察说，她的丈夫躺在地上死了。

几个小时之内，一伙伙警官先后到达，搜查房子，并做了相关调查。到杂货店的调查结果也与玛丽讲述的完全符合。黑夜到来，警察还在苦苦地搜寻案犯作案的凶器，但毫无头绪。这时，玛丽的羔羊腿已经烤制成熟，香气扑鼻。她就对辛苦侦查的警察说，自己本来为丈夫准备的晚饭——烤羊腿——已经准备好了，不吃怪可惜的。

经过一番推脱之后，已经饥肠辘辘的警察没有抵挡住羔羊腿香气的诱惑，纷纷走进厨房，心满意足地吃了起来。他们嘴里塞满了羊腿肉，但还是滔滔不绝地讨论着案情，你一言我一语地猜测着凶手可能会把凶器藏在什么地方。

听着他们塞满羊腿肉的嘴里发出的交谈声，玛丽·马洛尼"憋不住了，咯咯笑了起来"（Mary Maloney began to giggle）。

二、原作释读

达尔这篇小说阅读难度不大，情节单一。虽如此，却能以流畅文笔和扣人心弦的情节吸引读者一口气读下去。这就是达尔小说的魅力所在。

Lamb to the Slaughter[①]

The room was warm and clean, the curtains drawn, the two table lamps alight—hers and the one by the empty chair opposite. On the sideboard behind her, two tall glasses, soda water, whisky. Fresh ice cubes in the Thermos[②] bucket.

Mary Maloney was waiting for her husband to come home from work.

Now and again she would glance up at the clock, but without anxiety, merely to please herself with the thought that each minute gone by made it nearer the time when he would come. There was a slow smiling air about her, and about everything she did. The drop of the

---

① 本部小说原文出自"Roald Dahl. *The Best of Roald Dahl*[M]. England: Penguin Books Ltd., 2006"。The title is a play on the biblical references to lambs and sacrifices—a lamb being slaughtered is a symbol of the very vulnerable suffering the ultimate fate—death. It's not meant to be directly translated, such as who is the lamb. 本篇小说的标题取自《圣经》里有关羔羊与祭品的隐喻。"被屠宰的羔羊"象征极其脆弱者所遭受的最终命运——死亡。这个标题不是让读者去做字面上的理解,也不必去追究羔羊指的到底是什么。关于"如同被屠宰的羔羊(like a lamb to the slaughter)这一表达,举例如下:

like a lamb to the slaughter: 温顺地;服服帖帖地;胆怯地;听话地;天真烂漫地;容易上当地

Bob went into the exam room like a lamb to the slaughter. 鲍勃就像刑场一样进了考场。

Go like a lamb to the slaughter. "任人宰割"之意,其英文解释如下:

It means to await one's destructions with complete docility. One of the Israeli prophets, Isaiah says, "He was oppressed, and he was afflicted, yet he did not open his mouth; like a lamb that is led to the slaughter..." The lamb refers to Jesus who was crucified without resistance, just like a meek and gentle lamb.

② Thermos: *Noun* trademark of a vacuum flask(商标)膳魔师牌(真空保冷用具,如杯子等)

head as she bent over her sewing was curiously tranquil. Her skin—for this was her sixth month with child—had acquired a wonderful translucent① quality, the mouth was soft, and the eyes, with their new placid look, seemed larger, darker than before.

When the clock said ten minutes to five, she began to listen, and a few moments later, punctually as always, she heard the tyres on the gravel outside, and the car door slamming, the footsteps passing the window, the key turning in the lock. She laid aside her sewing, stood up, and went forward to kiss him as he came in.

"Hullo, darling," she said.

"Hullo," he answered. She took his coat and hung it in the closet. Then she walked over and made the drinks, a strongish one for him, a weak one for herself; and soon she was back again in her chair with the sewing, and he in the other, opposite, holding the tall glass with both his hands, rocking it so the ice cubes tinkled against the side.

For her, this was always a blissful time of day. She knew he didn't want to speak much until the first drink was finished, and she, on her side, was content to sit quietly, enjoying his company after the long hours alone in the house. She loved to luxuriate② in the presence of this man, and to feel—almost as a sunbather feels the sun that warm male glow that came out of him to her when they were alone together. She loved him for the way he sat loosely in a chair, for the way he came in a door, or moved slowly across the room with long strides. She loved the intent, far look in his eyes when they rested on her, the funny shape of

① translucent: *Adjective* permitting light to pass through but diffusing it so that persons, objects, etc., on the opposite side are not clearly visible 半透明的 (e.g. Frosted glass is translucent. 毛玻璃是半透明的。)

② luxuriate: *Verb* (used without object) to enjoy oneself without stint 沉溺 (e.g. She was luxuriating in a long bath. 她在享受一个长长的沐浴。)

the mouth, and especially the way he remained silent about his tiredness, sitting still with himself until the whisky had taken some of it away.

"Tired, darling?"

"Yes," he said. "I'm tired." And as he spoke, he did an unusual thing. He lifted his glass and drained it in one swallow although there was still half of it, at least half of it, left. She wasn't really watching him but she knew what he had done because she heard the ice cubes falling back against the bottom of the empty glass when he lowered his arm. He paused a moment, leaning forward in the chair, then he got up and went slowly over to fetch himself another.

"I'll get it!" she cried, jumping up.

"Sit down," he said.

When he came back, she noticed that the new drink was dark amber with the quantity of whisky in it.

"Darling, shall I get your slippers?"

She watched him as he began to sip the dark yellow drink, and she could see little oily swirls in the liquid because it was so strong.

"I think it's a shame," she said, "that when a policeman gets to be as senior as you, they keep him walking about on his feet all day long."

He didn't answer, so she bent her head again and went on with her sewing; but each time he lifted the drink to his lips, she heard the ice cubes clinking against the side of the glass.

"Darling," she said. "Would you like me to get you some cheese? I haven't made any supper because it's Thursday."

"No," he said.

"If you're too tired to eat out," she went on, "it's still not too late. There's plenty of meat and stuff in the freezer, and you can have it right here and not even move out of the chair."

Her eyes waited on him for an answer, a smile, a little nod, but he made no sign.

"Anyway," she went on, "I'll get you some cheese and crackers first."

"I don't want it," he said.

She moved uneasily in her chair, the large eyes still watching his face. "But you must have supper. I can easily do it here. I'd like to do it. We can have lamb chops. Or pork. Anything you want. Everything's in the freezer."

"Forget it," he said.

"But, darling, you must eat! I'll fix it anyway, and then you can have it or not, as you like."

She stood up and placed her sewing on the table by the lamp.

"Sit down," he said. "Just for a minute, sit down."

It wasn't till then that she began to get frightened.

"Go on," he said. "Sit down."

She lowered herself back slowly into the chair, watching him all the time with those large, bewildered eyes. He had finished the second drink and was staring down into the glass frowning.

"Listen," he said, "I've got something to tell you."

"What is it, darling? 'What's the matter?"

He had become absolutely motionless, and he kept his head down so that the light from the lamp beside him fell across the upper part of his face, leaving the chin and mouth in shadow. She noticed there was a little muscle moving near the corner of his left eye.

"This is going to be a bit of a shock to you, I'm afraid," he said. "But I've thought about it a good deal and I've decided the only thing to do is tell you right away. I hope you won't blame me too much."

And he told her. It didn't take long, four or five minutes at most, and she sat very still through it all, watching him with a kind of dazed horror as he went further and further away from her with each word.

"So there it is," he added. "And I know it's kind of a bad time to be telling you, but there simply wasn't any other way. Of course I'll give you money and see you're looked after. But there needn't really be any fuss. I hope not anyway. It wouldn't be very good for my job."

Her first instinct was not to believe any of it, to reject it all. It occurred to her that perhaps he hadn't even spoken, that she herself had imagined the whole thing. Maybe, if she went about her business and acted as though she hadn't been listening, then later, when she sort of woke up again, she might find none of it had ever happened.

"I'll get the supper," she managed to whisper, and this time he didn't stop her.

When she walked across the room she couldn't feel her feet touching the floor. She couldn't feel anything at all—except a slight nausea① and a desire to vomit. Everything was automatic now—down the stairs to the cellar, the light switch, the deep freeze, the hand inside the cabinet taking hold of the first object it met. She lifted it out, and looked at it. It was wrapped in paper, so she took off the paper and looked at it again.

A leg of lamb.

All right then, they would have lamb for supper. She carried it upstairs, holding the thin bone-end of it with both her hands, and as she went through the living-room, she saw him standing over by the window with his back to her, and she stopped.

"For God's sake," he said, hearing her, but not turning round. "Don't make supper for me. I'm going out."

At that point, Mary Maloney simply walked up behind him and without any pause she swung the big frozen leg of lamb high in the air

① nausea: *Noun* sickness at the stomach, especially when accompanied by a loathing for food and an involuntary impulse to vomit 作呕;恶心;反胃

and brought it down as hard as she could on the back of his head.

She might just as well have hit him with a steel club.

She stepped back a pace, waiting, and the funny thing was that he remained standing there for at least four or five seconds, gently swaying. Then he crashed to the carpet.

The violence of the crash, the noise, the small table overturning, helped bring her out of the shock. She came out slowly, feeling cold and surprised, and she stood for a while blinking at the body, still holding the ridiculous piece of meat tight with both hands.

All right, she told herself. So I've killed him.

It was extraordinary, now, how clear her mind became all of a sudden. She began thinking very fast. As the wife of a detective, she knew quite well what the penalty would be. That was fine. It made no difference to her. In fact, it would be a relief. On the other hand, what about the child? What were the laws about murderers with unborn children? Did they kill them both—mother and child? Or did they wait until the tenth month? What did they do?

Mary Maloney didn't know. And she certainly wasn't prepared to take a chance.

She carried the meat into the kitchen, placed it in a pan[①], turned the oven on high, and shoved it inside. Then she washed her hands and ran upstairs to the bedroom. She sat down before the mirror, tidied her face, touched up her lips and face. She tried a smile. It came out rather peculiar. She tried again.

"Hullo Sam," she said brightly, aloud.

The voice sounded peculiar too.

"I want some potatoes please, Sam. Yes, and I think a can of

① pan: *Noun* a container made of metal and used for cooking food in 平底锅

peas."

That was better. Both the smile and the voice were coming out better now. She rehearsed it several times more. Then she ran downstairs, took her coat, went out the back door, down the garden, into the street.

It wasn't six o'clock yet and the lights were still on in the grocery shop.

"Hullo Sam," she said brightly, smiling at the man behind the counter.

"Why, good evening, Mrs. Maloney. How're you?"

"I want some potatoes please, Sam. Yes, and I think a can of peas."

The man turned and reached up behind him on the shelf for the peas.

"Patrick's decided he's tired and doesn't want to eat out tonight," she told him. "We usually go out Thursdays, you know, and now he's caught me without any vegetables in the house."

"Then how about meat, Mrs. Maloney?"

"No, I've got meat, thanks. I got a nice leg of lamb, from the freezer."

"Oh."

"I don't much like cooking it frozen, Sam, but I'm taking a chance on it this time. You think it'll be all right?"

"Personally," the grocer said, "I don't believe it makes any difference. You want these Idaho[①] potatoes?"

---

① Idaho: *Noun* a state of the north-western US, bordering on British Columbia to the north and containing part of the Rocky Mountains; pop. 1,007,750 (1990); capital, Boise. It became the 43rd state of the US in 1890 爱达荷(美国西北部州,北面与不列颠哥伦比亚省接壤,包括部分洛基山脉;1990年人口1,007,750,首府博伊西;1890年成为美国第43个州。)

"Oh yes, that'll be fine. Two of those."

"Anything else?" The grocer cocked his head on one side, looking at her pleasantly. "How about afterwards? What you going to give him for afterwards?"

"Well what would you suggest, Sam?"

The man glanced around his shop. "How about a nice big slice of cheesecake[①]? I know he likes that."

"Perfect," she said. "He loves it."

And when it was all wrapped and she had paid she put on her brightest smile and said, "Thank you, Sam. Good night."

"Good night, Mrs. Maloney. And thank *you*."

And now, she told herself as she hurried back, all she was doing now, she was returning home to her husband and he was waiting for his supper; and she must cook it good, and make it as tasty as possible because the poor man was tired; and if, when she entered the house, she happened to find anything unusual, or tragic, or terrible, then naturally it would be a shock and she'd become frantic with grief and horror. Mind you, she wasn't *expecting* to find anything. She was just going home with the vegetables. Mrs. Patrick Maloney going home with the vegetables on Thursday evening to cook supper for her husband.

That's the way, she told herself. Do everything right and natural. Keep things absolutely natural and there'll be no need for any acting at all.

Therefore, when she entered the kitchen by the back door, she was humming a little tune to herself and smiling.

"Patrick!" she called. "How are you darling?"

---

① cheese cake: *Noun* (also "cheese cake") a cake having a firm custardlike texture, made with cream cheese, cottage cheese, or both, and sometimes topped with a jamlike fruit mixture 干酪饼

She put the parcel down on the table and went through into the living-room; and when she saw him lying there on the floor with his legs doubled up and one arm twisted back underneath his body, it really was rather a shock. All the old love and longing for him welled up inside her, and she ran over to him, knelt down beside him, and began to cry her heart out. It was easy. No acting was necessary.

A few minutes later she got up and went to the phone. She knew the number of the police station, and when the man at the other end answered, she cried to him, "Quick! Come quick! Patrick's dead!"

"Who's speaking?"

"Mrs. Maloney. Mrs. Patrick Maloney."

"You mean Patrick Maloney's dead?"

"I think so," she sobbed. "He's lying on the floor and I think he's dead."

"Be right over," the man said.

The car came over quickly, and when she opened the front door, two policemen walked in. She knew them both—she knew nearly all the men at that precinct[①]—and she fell right into Jack Noonan's arms, weeping hysterically. He put her gently into a chair, then went over to join the other one, who was called O'Malley, kneeling by the body.

"Is he dead?" she cried.

"I'm afraid he is. What happened?"

Briefly, she told her story about going out to the grocer and coming back to find him on the floor. While she was talking, crying and talking,

---

① precinct: *Noun* a district, as of a city, marked out for governmental or administrative purposes, or for police protection. 城镇中有某种用途或受限制的地区(N. Amer.) a district of a city or town as defined for police purposes(北美)警察管辖区;分管区

Noonan discovered a small patch of congealed[①] blood on the dead man's head. He showed it to O'Malley who got up at once and hurried to the phone.

Soon, other men began to come into the house. First a doctor, then two detectives, one of whom she knew by name. Later, a police photographer arrived and took pictures, and a man who knew about fingerprints. There was a great deal of whispering and muttering beside the corpse, and the detectives kept asking her a lot of questions. But they always treated her kindly. She told her story again, this time right from the beginning, when Patrick had come in, and she was sewing, and he was tired, so tired he hadn't wanted to go out for supper. She told how she'd put the meat in the oven—"it's there now, cooking"—and how she'd slipped out to the grocer for vegetables, and come back to find him lying on the floor.

"Which grocer?" one of the detectives asked.

She told him, and he turned and whispered something to the other detective who immediately went outside into the street.

In fifteen minutes he was back with a page of notes, and there was more whispering, and through her sobbing she heard a few of the whispered phrases "... acted quite normal very cheerful... wanted to give him a good supper... peas... cheesecake... impossible that she..."

After a while, the photographer and the doctor departed and two other men came in and took the corpse away on a stretcher. Then the fingerprint man went away. The two detectives remained, and so did the two policemen. They were exceptionally nice to her, and Jack Noonan

① congeal: *Verb* to change from a soft or fluid state to a rigid or solid state, as by cooling or freezing 使凝结;冻结(e. g. The oil at last is congealed into a white fat. 那层油最终凝结成了一种白色的油脂。)

asked if she wouldn't rather go somewhere else, to her sister's house perhaps, or to his own wife who would take care of her and put her up for the night.

No, she said. She didn't feel she could move even a yard at the moment. Would they mind awfully if she stayed just where she was until she felt better? She didn't feel too good at the moment, she really didn't.

Then hadn't she better lie down on the bed? Jack Noonan asked.

No, she said, she'd like to stay right where she was, in this chair. A little later perhaps, when she felt better, she would move.

So they left her there while they went about their business, searching the house. Occasionally one of the detectives asked her another question. Sometimes Jack Noonan spoke to her gently as he passed by. Her husband, he told her, had been killed by a blow on the back of the head administered with a heavy blunt instrument, almost certainly a large piece of metal. They were looking for the weapon. The murderer may have taken it with him, but on the other hand he may've thrown it away or hidden it somewhere on the premises.

"It's the old story," he said. "Get the weapon, and you've got the man."

Later, one of the detectives came up and sat beside her. Did she know, he asked, of anything in the house that could've been used as the weapon? Would she mind having a look around to see if anything was missing a very big spanner for example, or a heavy metal vase.

They didn't have any heavy metal vases, she said.

"Or a big spanner[1]?"

She didn't think they had a big spanner. But there might be some

---

① spanner: *Noun* a steel hand tool with a handle carrying jaws or a hole of particular shape designed to grip a nut or bolt head 扳手;扳钳

things like that in the garage.

The search went on. She knew that there were other policemen in the garden all around the house. She could hear their footsteps on the gravel outside, and sometimes she saw the flash of a torch through a chink① in the curtains. It began to got late, nearly nine she noticed by the clock on the mantel②. The four men searching the rooms seemed to be growing weary, a trifle③ exasperated④.

"Jack," she said, the next time Sergeant Noonan went by. "Would you mind giving me a drink?"

"Sure I'll give you a drink. You mean this whisky?"

"Yes, please. But just a small one. It might make me feel better."

He handed her the glass. "Why don't you have one yourself," she said. "You must be awfully tired. Please do. You've been very good to me."

"Well," he answered. "It's not strictly allowed, but I might take just a drop to keep me going."

One by one the others came in and were persuaded to take a little nip of whisky. They stood around rather awkwardly with the drinks in their hands, uncomfortable in her presence, trying to say consoling things to her. Sergeant Noonan wandered into the kitchen, came out quickly

---

① chink: *Noun* a narrow opening or crack, typically one that admits light(尤指透光的)裂口;裂缝

② mantel: (also called "mantelshelf") *Noun* a construction framing the opening of a fireplace and usually covering part of the chimney breast in a more or less decorative manner; a shelf above a fireplace opening 壁炉架;壁炉台

③ a trifle: *Adverb* to a small degree; somewhat 有点儿;稍微

④ exasperate: *Verb* to irritate or provoke to a high degree; annoy extremely 激怒;使气恼(e.g. She grew exasperated with his inability to notice anything. 他什么都没觉察到使她很是生气。)

and said, "Look, Mrs. Maloney. You know that oven of yours is still on, and the meat still inside."

"Oh dear me!" she cried. "So it is!"

"I better turn it off for you, hadn't I?"

"Will you do that, Jack. Thank you so much."

When the sergeant returned the second time, she looked at him with her large, dark, tearful eyes. "Jack Noonan," she said.

"Yes?"

"Would you do me a small favour—you and these others?"

"We can try, Mrs. Maloney."

"Well," she said. "Here you all are, and good friends of dear Patrick's too, and helping to catch the man who killed him. You must be terribly hungry by now because it's long past your supper time, and I know Patrick would never forgive me, God bless his soul, if I allowed you to remain in his house without offering you decent hospitality. Why don't you eat up that lamb that's in the oven? It'll be cooked just right by now."

"Wouldn't dream of it," Sergeant Noonan said.

"Please," she begged. "Please eat it. Personally I couldn't touch a thing, certainly not what's been in the house when he was here. But it's all right for you. It'd be a favour to me if you'd eat it up. Then you can go on with your work again afterwards."

There was a good deal of hesitating among the four policemen, but they were clearly hungry, and in the end they were persuaded to go into the kitchen and help themselves. The woman stayed where she was, listening to them through the open door, and she could hear them speaking among themselves, their voices thick and sloppy because their mouths were full of meat.

"Have some more, Charlie?"

"No. Better not finish it."

"She wants us to finish it. She said so. Be doing her a favour."

"Okay then. Give me some more."

"That is the hell of a big club the guy must've used to hit poor Patrick," one of them was saying. "The doc says his skull was smashed all to pieces just like from a sledgehammer①."

"That is why it ought to be easy to find."

"Exactly what I say."

"Whoever done it, they're not going to be carrying a thing like that around with them longer than they need."

One of them belched②. "Personally, I think it's right here on the premises."

"Probably right under our very noses. What you think, Jack?"

And in the other room, Mary Maloney began to giggle.

三、翻译探索

罗尔德·达尔的这部小说在英语世界中引起了广泛的讨论,讨论的焦点在于可怜的"羔羊"究竟指的是谁。在国内,很多人翻译过这部小说,但是对于题目的处理往往过于"直白",过早暴露的原本被作者"隐藏"起来的写作意图。比如,有人将题目译成《羊腿谋杀案》等。在这里,题目的处理做到了跟原文一样的"模糊性"。

宛若羔羊

房间里拉上了窗帘,温暖舒适、干净整齐。两盏桌灯亮了起来——她坐的位置前的桌子上有一盏,对面位置前的桌子上也有一盏。不过,对面位置的那把椅子空着。她身后的餐具橱柜上,放了两

---

① sledgehammer: *Noun* a large, heavy hammer used for such jobs as breaking rocks and driving in fence posts(用于锤岩石和篱笆打桩的)大锤

② belch: *Verb* (used without object) to eject gas spasmodically and noisily from the stomach through the mouth 打嗝

只高玻璃杯、苏打水和威士忌。膳魔师牌真空保冷桶里装的是冰块,刚刚冻好的。

玛丽·马洛尼正等着丈夫下班回家。

她不时地抬头瞅一眼时钟,但没有因为着急而感到不安,而是自娱自乐地想:时间每过一分,他的脚步声就会越近一点。她缓缓地微笑着,她做什么事情都是这样缓缓地微笑着。说来奇怪,她俯下身子、埋头干针线活的样子是那样的安详、宁静。由于处在妊娠期的第六个月里,她的皮肤光彩照人,几乎透亮了。她那张嘴柔软娇嫩,两只眼睛多了些柔顺、温和的目光,显得比以前更大、更黝黑。

时钟显示差五分十点的时候,她开始侧耳细听。没过多大功夫,就听到屋外轮胎碾压砾石路所发出的"啪啦、啪啦"的声音。这总是如此准确无误的。紧接着,车门"嘭"地关上,脚步声掠过窗户,钥匙开始在门锁里转动。她把针线活放到一边,站起来,迎头亲吻他一下。

"嗨,宝贝儿,"她说。

"嗨,"他回应一声。

她接过他的外衣,挂到壁橱里。然后,她走过去,开始倒喝的:为他倒了杯稍微烈点的,为自己倒了杯很柔和的。做完这些,立刻又坐到椅子上,继续干针线活。他则坐在对面,双手举着高玻璃杯摇一摇,再晃一晃,冰块碰撞着杯子内侧叮当作响。

对她来说,这始终是一天中幸福的时刻,令她快乐无比。她清楚,他只有第一杯酒下肚,才会打开话匣子。就她本身而言,独自一人度过了一天中的漫长时光之后,有了他的陪伴,哪怕安安静静地坐着,也是一种享受,她也就心满意足了。她就是喜欢在这个男人面前沉沦般地享受,几乎如同日光浴者享受阳光一般去享受他身上所散发出的那股暖暖的阳性气息——特别是他俩单独待在一起的时候。她爱他,爱他坐在椅子上那副松松垮垮的样子,爱他推门进来的样子,或者迈开大大的步子穿过房间的样子。四目相对时,她爱他那眼神——虽然热情专注,却也遥远陌生。她爱他,爱他的嘴型,令她忍俊不禁的嘴型——累死累活回来后,独自静坐、闭紧嘴巴、一言不发。

可是,一旦威士忌下肚,减缓了疲乏,样子就不一样啦。

“宝贝儿,累吗?”

“是的,”他回答。“很累。”他边说,边做出一个非同寻常之举:举起杯子,一口喝光,尽管喝光前杯子里还剩一半的酒——至少一半。她实际上没有看到他把酒喝光,但她知道,酒他是喝光了,因为他喝完放下胳膊的时候,她听到冰块撞击空杯子底儿所发出的声音。他停了一下,身体在椅子上向前倾斜着,随后“腾”地站起,慢慢走过去,自己要去再倒一杯。

“我给你倒!”她边喊,边一下子跳了起来。

“坐着别动,”他说。

他倒完酒回来时,她注意到,新倒的酒的颜色是深琥珀色的,那是威士忌加了量的缘故。

“宝贝儿,给你拿双拖鞋好吗?”

“不了。”

她看着他小口地喝着那杯新倒的深黄色的酒,看得出酒液表面泛起的一圈圈的、小小的漩涡,说明这酒太浓烈了。

“我觉得,有点说不过去的是,”她说,“像你这样老资历的警察,还整天步行巡视、走来走去的。”

他并没有回答。因此,她又埋头继续做针线活。但是,每次他端起杯子,放到唇边喝,她就能听到冰块撞击杯子内侧叮当作响。

“宝贝儿,”她说。“给你拿点乳酪,可以吗?今天周四,晚饭就没有做什么吃的。”

“不了,”他说。

“要是你累得不想出去吃的话,”她继续说,“我现在就去做点,还不算晚的。冰箱里冷冻了很多肉,还有吃的东西,你甚至不用离开椅子,马上就能吃得到。”

她看着他,等待回答,哪怕是微笑一下,或者轻轻点一下头,也算是回答了。可是,他没做任何表示。

“不管怎样,”她继续说,“我还是先拿点乳酪和饼干过来吧。”

“我不想吃,”他说。

她在椅子上动了动,感到有点不安。那双大眼,仍然看着他的脸。

"可是,晚饭你总得吃啊。不费劲的,我喜欢做。我俩可以吃羊排,或者猪肉。愿意吃什么你就吃什么,只要冰箱的冷冻室里有就成。"

"得啦,"他说。

"但是,宝贝儿,人是铁啊!我这就弄去,吃不吃由你。"

她站起来,针线活放到桌灯旁边。

"坐着别动,"他说。"别忙活了,就一小会儿。"

就在那一刻,她才突然害怕起来。

"对,就这样,"他说。"坐着别动。"

她坐在椅子上慢慢地向后靠去,却始终用她那双大大的、迷茫的眼睛看着他。他喝完第二杯,眼睛盯着杯子里面,皱起了眉头。

"听着,"他说。"我要跟你说点事儿。"

"什么事,宝贝儿?怎么啦?"

现在,他仿佛凝住一般,一动不动。他一直垂着脑袋,身旁的桌灯只能照在他脸部的上边部分,嘴和下巴就处在阴影之中了。她注意到,他左眼眼角附近一小块肌肉动了动。

"我想,这事儿对你来说会有点意想不到,"他说。"可是,我已经考虑了好久。我认为,最好现在立刻告诉你。我希望你不要对我有太多的指责。"

接着,他对她说了,总共也没用多长时间就说完了,至多四五分钟的样子。她始终静悄悄地坐在那儿听着。看着他每说完一个字,人也渐行渐远的时候,她感到头晕目眩、惊恐震颤。

"就是这样的,"他补充道。"我知道,现在告诉你,很不合时宜,但迫不得已,也没有其他法子。你放心,我会给你钱,还要确保你得到妥善的照料。但是,真的没有必要大呼小叫的。无论如何,我也不希望你大呼小叫地闹腾,那样对我的工作也没有任何好处。"

她的第一直觉就是,千万不要相信,这事儿不是真的。她突然想,他什么也没有说,整件事情都是她自己想象出来的。如果再忙忙这儿、忙忙那儿,仿佛没有听他说话一样,或许过一会,从恍惚中清醒过来后,就会发现刚才什么事情也未曾发生。

“我弄晚饭去，”她竭力低声说道，这次他没有说“不了”。

穿过房间的时候，她感觉不到自己的脚是贴着地板走的。除了轻微有点反胃，强烈感觉要呕吐外，她什么也感觉不到。现在，她做每件事情都不受自己支配，完全不由自主的——走下台阶，进入地窖，打开灯的开关，拉开冰箱冷冻室门，伸进手去，握住了首先摸到的东西。她把这个东西举着拿出来，看了一眼。东西用纸包裹着，她就揭开包装纸，又看了一眼。

原来是条羔羊腿。

那么，好吧，他俩晚饭就吃羔羊腿肉。她双手握紧羔羊腿细小的、带骨头的那一头儿，往楼上拿。经过起居室时，看到他站在窗户那边背对着她，她停了下来。

“看在老天的分上，”听到她走来，他头也没回地说。“别给我做晚饭了，我这就出去。”

就在那一刻，玛丽·马洛尼径直走到他身后，片刻也没有停歇，在空中高高地挥起那条大大的冷冻羔羊腿，用尽全力砸向他脑袋后部。

她这一砸，跟用钢制的棍棒砸相差无几。

她后退一步，等待着。有意思的一幕发生了：他仍然站在那儿，至少有四五秒钟，然后轻轻地摇晃几下，随即轰然倒下，摔倒在地毯上。

摔得很重，发出极大的声响，连小桌子也给掀翻在地。这一切倒让她回过神来。她渐渐清醒起来，感到浑身发冷、十分惊讶。她站立一会儿，眨着眼睛看着尸体，双手还是紧紧地握着那只羔羊腿，显得荒唐可笑。

她自言自语：这下可好，我竟然杀了他。

现在，就在突然之间，她头脑变得异常清醒起来，开始快速思考。她是这个死去警探的妻子，十分清楚会有什么样的惩罚等待着她。那倒也无所谓，对她而言，生还不如死呢，死也算是一种解脱。可又一想，没出生的孩子怎么办？对于怀孕期间犯有谋杀罪的人，法律是怎么说的呢？会把孩子和母亲一起处死吗？或者，等待十月怀胎分娩后，再处死？法律是怎么说的呢？

对此，玛丽·马洛尼一无所知。当然，她也没有做好准备要以身试法、冒险尝试的。

她把这块冻肉拿进厨房,放到一个平底锅中,调高烤箱温度,把锅猛的一下推了进去。然后,她把两手洗净,上楼进了卧室,坐到镜子前,整理一下头发,触摸一下双唇和脸颊,试着微笑了一下。但是,笑得怪怪的。于是,她又试着笑了一下。

“嘿,萨姆,”她试着大声地、欢快地说道。

这声音听起来也怪怪的。

“萨姆,请给我来些土豆。噢,对,我还想要一罐豌豆。”

好多了。这次,不管是微笑,还是声音都好多了。接着,她又排演了几次。练完后,她就下楼,拿起外衣,从后门出去,沿着花园走上了大街。

还没到六点呢,可杂货店的灯却点亮了。

“嘿,萨姆,”她一边欢快地打着招呼,一边冲柜台后面那个男子微笑着。

“嗨,晚上好,马洛尼太太。你好吗?”

“萨姆,请给我来些土豆。噢,对,我还想要一罐豌豆。”

那个男子转过身去,伸手去够身后货架上的豌豆。

“帕特里克感到很累,决定今晚不出来吃饭了,”她对他说,“要知道,我俩一般星期四出去吃晚饭。现在,他责备我,说家里什么蔬菜都没有了,可把我难为坏了。”

“那么,马洛尼太太,还买点肉回去吗?”

“不啦,我家里有肉的,谢谢。我家冰箱里冷冻了一条相当不错的羔羊腿。”

“哦,这样啊。”

“萨姆,我不大喜欢做冷冻的羔羊腿。但是,这次我就冒一把险试着做一下。你认为那东西好做吗?”

“就我自己来说,”杂货商说,“我认为,这东西冷冻不冷冻关系不大。你想要这些爱达荷州产的土豆吗?”

“哦,好的,很不错。就来两个吧。”

“还要别的吗?”杂货商把头歪向一侧,一脸高兴的样子看着她。

"然后，做什么？这吃完后，你给他做什么吃？"

"这个啊——你有什么建议吗，萨姆？"

这名男子环视一下自己的商店。"一大块香甜的干酪饼怎么样？我知道他喜欢那一口儿。"

"好极了，"她说。"他特别喜欢。"

东西都包好后，她付了钱，脸上露出最为灿烂的笑容，说道："谢谢你，萨姆。晚安。"

"晚安，马洛尼太太。也谢谢您。"

现在，一边往回赶，她一边思忖：她马上要做的，就是回到丈夫身边，他正等着吃晚饭呢；她一定要好好做一顿，尽可能做得香甜可口，因为可怜的丈夫累坏了；她一进家门，要是家中赶巧发生什么不同以往的、或者悲惨的、或者恐怖可怕的事情的话，她就会自然而然地大吃一惊，随后就会因悲伤和恐惧而发疯般无法自控。需要提醒的是，她不期望家中发生什么事的，她只是买完菜回家而已。也就是说，星期四的晚上，帕特里克·马洛尼太太买完菜，走回家，要为丈夫做晚饭呢。

她自言自语：就是这样的。一切都做得正确无误、自然流畅。所有的事情都要绝对地自然流畅，根本没有必要故意表演、矫揉造作。

因此嘛，从后门进入厨房之际，她独自哼起了小曲儿，面带着微笑。

"帕特里克！"她叫道。"怎么样啦，宝贝儿？"

那包东西放到桌子上后，她走进起居室。看到丈夫躺在地板上，两腿叠放着，一只胳膊扭到身后，压到了身体底下。这场景着实令她大吃一惊。随即，过去所有的爱以及对他的渴望在体内翻腾起来。她奔过去，在他身旁跪下，大哭起来，哭得伤心欲绝。简单得很，无需故意表演、矫揉造作的。

几分钟过后，她站起身，向电话走去。她知道警察局的电话号码。拨通后，另一端一个男子接了电话，她哭着说道："快！快来！帕特里克死了！"

"你是谁？"

"我是马洛尼太太，帕特里克·马洛尼太太。"

"你是说,帕特里克·马洛尼死了?"

"我想是的,"她啜泣着。"他躺在地板上,我想他是死了。"

"马上就赶过去,"那男子说道。

警车飞驰而来。她打开前门,两个警察走了进来,这两个她认识的。事实上,她认识那个分区里几乎所有的警员。她一下子扑到杰克·努南的两只胳膊中间,失声痛哭起来,简直无法控制。他轻轻地扶着她坐到一把椅子上,然后就跟另一个警察开始办案。那个警察名叫奥马利,正跪在尸体旁。

"他死了吗?"她大声问道。

"我想是的。发生什么事了?"

她讲了去杂货店,以及返回时发现他躺在地板上的前后经过,讲得很简短,而且边讲边哭,边哭边讲。努南发现死者头部有一小块血迹,已经凝结了,他就指给奥马利看。奥马利当即站起,匆忙奔向电话。

没过多久,又有几个警察进来。最先进来的是名医生,随后进来的是两个侦探,她知道其中一个的名字。过些时候,又有两个警察来了:一个是摄影专家,拍了现场;另一个是指纹专家,提取了指纹。这些人围在尸体旁边,嘀嘀咕咕、悄声细语说了很多。那两个侦探接二连三地问了她许多问题。但是,对她的态度始终是友好的。她又讲了一遍事情的经过,但这次是从最开始的地方讲起:帕特里克进屋,她在做针线活,他很累,累得不想出去吃晚饭。她讲到把羔羊腿放入烤箱的事:"瞧,现在还在里面烤着呢。"她还讲到出门到杂货店买菜的事,回来就发现他躺在地板上。

"哪家杂货店?"其中一个侦探问道。

她如实说了。他就转身对另一个侦探耳语了几句,那个侦探立马出去,走上大街。

十五分钟过后,他回来了,拿着一页纸,上面做了记录。两个侦探又低声耳语起来。她一边抽泣,一边听着,听出了他俩耳语中的只言片语:"……行为颇为正常……很是喜悦之情……晚饭想为他做些好吃的……豌豆……干酪饼……她不可能……"

过了一会儿,摄影专家和医生走了。另外两个人进来,用担架抬走了尸体。接着,指纹专家也离开了。两个侦探、还有开始那两个警察没有走,他们对她友好得不得了。杰克·努南问她是否愿意换个地方住,可以的话,到他妹妹家住,或者跟他妻子一起住,他妻子会照顾她,为她提供住处的。

她说了"不",感觉此刻半步也动不了。她就待在原地,直到感觉好一些,他们不会特别介意的。此刻,她感觉不太好,确实感觉不太好的。

那么,最好到床上躺一会,不是更好点吗?那是杰克·努南的请求。

她说了"不"。她就想呆在原地不动,就坐在这把椅子上。或许稍过一会,感觉好点儿,就能挪动了。

所以,他们就继续办案,搜查房间,让她自己在那儿待着。其中一个侦探会偶尔过来,再问一个问题。有的时候,杰克·努南经过她身边,会轻声地跟她说上一两句,说的意思是,她丈夫的死,是某种很沉的钝器击中脑袋后部导致的,几乎可以肯定的是,凶器是一块大大的金属制品。他们正在寻找凶器。凶手也许随身带走了,但也可能随手扔掉,或者藏到房子的某个角落。

"这属于老生常谈,"他说。"找到凶器,就等于找到凶手。"

后来,其中一个侦探走上前来,坐到她旁边。他问的是,她是否知道房间里有什么东西可能用来做凶器?她是否愿意看看周围有什么东西不见了,比如大个头的扳钳或沉重的金属花瓶什么的?

她的回答是,他们家里没有什么沉重的金属花瓶。

"或者,有大个头的扳钳吗?"

她记忆中没有这样的工具,但是,类似的东西车库里或许有的。

搜查还在继续。她知道,房子四周的花园里还有警察,听得见他们在外面砾石路上走动发出的脚步声,有时候还能透过窗帘的缝隙看到手电筒的光一闪一闪的。夜色越来越浓,她注意到壁炉台上的时钟指向了将近九点的位置。这四个人搜查着房间,似乎有些困倦萎靡,又稍微有点不耐烦了。

努南警长接下来一次经过她身边时,她问道:"杰克,能麻烦给我拿杯喝的吗?"

“当然可以,我给你拿。你是要这个威士忌吗?”

“是的,麻烦了。但是,只要一小杯。喝点我会感觉好些。”

他把玻璃杯递给她。

“你自己怎么不喝杯啊,”她说。“你一定是累得够呛。请喝吧。你一直对我那么好,很过意不去的。”

“噢,”他回答。“倒不是严令禁止喝酒的,但我可以喝一滴,也好继续破案。”

其他几个也陆续进来,在她的劝说下,每人都喝了点威士忌。他们手端酒杯站在她面前,显得有点尴尬,感觉有些不自在,尽力说些安慰她的话。努南警官溜达进厨房,随后立即出来,说道:“看啊,马洛尼太太。知道吗,你的那个烤箱还没关,羔羊腿还在里面烤着呢。”

“噢,我的天哪!”她叫道。“是还烤着啊!”

“我最好是帮你关掉,可以吗?”

“杰克,你要去关掉吗?真是太感谢了。”

杰克第二次从厨房返回时,她用那双大大的、黝黑的、饱含泪水的眼睛看着他。“杰克·努南,”她说。

“什么事?”

“你,还有其他三个,愿意帮我一个小忙吗?”

“马洛尼太太,我们会尽力的。”

“哦,”她说。“你们都在这儿,也都是我亲爱的帕特里克的好朋友,都来帮忙缉拿害死他的凶手。可到现在这个时候,早就超过了吃晚饭的时间,你们一定都饿得受不了。我知道,让你们呆在我家为他破案,却有失体面,没有好好招待你们,帕特里克永远都不会原谅我的。但愿上帝保佑他的灵魂。烤箱里那只羔羊腿,你们还是吃了吧。到现在,那肉烤的应该正是时候。”

“哪敢有这样的奢望啊。”杰克·努南说。

“拜托了,”她恳求道。“请吃吧。就我个人而言,我什么东西都碰不得的,当然不是指他生前房间里的东西,但是对你们就无所谓了。你们把羊腿肉吃完,就是帮我大忙了。吃完后,你们可以有劲再继续破案的。”

这四个当警察的一再谢绝，犹豫了好一阵子，但是很明显，他们都饿坏了。最终，他们给说动了，走进厨房，你一块、我一块地吃了起来。这位不简单的女子还是待在原地，听着他们走过厨房门发出的声响，也听见他们相互说着什么。但是，由于嘴里塞满了羔羊腿的肉，他们说起话来声音有些厚重、含糊。

“还要吗，查利？”

“不了，最好留点吧。”

“她要我们都吃光。她是这样说的，算是帮她一个大忙。”

“那样啊，好吧。再给我来些。”

“这家伙击中可怜的帕特里克用的那根棍子该是何等之大啊，”其中一个人说道。“咱们那医生说，他的颅骨都被击得粉碎，就好像抡起一把长柄大锤砸下去一样。”

“所以嘛，这个凶器是不难找到的。”

“这正是我要说的。”

“不管凶手是谁，凶器不用的时候，不会长时间带在身上的。”

其中一位打了一个饱嗝。

“就我个人看来，我想那凶器就藏在房子的某个角落。”

“或许就在我们大伙儿眼皮子底下呢。杰克，你什么想法？”

另一个房间里，玛丽·马洛尼憋不住了，咯咯笑了起来。

第二节 《通天之路》*The Way up to Heaven*

罗尔德·达尔的《通天之路》(The Way up to Heaven)首次发表在《纽约客》(The New Yorker)杂志 1954 年 2 月号上。后来，这篇故事收录到《吻了又吻》(Kiss Kiss)、《罗尔德·达尔小说精品集》(The Best of Roald Dahl)、《出乎意料的故事集》(Tales of the Unexpected)、《罗尔德·达尔选集》(The Roald Dahl Omnibus)、《罗尔德·达尔短篇故事集锦》(The Collected Short Stories of Roald Dahl)等书中。这部小说还被改编成电视系列剧——1979 年 5 月 19 日播映的《出乎意料

的故事集》(Tales of the Unexpected)第一部中的第九集(Episode 1.9),也被收录到由爱德华·皮瑟布里奇(Edward Petherbridge)朗读的有声读物《吻了又吻》(Kiss Kiss)中。这是颇具影响力的一部短篇小说。

一、原作导读

福斯特太太的一生之中,已经形成了一种近乎病态的恐惧感,干什么事情总是担心迟到或晚点。一旦发现自己有可能赶不上火车或飞机,她一只眼睛附近的一小块肌肉就会开始抽动。最为糟糕的是,她的丈夫尤金·福斯特先生似乎有意拿晚点这件事情来折磨她——每次总是拖到约定的出发时间过去一两分钟后才跟她离开家门出发。

故事发生的这一天,福斯特太太要独自离开家去探望远在巴黎的女儿及外孙。这是她第一次去巴黎,因此她疯狂般认为,自己会错过此行的航班。果不其然,坚持要送她到机场的丈夫最终不紧不慢地从家里出来钻进汽车、坐到她身旁时,她已经大大落后于预定的时刻了。所幸的是,她所乘坐的航班因天气原因推迟到第二天起飞。在她打到家里的电话中,福斯特先生劝说她回家过夜。

第二天准备离家赶往机场时,她的丈夫福斯特先生提议要她“顺路”送他一程到他要去的那家俱乐部。她知道,这“顺路”一送,她准会晚点,但无力反驳,只能听从。就在小汽车要开走的那一刻,福斯特先生借口说给女儿的礼物忘记带出来,又跑回家中取礼物了。福斯特先生离开座位后,福斯特夫人发现一个装礼物的小盒子被人使劲按进了坐垫之间的缝隙,于是,她也下车跑到房前要告诉他,说自己找到了那份礼物。

但是,在自家房子的正门前,她突然停住,听着里面的动静,而且是全神贯注地听着,身体约有十秒钟的时间僵住不动。接下来,她回转身体,往回跑向小汽车,告诉司机说时间已经来不及了,赶紧开车,而她的丈夫则会搭别人的车去俱乐部的。

她赶上了班机,到达了巴黎,跟几个外孙玩得不亦乐乎,尽享天伦之乐,而且她每周都给丈夫写信。六周后,就离开巴黎回家,但在动身前,给丈夫发了封电报。尽管如此,下飞机后,她发现丈夫并没有前来接机。打出租车回到家、打开家门之际，她闻到空气中有一股奇怪的味道。于是，她心满意足地进了丈夫的书房，打电话叫来了电梯维修工。

打完电话后，"她把听筒放回话机，就坐在丈夫的书桌那儿耐心等待着，等着要派的人过来。派的人很快就会过来为她修理电梯了。"（She replaced the receiver and sat there at her husband's desk, patiently waiting for the man who would be coming soon to repair the lift.）

二、原作释读

这篇小说中，达尔用笔细腻，对人物的刻画惟妙惟肖。理解起来，难度不大。

The Way up to Heaven①

All her life, Mrs. Foster had had an almost pathological② fear of missing a train, a plane, a boat, or even a theatre curtain. In other respects, she was not a particularly nervous woman, but the mere thought of being late on occasions like these would throw her into such a state of nerves that she would begin to twitch③. It was nothing much—just a tiny vellicating④ muscle in the corner of the left eye, like a secret wink—but the annoying thing was that it refused to disappear until an hour or so after the train or plane or whatever it was had been safely caught.

It was really extraordinary how in certain people a simple

---

① 本部小说原文出自"Roald Dahl. *The Best of Roald Dahl*[M]. England: Penguin Books Ltd., 2006"。

② pathological: *Adjective* (informal) compulsive; obsessive（非正式）强迫性神经官能症的；病态的

③ twitch: *Verb* give or cause to give a short, sudden jerking or convulsive movement 抽动；使抽动

④ vellicate: *Verb* twitch 抽动

apprehension about a thing like catching a train can grow into a serious obsession. At least half an hour before it was time to leave the house for the station, Mrs. Foster would step out of the elevator all ready to go, with hat and coat and gloves, and then, being quite unable to sit down, she would flutter① and fidget② about from room to room until her husband, who must have been well aware of her state, finally emerged from his privacy and suggested in a cool dry voice that perhaps they had better get going now, had they not?

Mr. Foster may possibly have had a right to be irritated by this foolishness of his wife's, but he could have had no excuse for increasing her misery by keeping her waiting unnecessarily. Mind you, it is by no means certain that this is what he did, yet whenever they were to go somewhere, his timing was so accurate—just a minute or two late, you understand and his manner so bland③ that it was hard to believe he wasn't purposely inflicting a nasty private little torture of his own on the unhappy lady. And one thing he must have known—that she would never dare to call out and tell him to hurry. He had disciplined her too well for that. He must also have known that if he was prepared to wait even beyond the last moment of safety, he could drive her nearly into hysterics. On one or two special occasions in the later years of their married life, it seemed almost as though he had wanted to miss the train simply in order to intensify the poor woman's suffering.

Assuming (though one cannot be sure) that the husband was guilty,

---

① flutter: *Verb* [with adverbial of direction] (of a person) move restlessly or uncertainly(人)奔忙;忙乱

② fidget: *Verb* [no obj.] make small movements, especially of the hands and feet, through nervousness or impatience 坐立不安;手足无措

③ bland: *Adjective* lacking strong features or characteristics and therefore uninteresting 特点不鲜明的;枯燥乏味的

what made his attitude doubly unreasonable was the fact that, with the exception of this one small irrepressible foible[1], Mrs. Foster was and always had been a good and loving wife. For over thirty years, she had served him loyally and well. There was no doubt about this. Even she, a very modest woman, was aware of it, and although she had for years refused to let herself believe that Mr. Foster would ever consciously torment her, there had been times recently when she had caught herself beginning to wonder.

Mr. Eugene Foster, who was nearly seventy years old, lived with his wife in a large six-storey house in New York City, on East Sixty-second Street, and they had four servants. It was a gloomy place, and few people came to visit them. But on this particular morning in January, the house had come alive and there was a great deal of bustling about. One maid was distributing bundles of dust sheets to every room, while another was draping[2] them over the furniture. The butler was bringing down suitcases and putting them in the hall. The cook kept popping up from the kitchen to have a word with the butler, and Mrs. Foster herself, in an old-fashioned fur coat and with a black hat on the top of her head, was flying from room to room and pretending to supervise these operations. Actually, she was thinking of nothing at all except that she was going to miss her plane if her husband didn't come out of his study soon and get ready.

"What time is it, Walker?" she said to the butler as she passed him.

"It's ten minutes past nine, Madam."

---

① foible: *Noun* a minor weakness or eccentricity in someone's character 性格上的小缺点；怪癖

② drape: *Verb* [with obj. and adverbial] arrange (cloth or clothing) loosely or casually on or round something 将（布）随便地披在……上；松松地围在……上

"And has the car come?"

"Yes, Madam, it's waiting. I'm just going to put the luggage in now."

"It takes an hour to get to Idlewild," she said. "My plane leaves at eleven. I have to be there half an hour beforehand for the formalities[1]. I shall be late. I just know I'm going to be late."

"I think you have plenty of time, Madam," the butler said kindly. "I warned Mr. Foster that you must leave at nine – fifteen. There's still another five minutes."

"Yes, Walker, I know, I know. But get the luggage in quickly, will you please?"

She began walking up and down the hall, and whenever the butler came by, she asked him the time. This, she kept telling herself, was the *one* plane she must not miss. It had taken months to persuade her husband to allow her to go. If she missed it, he might easily decide that she should cancel the whole thing. And the trouble was that he insisted on coming to the airport to see her off.

"Dear God," she said aloud, "I'm going to miss it. I know, I know, I know I'm going to miss it." The little muscle beside the left eye was twitching madly now. The eyes themselves were very close to tears.

"What time is it, Walker?"

"It's eighteen minutes past, Madam."

"Now I really will miss it!" she cried. "Oh, I wish he would come!"

This was an important journey for Mrs. Foster. She was going all alone to Paris to visit her daughter, her only child, who was married to a

---

① formality: *Noun* [count noun] (usu. as "formalities") a thing that is done simply to comply with requirements of etiquette, regulations, or custom 礼节;正式手续;俗套

Frenchman. Mrs. Foster didn't care much for the Frenchman, but she was fond of her daughter, and, more than that, she had developed a great yearning to set eyes on her three grandchildren. She knew them only from the many photographs that she had received and that she kept putting up all over the house. They were beautiful, these children. She doted on them, and each time a new picture arrived she would carry it away and sit with it for a long time, staring at it lovingly and searching the small faces for signs of that old satisfying blood likeness that meant so much. And now, lately, she had come more and more to feel that she did not really wish to live out her days in a place where she could not be near these children, and have them visit her, and take them for walks, and buy them presents, and watch them grow. She knew, of course, that it was wrong and in a way disloyal to have thoughts like these while her husband was still alive. She knew also that although he was no longer active in his many enterprises, he would never consent to leave New York and live in Paris. It was a miracle that he had ever agreed to let her fly over there alone for six weeks to visit them. But, oh, how she wished she could live there always, and be close to them!

"Walker, what time is it?"

"Twenty-two minutes past, Madam."

As he spoke, a door opened and Mr. Foster came into the hall. He stood for a moment, looking intently at his wife, and she looked back at him—at this diminutive[①] but still quite dapper[②] old man with the huge bearded face that bore such an astonishing resemblance to those old

---

① diminutive: *Adjective* extremely or unusually small 极小的;非常小的

② dapper: *Adjective* (typically of a man) neat and trim in dress, appearance, or bearing(尤指男子)整洁的;衣冠楚楚的

photographs of Andrew Carnegie[①].

"Well," he said, "I suppose perhaps we'd better get going fairly soon if you want to catch that plane."

"Yes, dear—yes! Everything's ready. The car's waiting."

"That's good, he said. With his head over to one side, he was watching her closely. He had a peculiar way of cocking the head and then moving it in a series of small, rapid jerks. Because of this and because he was clasping his hands up high in front of him, near the chest, he was somehow like a squirrel standing there—a quick clever old squirrel from the Park.

"Here's Walker with your coat, dear. Put it on."

"I'll be with you in a moment," he said. "I'm just going to wash my hands."

She waited for him, and the tall butler stood beside her, holding the coat and the hat.

"Walker, will I miss it?"

"No, Madam," the butler said. "I think you'll make it all right."

Then Mr. Foster appeared again, and the butler helped him on with his coat. Mrs. Foster hurried outside and got into the hired Cadillac. Her husband came after her, but he walked down the steps of the house slowly, pausing halfway to observe the sky and to sniff the cold morning air.

"It looks a bit foggy," he said as he sat down beside her in the car.

---

① Andrew Carnegie (1835 - 1919), Scottish-born American industrialist and philanthropist. He built up a fortune in the steel industry in the US, then retired from business in 1901 and devoted his wealth to charitable purposes, in particular libraries, education, and the arts. 安德鲁·卡内基(1835—1919,生于苏格兰的美国工业家、慈善家,在美国钢铁业积累了财富,随后于1901年退休,将其财产用于慈善事业,尤其用于图书馆、教育和艺术方面。)

"And it's always worse out there at the airport. I shouldn't be surprised if the flight's cancelled already."

"Don't say that, dear—please."

They didn't speak again until the car had crossed over the river to Long Island①.

"I arranged everything with the servants," Mr. Foster said. "They're all going off today. I gave them half-pay for six weeks and told Walker I'd send him a telegram when we wanted them back."

"Yes," she said. "He told me."

"I'll move into the club tonight. It'll be a nice change staying at the club."

"Yes, dear. I'll write to you."

"I'll call in at the house occasionally to see that everything's all right and to pick up the mail."

"But don't you really think Walker should stay there all the time to look after things?" she asked meekly②.

"Nonsense. It's quite unnecessary. And anyway, I'd have to pay him full wages."

"Oh yes," she said. "Of course."

"What's more, you never know what people get up to when they're left alone in a house," Mr. Foster announced, and with that he took out a cigar and, after snipping off the end with a silver cutter, lit it with a

---

① Long Island: *Noun* an island on the coast of New York State. Its western tip, comprising the New York districts of Brooklyn and Queens, is separated from Manhattan and the Bronx by the East River and is linked to Manhattan by the Brooklyn Bridge 长岛(纽约州沿海岛屿,西端包括布鲁克林和昆斯等纽约区,被东河与曼哈顿和布朗克斯分隔,由布鲁克林桥与曼哈顿相连。)

② meek: *Adjective* quiet, gentle, and easily imposed on; submissive 娴静的;温顺的;顺从的

gold lighter.

She sat still in the car with her hands clasped together tight under the rug.

"Will you write to me?" she asked.

"I'll see," he said. "But I doubt it. You know I don't hold with letter-writing unless there's something specific to say."

"Yes, dear, I know. So don't you bother."

They drove on, along Queen's Boulevard, and as they approached the flat marshland on which Idlewild is built, the fog began to thicken and the car had to slow down.

"Oh dear!" cried Mrs. Foster. "I'm sure I'm going to miss it now! What time is it?"

"Stop fussing," the old man said. "It doesn't matter anyway. It's bound to be cancelled now. They never fly in this sort of weather. I don't know why you bothered to come out."

She couldn't be sure, but it seemed to her that there was suddenly a new note in his voice, and she turned to look at him. It was difficult to observe any change in his expression under all that hair. The mouth was what counted. She wished, as she had so often before, that she could see the mouth clearly. The eyes never showed anything except when he was in a rage.

"Of course," he went on, "if by any chance it *does* go, then I agree with you—you'll be certain to miss it now. Why don't you resign yourself to that?"

She turned away and peered through the window at the fog. It seemed to be getting thicker as they went along, and now she could only just make out the edge of the road and the margin of grassland beyond it. She knew that her husband was still looking at her. She glanced at him again, and this time she noticed with a kind of honor that he was staring intently at the little place in the corner of her left eye where she could feel the muscle twitching.

"Won't you?" he said.

"Won't I what?"

"Be sure to miss it now if it goes. We can't drive fast in this muck[1]."

He didn't speak to her any more after that. The car crawled on and on. The driver had a yellow lamp directed on to the edge of the road, and this helped him to keep going. Other lights, some white and some yellow, kept coming out of the fog towards them, and there was an especially bright one that followed close behind them all the time.

Suddenly, the driver stopped the car.

"There!" Mr. Foster cried. "We're stuck. I knew it."

"No, sir," the driver said, turning round. "We made it. This is the airport."

Without a word, Mrs. Foster jumped out and hurried through the main entrance into the building. There was a mass of people inside, mostly disconsolate[2] passengers standing around the ticket counters. She pushed her way through and spoke to the clerk.

"Yes," he said. "Your flight is temporarily postponed. But please don't go away. We're expecting this weather to clear any moment."

She went back to her husband who was still sitting in the car and told him the news. "But don't you wait, dear," she said. "There's no sense in that."

"I won't," he answered. "So long as the driver can get me back. Can you get me back, driver?"

"I think so," the man said.

---

① muck: *Noun* [*Mass Noun*] dirt, rubbish, or waste matter 污垢;垃圾;废物

② disconsolate: *Adjective* very unhappy and unable to be comforted 不开心的;郁郁寡欢的

"Is the luggage out?"

"Yes, sir."

"Good-bye, dear," Mrs. Foster said, leaning into the car and giving her husband a small kiss on the coarse grey fur of his cheek.

"Good-bye," he answered. "Have a good trip."

The car drove off, and Mrs. Foster was left alone.

The rest of the day was a sort of nightmare for her. She sat for hour after hour on a bench, as close to the airline counter as possible, and every thirty minutes or so she would get up and ask the clerk if the situation had changed. She always received the same reply—that she must continue to wait, because the fog might blow away at any moment. It wasn't until after six in the evening that the loudspeakers finally announced that the flight had been postponed until eleven o'clock the next morning.

Mrs. Foster didn't quite know what to do when she heard this news. She stayed sitting on her bench for at least another half-hour, wondering, in a tired, hazy sort of way, where she might go to spend the night. She hated to leave the airport. She didn't wish to see her husband. She was terrified that in one way or another he would eventually manage to prevent her from getting to France. She would have liked to remain just where she was, sitting on the bench the whole night through. That would be the safest. But she was already exhausted, and it didn't take her long to realize that this was a ridiculous thing for an elderly lady to do. So in the end she went to a phone and called the house.

Her husband, who was on the point of leaving for the club, answered it himself. She told him the news, and asked whether the servants were still there.

"They've all gone," he said.

"In that case, dear, I'll just get myself a room somewhere for the night. And don't you bother yourself about it at all."

"That would be foolish," he said. "You've got a large house here at your disposal. Use it."

"But, dear, it's *empty*."

"Then I'll stay with you myself"

"There's no food in the house. There's nothing."

"Then eat before you come in. Don't be so stupid, woman. Everything you do, you seem to want to make a fuss about it."

"Yes," she said. "I'm sorry. I'll get myself a sandwich here, and then I'll come on in."

Outside, the fog had cleared a little, but it was still a long, slow drive in the taxi, and she didn't arrive back at the house on Sixty – second Street until fairly late.

Her husband emerged from his study when he heard her coming in. "Well," he said, standing by the study door, "how was Paris?"

"We leave at eleven in the morning," she answered. "It's definite."

"You mean if the fog clears."

"It's clearing now. There's a wind coming up."

"You look tired," he said. "You must have had an anxious day."

"It wasn't very comfortable. I think I'll go straight to bed."

"I've ordered a car for the morning," he said. "Nine o'clock."

"Oh, thank you, dear. And I certainly hope you're not going to bother to come all the way out again to see me off."

"No," he said slowly. "I don't think I will. But there's no reason why you shouldn't drop me at the club on your way."

She looked at him, and at that moment he seemed to be standing a long way off from her, beyond some borderline. He was suddenly so small and far away that she couldn't be sure what he was doing, or what he was thinking, or even what he was.

"The club is downtown," she said. "It isn't on the way to the airport."

"But you'll have plenty of time, my dear. Don't you want to drop me at the club?"

"Oh, yes—of course."

"That's good. Then I'll see you in the morning at nine."

She went up to her bedroom on the second floor, and she was so exhausted from her day that she fell asleep soon after she lay down.

Next morning, Mrs. Foster was up early, and by eight-thirty she was downstairs and ready to leave.

Shortly after nine, her husband appeared. "Did you make any coffee?" he asked.

"No, dear. I thought you'd get a nice breakfast at the club. The car is here. It's been waiting. I'm all ready to go."

They were standing in the hall—they always seemed to be meeting in the hall nowadays—she with her hat and coat and purse, he in a curiously cut Edwardian① jacket with high lapels.

"Your luggage?"

"It's at the airport."

"Ah yes," he said. "Of course. And if you're going to take me to the club first, I suppose we'd better get going fairly soon, hadn't we?"

"Yes!" she cried. "Oh, yes—*please*!"

"I'm just going to get a few cigars. I'll be right with you. You get in the car."

She turned and went out to where the chauffeur was standing, and he opened the car door for her as she approached.

"What time is it?" she asked him.

---

① Edwardian: *Adjective* of, relating to, or characteristic of the reign of King Edward VII(与)爱德华七世(有关)的;(有)爱德华七世时代特点的

"About nine-fifteen."

Mr. Foster came out five minutes later, and watching him as he walked slowly down the steps, she noticed that his legs were like goat's legs in those narrow stovepipe trousers that he wore. As on the day before, he paused halfway down to sniff the air and to examine the sky. The weather was still not quite clear, but there was a wisp of sun coming through the mist.

"Perhaps you'll be lucky this time," he said as he settled himself beside her in the car.

"Hurry, please," she said to the chauffeur. "Don't bother about the rug. I'll arrange the rug. Please get going. I'm late."

The man went back to his seat behind the wheel and started the engine.

"Just a moment!" Mr. Foster said suddenly. "Hold it a moment, chauffeur, will you?"

"What is it, dear?" She saw him searching the pockets of his overcoat.

"I had a little present I wanted you to take to Ellen," he said. "Now, where on earth is it? I'm sure I had it in my hand as I came down."

"I never saw you carrying anything. What sort of present?"

"A little box wrapped up in white paper. I forgot to give it to you yesterday. I don't want to forget it today."

"A little box!" Mrs. Foster cried. "I never saw any little box!" She began hunting frantically in the back of the car.

Her husband continued searching through the pockets of his coat.

Then he unbuttoned the coat and felt around in his jacket. "Confound[①] it," he said, "I must've left it in my bedroom. I won't be a moment."

"Oh, *please*!" she cried. "We haven't got time! *Please* leave it! You can mail it. It's only one of those silly combs anyway. You're always giving her combs."

"And what's wrong with combs, may I ask?" he said, furious that she should have forgotten herself[②] for once.

"Nothing, dear, I'm sure. But..."

"Stay here!" he commanded. "I'm going to get it."

"Be quick, dear! Oh, *please* be quick!"

She sat still, waiting and waiting.

"Chauffeur, what time is it?"

The man had a wristwatch, which he consulted. "I make it nearly nine-thirty."

"Can we get to the airport in an hour?"

"Just about."

At this point, Mrs. Foster suddenly spotted a corner of something white wedged[③] down in the crack of the seat on the side where her husband had been sitting. She reached over and pulled out a small paper-wrapped box, and at the same time she couldn't help noticing that it was wedged down firm and deep, as though with the help of a pushing hand.

"Here it is!" she cried. "I've found it! Oh dear, and now he'll be up there forever searching for it! Chauffeur, quickly—run in and call

---

① confound: *Exclamation* (dated) used to express anger or annoyance(旧)(用于表达愤怒、烦恼)讨厌;该死

② forget oneself: to act in a socially unacceptable way because one has lost control of one's emotions 失去理智

③ wedge: *Verb* [with obj.] fix in position using a wedge 楔入;楔进

him down, will you please?"

The chauffeur, a man with a small rebellious Irish mouth, didn't care very much for any of this, but he climbed out of the car and went up the steps to the front door of the house. Then he turned and came back. "Door's locked," he announced. "You got a key?"

"Yes—wait a minute." She began hunting madly in her purse. The little face was screwed up tight with anxiety, the lips pushed outward like a spout.

"Here it is! No I'll go myself. It'll be quicker. I know where he'll be."

She hurried out of the car and up the steps to the front door, holding the key in one hand. She slid the key into the keyhole and was about to turn it—and then she stopped. Her head came up, and she stood there absolutely motionless, her whole body arrested① right in the middle of all this hurry to turn the key and get into the house, and she waited—five, six, seven, eight, nine, ten seconds, she waited. The way she was standing there, with her head in the air and the body so tense, it seemed as though she were listening for the repetition of some sound that she had heard a moment before from a place far away inside the house.

Yes—quite obviously she was listening. Her whole attitude② was a listening one. She appeared actually to be moving one of her ears closer and closer to the door. Now it was right up against the door, and for still another few seconds she remained in that position, head up, ear to door, hand on key, about to enter but not entering, trying instead, or so it seemed, to hear and to analyse these sounds that were coming faintly from this place deep within the house.

---

① arrest: *Verb* stop or check (progress or a process) 阻挡(进程);抑制

② attitude: *Noun* a position of the body proper to or implying an action or mental state 姿势;姿态

Then, all at once, she sprang to life again. She withdrew the key from the door and came running back down the steps.

"It's too late!" she cried to the chauffeur. "I can't wait for him, I simply can't. I'll miss the plane. Hurry now, driver, hurry! To the airport!"

The chauffeur, had he been watching her closely, might have noticed that her face had turned absolutely white and that the whole expression had suddenly altered. There was no longer that rather soft and silly look. A peculiar hardness had settled itself upon the features. The little mouth, usually so flabby①, was now tight and thin, the eyes were bright, and the voice, when she spoke, carried a new note of authority.

"Hurry, driver, hurry!"

"Isn't your husband travelling with you?" the man asked, astonished.

"Certainly not! I was only going to drop him at the club. It won't matter. He'll understand. He'll get a cab. Don't sit there talking, man. Get going! I've got a plane to catch for Paris!"

With Mrs. Foster urging him from the back seat, the man drove fast all the way, and she caught her plane with a few minutes to spare. Soon she was high up over the Atlantic, reclining comfortably in her aeroplane chair, listening to the hum of the motors, heading for Paris at last. The new mood was still with her. She felt remarkably strong and, in a queer sort of way, wonderful. She was a trifle breathless with it all, but this was more from pure astonishment at what she had done than anything else, and as the plane flew farther and farther away from New York and East Sixty-second Street, a great sense of calmness began to settle upon

---

① flabby: *Adjective* (of a part of a person's body) soft, loose, and fleshy (人体某一部位)松弛的;冗赘的

her. By the time she reached Paris, she was just as strong and cool and calm as she could wish.

She met her grandchildren, and they were even more beautiful in tho flesh[①] than in their photographs. They were like angels, she told herself, so beautiful they were. And every day she took them for walks, and fed them cakes, and bought them presents, and told them charming stories.

Once a week, on Tuesdays, she wrote a letter to her husband—a nice, chatty letter—full of news and gossip, which always ended with the words "Now be sure to take your meals regularly, dear, although this is something I'm afraid you may not be doing when I'm not with you."

When the six weeks were up, everybody was sad that she had to return to America, to her husband. Everybody, that is, except her. Surprisingly, she didn't seem to mind as much as one might have expected, and when she kissed them all good - bye, there was something in her manner and in the things she said that appeared to hint at the possibility of a return in the not too distant future.

However, like the faithful wife she was, she did not overstay her time. Exactly six weeks after she had arrived, she sent a cable to her husband and caught the plane back to New York.

Arriving at Idlewild, Mrs. Foster was interested to observe that there was no car to meet her. It is possible that she might even have been a little amused. But she was extremely calm and did not overtip the porter who helped her into a taxi with her baggage.

New York was colder than Paris, and there were lumps of dirty snow lying in the gutters of the streets. The taxi drew up before the house on

① in the flesh: in person rather than via a telephone, film, the written word, or other means 当面

Sixty – second Street, and Mrs. Foster persuaded the driver to carry her two large cases to the top of the steps. Then she paid him off and rang the bell. She waited, but there was no answer. Just to make sure, she rang again, and she could hear it tinkling shrilly far away in the pantry①, at the back of the house. But still no one came.

So she took out her own key and opened the door herself.

The first thing she saw as she entered was a great pile of mail lying on the floor where it had fallen after being slipped through the letter box. The place was dark and cold. A dust sheet was still draped over the grandfather clock②. In spite of the cold, the atmosphere was peculiarly oppressive, and there was a faint and curious odour in the air that she had never smelled before.

She walked quickly across the hall and disappeared for a moment around the corner to the left, at the back. There was something deliberate and purposeful about this action; she had the air of a woman who is off to investigate a rumour or to confirm a suspicion. And when she returned a few seconds later, there was a little glimmer③ of satisfaction on her face.

She paused in the centre of the hail, as though wondering what to do next. Then, suddenly, she turned and went across into her husband's study. On the desk she found his address book, and after hunting through it for a while she picked up the phone and dialled a number.

"Hello," she said. "Listen—this is Nine East Sixty-second Street...Yes, that's right. Could you send someone round as soon as

---

① pantry: *Noun* a small room or cupboard in which food, crockery, and cutlery are kept 餐具室;食品储藏室;碗橱;食品柜

② grandfather clock: *Noun* a clock in a tall free-standing wooden case, driven by weights (装在高高的木匣中靠重力驱动的)落地式大摆钟

③ glimmer: *Noun* a faint or wavering light 微光;闪烁的光

possible, do you think? Yes, it seems to be stuck between the second and third floors. At least, that's where the indicator's pointing… Right away? Oh, that's very kind of you. You see, my legs aren't any too good for walking up a lot of stairs. Thank you so much. Good-bye."

She replaced the receiver and sat there at her husband's desk, patiently waiting for the man who would be coming soon to repair the lift.

三、翻译探索

本篇小说翻译起来,难度不大,但要用流畅的汉语传达出原作的风格和对人物的细腻刻画,也不是一件容易的事情。

通天之路

福斯特太太的一生之中,已经形成了一种近乎病态的恐惧感,总是担心赶不上火车、飞机、轮船,甚至害怕错过剧院的启幕时间。除此之外,她倒不是一个特别紧张兮兮的人。但是,只要一想到上述场合自己要迟到了,她就会提心吊胆,部分肌肉就开始抽搐,整个人就深陷这种状态而无法自拔。其实,也不是什么大幅度的抽搐,只是左眼眼角肌肉微微抽动,就像眼睛不为人知地一眨一眨似的。但是,令人烦恼的是,这种抽动不会马上消失,而是在安安全全地赶上火车、飞机——或者什么要赶上的——大约一个小时过后,才会消失。

在某些人身上,对于像赶火车这种事情所产生的稀松平常的恐惧心理,竟然会演变成一种严重的强迫症,这真的是匪夷所思。在离家去车站前至少半小时,福斯特太太就会跨出电梯,全副武装地准备出发了:帽子戴好、衣服穿好、手套戴上。此时,坐是坐不稳的。于是,她就从一个屋子走到另一个屋子,忧心忡忡、焦虑不安,一直持续到她丈夫出现。这位做丈夫的在出现之前,一直清静独处、自享其乐。他一定早就意识到她的这种状态,因此,他一出现,就镇定自若地用一种干巴巴的声音建议,他们最好现在就出发,难道不该出发了吗?

对于妻子这种荒谬愚蠢的行为,福斯特先生或许早就有权大发雷霆的,但却也没有任何借口对她的悲惨境遇采取变本加厉的手段,比如说,让她没有必要的一直等下去。需要提醒的是,也绝对不能百分百地肯定,他曾经这样做过。然而,无论什么时候他俩要去什么地方,他把时间掐得都是那么的精确——每次就晚一两分钟,这你就理解去吧。每一次他的那种"晚"总是千篇一律,你很难相信他不是故意卑鄙地将自己心存的那点小小的折磨之意强加给自己不幸的老婆。但是,有一件事,他一定十分清楚:她向来不敢大声喊叫,也不敢催促他。这一点,他把她管教得相当驯服了。他一定也十分清楚:要是超过了准时到达的时间界限,他还不准备出发的话,准能把她逼到歇斯底里的程度。他俩结完婚以后的那几年时间里,在一两种特殊的场合下,他就是有意打算赶不上火车,看起来似乎就是加强这个可怜兮兮的女人受折磨的程度。

假设——因为谁也不敢肯定——这个做丈夫的是有罪的,那么,排除上述这一个小小的、对妻子不负责任的偏好外,让他的态度加倍失去理智的原因就是,福斯特太太自始至终是一位充满爱心的好妻子。三十多年以来,毫无疑问的是,她对丈夫忠贞不渝、体贴入微。她是一个不喜欢张扬的女性,但也意识到自己的这一点。多年以来,尽管她十分不愿意相信自己的丈夫心存故意折磨过自己,可是,最近有些时候她有意无意会往这方面想。

尤金·福斯特将近七十岁,跟妻子一起住在一座六层楼的大房子中,房子坐落在东62大街。他俩请了四个佣人。由于房子地处偏僻,没几个人来看他们。可是,一月份的这天早晨很是特别,整座房子热闹起来,一片繁忙的景象。其中有一个佣人往各个房间送防尘套,另一个佣人就忙着往家具上蒙;男管家一个个往楼下搬手提箱,放到大厅里;厨师不时地从厨房奔出来,跟男管家说着什么;福斯特太太本人呢,则穿了一件老款式的皮大衣,头戴一顶黑色的帽子,从一个房间奔向另一房间,装模作样地监督这一切。而实际上,这一切她都没有放在心上,只是一味地想,要是她丈夫不快点从书房出来、做好出发准备的话,就赶不上飞机了。

"沃克,几点了?"经过男管家身旁时,她问道。

“九点过十分,夫人。”

“车到了吗?”

“是的,夫人。在外面等着呢。我现在正要把行李放到车里。”

“到艾德怀尔德机场需要一个小时时间,”她说。“我乘坐的飞机十一点起飞。还要提前半个小时到那里,办理登机手续。我要赶不上了,我刚刚才知道,我要迟到了。”

“夫人,我想你时间足够的,”男管家心怀好意地说。“我提醒过福斯特先生,说你九点十五必须出发。还有五分钟呢。”

“没错,沃克,我知道,我知道。可是,快点放行李,可以吗?”

她开始在大厅里来回走动。男管家经过一次,她就问一次时间。她不断告诫自己:这趟飞机是万万不能错过的。好几个月以来,软磨硬泡之下,她丈夫才同意她去的。要是她赶不上的话,她丈夫就会轻而易举做出决定,让她把整个行程一笔勾销。但是,麻烦就麻烦在,他硬是要到机场为她送行。

“仁慈的老天啊,”她大声说,“快要赶不上了。我知道,我知道,我就知道我要赶不上了。”现在,她左眼边那小块肌肉开始抽搐,疯狂地抽动,那双眼睛也饱含泪水。

“几点了,沃克?”

“十八分了,夫人。”

“现在,真的要赶不上啦!”她叫道。“噢,真希望他这就出来!”

对于福斯特太太来说,这是一次重要的旅行。她要去巴黎看她的独生女儿,女儿嫁给了法国人。她不怎么喜欢这位法国女婿,但很喜欢自己的女儿。不仅如此,她还极其渴望看一眼女儿生下的这三个孙辈的孩子。她只是从不断寄来的照片中看到过这些孩子,而且寄来一张,她就挂上一张,整座房子都挂满了。这几个孩子都很漂亮,令她十分喜爱。每次寄来一幅新照片,她就先拿过去,坐下来端详很长时间,慈爱的目光长久地盯着照片,还抚摸着照片上一张张的小脸,看看有没有令人满意的迹象能表明世代相传的血缘关系。要知道,血是浓于水的。目前,尤其是最近一段时间以来,她越来越强烈地感觉到,生活中的每一天不能没有这些孩子。她真心希望这几个孩子能随时来看她,她带着他们去溜达,给他们买礼物,看着他们逐渐长大。可是,她当然知道,她的丈夫还活在这个世界上,所以她这样希望就是不对的,而且从某种程度上来说,她的这些愿望就不是对丈夫忠贞不渝了。她也知道,尽管他在多家企业中已不再吃香,但也永远不会同意离开纽约、到巴黎居住的。他总算同意让她一个人飞过去呆上六个星期、看看孩子们,这本身就算是破天荒了。哦,可是,她多么希望能永远住在那里、住在他们身边啊!

“沃克,几点了?”

“二十二分了,夫人。”

男管家的声音刚落,一扇门就打开了,福斯特先生走进了大厅。他站立一会,凝视着他的妻子。他妻子也看着年迈的他——身材异常矮小,但依然那样衣冠楚楚,脸上一大片络腮胡子,模样与安德鲁·卡内基的那些老照片比较起来,具有惊人的相似之处。

“噢,”他说,“要想赶上那班飞机的话,我想,我们或许最好快些出发。”

“是,亲爱的——对!都准备好了,车也在等着呢。”

“太好了,”他说。他把头歪向一侧,仔细看着她。他歪头的样式很是奇特,边歪边一抖一抖的,幅度很小,速度却很快。正因为这一点,再加上两只手紧紧抱起放到了靠近胸前的位置,他整个人看起来就像是一只松鼠站在那儿——从公园里跑出来的一只反应敏捷、聪明伶俐的老松鼠。

“亲爱的,这是沃克为你拿来的外衣,披上吧。”

“我去去就来,”他说。“我只是想上趟卫生间。”

她等着他,高个子男管家也站在那儿等着,手里还拿着外衣和帽子。

“沃克,我能赶上吗?”

“能的,夫人,”男管家说。“我想,时间不多不少,刚好能赶上。”

接着,福斯特先生又出来了,男管家就帮他穿上外衣。福斯特太太立马奔出屋子,钻进租来的凯迪拉克。她丈夫跟随其后,看了天空一眼,随即用鼻子吸入一些早晨的寒冷空气。

“看起来有点雾蒙蒙的,”他钻入车中,坐到她身边,说道。“机场那边雾总是会更大一些。要是航班已经取消，也在意料之中。”

“亲爱的，不要那样说。拜托。”

他俩不再说话。车过了河到达长岛时，才开始讲话。

“我都跟佣人交代好了，”福斯特先生说。“今儿起，给他们放假，放六个星期。其间，工资减半。我告诉沃克说，什么时候要他们回来，就什么时候给他拍一份电报。”

“好的，”她说。“他对我说过了。”

“我今晚就搬进俱乐部住。待在俱乐部，换换环境，很不错的。”

“好吧，亲爱的。我会给你写信的。”

“我偶尔也回咱家房子一趟，看看有什么不妥之处，顺便也取一下邮件。”

“可是，让沃克一直待在咱们房子里照看那里的一切，你真的认为没有必要吗？”她问道，显露出一副温顺的样子。

“瞎扯，相当没有必要。不管待不待，我得给他付全额工资的。”

“哦，好的。”她说。“当然可以啦。”

“更何况，你永远也预料不到，把一个人单独留在一座房子里，他会干些什么，”福斯特先生说。然后，拿出一支雪茄，用一把银色的切割器“咔嚓”一声剪去末端，再用一个金色的打火机“啪”地点燃。

她静静地坐在车里，双手紧紧地扣在一起，放到盖膝毯下面。

“你会给我写信吗？”她问道。

“看情况吧，”他回答。“但，恐怕写不上。你知道的，要是没有什么特定的事情要说，我是提不起笔来写信的。”

“好吧，亲爱的。我知道了。所以，你也别放在心上了。”

他们继续向前，驶过了女王大街。就在他们接近那块平坦的沼泽地时，大雾开始变浓，车不得不放慢速度。艾德怀尔德机场就是在那块沼泽地上修建起来的。

“噢，天哪！”福斯特太太叫了起来。“我敢肯定，现在赶不上飞机啦！几点了？”

“不要大呼小叫的，”老头说。“不管怎么说，也不打紧的。现在，航班注定要取消了。这种天气，飞机永远也飞不起来。真不明白,你为什么不嫌麻烦硬要出来一趟。”

她还不能确定究竟能否起飞。但是突然间,她似乎听出她丈夫的语气带有一种从未有过的腔调。于是,她转身看了他一眼,但在那大片胡须的掩盖下,却看不出他的表情有任何变化。除了愤怒,他的眼睛从来没有表露出任何的神情。此时,嘴就至关重要了。她跟以往一样,希望能够看清他的嘴。

“当然啦,”他继续说,“要是凑巧航班真的没有取消,我同意你刚才说的——你现在一定是赶不上了。为什么不接受这个事实呢?”

她转过身去,透过车窗看着外面的迷雾。越往前行驶,大雾似乎就越浓。现在,她只能刚好辨认出路的边沿,还能隐约看到路旁远处草地的边缘部分。她知道,她丈夫仍然看着她。于是,她又回头瞥了他一眼。这一次,她注意到,他使劲盯着她左眼眼角那一小块地方,她也感觉到那地方的肌肉在抽搐。这时候,她产生了某种恐惧感。

“难道不是吗?”他问道。

“难道不是什么?”

“难道不是一定赶不上了吗——如果航班真的没有取消的话?天气这样糟糕,我们开不快的。”

说完这话之后,他就没再说什么。车简直是向前爬行,不停地爬行。司机打开黄灯,照亮了路的边沿,这才不至于停滞不前。其他车的车灯,有白色的、有黄色的,不断透过迷雾向他们照射过来。其中有辆车,自始至终紧跟在他们后面,车灯特别耀眼。

突然间,司机把车停住了。

“看吧!”福斯特先生喊道。“我就知道,卡住不动了吧。”

“不是的,先生,”司机转头说道。“我们到了。这就是机场。”

福斯特太太一声不响地跳下车,匆忙通过大门进入楼内。里面有一大堆人,其中大多数乘客都站在售票柜台的周围,一个个闷闷不乐的样子。她挤上前来,询问其中一位工作人员。

“是的,”这位工作人员说。“你要乘坐的航班暂时推迟了。但是,请不要走开。我们预测,这种天气随时会放晴的。”

她回到她丈夫身边,把这一消息告诉了他,他仍然坐在车里。

“回去吧，亲爱的，”她说。“等我毫无意义。”

“我不等了，”他回答。“只要司机能把我送回去，我就不等了。司机，你能把我送回去吗?”

“我想可以的，”司机说。

“行李拿出去了吗?”

“是的，先生。”

“再见，亲爱的，”福斯特太太边说，边把身体探入车内，在她丈夫脸颊上轻轻吻了一下，吻到的是那里粗糙的、灰色的软毛。

“再见，”他回应道。“旅途愉快!”

车开走了，留下福斯特太太一个人待在机场。

对她来说，这一天的其余时间犹如梦魇一般。她坐在尽可能靠近售票柜台的一条长凳上，时间过去一个小时又一个小时，而且每过半个小时，她就起身问一下那个工作人员，情况是否好转。每次得到的答案都是一样的，那就是，必须继续等待，因为浓雾随时有可能散尽。直到晚上六点过后，扬声器最终才广播说，航班延期到第二天上午十一点。

刚听到这一消息的时候，福斯特太太不是很清楚该怎么办。她仍旧坐在那条长登上，足足又过去半个小时，其间她反复地思考今晚要在哪里过夜——思考得大脑疲惫不堪，思考得眼前迷雾蒙蒙。她很不愿意离开机场，也不希望看到她丈夫。她感到，他最终会千方百计、想方设法阻止她，让她去不成法国。一想到这一点，她就恐惧万分。她宁愿待在原地不动，一整夜坐在长登上，那会是最安全的。可问题是，她已经筋疲力尽，而且她很快就意识到，一个上了年纪的女人这样做是很荒唐愚蠢的。所以，最终她还是走向话机，给家里打了个电话。

她丈夫接了电话，当时他正要离家去俱乐部呢。她把消息告诉了他，问他家里是否还有佣人没有走。

“他们都走了，”他说。

“那样的话，亲爱的，我就到什么地方随便找一个房间睡下，你就不用操心了。”

“那样做很愚蠢,”他说。“家里房子这么大,睡哪间都可以的。回来睡吧。”

“但是,亲爱的,家里空无一人呀。”

“那么,我就待在家里陪你。”

“家里没有吃的,什么吃的都没有。”

“那就吃完再进屋。不要愚蠢透顶,老婆。你做什么事,似乎都喜欢挑来挑去的。”

“是的,”她说。“很抱歉。我就在机场这儿吃个三明治,吃完就回家。”

外面,浓雾散去一点点,但是出租车还是开得很慢,开了很长时间。到达62大街,进入家门的时候,时间已经相当晚了。

听到她进屋的声音,她丈夫就从书房里出来了。“说说看,”他站在书房门口说,“巴黎怎么样?”

“我们上午十一点出发,”她回答。“这次确定无疑了。”

“你意思是说,要是大雾散去的话。”

“现在就要散了,因为起风了。”

“你看起来很累啊,”他说。“这一天你过得一定焦虑不安。”

“反正不是很舒适、惬意。我想,我就直接上床睡下了。”

“我已经为上午预订了一辆车,”他说。“九点钟。”

“哦,谢谢你,亲爱的。我当然希望,你不用再麻麻烦烦一路送我了。”

“不送你,”他慢慢说。“我想我不去送了。但是,没有理由不把我顺路送到俱乐部的。”

她看了看他,就在那一刻,他似乎离她很远很远,站到了某个边界线之外了。就在突然之间,他变得如此渺小、如此遥远,她无法肯定他要做什么、正在想什么,也无法肯定他是一个什么样的人。

“俱乐部在闹市区,”她说。“况且,到机场也不顺路。”

“可是,我亲爱的,你时间很充裕。难道你不想把我捎到俱乐部吗?”

“哦,好的——当然想。”

“那就好。那就早晨九点见。”

她上楼进了卧室，卧室在三楼。这一天的折腾把她弄得筋疲力尽，一躺下就很快睡着了。

第二天早晨，福斯特太太早早起来，八点半就下了楼，做好了出发的准备。

刚过九点，她丈夫也露面了。“冲咖啡没有？”他问道。

“没有呢，亲爱的。我还以为你会到俱乐部好好吃顿早餐的。要的车到了，等了好一阵子，我准备出发了。”

他俩站在大厅里，这阵子他俩似乎总在大厅里见面。这一次，她戴上了帽子，穿好了衣服，手里还拿着一只小手提包；他穿了件剪裁得稀奇古怪的夹克衫，翻领高高竖起，属于爱德华七世那个时代的服装风格。

“你的行李呢？”

“存放在机场了。”

“噢，是的。”他说。“想起来啦。要是你先把我捎到俱乐部，我想我们最好尽早出发，对吧？”

“正是！”她大声说。“喔，正是——走吧！”

“我去拿几支雪茄来。去去就来，你先上车。”

她转身出门，走向司机站立的地方。司机见她走近，就拉开了车门。

“几点了？”她问司机。

“大概九点十五。”

五分钟后，福斯特先生出来了。看着他慢腾腾走下台阶，她注意到，在他穿的那条窄窄的烟筒裤的衬托下，他的两条腿就像是山羊的腿。就像昨天下台阶的时候一样，他下到半道暂停下来，用鼻子吸入一些空气，检查一下天空状况。天仍然不是很晴朗，但是却有一束阳光透过迷雾照射下来。

“或许这次你运气会不错的，”上车在她旁边坐定后，他说。

“请快开车吧，”她对司机说。“盖膝毯不用麻烦你弄了，我自己会搞定的。请出发吧，我要晚了。”

于是，司机就返回，坐到方向盘后面，发动了引擎。

“等一会儿!”福斯特先生冷不防说道。“司机,等一会儿,行吗?”

“怎么啦,亲爱的?”她看到他在外衣兜里摸索着。

“我有一件小礼物想让你带给爱伦,”他说。“现在,我到底把它放哪儿了？我敢肯定,下楼的时候手里还拿着呢。”

“我可从来没有看到你拿着什么啊？什么样的礼物?”

“是一个小盒子,外面包着白纸。昨天忘了给你,今天我可不想忘记。”

“一个小盒子!”福斯特夫人叫道。“我可从来没有看到什么小盒子啊!”说完,她就开始拼命地在车后部寻找起来。

她丈夫继续摸索,这次摸的是外衣兜子。接着,解开外衣扣子,在夹克衫上摸来摸去。“真该死,”他说,“一定是落到卧室里了。我去去就来。”

“噢,拜托啊!”她叫道。“我们没时间啦！别拿啦！可以邮寄的。不管怎么说,那礼物只不过是一把微不足道的梳子而已,你哪次送的不是梳子啊。”

“梳子怎么啦,我能问问吗?”他说。这次她竟然忘乎所以,他感到十分生气。

“亲爱的,我敢肯定,不给礼物也没有什么大不了的。但是……”

“待着别动!”他发号施令了。“我去取一下。”

“快点啊,亲爱的。喔,请快点啊!”

她静静坐着,等了又等。

“司机,几点了?”

这个开车的男子戴了一块手表,于是,他看了看。“快到九点半了。”

“一个小时之内我们能到机场吗?”

“将将巴巴能。”

就在此时,福斯特太太一下子看到一种白色的什么东西的一角,这个东西楔入她旁边座位的缝隙中,那座位她丈夫刚刚还坐过。她俯身去够,拉出一个小小的、白纸包裹的盒子。与此同时,她自然而然地注意到,这个小盒子紧紧地嵌进缝隙处——很紧、很深,就好像用手使劲压进去的一样。

"在这儿呢!"她喊道"我找到了!哦,亲爱的,现在他一定在楼上不停地找来找去。司机啊,快点帮个忙——跑进去把他喊下来,可以吗?"

开车的男子长有爱尔兰人的嘴形,嘴很小,颇具叛逆精神。他对这一切不是很在意,但还是从车里出来,走上台阶,来到房子前门,随即转身回来。"门锁着呢,"他说道。"你有钥匙吗?"

"有的——等一下。"她开始在小手提包里狂乱翻找。她的那张小脸绷得紧紧的,一脸的焦虑和不安。双唇向外撅起,就像植物发了芽一般模样。

"给你!不——我自己去会更快些。我知道他在哪儿。"

她匆匆忙忙下了车,走上台阶,来到前门,一只手拿着钥匙。钥匙插入锁孔,刚要转动,结果却戛然而止,停了下来。她站在门那儿,头靠门近一些,整个身体僵住一般一动不动的,摆出一副匆忙要转动钥匙、随后进入房间的样子。她僵直地等着——五秒、六秒、七秒、八秒、九秒、十秒——等待着。她头仰起来,还是那样站立着,绷紧了身体,看起来似乎要听到某种声音再重复一遍,而这种声音她刚听到过,是从房子的深处传出来的。

是的,很明显,她是在听,摆出的正是一副倾听的姿态。外表看起来,她实际上把耳朵越来越近地向门贴去。现在,这只耳朵正好贴到门上,贴了好几秒钟。同时,头抬起,手把钥匙,身体要进去,但却没有往里走,而是——或者似乎是——倾听、分析那些从房内深处传出来的声音,声音很微弱。

接着,她一下子跳了起来,整个人又活了。她从门上拔下钥匙,沿着台阶跑了回来。

"不赶趟啦!"她对司机喊道。"不能等他了,就是等不了啦。飞机要赶不上了。司机,现在赶快走,赶快!去机场!"

要是司机当时仔细看看她的话,或许就会注意到:她的脸变得煞白煞白,脸上的表情突然变了样——看不到温柔体贴、傻里傻气的样子了;脸上有的只是坚毅和刚强,很是奇特。那张小嘴通常是那样的松弛,现在却绷得又紧又薄,两只眼睛睁得亮亮的。说起话来,声音中增添了一种新的腔调,颇具权威性。

"赶快,司机,赶快走!"

"你丈夫不跟你一起旅行吗?"司机问道,十分吃惊。

"当然不啦!他只不过要我把他捎到俱乐部。不打紧,他会理解的。他会打出租车去。伙计,不要光坐在那儿说话,走啊!我要赶飞机去巴黎。"

在后座福斯特太太的催促下,司机一路开得很快。上飞机时,就剩几分钟时间了。很快,飞机高高升起,飞行在大西洋的上空。舒舒服服地坐在飞机椅子上,听着飞机马达低沉的嗡嗡声,她终于能向巴黎飞去了。她身上还洋溢着以前没有过的情绪状态。她感到刚强无比,感觉从来没有这么好过,很是奇特。因此,她还有点喘不过气来。其实,她喘不过气来,倒不是因为别的什么原因,而是因为对自己的所作所为惊讶不已。随着飞机离开东62大街及纽约越来越远,她也越来越感觉平静和镇定。到达巴黎的时候,她恢复到以往的刚强、镇定和平静了。

她见到那几个孙辈的孩子。当面见到这几个活生生的孩子,感觉比照片上见到的漂亮多了。她对自己说,这几个孩子就像天使,漂亮无比。每天她都带着他们去溜达,给他们吃蛋糕,买礼物给他们,还给他们讲一些令人陶醉的故事。

每个周二,她都要给丈夫写一封信,每一封信写得都细致入微、轻松活泼,每封信都有新鲜事、家常话,每封信都是以这样的话结尾:"现在,亲爱的,一定要按时吃饭。可是,我知道,我不在你身边,吃饭这件事我担心你不会按我的意思去做。"

六周的时间结束之际,她要返回美国,回到丈夫身边了,大家没有一个不感到伤心的。也可以说,除了她之外,大家都伤心。令人意想不到的是,她并不像大家想象的那样在意这次分别。与大家伙儿一个个吻别之际,她的言谈举止似乎含有这样的暗示:用不了多长时间,她就有可能再次回来。

无论如何,身为一个对丈夫忠贞不渝的妻子,她没有逾期多待。自到达之日算起,正好六个星期的时候,她就给丈夫发了一封电报,然后登上飞机回纽约了。

到达艾德怀尔德机场后，福斯特太太饶有兴趣地发现，没有车前来接她。对此，她也有可能感觉有一点开心，但是，她没有过于张扬，搬运工帮忙把行李放入出租车内时，她并没有多给小费。

纽约比巴黎可冷多了，街沟里还可以看到一块块脏兮兮的残雪。出租车到达62大街，停在那座房子前面。福斯特太太说动了司机，帮她把两只大箱子搬到台阶顶部。然后，她付清了钱，就去按门铃，按完后就等着，但是没有人来开门。怕里面听不见，她又按了一下。这一次，她甚至听到远在房后的食品储藏室也回荡着"叮当叮当"刺耳的门铃声。但是，还是没有人来开门。

所以，她掏出自己的钥匙，亲自打开了门。

一进屋，首先映入眼帘的是地板上的一大堆邮件，是塞进邮箱后掉落到地板上的。整个屋子又黑又冷，那只落地式大摆钟还用防尘罩罩着。姑且不管寒冷与否，整个屋子气氛异常压抑，空气中弥漫着一股微弱的、古怪的味道，这种味道她以前从没有闻到过。

她快速穿过大厅，来到后边，绕着角落向左拐，就暂时看不到她了。她的这一行为有点故作姿态之嫌，这种姿态是一个女子所特有的：或者要开始对外面的谣传开始调查，或者要开始对内心的怀疑加以确认。几秒钟过后返回时，她的脸上微微闪现出一丝满意的光芒。

她在大厅中间停下来，好像在思考下一步该做什么。接着，她突然转身走进丈夫的书房。在书桌上，她找到一本地址簿，翻了一会儿，就拿起电话，拨通了一个号码。

"嗨，你好，"她说。"听着——这里是东62大街9号……是的，没错。尽快派一个人过来，你认为可能吗？是的，似乎卡到二楼和三楼之间，至少，这是楼层指示器指示的位置……马上吗？哦，太感谢你了。要知道，我腿脚不再那么灵便，无法爬那么多楼梯。十分感谢。再见。"

她把听筒放到话机上，就坐在她丈夫的书桌那儿耐心等待着，等着要派的人过来。派的人很快就会过来为她修理电梯。

第三章 战争创伤

人人都希望和平，讨厌战争。然而，战争有时是不可避免的。战争会引燃人们的厌战情绪，正如美国摇滚艺术家鲍勃·迪伦（Bob Dylan）在《答案在风中飘荡》一歌中所唱的那样：

How many roads must a man walk down
Before you call him a man?
How many seas must a white dove sail
Before she sleeps in the sand?
Yes, how many times must the cannon balls fly
Before they're forever banned?
The answer my friend is blowin' in the wind
The answer is blowin' in the wind. ①

其中文意思大致如下：

要走多少条路的人

① 参见"Lyrics Freak"，网址：http://www.lyricsfreak.com/

才能被称为真正的人？
白鸽飞过大海多少遍
才能安眠于沙滩？
噢，炮弹越过天空多少次
才能永远被禁止？
朋友啊，答案在风中飘荡——
答案在这风中飘荡。①

鲍勃·迪伦的这一小节歌词可谓一语道破天机，充分揭示了人们的厌战情绪。的确，战争不是人们想要的，一旦发生了战争，就会给人们带来无尽的创伤。创伤有身体上的，也有精神上的。肢体伤残等身体创伤，人们还能克服，但是，失眠、孤独等精神创伤恐怕就难以克服，使人难以融入社会，甚至造成心灵上的伤痛，衍生出各种心理疾病。这恐怕就是战争带来的最大的创伤了。

深受战争创伤之苦的"士兵"，时常会出现"幻象"，时常会忆起"美好昨日"，但他们不乏面临同样问题的伙伴，时常会发现"如你之人"。

这就是罗尔德·达尔笔下的战争给人留下的种种创伤。

第一节　《美好昨日》*Yesterday Was Beautiful*

罗尔德·达尔的《美好昨日》(Yesterday Was Beautiful)首次发表在《向你飞跃》(Over to You)一书中。后来，这篇故事又收录到《罗尔德·达尔短篇故事集锦》(The Collected Short Stories of Roald Dahl)以及《五部畅销书集》(5 Bestsellers)等书中。这部小说情节简单，描写的是第二次世界大战时期的一个场景。《向你飞跃》是罗尔德·达

① 这一小儿段歌词为著者所译。

尔在第二次世界大战期间当皇家空军飞行员所经历的一些故事的集锦。这些故事中,有的主人公是“隐身”的,但可以想象是作家达尔的化身。

一、原作导读

英国皇家空军的一名飞行员因格莱赛从战斗机座舱弹射跳伞,降落到希腊的一座小岛上。落地时,他扭伤了脚踝骨。现在,他要做的就是在岛上找到一条小船,好坐船渡到对岸的陆地上去。但问题是,他降落的那个小岛上的那个村庄里几乎找不到人了。

找来找去,他最终发现了一位老人,老人坐在一个水槽附近的阴影里。他问老人,是否认识村子里拥有船只的人,但老人懵懵懂懂,脸上一点表情都没有。老人没有回答,而是问德国鬼子什么时候会再来。飞行员对老人说,他们今天是不会再来了。老人接着说,村子人已经没有人了,他不明白德国鬼子为什么还来轰炸。

因格莱赛又问了问老人关于什么人有船的事情。老人告诉他,村子里有一个叫约安尼斯·斯皮拉吉斯的人拥有一条船,约安尼斯曾经住在靠近海边的一所房子里,但那所房子已经被德国飞机炸毁了。约安尼斯现在住在安东尼娜·安热卢的房子里。老人还说,约安尼斯目前可能不在,但是,他的妻子安娜会在的。飞行员刚要动身去找船主,老人又对他说,德国鬼子轰炸的时候,约安尼斯和安娜的女儿玛丽亚当时正好都在家。

飞行员找到了安东尼娜·安热卢的房子,敲开房门,有人出来带他进去见安娜。他对安娜说,他要找她的丈夫,因为他听说她的丈夫有条船。年迈的安娜问他,德国人跑哪去了。他告诉她,德国人在拉米亚附近,今天不会再来了。安娜却说,德国兵每天都来轰炸,没完没了地轰炸,只要你闭上眼睛再睁开眼睛,然后到外面一看,房子就纷纷化为灰烬,人也跟着遭殃。她问他杀死了多少鬼子,他回答说他尽可能多地去杀鬼子。她对他说,他要把所有的德国鬼子都杀光,不管男女老少。接着,她又问他来干什么。他说来找约安尼斯,于是,她领着他来到门口,指向了水槽附近那位老人。

"他在那儿,"她说道。"那就是他。"("There he is," she said. "That's him.")

最后,"这位飞行员看了看那个人,然后转身要对老妇人说点什么,但是,老妇人已经进屋,消失不见了。"(The pilot looked at the man. Then he turned to speak to the old woman, but she had disappeared into the house)

二、原作释读

昨日很美好。的确如此。人们追忆昔日的美好时光,痛恨战争带来的伤痛。达尔的这篇小说篇幅不长,选取了一个视角来揭示战争的残酷。

Yesterday Was Beautiful[①]

He bent down and rubbed his ankle where it had been sprained[②] with the walking so that he couldn't see the ankle bone. Then he straightened up and looked around him. He felt in his pocket for a packet of cigarettes, took one out and lit it. He wiped the sweat from his forehead with the back of his hand and he stood in the middle of the street looking around him.

"Dammit[③], there must be someone here," he said aloud, and he felt better when he heard the sound of his voice.

He walked on, limping, walking on the toe of his injured foot, and

① 本部小说原文出自"Roald Dahl. *The Collected Short Stories of Roald Dahl*[M]. England: Penguin Books Ltd., 1992"。

② sprain: *Verb* [with obj.] wrench or twist the ligaments of (an ankle, wrist, or other joint) violently so as to cause pain and swelling but not dislocation 扭伤(脚踝,手腕,其他关节)

③ dammit: *Exclamation* used to express anger and frustration 该死;真他妈的

when he turned the next corner he saw the sea and the way the road curved around between the ruined houses and went on down the hill to the edge of the water. The sea was calm and black. He could clearly make out the line of hills on the mainland in the distance and he estimated that it was about eight miles away. He bent down again to rub his ankle. "God dammit," he said. "There must be some of them still alive." But there was no noise anywhere, and there was a stillness about the buildings and about the whole village which made it seem as though the place had been dead for a thousand years.

Suddenly he heard a little noise as though someone had moved his feet on the gravel and when he looked around he saw the old man. He was sitting in the shade on a stone beside a water trough①, and it seemed strange that he hadn't seen him before.

"Health to you," said the pilot. "Ghia son."②

He had learned Greek from the people up around Larissa and Yanina.

The old man looked up slowly, turning his head but not moving his shoulders. He had a grayish-white beard. He had a cloth cap on his head and he wore a shirt which had no collar. It was a grey shin with thin black stripes. He looked at the pilot and he was like a blind man who looks towards something but does not see.

"Old man, I am glad to see you. Are there no other people in the village?"

There was no answer.

The pilot sat down on the edge of the water trough to rest his ankle.

---

① trough: *Noun* a long, narrow open container for animals to eat or drink out of (给动物进食或饮水的)槽

② Ghia son: 这里采用音译来对等传达,应是当地语(希腊语)"Health to you"的意思

"I am Inglese," he said. "I am an aviator who has been shot down and jumped out by the parachute. I am Inglese."

The old man moved his head slowly up and down. "Inglesus[①]," he said quietly. "You are Inglesus."

"Yes, I am looking for someone who has a boat. I wish to go back to the mainland."

There was a pause, and when he spoke, the old man seemed to be talking in his sleep. "They come over all the time," he said. "The Germanoi[②] they come over all the time." The voice had no expression. He looked up into the sky, then he turned and looked behind him in the sky. "They will come again today, Inglese. They will come again soon." There was no anxiety in his voice. There was no expression whatsoever. "I do not understand why they come to us," he added.

The pilot said, "Perhaps not today. It is late now. I think they have finished for today."

"I do not understand why they come to us, Inglese. There is no one here."

The pilot said, "I am looking for a man who has a boat who can take me across to the mainland. Is there a boat owner now in the village?"

"A boat?"

"Yes." There was a pause while the question was considered.

"There is such a man."

"Could I find him? Where does he live?"

"There is a man in the village who owns a boat."

"Please tell me what is his name?"

---

① Inglesus：主人公的名字"Inglese"的非标准发音形式

② Germanoi：当地人对"German"的一种发音形式

The old man looked up again at the sky. "Joannis is the one here who has a boat."

"Joannis who?"

"Joannis Spirakis," and he smiled. The name seemed to have a significance for the old man and he smiled.

"Where does he live?" the pilot said. "I am sorry to be giving you this trouble."

"Where he lives?"

"Yes."

The old man considered this too. Then he turned and looked down the street towards the sea. "Joannis was living in the house nearest to the water. But his house isn't any more. The Germans hit it this morning. It was early and it was still dark. You can see the house isn't any more. It isn't any more."

"Where is he now?"

"He is living in the house of Antonina Angelou. That house there with the red colour on the window." He pointed down the street.

"Thank you very much. I will go and call on the boat owner."

"Ever since he was a boy," the old man went on, "Joannis has had a boat. His boat is white with a blue line around the top," and he smiled again. "But at the moment I do not think he will be in the house. His wife will be there. Anna will be there, with Antonina Angelou. They will be home."

"Thank you again. I will go and speak to his wife."

The pilot got up and started to go down the street, but almost at once the man called after him, "Inglese."

The pilot turned.

"When you speak to the wife of Joannis—when you speak to Anna... you should remember something." He paused, searching for words. His voice wasn't expressionless any longer and he was looking up at the pilot.

"Her daughter was in the house when the Germanoi came. It is just something that you should remember."

The pilot stood on the road waiting.

"Maria. Her name was Maria."

"I will remember," answered the pilot. "I am sorry." He turned away and walked down the hill to the house with the red windows. He knocked and waited. He knocked again louder and waited. There was the noise of footsteps and the door opened.

It was dark in the house and all he could see was that the woman had black hair and that her eyes were black like her hair. She looked at the pilot who was standing out in the sunshine.

"Health to you," he said. "I am Inglese."

She did not move.

"I am looking for Joannis Spirakis. They say that he owns a boat."

Still she did not move.

"Is he in the house?"

"No "Perhaps his wife is here. She could know where he is."

At first there was no answer. Then the woman stepped back and held open the door. "Come in, Inglesus," she said.

He followed her down the passage and into a back room. The room was dark because there was no glass in the windows—only patches of cardboard. But he could see the old woman who was sitting on the bench with her arms resting on the table. She was tiny. She was small like a child and her face was like a little screwed-up[①] ball of brown paper.

---

① screwed-up: *Adjective* [attrib.] (of paper or fabric) crumpled or crushed into a ball (纸,织物)揉(或挤压)成一团的

(of a person's face or eyes) crumpled, especially because of worry or effort (脸、眼部,尤指因忧虑、辛苦)起皱的

"Who is it?" she said in a high voice.

The first woman said, "This is an Inglesus. He is looking for your husband because he requires a boat."

"Health to you, Inglesus," the old woman said.

The pilot stood by the door, just inside the room. The first woman stood by the window and her arms hung down by her sides.

The old woman said, "Where are the Germanoi?" Her voice seemed bigger than her body.

"Now they are around Lamia."

"Lamia." She nodded. "Soon they will be here. Perhaps tomorrow they will be here. But I do not care. Do you hear me, Inglesus, I do not care." She was leaning forward a little in her chair and the pitch of her voice was becoming higher. "When they come it will be nothing new. They have already been here. Every day they have been here. Every day they come over and they bom[①] bom bom and you shut your eyes and you open them again and you get up and you go outside and the houses are just dust and the people." Her voice rose and fell.

She paused, breathing quickly, then she spoke more quietly. "How many have you killed, Inglesus?"

The pilot put out a hand and leaned against the door to rest his ankle.

"I have killed some," he said quietly.

"How many?"

"As many as I could, old woman. We cannot count the number of men."

"Kill them all," she said softly. "Go and kill every man and every

---

① bom：当地人对飞机轰炸声的一种真实的模仿，应是"bomb"的一种非标准发音形式

woman and baby. Do you hear me, Inglesus? You must kill them all." The little brown ball of paper became smaller and more screwed up. "The first one I see I shall kill." She paused. "And then, Inglesus, and then later, his family will hear that he is dead."

The pilot did not say anything. She looked up at him and her voice was different. "What is it you want, Inglesus?"

He said, "About the Germanoi, I am sorry. But there is not much we can do."

"No," she answered, "there is nothing. And you?"

"I am looking for Joannis. I wish to use his boat."

"Joannis," she said quietly, "he is not here. He is out."

Suddenly she pushed back the bench, got to her feet and went out of the room. "Come," she said. He followed her down the passage towards the front door. She looked even smaller when she was standing than when she was sitting down and she walked quickly down the passage towards the door and opened it. She stepped out into the sunshine and for the first time he saw how very old she was.

She had no lips. Her mouth was just wrinkled skin like the rest of her face and she screwed up① her eyes at the sun and looked up the road.

"There he is," she said. "That's him." She pointed at the old man who was sitting beside the drinking trough.

The pilot looked at the man. Then he turned to speak to the old woman, but she had disappeared into the house.

---

① screw up: (of the muscles of one's face or around one's eyes) contract, typically so as to express emotion or because of bright light(面部或眼睛周围的肌肉,尤指为表达情感或因强光刺激)收缩;皱紧

三、翻译探索

本篇的理解和翻译难度都不算大。有几处涉及当地语的表达,根据上下文的关联性,采取了"异化"处理方式。

美好昨日

他弯下腰,伸手去揉搓脚踝部位,那个部位走路的时候扭伤了,而且肿得连凸出的脚踝骨都看不见了。随后,他直起身,眼睛向四周观瞧,然后从衣兜里摸出一盒香烟,从中抽出一支,随手点着。他站在大街中央,用手背擦去额头的汗水,眼睛再一次向周围观瞧。

"真该死,这儿不会一个人都没有的。"他大声说道。听到了自己的声音后,他感觉好多了。

他用受伤那只脚的脚趾尖儿点地,一瘸一拐地继续走着。转过下一个街角,他一眼就看到了大海,还看到马路在被炸毁的房屋间弯曲地向前延伸开去。于是,他走下小山,来到了海边。大海风平浪静,黑幽幽的一片。他可以清清楚楚地看见远处大陆上一座座小山的轮廓,估计距离也就十二公里吧。他再一次弯下腰,揉搓自己的脚踝部位。"真他妈的该死,"他骂道。"肯定会有几个人活下来的。"可问题是,到处都是静悄悄的,幸存的建筑物里一点声音都没有,整个村子一点声音都没有,这个地方看起来似乎已经沉寂了一千年之久。

突然之间,他听到了一点轻微的声音,就好像有人在砾石地面上挪动脚步时发出的声音。向周围一看,他看见了一位老人,老人坐在阴影下的一块石头上,旁边是一个水槽。奇怪的是,在这之前,他竟然没有看见这位老人。

"愿你健康,"这位飞行员说道,"吉阿薮。"他又用当地话补充道。

在拉里萨以及亚尼纳呆着的时候,他从当地人那里学了些希腊语。

这位老人慢慢抬起头,转了过来,但是,肩膀并没有转过来。老人胡须灰白，头戴一顶布帽子，上身穿了一件衬衫，衬衫是灰色的，带有黑色的细条纹，上面没有领子。老人看了看眼前这名飞行员，那架势好似盲人面对着某个看不见的东西。

“老人家，看见你，我很高兴。村子里还有其他人吗？”

没有回答。

这位飞行员在水槽边坐下，好让自己的脚踝放松一下。

“我叫因格莱赛，”他说，“我是一名飞机驾驶员，我的飞机被击落，我跳伞逃生。我叫因格莱赛。”

老人慢慢地上下移动着脑袋。“因格莱瑟，”他安静地说，“你叫因格莱瑟。”

“是的，我想找一位拥有小船的人，希望借船返回大陆那边。”

停顿了一会。随后，老人说起话来就如同在睡梦中还没有醒来一般。“他们总是从上方来袭，”老人说。“德国鬼子总是从上方来袭。”他说起话来，面无表情。他抬起头看了看天空，然后转身看了看身后的天空。“因格莱赛，他们今天还会来的。他们很快就会来的。”这次，他把名字说对了，但从他的声音里听不出半点儿焦虑，脸上也看不出什么表情。“他们为什么袭击我们，我不明白，”他补充道。

这位飞行员说：“或许今天不会来了，现在太晚了。我想，他们今天的任务已经完成了。”

“因格莱赛，他们为什么袭击我们，我不明白。这儿哪里还有什么人啊。”

飞行员说：“我在找一个拥有小船的人，好让他带我渡过大海、回到大陆那边。现在，村子里有人拥有小船吗？”

“小船？”

“是的。”暂停了一会儿，老人在思考这个问题。

“倒是有这样一个人。”

“我能找到他吗？他住在哪儿？”

“村子里有一个人拥有一条小船。”

“拜托你告诉我，他叫什么名字呢？”

老人又抬头看了看天空。“拥有一条小船的人名字叫约安尼斯。”

“约安尼斯什么?”

“约安尼斯·斯皮拉吉斯,”说完,他微笑了一下。这个名字对老人来说,似乎意义重大,因此,他微笑了一下。

“他住在哪儿?”飞行员问道。“给你添麻烦,我很抱歉。”

“他住在哪儿?”

“是的。”

对于这个问题,老人也思考了一下。随后,他转过身,向大街的下方看去,大街直通大海。“斯皮拉吉斯曾经一直住在最靠近海边的那座房子里,可是,如今那房子已经不在了。今天早晨,德国鬼子击中了房子,是在今天很早的时候,当时天还没亮呢。你可以看见,那房子已经不见了,房子已经不在那儿了。”

“他人呢,现在在哪儿?”

“他现在住在安东尼娜·安热卢的房子里,就在那边,红色窗户的那座房子。”他指着大街的下方。

“太谢谢你了,我这就去拜访船主。”

“约安尼斯还是一个孩子的时候,”老人继续说,“就拥有一条小船,小船是白色的,顶部边缘划上了蓝色的线条。”说完,他又微笑了一下。“但是,此时此刻,他不会在房子里的。他妻子会在的——安娜会在的,还有安东尼娜·安热卢,她们都会在家的。”

“再次感谢,我这就去跟他妻子说。”

这位飞行员起身,打算沿着大街走下去,但是,几乎与此同时,老人从后面叫住了他:“因格莱赛。”

飞行员转过身来。

“跟约安尼斯妻子说话时——跟安娜说话时……你应该记住点什么。”他停了一下,寻找着能表达自己意思的词语。这时,他的声音里也不像刚才那样没有任何的表情了。他边说边看着飞行员。

“德国鬼子来袭时,她的女儿当时在家。这一点,你应该记住。”

飞行员站在道路中间,等着他把话说完。

“玛丽亚。对,她的名字曾经叫玛丽亚。”

"我会记住的，"飞行员回答。"我很难过。"

他转过身，走下小山，来到红色窗户的那座房子门前。他敲了敲门，等待着。又大声敲了敲门，继续等待着。房子里传来了脚步声，房门打开了。

房子里面很暗，他只能看到，出来开门的这位妇女的头发是黑色的，她的眼睛跟她的头发一样，也是黑色的。她看了看站在外面明媚阳光下的这位飞行员。

"祝你健康，"他说。"我叫因格莱赛。"

她站在那儿一动没动。

"我要找约安尼斯·斯皮拉吉斯。有人说，他拥有一条小船。"

她站在那儿，还是一动没动。"他在房子里吗？"

"不在。"

"或许他妻子在吧，她能知道他在什么地方。"

刚开始的时候，这位妇女没有回答。接下来，她手把着门，不让其关闭，向后退了一步。"进来吧，因格莱瑟，"她说。

他跟着她沿着过道走进里面的一个房间，房间很黑，因为窗户没有玻璃，只是钉着一块块的硬纸板。即便这样，他也能看清，屋里有一位老妇人，坐在长凳上，两只胳膊放在桌子上。这位老妇人很是矮小，看上去就像是一个小孩子，她的脸就像是一个被揉搓后挤压到一起的棕色小纸球。

"这人是谁？"她高声问道。

给他开门的妇女说道："这位是因格莱瑟。他要找你的丈夫借小船用。"

"愿你健康，因格莱瑟，"老妇人说道。

飞行员站在门边，站在刚好跨进房间的位置上。给他开门的妇女站在窗户附近，两只胳膊从身体两侧垂下。

老妇人说："德国鬼子哪里去了？"她的声音听起来比她的体型更大一些。

"现在，他们盘踞在拉米亚。"

"拉米亚，"她说完点了点头。"用不了多久，他们就会到这里来的。或许明天吧,他们就会到这里来,但是,我不在意的。因格莱瑟,你听见我说话了吗?我说,我不在意。"她坐在椅子上将身体向前倾斜一点,说话的音调提高了一些。"即使他们来了,也没有什么新奇的,他们已经来过多少次了。他们每天都来,每天都飞过来,轰了又轰,炸了又炸。你闭上眼睛,再睁开眼睛,起床走到外边一看,房子纷纷化为灰烬,还有那些可怜的人们。"她说话时,声音忽高忽低的。

她停了下来,快速喘了几口气,接着又颇为安静地说:"因格莱瑟,你干掉过多少?"

这位飞行员伸出一只手,靠在门上,好让脚踝放松一下。

"我干掉了一些,"他平静地说道。

"多少?"

"老妇人,我尽可能多地将他们干掉,但我们没法清点数目。"

"把他们统统干掉,"她轻声说道。"去,干掉所有的男人、女人和婴儿。因格莱瑟,你听见我说的吗?你一定要把他们统统干掉。"她那棕色小纸球般的脑袋变得更小、更往一起揉搓、挤压起来。"我会干掉我第一眼看到的,"说完,她暂停了一下。"接下来,因格莱瑟,用不了多久,他的家人就会听说,他已经死了。"

这位飞行员什么都没有说。于是,她抬头看了看他,说话的语调也大不相同了。"你想要什么来着,因格莱瑟?"

他说道:"关于德国鬼子,我很抱歉,可问题是,我们也无能为力,做不了太多。"

"不,"她回应,"这没什么。你想要……"

"我来找约安尼斯,我希望借他的小船用一用。"

"约安尼斯,"她静静地说。"他不在这儿,出去了。"

突然之间,她将长凳往后一推,站起来,走出了房间。"随我来,"她说道。他跟着她沿着过道走向正门。她站起来的样子甚至比她坐着的样子更加矮小。只见她沿着过道快速走向门口,打开了门,跨出门槛,站在阳光下。此时,他第一次看见,她是多么的衰老。

她的上下嘴唇都没有了,嘴部就是一些起了皱纹的皮肤,跟脸上其他部分的皮肤一样。她冲着太阳收紧了双眼,然后向马路的上方看去。

“他在那儿，”她说道。“那就是他。”她指向坐在饮水槽旁边的那位老人。

这位飞行员看了看那个人，然后转身要对老妇人说点什么，但是，老妇人已经进屋，消失不见了。

第二节 《如你之人》*Someone like You*

罗尔德·达尔的《如你之人》(Someone like You)首次发表在《向你飞跃》(Over to You)一书中。后来，这篇故事又收录到《罗尔德·达尔短篇故事集锦》(The Collected Short Stories of Roald Dahl)以及《五部畅销书集》(5 Bestsellers)等书中。《向你飞跃》是罗尔德·达尔二战期间在皇家空军服役时所经历的一些故事的集锦。这些故事中，有的主人公是“隐性”的，但可以想象是作家罗尔德·达尔的化身。

一、原作导读

本篇小说里的叙述者是“隐姓埋名”的“我”，作家达尔始终没有交代“我”是何许人也，但不妨将之视作罗尔德·达尔本人的化身。

一家酒吧里，两名轰炸机飞行员——其中一名是叙述者“我”——正在喝酒。他们俩一边喝酒一边讨论着眼下这场战争。其中一位飞行员从战争一爆发就开始参战，并对战争中人的命运的随意性感到深深的困扰。他说，每一次空袭过程中，他都不停地想，释放炸弹之际要是偏离那么一点点——就往一侧偏那么一小点儿，那么，他投下的炸弹就会落到别的什么人身上；炸弹要投到谁的身上，要炸死哪十个人、哪二十个人、哪一百个人完全取决于他自己。现在，他每次飞行都在思考这个问题。

他们俩都认为，不管是谁，在某个时候，都会有所偏离的。接着，他们说起了一个叫斯汀克尔的飞行员同行。有一次执行任务前，斯汀克尔被迫将自己养的狗留下，回来后狗就找不到了。从那之后，斯汀克尔就变得疯疯癫癫,走到哪里都跟自己的狗说话,而实际上他的身边根本就没有狗。

喝着喝着,他们俩讨论起“驾车等待”这个问题。所谓“驾车等待”,就是在离开一个交叉路口前,等待二十秒钟,这样做就比不等待会少撞一次车、少撞一个人。接着,他们俩开始大赞酒吧里那个漂亮女子的“美妙的胸部”。接着,那位持宿命论观点的飞行员就说,他敢打赌他炸死过很多比酒吧里那个女孩更加漂亮的女子;他甚至好奇地想,要是酒吧里所有的人都跌倒在地死去,会发生什么样的情况。

他们俩喝完酒,走出酒吧,来到大街上,要打出租车去另一个地方,再喝些威士忌。等待过程中,“我”这样写道:“我们俩透过车头灯的一束束光柱,看到丝丝细雨飘落而下。我们俩就这样站在那儿,等待着一辆出租车的到来。”(We could see the drizzle falling through the beams of their headlights and we stood there waiting for a taxi.)

二、原作释读

战争过后,到处都是“如你之人”——疯疯癫癫,甚至高谈阔论。读完达尔的这篇小说,你甚至会发现,你跟小说中的人物原来如此相像。

Someone like You[①]

“BEER?”

“Yes, beer.”

I gave the order and the waiter brought the bottles and two glasses. We poured out our own, tipping[②] the glasses and holding the tops of the bottles close to the glass.

“Cheers,” I said.

---

① 本部小说原文出自“Roald Dahl. *The Collected Short Stories of Roald Dahl*[M]. England: Penguin Books Ltd., 1992”。

② tip: *Verb* be or cause to be in a sloping position with one end or side higher than the other 使倾斜(或侧倾)

He nodded. We lifted our glasses and drank.

It was five years since I had seen him, and during that time he had been fighting the war. He had been fighting it right from the beginning up to now and I saw at once how he had changed. From being a young, bouncing boy, he had become someone old and wise and gentle. He had become gentle like a wounded child. He had become old like a tired man of seventy years. He had become so different and he had changed so much that at first it was embarrassing for both of us and it was not easy to know what to say.

He had been flying in France in the early days and he was in Britain during the Battle[1]. He was in the Western Desert[2] when we had nothing

---

① Battle：这里指第二次世界大战期间的"Battle of Britain"，即"不列颠战役"

② Western Desert：Egyptian name for Libyan Desert 埃及人对"利比亚大沙漠"的别称

and he was in Greece and Crete[①]. He was in Syria[②] and he was at Habbaniya during the rebellion. He was at Alamein[③]. He had been flying in Sicily[④] and in Italy and then he had gone back and flown again from England. Now he was an old man.

He was small, not more than five feet six, and he had a pale, wide-open face which did not hide anything, and a sharp pointed chin. His eyes were bright and dark. They were never still unless they were looking into your own. His hair was black and untidy. There was a wisp of it always hanging down over his forehead; he kept pushing it back with his

---

① Crete: a Greek island in the eastern Mediterranean; pop. 536,980 (1991); capital, Heraklion. It is noted for the remains of the Minoan civilization which flourished there in the 2nd millennium B. C. It fell to Rome in 67 B. C. and was subsequently ruled by Byzantines, Venetians, and Turks. Crete played an important role in the Greek struggle for independence from the Turks in the late 19th and early 20th centuries, becoming administratively part of an independent Greece in 1913. Greek name Kríti. 克里特岛(地中海东部一希腊岛屿),1991年人口536,980,首都伊拉克利翁,因公元前两千年繁荣的弥诺斯文化遗产闻名;公元前67年向罗马称臣,后相继被拜占庭人、威尼斯人和土耳其人统治;克里特岛在19世纪末和20世纪初希腊为争取独立而与土耳其进行的斗争中起了重要作用,1913年成为独立的希腊的一个行政区。希腊语名"Kríti"。)

② Syria: a country in the Middle East with a coastline on the eastern Mediterranean Sea; pop. 12,824,000 (est. 1991); official language, Arabic; capital, Damascus 叙利亚(中东国家,位于地中海东岸;1991年估计人口12,824,000;官方语言是阿拉伯语;首都大马士革。)

③ Alamein: 阿拉曼(埃及北部一村庄,第二次世界大战战场。)

④ Sicily: a large Italian island in the Mediterranean, off the south-western tip of Italy; capital, Palermo. It is separated from the Italian mainland by the Strait of Messina and its highest point is the volcano Mount Etna. Italian name Sicilia 西西里岛(地中海上的一座意大利大岛,位于意大利西南端外海,首府巴勒莫。墨西拿海峡将它与意大利大陆分开,最高点是埃特纳火山。意大利语名"Sicilia"。)

hand.

For a while we were awkward and did not speak. He was sitting opposite me at the table, leaning forward a little, drawing lines on the dew of the cold beer-glass with his finger. He was looking at the glass, pretending to concentrate upon what he was doing, and to me it seemed as though he had something to say, but that he did not know how to say it. I sat there and picked nuts out of the plate and munched[①] them noisily, pretending that I did not care about anything, not even about making a noise while eating.

Then without stopping his drawing on the glass and without looking up, he said quietly and very slowly, "Oh God, I wish I was a waiter or a whore or something."

He picked up his glass and drank the beer slowly and all at once, in two swallows. I knew now that there was something on his mind and I knew that he was gathering courage so that he could speak.

"Let's have another," I said.

"Yes, let's have a whisky."

"All right, whisky."

I ordered two double Scotches[②] and some soda, and we poured the soda into the Scotch and drank. He picked up his glass and drank, put it down, picked it up again and drank some more. As he put down the glass the second time, he leaned forward and quite suddenly he began to talk.

"You know," he said, "you know I keep thinking during a raid, when we are running over the target, just as we are going to release our

---

① munch: *Verb* [with obj.] eat (something) with a continuous and often audible action of the jaws 用力咀嚼;出声地咀嚼

② Scotch: *Noun* 苏格兰人;苏格兰威士忌

bombs, I keep thinking to myself, shall I just jink[1] a little; shall I swerve a fraction to one side, then my bombs will fall on someone else. I keep thinking, whom shall I make them fall on; whom shall I kill tonight. Which ten, twenty or a hundred people shall I kill tonight. It is all up to me. And now I think about this every time I go out."

He had taken a small nut and was splitting it into pieces with his thumb – nail as he spoke, looking down at what he was doing because he was embarrassed by his own talk.

He was speaking very slowly. "It would just be a gentle pressure with the ball of my foot upon the rudder-bar[2]; a pressure so slight that I would hardly know that I was doing it, and it would throw the bombs on to a different house and on to other people. It is all up to me, the whole thing is up to me, and each time that I go out I have to decide which ones shall be killed. I can do it with the gentle pressure of the ball of my foot upon the rudder-bar. I can do it so that I don't even notice that it is being done. I just lean a little to one side because I am shifting my sitting position. That is all I am doing, and then I kill a different lot of people."

Now there was no dew left upon the face of the glass, but he was still running the fingers of his right hand up and down the smooth surface.

"Yes," he said, "it is a complicated thought. It is very far-reaching; and when I am bombing I cannot get it out of my mind. You see it is such a gentle pressure with the ball of the foot; just a touch on the rudder-bar and the bomb-aimer wouldn't even notice. Each time I go

---

① jink: *Verb* [no obj.] change direction suddenly and nimbly, as when dodging a pursuer 躲闪;闪避

② rudder bar: a flat piece of wood or metal at the back of a boat or aircraft, moved from side to side in order to control the direction of travel 方向舵;脚蹬

out, I say to myself, shall it be these or shall it be those? Which ones are the worst? Perhaps if I make a little skid to the left I will get a houseful of lousy women-shooting German soldiers, or perhaps if I make that little skid I will miss getting the soldiers and get an old man in a shelter. How can I know? How can anyone know these things?"

He paused and pushed his empty glass away from him into the middle of the table.

"And so I never jink," he added, "at least hardly ever."

"I jinked once," I said, "ground-strafing I thought I'd kill the ones on the other side of the road instead."

"Everybody jinks," he said. "Shall we have another drink?"

"Yes, let's have another."

I called the waiter and gave the order, and while we were waiting, we sat looking around the room at the other people. The place was starting to fill up because it was about six o'clock and we sat there looking at the people who were coming in. They were standing around looking for tables, sitting down, laughing and ordering drinks.

"Look at that woman," I said. "The one just sitting down over there."

"What about her?"

"Wonderful figure," I said. "Wonderful bosom. Look at her bosom."

The waiter brought the drinks.

"Did I ever tell you about Stinker?" he said. "Stinker who?"

"Stinker Sullivan in Malta[①]."

---

① Malta: an island country in the central Mediterranean, about 100 km (60 miles) south of Sicily; pop. 356,000 (est. 1991); official languages, Maltese and English; capital, Valletta 马耳他(地中海中部岛国,西西里岛以南约100公里,即60英里;1991年估计人口356,000;官方语言马耳他语和英语;首都瓦莱塔。)

"No."

"About Stinker's dog?"

"No."

Stinker had a dog, a great big Alsatian①, and he loved that dog as though it was his father and his mother and everything else he had, and the dog loved Stinker. It used to follow him around everywhere he went, and when he went on ops② it used to sit on the tarmac③ outside the hangars④ waiting for him to come back. It was called Smith. Stinker really loved that dog. He loved it like his mother and he used to talk to it all day long."

"Lousy whisky," I said.

"Yes, let's have another."

We got some more whisky.

"Well anyway," he went on, "one day the squadron got orders to fly to Egypt. We had to go at once; not in two hours or later in the day, but at once. And Stinker couldn't find his dog. Couldn't find Smith anywhere. Started running all over the aerodrome⑤ yelling for Smith and going mad yelling at everyone asking where he was and yelling Smith

---

① Alsatian: *Noun* (Brit.) a large dog of a breed typically used as guard dogs or for police work (英国英语)(用于警卫或协助警察的)阿尔萨斯牧羊犬,亦称"German shepherd"

② ops: 本文中应该是"operations"(军事行动)的简称

③ tarmac: *Noun* [*Mass Noun*] (trademark in the UK) material used for surfacing roads or other outdoor areas, consisting of broken stone mixed with tar(英商标)柏油碎石

④ hangar: *Noun* a large building with extensive floor area, typically for housing aircraft 飞机棚;飞机库

⑤ aerodrome: *Noun* (Brit.) a small airport or airfield(英国英语)小型飞机(降落)场

Smith all over the aerodrome. Smith wasn't anywhere."

"Where was he?" I said.

"He wasn't there and we had to go. Stinker had to go without Smith and he was mad as a hatter[①]. His crew said he kept calling up over the radio asking if they'd found him. All the way to Heliopolis[②] he kept calling up Malta saying, have you got Smith, and Malta kept saying no, they hadn't."

"This whisky is really terrible," I said.

"Yes. We must have some more."

We had a waiter who was very quick.

"I was telling you about Stinker," he said.

"Yes, tell me about Stinker."

"Well, when we got to Egypt he wouldn't talk about anything except Smith. He used to walk around acting as though the dog was always with him. Damn fool walked around saying, 'Come on, Smith, old boy come on,' and he kept looking down and talking to him as he walked along. Kept reaching down and patting the air and stroking this bloody dog that wasn't there."

"Where was it?"

"Malta, I suppose. Must have been in Malta."

"Isn't this awful whisky?"

"Terrible. We must have some more when we've finished this."

---

① (as) mad as a hatter: informal completely insane 极疯狂;狂怒(e. g. He's indisputably a genius, but he's also mad as a hatter. 毋庸置疑,他是个天才,但也是个疯疯癫癫的人。)

② Heliopolis: an ancient Egyptian city situated near the apex of the Nile delta at what is now Cairo. It was the original site of the obelisks known as Cleopatra's Needles 太阳城(古埃及城市,位于尼罗河三角洲顶端现开罗所在地,为克娄巴特拉方尖柱碑的原址。)

"Cheers."

"Cheers."

"Waiter. Oh waiter. Yes; again."

"So Smith was in Malta."

"Yes," he said. "And this damn fool Stinker Sullivan went on like this right up to the time he was killed."

"Must have been mad."

"He was. Mad as a hatter. You know once he walked into the Sporting Club at Alexandria① at drinking time."

"That wasn't so mad."

"He walked into the big lounge and as he went in he held the door open and started calling his dog. Then when he thought the dog had come in he closed the door and started walking right down the length of the room, stopping every now and then and looking round and saying, 'Come on, Smith, old boy, come on.' He kept flipping his fingers. Once he got down under a table where two men and two women were drinking. He got on to his hands and knees and said, 'Smith, come on out of there; come here at once,' and he put out his hand and started dragging nothing at all from under the table. Then he apologized to the people at the table. 'This is the hell of a dog,' he said to them. You should have seen their faces. He went on like that all down the room and when he came to the other end he held the door open for the dog to go out and then went out after it."

"Man was mad."

"Mad as a hatter. And you should have seen their faces. It was full of people drinking and they didn't know whether it was them who were

① Alexandria: *Noun* the chief port of Egypt; pop. 3,170,000 (est. 1990). Alexandria was a major centre of Hellenistic culture 亚历山大港(埃及主要港口,1990年估计人口3,170,000;曾是希腊文化的重要中心。)

crazy or whether it was Stinker. They kept looking up at each other to make sure that they weren't the only ones who couldn't see the dog. One man dropped his drink."

"That was awful."

"Terrible."

The waiter came and went. The room was full of people now, all sitting at little tables, talking and drinking and wearing their uniforms. The pilot poked the ice down into his glass with his finger.

"He used to jink too," he said.

"Who?"

"Stinker. He used to talk about it."

"Jinking isn't anything," I said. "It's like not touching the cracks on the pavement when you're walking along."

"Balls[1]. That's just personal. Doesn't affect anyone else."

"Well, it's like car-waiting."

"What's car-waiting?"

"I always do it," I said.

"What is it?"

"Just as you're going to drive off, you sit back and count twenty, then you drive off."

"You're mad too," he said. "You're like Stinker."

"It's a wonderful way to avoid accidents. I've never had one in a car yet; at least, not a bad one."

"You're drunk."

"No, I always do it."

"Why?"

---

① balls: *Plural Noun* [treated as sing.] (Brit.) nonsense; rubbish (often said to express strong disagreement) (英)废话,胡话(常用于表达强烈不满)

"Because then if someone was going to have stepped off the kerb① in front of your car, you won't hit them because you started later. You were delayed because you counted twenty, and the person who stepped off the kerb whom you would have hit—you missed him."

"Why?"

"He stepped off the kerb long before you got there because you counted twenty."

"That's a good idea."

"I know it's a good idea."

"It's a bloody marvellous idea."

"I've saved lots of lives. And you can drive straight across intersections because the car you would have hit has already gone by. It went by just a little earlier because you delayed yourself by counting twenty."

"Marvellous."

"Isn't it?"

"But it's like jinking," he said. "You never really know what would have happened."

"I always do it," I said.

We kept right on drinking.

"Look at that woman," I said.

"The one with the bosom?"

"Yes, marvellous bosom."

He said slowly, "I bet I've killed lots of women more beautiful than that one."

"Not lots with bosoms like that."

---

① kerb (A. E. curb): *Noun* a stone edging to a pavement or raised path (人行道,凸起小道的)石砌路缘

"I'll bet I have. Shall we have another drink?"

"Yes, one for the road."

"There aren't any other women with bosoms like that," I said. "Not in Germany anyway."

"Oh yes there are. I've killed lots of them."

"All right. You've killed lots of women with wonderful bosoms."

He leaned back and waved his hand around the room. "See all the people in this room," he said.

"Yes."

"Wouldn't there be a bloody row if they were all suddenly dead; if they all suddenly fell off their chairs on to the floor dead?"

"What about it?"

"Wouldn't there be a bloody row?"

"Certainly there'd be a row."

"If all the waiters got together and put stuff in all the drinks and everyone died."

"There'd be a godalmighty row."

"Well, I've done that hundreds of times. I've killed more people than there are in this room hundreds of times. So have you."

"Lots more," I said. "But that's different."

"Same sort of people. Men and women and waiters. All drinking in a pub."

"That's different."

"Like hell[①] it is. Wouldn't there be a bloody row if it happened here?"

"Bloody awful row."

---

① like hell: (informal) used in ironic expressions of scorn or disagreement (用讽刺口吻表示轻蔑或不同意)见鬼;决不;才不

"But we've done it. Lots of times."

"Hundreds of times," I said. "This is nothing."

"This is a lousy place."

"Yes, it's lousy. Let's go somewhere else."

"Finish our drinks."

We finished our drinks and we both tried to pay the bill, so we tossed for it and I won. It came to sixteen dollars and twenty-five cents. He gave the waiter a two-dollar tip.

We got up and walked around the tables and over to the door.

"Taxi," he said.

"Yes, must have a taxi."

There wasn't a doorman. We stood out on the kerb waiting for a taxi to come along and he said, "This is a good town."

"Wonderful town," I said. I felt fine. It was dark outside, but there were a few street-lamps, and we could see the cars going by and the people walking on the other side of the street. There was a thin, quiet drizzle falling, and the wetness on the black street shone yellow under the lights of the cars arid under the street-lamps. The tyres of the cars hissed on the wet surface.

"Let's go to a place which has lots of whisky," he said. "Lots of whisky and a man with egg on his beard serving it."

"Fine."

"Somewhere where there are no other people but just us and the man with egg on his beard. Either that."

"Yes," I said. "Either that or what?"

"Or a place with a hundred thousand people in it."

"Yes," I said. "OK."

We stood there waiting and we could see the lights of the cars as they came round the bend over to the left, coming towards us with the tyres swishing[①] on the wet surface and going past us up the road to the bridge which goes over the river. We could see the drizzle falling through the beams of their headlights and we stood there waiting for a taxi.

三、翻译探索

本篇在翻译的整体处理上，比较好把握，但是麻烦之处是一些地名的处理，要本着认真负责的态度一一落实，有时需要多方查证。

如你之人

"喝啤酒？"

"好，啤酒。"

于是，我要了啤酒。男侍者拿来两瓶啤酒、两只杯子。我们开始各自倒酒：将杯子倾斜一下，握着瓶颈靠上的部位，贴近杯子，往里面倒。

"干杯，"我说。

他点了点头，于是，我们举起杯子，喝了起来。

我已经有五年没有见到他了。其间，他一直不停地转战，"不列颠战役"一爆发，他就参战，一直战斗到今天。所以，一看到他，我就立刻看出他的变化有多大。他已不再是一名年轻的、活力十足的男孩子，而是变成了一个年迈、老练、温和之人。他温和得像一个受了伤的孩子，年迈得如同一位年届七十的困倦老者。他与以前判若两人，变化巨大，以至于刚开始的时候，我们两个都尴尬无比，竟不知道该说些什么。

早期的日子里，他一直在法国执行飞行任务。战争期间，他转到了英国。我们无所事事的时候，他去往利比亚大沙漠执行任务，又去了希腊，包括其中的克里特岛，还去过叙利亚。伊拉克发生叛乱那段

---

① swish: *Verb* [no obj., with adverbial of direction] move with a hissing or rushing sound 刷的（或嗖的）行进

时间,他去过那里的哈班尼亚。他还去过阿拉曼,还去过意大利,曾经一度在其中的西西里岛作战过。然后返回,又回到英国作战。现在,看上去他就像一位年迈苍苍的老者。

他个子不高,不足一米六八,尖尖的下巴,宽宽的脸,脸色灰白,脸上什么事儿都藏不住,一览无遗。他的两只眼睛明亮、黝黑,不停地转来转去,只有和你对视的时候,才会停下来。他一头黑发乱蓬蓬的,其中有一绺还总是从额头部位悬垂下来,于是乎,他就不停地用手往后拢。

有好一阵儿,我们两个人都很尴尬,没有说话。他坐在我对面,身体稍微向前倾斜,手指在啤酒杯表面凝结的凉霜上画着线条。他瞧着杯子,假装集中精力画着线条。在我看来,他好像有话要说,但不知从何说起。我坐在那儿,从盘子里挑拣出坚果,"咔嚓、咔嚓"使劲嚼了起来,装出一副对什么都满不在乎的样子,哪怕是吃东西弄出声响来,也不在乎。

接下来,他继续在杯子上画着,头也没有抬起来,安静而缓慢地说:"噢,上帝啊,多希望我自己做个男侍,或者男妓什么的啊。"

他拿起杯子,慢慢地将里面的啤酒全部喝完,两口就咽了下去。现在,我知道,他心里有谱了,我也知道,他在为自己鼓劲,以便将心里的话说出来。

"我们换一种酒,"我说。

"好的。我们喝威士忌吧。"

"好的,就威士忌啦。"

我要了两份双倍浓度的苏格兰威士忌,还有一些苏打水。我们将苏打水倒入威士忌,喝了起来。他拿起杯子,喝了一口,放下杯子,又拿起杯子,多喝了一些。第二次放下杯子的时候,他倚身向前,冷不防地说了起来。

"要知道,"他说,"要知道,一次空袭过程中,我一直在想,我们飞临目标上空、就要释放炸弹之时,我自己不停地想:我要是偏离一点点,就往一侧偏那么一小点儿,那么,我投下的炸弹就会落到别的什么人身上。我不停地想:炸弹要投到谁的身上,今晚会要谁的命,今晚我会炸死哪十个人、哪二十个人、哪一百个人呢。这完全取决于我。现在,每次飞行我都想这个问题。”

他一边说话,一边拿起一枚小坚果,用大拇指指甲将其弄碎,同时,低着头看着自己的动作,为自己所说的话感到局促不安。

他讲得很慢。“大脚趾只需在方向舵脚蹬上轻轻那么一压,压得极其轻微,我几乎感觉不到自己压了一下。这样就会导致炸弹投到另一座房子上,投到另外一些人身上。这完全取决于我,这一切都取决于我。每一次飞行,我必须得决定要炸死哪些对象,至于哪些对象被炸死,我只需用大脚趾在方向舵脚蹬上轻轻那么一压。做到了这一点之后,我甚至丝毫没有察觉到我已经做到了这一点。由于更换坐姿,我就向一侧倾斜一点点,对啊,就是倾斜那么一点点,我就会炸死另一批人。”

现在,杯子表面已经没有凝霜了,但是,他依然用右手的手指头沿着杯子光滑的表面,上上下下画个不停。

“对的,”他说,“这是一个复杂的思想,意义深远。执行轰炸任务时,这个思想我无法摆脱。你知道,用大脚指就这样轻轻地一压,就这样轻轻触碰一下方向舵脚蹬,轰炸瞄准手甚至连察觉都察觉不出来。每次飞行时,我就对自己说,是炸死这些人呢,还是炸死那些人呢?哪些人最坏呢?或许,要是我向左侧稍微打一点滑,就会炸死一屋子向女性开枪的、该死的德国兵。或许,要是稍微打那么一点滑,就不会命中那些德国兵,而是炸死了避难所里的一位老人。我怎么会知道结果呢?谁又会知道这么多呢?”

他停了下来,将空杯子推开,推到桌子中央。

“所以说嘛,我从来没有出过偏差,他补充道。“至少,几乎没出过偏差。”

“我出过一次偏差,”我说。“我想,那一次我执行的是低空扫射任务,却要了路另一边那几个人的命。”

“谁都会出偏差的,”他说。“我们再来一杯好吗?”

“好的,再喝一杯吧。”

我叫来男侍者,点了酒。坐在那儿等着上酒的当儿,我们向屋子周围看了看,看了看屋子里其他人。屋子里聚的人越来越多了,因为当时已是六点钟的光景。我们坐在那儿,看着进来的人,那些人进来后就四处找空座位,找到后坐下,边笑边点喝的东西。

“看看那个女的,”我说。“就在那边,刚刚坐下来的那个。”

“她怎么啦?”

“体形美极了,”我说。“胸部美极了。看看她的胸部啊。”

男侍者拿酒过来了。

“我跟你提过斯汀克尔没有?”他问。

“斯汀克尔姓什么?”

“斯汀克尔姓沙利文,他在马耳他。”

“没有。”

“有关斯汀克尔的那条狗呢?”

“没有。”

“斯汀克尔养了一条狗,是一条大块头的阿尔萨斯犬。他很爱那条狗,那条狗就好像是他的父母,可以说,是他的全部,那条狗也很爱他。他走到哪儿,那条狗就跟到哪儿。每当他执行任务,那条狗就经常坐在机库外面的柏油碎石跑道上,等着他回来。狗的名字叫史密斯。斯汀克尔真的很爱那条狗。就像爱自己的母亲一样,爱着那条狗,经常整天跟它说话。”

“这威士忌真差劲儿啊,”我说。

“是的,再来一杯吧。”

我们又要了些威士忌。

“噢,不管怎么说,”他继续说,“有一天,中队接到命令,要飞往埃及,必须得马上出发。不是两个小时之后出发,也不是晚些时候出发,而是立刻出发。情急之下,斯汀克尔找不到他的那条狗了,哪儿都找不到。于是,他就开始满飞机场跑,边跑边喊着史密斯的名字,疯一般呼喊,逢人就大声问:看到史密斯没有?他跑遍了整个机场,不断喊着:史密斯、史密斯,但是,哪儿都没有史密斯的踪影。”

“史密斯在哪儿呢?”我问。

“史密斯不在机场那儿,但我们必须得出发了。在找不到史密斯的情况下，斯汀克尔必须得出发了，因此，他愤怒到了极点。他的机组人员说，他通过无线电，一个劲儿地问，是否有人看见了史密斯。在飞往太阳城的途中，他一直呼叫马耳他，问是否找到了史密斯。马耳他那边的人不断地回答，没有，还没有找到。”

“这种威士忌真是糟糕，”我说。

“没错。我们必须再来一些。”

男侍者快手快脚，动作麻利。

“我要跟你讲讲斯汀克尔的事儿，”他说。

“是的，跟我讲讲吧。”

“噢，我们到达埃及后，除了史密斯，他什么都不说。他常常走来走去，他走路的样子就好像狗时刻跟在他的左右。他一副发傻的样子，走来走去，边走边说：‘来啊，史密斯。老伙计，来啊。’同时，他一个劲儿低头看，边走边跟史密斯交谈，还一个劲儿俯身，然后拍拍，抚摸着那条并不存在的破狗。”

“狗在哪儿?”

“在马耳他啊，我想。一定在马耳他。”

“这种威士忌，难道不是很难喝吗?”

“真差劲儿。这些喝完，一定再喝点别的。”

“干杯。”

“干杯。”

“侍者，喂，侍者。是的，再来些。”

“那么说，史密斯在马耳他啦。”

“是的，”他说。“但是，这个傻乎乎的斯汀克尔·沙利文一直这样疯疯癫癫的，直到他死前的那一刻。”

“一定是疯了。”

“他是疯了，疯得不亦乐乎。要知道，有一次，他走进亚历山大港一家叫博彩俱乐部的地方，当时，大家都在里面喝酒呢。”

“那个举动不算太疯狂。”

“他走进宽敞的客厅，刚一进门，就将门把住，不让其关闭，同时呼唤他的狗。然后，他认为自己的狗已经进来之后，就关上门，从屋子一头一直走到另一头,不时地停下来,向四周看看,说道:'来啊,史密斯。老伙计,来吧。'他还不停地弹着自己的手指。有一次,他钻到一张桌子底下,当时,两男、两女正坐在桌子旁喝酒呢。只见他双手着地,跪在那儿,说:'史密斯,从那儿给我出来,马上到我这边来。'于是,他伸出手,开始从桌子底下往外拽狗,其实什么都没有。之后,他向桌旁的人道歉。'真是一条该死的狗,'他对桌旁的人说。你真应该看看那些人脸上表情啊。他就是如此这般走过整个屋子,走到屋子另一头的时候,他把住门,不使其关闭,让狗先走了出去。然后,他跟着狗走了出去。"

"这人是疯了。"

"疯得不亦乐乎。你真应该看看那些人脸上表情啊。当时,屋子里尽是些喝酒的人,他们都不甚清楚,是他们疯了,还是斯汀克尔疯了。那些人不停地你看看我,我看看你,以确定自己不是唯一看不见狗的人,其中一人还把酒洒到了地上。"

"那真是糟糕啊。"

"糟透了。"

男侍者过来,又走开。现在,房间里聚满了客人,大家都穿着制服,都坐在小桌子旁,一边喝着酒,一边交谈着。这位飞行员用手指将杯子里的冰块往下戳。

"他也经常出现偏差,"他说。

"谁?"

"斯汀克尔啊,他经常谈起自己出过偏差的事儿。"

"出偏差不算什么事儿,"我说。"就像在人行道上行走,避不开路面的缝隙。"

"胡扯。那只是个人的问题,不能影响他人的。"

"噢,这如同驾车等待。"

"什么叫驾车等待?"

"我总是这样做的,"我说。

"怎么回事?"

"就在你要驾车离开之际,你就向后一仰,数二十个数,然后再开走。”

“你也疯了，”他说。“你跟斯汀克尔一样。”

“避免发生交通事故，这种方式很完美。我这样开车从未发生一次事故，至少一次严重事故也没有发生过。”

“你喝多了。”

“没喝多。我一直这样做的。”

“为什么？”

“因为当时，要是有人在你前面跨步走下人行道，你不会撞到那个人，因你开车起步较晚。你启动推迟，因为你数了二十个数。那个跨步走下人行道的人，你本来是会撞上的，但却错开了。”

“为什么？”

“远在你到达、撞上他之前，他就已经跨步走下了人行道，就是因为你数了二十个数。”

“你那主意不错。”

“我知道，是个不错的主意。”

“相当美妙的一个主意。”

“我救了很多人的命。你只管径直开车穿过交叉路口，因为原本你要撞上的那辆车已经驶远。那辆车比你早一点开了过去，就是因为你自己数到二十，耽搁了一下。”

“美妙之极。”

“的确如此。”

“可是，这跟飞行出现偏差很像啊，”他说。“你永远都不会知道，到底会发生什么情况。”

“我经常这样做的，”我说。

我们继续喝起酒来。

“看看那个女的，”我说。

“胸大的那个？”

“对，美妙的胸部。”

他慢腾腾地说：“我敢打赌，我杀死过许许多多比她更漂亮的女子。”

"但没有一个有她那样的双乳。"

"我敢打赌,有的。我们再喝一杯好吗?"

"好的,来一杯好在路上喝。"

"哪个女人都不会有像她那样的乳房了,"我说。"起码,德国是没有了。"

"噢,不,有的。我就杀死过很多、很多那样的。"

"好吧,就算你杀死过许许多多有那样美妙乳房的女子啦。"

他向后倚身,一只手朝屋子四周指了指。"看到屋子里所有的人了吧,"他说。

"看到了。"

"如果他们突然间死掉,会不会摆成很长的一列呢?要是突然之间,他们一下子都从椅子上跌落身亡,会不会摆成很长的一列呢?"

"那会怎么样?"

"难道不会摆成很长的一列吗?"

"当然会的。"

"要是所有的侍者联手往酒里放点什么东西进去、没有一个生还的话。"

"那样就会摆成老长的一列啦。"

"噢,那样的事我已经干过好几百次了。我已经好几百次干过类似的事情,杀死的人比这屋子里的要多得多。你也一样。"

"还要多得多,"我说。"但是,不一样的啊。"

"都是一样的人啊,男的、女的,还有侍者,都在一个酒吧里喝酒。"

"那可不一样的。"

"没有什么不一样的。要是这儿发生那样的事儿,死者难道不会摆成一大长列吗?"

"相当、相当长的一列啊。"

"可是,我们做过这样的事儿,做过好几百次了。"

"嗯,好几百次了,"我说。"这没什么啊。"

"这个地方很差劲儿。"

"没错,是很差劲儿。我们去别的地方吧。"

"先喝完吧。"

喝完后,我们俩都抢着要付账,于是,我们投币决定谁付,最终我赢了。我一共花了十六美元二十五美分,他给了侍者两块钱的小费。

我们站起身,绕过一张张桌子,走到了门口。

"出租车,"他说。

"对,一定得打出租车。"

这家没有门卫帮忙叫出租车,于是,我们站在马路的镶边石旁边,等着出租车过来。他说:"这座城镇不错。"

"美妙的城镇,"我说,感觉不错。外面黑了下来,但是,几盏街灯已经亮起,我们可以看到车来车往,街道的另一侧有人在行走。淅淅沥沥的毛毛雨静静地落下,在车灯以及街灯的映照下,湿乎乎的黝黑街面发射出黄色的光亮。汽车的轮胎压在湿漉漉的路面上,发出"嗞嗞"的声音。

"我们去一个威士忌很多、很多的地方,"他说。"很多、很多的威士忌,还有胡子上粘着蛋渣的人为我们端上酒来。"

"不错。"

"去一个没有其他人的地方,那里只有我们俩,再加上那个胡子上粘着蛋渣的人。或者去……"

"好的,"我说。"或者去什么样的地方?"

"或者,去一个有成千上万人的地方。"

"好的,"我说。"可以。"

我们站在那儿等着出租车,看见一辆辆车亮起灯,绕过弯道,向左拐,朝我们这边驶来,轮胎与湿漉漉的路面摩擦,发出"刷刷"的声音。这些车从我们身旁掠过,沿着马路驶向一座通向河流的桥梁。我们俩透过车头灯的一束束光柱,看到丝丝细雨飘落而下。我们俩就这样站在那儿,等待着一辆出租车的到来。

第三节 《士兵幻象》*The Soldier*

罗尔德·达尔的《士兵幻象》(The Soldier)首次发表在《如你之人》(Someone like You)一书中。后来,这篇故事又收录到《罗尔德·达尔短篇故事集锦》(The Collected Short Stories of Roald Dahl)、《罗尔德·达尔选集》(The Roald Dahl Omnibus)以及《五部畅销书集》(5 Bestsellers)等书中。1956 年上演一部三幕歌剧《士兵幻象》就是根据罗尔德·达尔的这部小说改编的。

一、原作导读

罗伯特是一位从战场上返乡的士兵,但却是一个有着多重问题的士兵。他的神经似乎受到了某种程度的损伤,令他很难能感觉到炎热或疼痛,但他渴望回到年轻时在海边度假的美好时光里。

罗伯特已经成家,娶了一个名叫埃德娜的女子为妻,但是,埃德娜似乎以折磨他为乐——至少他是这么想的。无论何时听到头顶上方有飞机飞过,他都会感到战战兢兢的。他相信,是埃德娜将浴室里冷、热水龙头颠倒过来的,也是埃德娜将家门把手左右颠倒过来的。她这样做,就是为了把他搞迷糊。他还看到有人将脸贴到窗户上往屋内观瞧,夜晚出门还听到有人尾随着。

一天夜里回家时,“就在手指触碰到把手的那一刻,某种体积虽小但威力猛烈的东西在他的脑袋里炸开了,而且,伴随着这种爆炸,狂怒、愤慨、恐惧也喷涌而出。他打开门,进屋后随手快速将门带上,大喊:‘埃德娜,你在吗?’”(—and the moment the fingers touched the knob, something small but violent exploded inside his head and with it a surge of fury and outrage and fear. He opened the door, shut it quickly behind him and shouted “Edna, are you there?”)

他迈进家门,上楼直奔埃德娜而去,但却发现待在屋子里的不是埃德娜,而是另外一个女人。这个女人声称自己是埃德娜的朋友,名叫玛丽,并要求他将手中的刀放下。罗伯特告诉“玛丽”说,尽管他爱埃德娜,但埃德娜却是个残忍的、坏透了的下贱小女人。他对她说,她看起来像埃德娜,并说埃德娜“长了一个棕色的小痣,很有意思,就长在左耳朵后面。”(... has a funny little brown mole just behind her left ear.)

接着,他就要上前查看她的左耳朵后边是否长有一颗像埃德娜那样的小痣。他面带微笑,慢慢地向她靠近。等他靠近时,“她的右手快速伸出,在他脸前狠狠地扇了一巴掌,速度之快,他都没有看清是怎么一回事儿。他在床上坐下、开始哭泣时,她从他手中夺下那把刀,飞速走出房间,奔下楼梯,赶到了门厅里放电话的地方。”(... with a quick right hand, so quick he never saw it coming, she smacked him hard across the front of the face. And when he sat down on the bed and began to cry, she took the knife from his hand and went swiftly out of the room, down the stairs to the hall, where the telephone was.)

二、原作释读

这是一篇带有“意识流”色彩的小说,角度的切换有时令人摸不着头脑。这也是理解上的难点。

The Soldier[①]

It was one of those nights that made him feel he knew what it was like to be a blind man; not the shadow of an image for his eyes to discern, not even the forms of the trees visible against the sky.

Out of the darkness he became aware of small rustling noises in the hedge, the breathing of a horse some distance away in the field, the soft thud[②] of a hoof as it moved its foot; and once he heard the rush of a bird

---

① 本部小说原文出自“Roald Dahl. *The Collected Short Stories of Roald Dahl*[M]. England: Penguin Books Ltd., 1992”。

② thud: *Noun* a dull, heavy sound, such as that made by an object falling to the ground 砰(或嘭)的一声

flying past him low overhead.

"Jock," he said, speaking loud. "We'll go home now." And he turned and began to walk back up the slope of the lane, the dog pulling ahead, showing the way in the dark.

It must be nearly midnight, he thought. That meant that soon it would be tomorrow. Tomorrow was worse than today. Tomorrow was the worst of all because it was going to become today—and today was now.

Today had not been very nice, especially that business with the splinter①.

Stop it, he told himself. There isn't any sense thinking about it. It doesn't do anyone any good thinking about things like that. Think about something else for a change. You can kick out a dangerous thought, you know, if you put another in its place. Go right back as far as you can go. Let's have some memories of sweet days. The seaside holidays in the summer, wet sand and red buckets and shrimping nets and the slippery seaweedy rocks and the small clear pools and sea anemones② and snails and mussels③ and sometimes one grey translucent shrimp hovering deep down in the beautiful green water.

But how *could* that splinter have got into the sole of his foot without him feeling it?

It is not important. Do you remember hunting for cowries④ along the margin of the tide, each one so fine and perfect it became a precious

---

① splinter: *Noun* a small, thin, sharp piece of wood, glass, or similar material broken off from a larger piece (木头、玻璃等材料的)碎片;裂片;尖片

② anemone = sea anemone 海葵

③ mussel: *Noun* a marine bivalve which uses byssus threads to anchor to a firm surface 贻贝

④ cowry: (also "cowrie") *Noun* (plural cowries) a marine mollusc which has a glossy, brightly patterned domed shell with a long, narrow opening 贝壳

jewel to be held in the hand all the way home; and the little orange-coloured scallops, the pearly oyster shells, the tiny bits of emerald glass, a live hermit crab, a cockle①, the spine of a skate②, and once, but never to be forgotten, the dry seawashed jawbone of a human being with teeth in it, white and wonderful among the shells and pebbles. Oh Mummy, look what I've found! Look, Mummy, look!

But to go back to the splinter. She had really been rather unpleasant about that.

"What do you mean, you didn't notice?" she had asked, scornful.

"I just didn't notice, that's all."

"I suppose you're going to tell me if I stick a pin into your foot you won't feel it?"

"I didn't say that."

And then she had jabbed him suddenly in the ankle with the pin she had been using to take out the splinter, and he hadn't been watching so he didn't know about it till she had cried out in a kind of horror. And when he had looked down, the pin was sticking into the flesh all by itself behind the anklebone, almost half of it buried. "Take it out," he had said. "You can poison someone like that."

"You mean you can't *feel* it?"

"Take it out, will you?"

"You mean it doesn't hurt?"

"The pain is terrible. Take it out."

"What's the *matter* with you?"

"I said the pain is terrible. Didn't you hear me?"

---

① cockle: *Noun* an edible burrowing bivalve mollusc with a strong ribbed shell 鸟蛤

② skate: *Noun* (*Plural* same or skates) a typically large marine fish of the ray family with a cartilaginous skeleton and a flattened diamond – shaped body 鳐鱼

Why did they do things like that to him?

When I was down beside the sea, a wooden spade they gave to me, to dig the sandy shore. My holes were empty as a cup, and every time the sea came up, till it could come no more.

A year ago the doctor had said, "Shut your eyes. Now tell me whether I'm pushing this toe up or down."

"Up," he had said.

"And now?"

"Down. No, up. I think it's up."

It was peculiar that a neuro-surgeon should want to play with his toes.

"Did I get them all right, doctor?"

"You did very well."

But that was a year ago. He had felt pretty good a year ago. The sort of things that happened now never used to happen then. Take, for example, just one item—the bathroom tap.

Why was the hot tap in the bathroom on a different side this morning? That was a new one.

It is not of the least importance, you understand, but it would be interesting to know why.

Do you think she could have changed it over, taken a spanner and a pipe-wrench① and sneaked in during the night and changed it over?

Do you? Well—if you really want to know—yes. The way she'd been acting lately, she'd be quite capable of doing that.

A strange and difficult woman, that's what she was. Mind you, she used not to be, but there's no doubt at all that right now she was as

① pipe-wrench: an adjustable tool like a spanner, used forhandling pipes 管扳手;管钳子

strange and difficult as they come. Especially at night.

Yes, at night. That was the worst time of all—the night.

Why, when he put out his right hand in bed at night, could his fingers not feel what they were touching? He had knocked over the lamp and she had woken up and then sat up suddenly while he was feeling for it on the floor in the dark.

"What are you doing now?"

"I knocked over the lamp. I'm sorry."

"Oh Christ," she had said. "Yesterday it was the glass of water. What's the *matter* with you?"

Once, the doctor had stroked the back of his hand with a feather, and he hadn't been able to feel that either. But he had felt it when the man scratched him with a pin.

"Shut your eyes. No—you mustn't look. Shut them tight. Now tell me if this is hot or cold."

"Hot."

"And this?"

"Cold."

"And this?"

"Cold. I mean hot. Yes, it's hot, isn't it?"

"That's right," the doctor had said. "You did very well."

But that was a year ago.

Why were the switches on the walls, just lately, always a few inches away from the well-remembered places when he felt for them in the dark?

Don't think about it, he told himself. The only thing is not to think about it.

And while we're on the subject, why did the walls of the living-room take on a slightly different shade of colour each day?

Green and blue-green and blue; and sometimes—sometimes slowly swimming like colours seen through the heat-haze of a brazier[1].

One by one, neatly, like index cards out of a machine, the little questions dropped.

Whose face appeared for one second at the window during dinner? Whose eyes?

"What are you staring at?"

"Nothing," he had answered. "But it would be nice if we could draw the curtains, don't you think?

"Robert, what were you staring at?"

"Nothing,"

"Why were you staring at the window like that?"

"It would be nice if we could draw the curtains, don't you think?" he had answered.

He was going past the place where he had heard the horse in the field and now he could hear it again; the breathing, the soft hoof thuds, and the crunch of grass-cropping that was like the noise of a man munching celery[2].

"Hello old horse," he said, calling loud into the darkness. "Hello old horse over there."

Suddenly he heard the footsteps behind him, slow, long-striding footsteps close behind, and he stopped. The footsteps stopped. He turned around, searching the darkness.

"Good evening," he said, "You here again?"

In the quiet that followed he could hear the wind moving the leaves in the hedge.

"Are you going my way?" he said.

---

① brazier: *Noun* portable heater consisting of a pan or stand for holding lighted coals 火盆

② celery: *Noun* Apium graveolens var. dulce, family Umbelliferae 芹菜

Then he turned and walked on, the dog still pulling ahead, and the footsteps started after him again, but more softly now, as though the person were walking on toes.

He stopped and turned again.

"I can't see you," he said, "because it's so dark. Are you somcono I know?"

Again the silence, and the cool summer wind on his cheeks, and the dog tugging on the leash to get home.

"All right," he called. "You don't have to answer if you don't want to. But remember I know you're there."

Someone trying to be clever.

Far away in the night, over to the west and very high, he heard the faint hum of an aeroplane. He stopped again, head up, listening.

"Miles away," he said. "Won't come near here." But why, when one of them flew over the house, did everything inside him come to a stop, and his talking and what he was doing, while he sat or stood in a sort of paralysis waiting for the whistle-shriek of the bomb. That one after dinner this evening.

"Why did you duck① like that?" she asked, "Duck?"

"Why did you duck? What are you ducking for?"

"Duck?" he had said again. "I don't know what you mean."

"I'll say you don't," she had answered, staring at him hard with those hard, blue-white eyes, the lids dropping slightly, as always when there was contempt. The drop of her eyelids was something beautiful to him, the half-closed eyes and the way the lids dropped and the eyes became hooded when her contempt was extreme.

---

① duck: *Verb* [no obj.] lower the head or the body quickly to avoid a blow or missile or so as not to be seen (为躲避袭击等)突然低下头;突然弯身

Yesterday, lying in bed in the early morning, when the noise of gunfire was just beginning far away down the valley, he had reached out with his left hand and touched her body for a little comfort.

"What on earth are you doing?"

"Nothing, dear."

"You woke me up."

"I'm sorry."

It would be a help if she would only let him lie closer to her in the early mornings when he began to hear the noise of gunfire.

He would soon be home now. Around the last bend of the lane he could see a light glowing pink through the curtain of the living-room window, and he hurried forward to the gate and through it and up the path to the front door, the dog still pulling ahead.

He stood on the porch, feeling around for the door - knob in the dark.

It was on the right when he went out. He distinctly remembered it being on the right-hand side when he shut the door half an hour ago and went out.

It couldn't be that she had changed *that* over too? Just to fox him? Taken a bag of tools and quickly changed it over to the other side while he was out walking the dog?

He moved his hand over to the left—and the moment the fingers touched the knob, something small but violent exploded inside his head and with it a surge of fury and outrage and fear. He opened the door, shut it quickly behind him and shouted "Edna, are you there?"

There was no answer so he shouted again, and this time she heard him.

"What do you want now? You woke me up."

"Come down here a moment, will you. I want to talk to you."

"Oh for heaven's sake[①]," she answered. "Be quiet and come on up."

"Come here!" he shouted. "Come here at once!"

"I'll be damned if I will. You come here."

The man paused, head back, looking up the stairs into the dark of the second floor. He could see where the stair-rail curved to the left and went on up out of sight in the black towards the landing and if you went straight on across the landing you came to the bedroom, and it would be black in there too.

"Edna!" he shouted. "Edna!"

"Oh go to hell."

He began to move slowly up the stairs, treading quietly, touching the stair-rail for guidance, up and around the lefthand curve into the dark above. At the top he took an extra step that wasn't there; but he was ready for it and there was no noise. He paused awhile then, listening, and he wasn't sure, but he thought he could hear the guns starting up again far away down the valley, heavy stuff mostly, seventy-fives and maybe a couple of mortars[②] somewhere in the background.

Across the landing now and through the open doorway—which was easy in the dark because he knew it so well—through on to the bedroom carpet that was thick and soft and pale grey although he could not feel or see it.

In the centre of the room he waited, listening for sounds. She had gone back to sleep and was breathing rather loud, making the slightest

---

① for heaven's sake: used to express impatience, annoyance, urgency, or desperation 看在上帝分上;天哪;哎呀;我求你(用于表达不耐烦、生气、紧迫或绝望)

② mortar: *Noun* a short smooth-bore gun for firing shells (technically called bombs) at high angles 迫击炮

little whistle with the air between her teeth each time she exhaled. The curtain flapped[①] gently against the open window, the alarm-clock tick-tick-ticked beside the bed.

Now that his eyes were becoming accustomed to the dark he could just make out the end of the bed, the white blanket tucked in under the mattress, the bulge of her feet under the bedclothes; and then, as though aware of the presence of the man in the room, the woman stirred. He heard her turn, and turn again. The sound of her breathing stopped. There was a succession of little movement-noises and once the bedsprings creaked, loud as a shout in the dark.

"Is that you, Robert?"

He made no move, no sound.

"Robert, are you there?"

The voice was strange and rather unpleasant to him.

"Robert!" She was wide awake now. "Where are you?"

Where had he heard that voice before? It had a quality of stridence[②], dissonance[③], like two single high notes struck together hard in discord. Also there was an inability to pronounce the R of Robert. Who was it that used to say Wobert[④] to him?

"Wobert," she said again. "What are you doing?"

Was it that nurse in the hospital, the tall one with fair hair? No, it was further back. Such an awful voice as that he ought to remember.

---

① flap: *Verb* [no obj.] (of something attached at one point or loosely fastened) flutter or wave around (附着于一点或系得不紧的东西)摆动;飘动;飘舞

② stridence: *Noun* a sound that is loud, unpleasant, and rough 刺耳的声音

③ dissonance: *Noun* [*Mass Noun*] (Music) lack of harmony among musical notes(乐)不协和音

④ Wobert:主人公"Robert"的非标准发音形式

Give him a little time and he would get the name.

At that moment he heard the snap of the switch of the bedside lamp and in the flood of light he saw the woman half-sitting up in bed, dressed in some sort of a pink nightdress. There was a surprised, wide-eyed expression on her face. Her cheeks and chin were oily with cold cream.

"You better put that thing down," she was saying, "before you cut yourself."

"Where's Edna?" He was staring at her hard.

The woman, half-sitting up in bed, watched him carefully. He was standing at the foot of the bed, a huge, broad man, standing motionless, erect, with heels together, almost at attention, dressed in his dark-brown, woolly, heavy suit.

"Go on," she ordered. "Put it down."

"Where's Edna?"

"What's the matter with you, Wobert?"

"There's nothing the matter with me. I'm just asking you where's my wife?"

The woman was easing herself up gradually into an erect sitting position and sliding her legs towards the edge of the bed. "Well," she said at length, the voice changing, the hard blue-white eyes secret and cunning, "if you really want to know, Edna's gone. She left just now while you were out."

"Where did she go?"

"She didn't say."

"And who are you?"

"I'm just a friend of hers."

"You don't have to shout at me," he said. "What's all the excitement?"

"I simply want you to know I'm not Edna."

The man considered this a moment, then he said, "How did you know my name?"

"Edna told me." slightly he paused, studying her closely, still slightly puzzled, but much calmer now, his eyes calm, perhaps even a little amused the way they looked at her. "I think I prefer Edna."

In the silence that followed they neither of them moved. The woman was very tense, sitting up straight with her arms tense on either side of her and slightly bent at the elbows, the hands pressing palms downward on the mattress.

"I love Edna, you know. Did she ever tell you I love her?"

The woman didn't answer.

"I think she's a bitch. But it's a funny thing I love her just the same."

The woman was not looking at the man's face; she was watching his right hand.

"Awful cruel little bitch, Edna."

And a long silence now, the man standing erect, motionless, the woman sitting motionless in the bed, and it was so quiet suddenly that through the open window they could hear the water in the millstream[①] going over the dam far down the valley on the next farm.

Then the man again, speaking calmly, slowly, quite impersonally: "As a matter of fact, I don't think she even likes me any more."

The woman shifted closer to the edge of the bed. "Put that knife down," she said, "before you cut yourself."

"Don't shout, please. Can't you talk nicely?" Now, suddenly, the man leaned forward, staring intently into the woman's face, and he raised

① millstream: *Noun* the flowing water that drives a mill wheel 磨坊水车的动力水流

his eyebrows①. "That's strange," he said. "That's very strange."

He took a step forward, his knees touching the bed. "You look a bit like Edna yourself."

"Edna's gone out. I told you that."

He continued to stare at her and the woman kept quite still, the palms of her hands pressing deep into the mattress.

"Well," he said. "I wonder."

"I told you Edna's gone out. I'm a friend of hers. My name is Mary."

"My wife," the man said, "has a funny little brown mole just behind her left ear. You don't have that, do you?"

"I certainly don't."

"Turn your head and let me look."

"I told you I didn't have it."

"Just the same, I'd like to make sure."

The man came slowly around the end of the bed. "Stay where you are," he said. "Please don't move." And he came towards her slowly, watching her all the time, a little smile touching the corners of his mouth.

The woman waited until he was within reach, and then, with a quick right hand, so quick he never saw it coming, she smacked him hard across the front of the face. And when he sat down on the bed and began to cry, she took the knife from his hand and went swiftly out of the room, down the stairs to the hall, where the telephone was.

三、翻译探索

① raise one's eyebrows (or an eyebrow): show surprise, disbelief, or mild disapproval 抬眉;扬眉(表示吃惊、不信或轻度反对)

士兵幻象

那些日子的夜晚里,他感觉,自己了解了一个眼睛看不见的人的感受:丝毫的影像都辨别不出来,就连在夜空映衬下的那些树的可见轮廓,也看不出来。这个夜晚也是如此。

黑暗之中,他隐约觉察到,树篱里有些东西在沙沙作响,田野里很远的地方,一匹马在呼吸,还有那匹马移动蹄子时发出的轻微而沉闷的"砰砰"声。有一次,他听到一只鸟儿在头顶上方很低的地方,扑棱着翅膀疾飞而过。

"乔克,"他说,声音很大。"现在,我们回家。"他转过身,沿着小路的斜坡开始往回走。那条狗奋力赶在前头,在黑暗中为他引路。

他琢磨着,一定是接近午夜了,那就意味着明天很快就会到来,而明天比今天还要糟糕。所有的日子中,明天糟糕透顶,因为明天会变成今天,而今天就是现在这个时候。

今天不是很美妙,特别是想到了那根刺的事情。

他对自己说,不要想这事儿,想这事儿没有任何意义——想诸如此类的事情对谁都不会有任何的好处。换换样儿,想想别的事情吧。你知道的,要是你用另一件事儿置换这件事儿,危险的念头就会被踢到九霄云外。尽可能远地去追忆吧,尽可能追忆一些甜蜜的日子吧。比如,夏季在海边度过的假日——湿润的沙滩、红色的水桶、捕虾的网具、滑溜溜的长满海藻的岩石、清澈见底的小水洼、海葵、海螺、贻贝。有时候,在美丽的碧绿的海水中,还有一只半透明的灰色小虾潜在深处游来游去。

可是,那根刺扎进他的脚底,他怎么会没有感觉到呢?

这事儿不重要。沿着潮水的边缘找寻贝壳,每一只贝壳都那么精致、完美,握在手里一路走回家,就像握着珍贵的珠宝似的,还记得吗?我找到了橘黄色的扇贝、珍珠色的牡蛎壳、一小块一小块翡翠色的玻璃、会动的寄居蟹、鸟蛤、鳐鱼的脊椎骨,还记得吗?有一次,我一辈子也忘不了,竟然发现了一只被海水冲刷过的、干巴巴的人下颌骨,上面还有牙齿。这只下颌骨白白的,镶嵌在一些贝壳和鹅卵石之间，很是奇妙。噢，妈咪，看看我找到了什么！看啊，妈咪，快看！

且慢，还是回到那根刺的事情上吧。对于那件事，她着实不很愉快。

“你说没有注意到，那是什么意思？”她说，有点蔑视的意味。

“我就是没有注意到，就那个意思。”

“我想，你要对我说，要是我将大头针扎进你的脚里，你也不会有感觉，是不是呢？”

“我没那样说。”

接着，突然之间，她将自己一直使用的大头针扎进了我的踝关节，要把那根刺挑出来。他一直没有看她，若不是她大声喊叫起来，声音中带着一丝的恐惧，他还不知道大头针扎了进去。他向下一看，发现大头针已经扎进了踝骨后面的肌肉里，几乎有一半的长度已经扎了进去。

“把针拔出来，”他说。“那样，会让人染毒的。”

“你的意思是说，你感觉不到针扎进去了？”

“把针拔出来，好吗？”

“你的意思是说，扎进去不疼吗？”

“疼得厉害，把针拔出来。”

“你这是怎么了？”

“我说过了，疼得厉害。难道你没有听见吗？”

他们为什么要对他做出那样的事情呢？

我走下来到了海边，他们给了我一把木铲子，用来挖海边的沙子。我挖出的沙坑空空的，就像一个个空杯子。每次里面都能冒出些海水，直到有一次，海水再也冒不出来了。

一年前，医生说过：“闭上眼睛。现在，告诉我，这只脚趾，我是向上推，还是向下推。”

“向上，”他说道。

“那么，现在呢？”

“向下。不，是向上。我想，是向上。”

奇特的是，一名神经外科医生竟然还玩弄起脚趾。

“医生,我都说对了吗?”

“说得很不错。”

可是,那是一年前的事情了。一年前,他的状态很好。现在发生的这类事情,那时候从来都没有发生过。拿一个东西做例子吧,那就是浴室的水龙头。

今天早晨,浴室里的热水龙头为什么出现在不同的一侧?那是一只新安装的龙头。

这事儿一点都不重要,你明白的。但是,知道了原因所在,会是很有意思的事情。

你认为,她有可能已经将水龙头颠倒过来吗?拿起一个扳手和一把管钳,趁着黑夜悄悄溜进去,把水龙头调换位置,她能做到吗?

你认为能吗?好吧,要是你想知道答案的话,那么,答案就是:能。从她最近的行为举止来看,她是相当有能力做到那一点的。

真是一名奇怪而挑剔的女子,这就是她的本来面目。请注意,她以前可不是这个样子,但毫无疑问的是,现在她既奇怪得很,又挑剔得很,特别是在夜晚。

没错,在夜晚。所有的时间段中,夜晚是最糟糕的一段时间。

在夜晚,他躺在床上伸出了右手,为什么他的手指感觉不到触碰到的东西呢?他碰翻了床头灯。随之,她醒来,突然坐起,而他正在黑暗中的地板上摸索着床头灯。

“你在干什么呢?”

“我把床头灯碰翻了,很抱歉。”

“哦,天哪,”她说。“昨天碰翻的是装了水的杯子。你这是怎么了?”

有一次,医生用一根羽毛轻拂他的手背,他也未能感觉到,但是,当医生用大头针刮擦时,他感觉到了。

“闭上眼睛。不,你千万别看。紧闭双眼。现在,告诉我,这是热的,还是冷的。”

“热的。”

“这个呢?”

"冷的。"

"那么,这个呢?"

"冷的。我的意思是,热的。是的,这是热的,对不对?"

"说的没错,"医生说。"你说得很好。"

但是,那是一年前的事情了。

就在最近,在黑夜里,他触摸墙上的开关时,明明非常清楚地记得开关的位置,为什么总差那么几厘米呢?

他对自己说,不要想这件事儿了。唯一要做的事情,就是不要想这件事儿。

可是,既然谈到这个话题,为什么起居室的墙壁每一天都呈现出略微不同的色调呢?

绿色、蓝绿色、蓝色,有时候——有时候,颜色还会慢慢浮动、游移,就像透过火盆的热气流看到的颜色样子。

小问题一个接着一个,干净利落地蹦了出来,就像从一台机器里输出的索引卡片一样。

吃晚饭的时候,谁的脸在窗户那儿露出一秒钟?谁的眼睛?

"你盯着什么东西看呢?"

"没什么,"他回答。"可是,要是把窗帘放下来,会很不错的,难道你不这样认为吗?"

"罗伯特,你盯着什么东西看呢?"

"没什么。"

"你为什么那个样子盯着窗户看呢?"

"要是把窗帘放下来,会很不错的,难道你不这样认为吗?"他说。

他正从田野的那个地方走过,在那里听到过马的呼吸声。现在,他又听到了这种声音——呼吸声,还有马蹄移动发出的轻微、低沉的"砰砰"声,还有马啃青草时发出的"嘎吱、嘎吱"的声响,就像人用力咀嚼芹菜发出的噪音。

"嗨,老马,"他冲着黑暗大声叫道。"嗨,那边的老马。"

突然之间,他听到身后有脚步声——步伐缓慢,每一步跨的距离都很长——就从紧靠身后的位置传来。他停了下来,后面的脚步声也停止了。他转过身,往黑暗中搜索。

“晚上好,”他招呼道。“你又来了吗?”

接着,一阵安静之中,他听到风吹动了树篱的叶子。

“你跟我同路吗?”他问。

然后,他转回身,继续赶路。那条狗仍然奋力走在前头引路,身后的脚步声再次响起,但是,这次的声音更轻一些,就好像后面那人踮起脚尖走路似的。

他停了下来,又转过身去。

“我看不见你,”他说,“因为天太黑了。我们认识吗?”

又是一阵沉默。夏日凉爽的风吹上了他的脸颊,那条狗用力拉动皮带要往家走。

“那好吧,”他叫道。“要是你不想回答,就不用回答,但是要记住,我知道你在那儿。”

有人摆谱要聪明呢。

夜晚很远的地方——最西边很高的地方,他听到飞机微弱的“嗡、嗡、嗡”的声音。他又停了下来,仰起头,听着。

“远着呢,”他说。“不会飞来、靠近这里的。”

可是,其中一架飞机飞过房屋上空时,他内心的一切以及他的言谈举止戛然而止,整个人等待炸弹的呼啸声和爆炸声——不管当时是坐着,还是几乎瘫痪一样站立着。今天傍晚吃完饭后出现的那架飞机,就令他有着同样的感觉。

“你为什么像那样突然弯身?”她问。

“突然弯身?”

“你为什么突然弯身?你突然弯身干什么?”

“突然弯身?”他又说了一遍。“我不明白你说的是什么意思。”

“我说的是,你不要那样,”她回答,使劲盯着他。她那双眼睛很尖刻,呈蓝白色,眼皮轻微下垂——只要露出轻蔑的神情,就会这样。对他来说,她眼皮下垂是某种美好的事情——半睁半闭的双眼,还有眼皮下垂的样子。要是她的轻蔑之情达到了极端,她的眼睛就会完全闭上。

昨天早晨很早的时候，他躺在床上，山谷下方很远的地方传来了枪炮声，他伸出左手，触摸她的身体，欲寻求一点安慰。

"你到底在干什么呢？"

"没干什么，亲爱的。"

"你把我弄醒了。"

"我很抱歉。"

每天早晨很早的时候，只要听到了枪炮声，她如果让他躺得靠她更近一些，他就会有所缓解。

现在，他很快就要到家了。绕过小路的最后一个转弯处，他就能看见，一盏灯透过起居室的窗帘发出粉红色的光芒。于是，他匆忙上前，走到大门口。他穿过大门，沿着小径走近正门，那条狗仍然奋力向前引路。

他站在门廊里，黑暗中摸索着门把手。

出门时，门把手在右侧。他清晰地记得，半小时前出去、关上门的时候，把手是在右手边的。

她已经将门把手颠倒位置，没有这种可能吗？就是为了迷惑他？趁他出去遛狗的工夫，拿出一袋子工具，快速将门把手换到另一边了吗？

他将手移向左边。就在手指触碰到把手的那一刻，某种体积虽小但威力猛烈的东西在他的脑袋里炸开了，而且，伴随着这种爆炸，狂怒、愤慨、恐惧也喷涌而出。他打开门，进屋后随手快速将门带上，大喊："埃德娜，你在吗？"

没有回应，于是，他又大喊一声。这一次，她听到了。

"现在，你想要干什么？你吵醒我了。"

"下来，到这儿来一会儿，拜托。我想跟你谈谈。"

"哦，天呐，"她说。"安静下来，上来吧。"

"到这儿来！"他喊道。"立马到这儿来！"

"我要是下去，我就不叫埃德娜。你过来。"

这名男子暂停了一下，转回头，向楼梯上方看去，看向楼上的黑暗处。他能够看得到，楼梯扶手向左边弯曲，然后继续向上延伸，直至消失在黑暗中的楼梯平台处。要是穿过平台,径直往前走,就会走进卧室,但那里也会漆黑一片。

“埃德娜!”他喊道。“埃德娜!”

“噢,见鬼去吧。”

他开始慢腾腾地走上楼梯,双脚轻抬轻放,手触摸着楼梯扶手来引导自己,绕着左手边弯曲的弧线,走入上方的黑暗之中。到达顶部,他多迈了一级台阶,而实际上,所有台阶都已经迈完了。但是,他已经抬起脚要迈上台阶的,可却没有发出任何的声响。他暂停一会儿,倾听着。他想——但不十分肯定,他能够听见很远的山谷里又响起了枪炮声,多数是重火力的家伙发出的声音,有“75型”发出的声音,间或还听得见两三门迫击炮的声音,像是一种陪衬。

现在,穿过了楼梯平台。门开着,他走了进去。黑暗中,从门口走进卧室很是轻松,因为他熟悉这里的一切:进去就是卧室的地毯,地毯很厚、很软,呈浅灰色——尽管他摸不出来,也看不见。

在屋子的中央,他停下来,等待着,听听有什么动静。她又睡着了,呼吸声相当大——每次呼出的气体在上下牙齿间发出轻微的呼哨声。窗帘轻轻地摆动,拍打着开着的窗户,床边的闹钟发出“滴答、滴答、滴答”的声音。

由于眼睛逐渐适应了黑暗的环境,他能够辨别出哪里是床尾了——白色的毯子掖进床垫的底下,她的双脚从铺盖下面鼓了出来。接着,好像意识到丈夫出现在了屋子里,这位妻子醒了。他听见她翻身的声音。接着,她又翻了一个身。呼吸的声音听不见了,却听见某些小幅度的动作所发出的窸窣的声响。有一次,床下的弹簧“嘎吱”一声响,响动之大,好似有人在黑暗中大喊一声。

“是你吗,罗伯特?”

他没有动弹,也没有吱声。

“罗伯特,你在那儿吗?”

对他而言,这种声音很是怪异,令人感到相当不愉快。

“罗伯特!”现在,她完全醒来了。“你在哪儿?”

以前在什么地方听到过那种声音呢?那声音刺耳、不和谐,就像两个高音符很不和谐地使劲撞击到一起。另外,"罗伯特"这个名字的第一个字"罗"的音也没发好,发成了"沃"。以前谁经常说"沃伯特"来着呢?

"沃伯特,"她又这样说。"你在干什么?"

是医院里的那名护士吗?是个子高高、头发浅色的那名护士吗?不是。那声音还得往前追溯。像那样令人不快的声音,他应该记得。给他一点时间,他就会想起那人的名字来。

就在那一刻,他听到床头灯的开关"啪"的一声打开了。在耀眼炫目的灯光下,他看到她从床上半坐起来,身上穿的是粉红色的睡衣。她圆睁双目,脸上露出一副吃惊的表情,脸颊和下巴由于涂抹了雪花膏而显得油光光的。

"你最好把那东西放下,"她当时说道,"以免砍到你自己。"

"埃德娜在哪里?"他使劲儿盯着她。

这位女子半坐在床上,仔细打量着他。他站在床脚处,一动不动地站着,挺胸抬头,脚后跟并拢,几乎以立正姿势站立着。他身穿一套厚重的、深棕色的羊毛衣服,是位肩膀宽宽的大块头男子。

"快啊,"她命令道。"把那东西放下。"

"埃德娜在哪儿?"

"你这是怎么了,沃伯特?"

"没怎么了。我只是问你:我的妻子在哪里?"

这位女子不慌不忙地慢慢起身,笔直坐了起来,将双腿滑向床边。"哦,"她最终开口说道,说话的声音变了样,那双尖刻的蓝白色眼睛神秘莫测、阴险奸诈。"要是你想知道答案的话,埃德娜走了。她刚刚离开,就在你刚才出去的时候。"

"她去哪里了?"

"她没有说。"

"那么,你是谁?"

"我只是她的一个朋友。"

"你没有必要对我呼来喊去的,"他说。"你大呼小叫是为了什么?"

"我只不过是想让你知道,我不是埃德娜。"

这位男子考虑了一会儿这句话的意思,然后说:"你怎么知道我的名字?"

"埃德娜告诉我的。"

他又停了下来,仔细打量着她,仍然有点儿疑惑不解,但是现在,他平静多了。他的双眼平静下来,而且,从他看她的样子上看,他的眼中甚至还有点愉悦的色彩。

"我想,我更喜欢埃德娜。"

在接下来的沉默之中,他们两个谁都没有动一下。这位女子紧绷着身体,笔直坐着,两只胳膊也紧绷着放到身体两侧,胳膊肘那儿稍微弯曲一点儿,两只手的手掌朝下按压在床垫上。

"你知道,我爱埃德娜。她没有对你说过我爱她吗?"

女子没有作答。

"我想,她是一个下贱的女人,但有意思的是,我还照样爱她。"

女子没有看男子的脸,而是看着他的右手。

"埃德娜,这个残忍的、坏透了的下贱小女人。"

现在,一阵长时间的沉默。男子一动不动地笔直站立着,女子一动不动地坐在床上。突然之间,房间里安静得出奇。通过打开着的窗户,他们能够听见山谷下方很远的一座农场里,磨坊水车的水流流过堤坝的声音。

接着,这名男子又开始说话了,平静而缓慢,语调相当的冷淡:"事实上,我认为,她甚至不再喜欢我了。"

这位女子改变了位置,离床沿更近一些。"放下那把刀,"她说,"以免砍到你自己。"

"请不要喊叫。难道你不能好好说话吗?"现在,突然之间,男子倚身向前,目不转睛地盯着女子的脸,吃惊地扬起了眉毛。"这很奇怪,"他说。"这也太奇怪了。"

他向前迈出一步,双膝触到了床沿。

"你看起来有点像埃德娜。"

"埃德娜出去了,我告诉过你的。"

他继续盯着她看，而她却依然相当安静，双手的手掌将床垫深深地按压下去。

“噢，”他说。“我还是好奇。”

“我对你说过，埃德娜出去了。我是她的一个朋友，我的名字叫玛丽。”

“我的妻子，”这名男子说道，“长了一个棕色的小痣，很有意思，就长在左耳朵后面。你没有那样的痣，对吧？”

“我当然没有。”

“把头转一下，让我看一看。”

“我告诉过你，我没有。”

“我仍然要看一看，想确定一下。”

男子慢慢地绕到床尾。“待在原地，”他说。“请不要移动。”他慢慢地走近她，嘴角露出一点儿微笑，眼睛却始终没有从她身上移开。

女子等待着，等着他走到自己可以够得到的范围，然后，她的右手快速伸出，在他脸上狠狠地扇了一巴掌，速度之快，他都没有看清是怎么一回事儿。他在床上坐下、开始哭泣时，她从他手中夺下那把刀，飞速走出房间，奔下楼梯，赶到了门厅里放电话的地方。

第四章 战场硝烟

血腥战场，硝烟弥漫。

“废墟之中”，惨剧上演；“坠机余生”，沙漠脱险；“希腊孤女”，捍卫家园。

这就是罗尔德·达尔笔下硝烟四起的战场——战场上有浴血奋战的场景，有搏击长空的壮烈，有单枪匹马的执著，有同仇敌忾的愤怒。

待战场硝烟散尽，有谁会记得他们？走进罗尔德·达尔的战争画卷，去体会那真实的场景，去回忆那不该忘却的记忆。

第一节 《废墟之中》*In the Ruins*

罗尔德·达尔的《废墟之中》(In the Ruins)首次发表在《国王》(King)杂志1964年某期上。后来，这篇故事又收录到《年度最佳科幻作品集》(The Year's Best S-F)以及《恐怖故事小册子：微型恐怖故事集》(The Little Book of Horrors: Tiny Tales of Terror)等书中。

这部小说篇幅极短，可以说是罗尔德·达尔短篇小说中最短的一篇了，相当于今天所说的“微型小说”或者“小小说”。尽管篇幅短小,但读后却令人毛骨悚然,甚至不寒而栗。达尔以极短的篇幅,揭示了战争的残酷。正如克里斯廷·霍华德(Kristine Howard)所言:“这是一篇很短但却令人反胃的小故事。我猜测,达尔写出这篇的原意是为填补杂志的空余版面。这篇小说后来只重新刊印了几次。”①

一、原作导读

这篇超短篇小说的叙述者是“我”——算是“隐性”的叙述者,不妨将“我”看作是作者罗尔德·达尔的化身。

趁着战争的间隙,“我”行走在战争留下的残砖碎石中。那里原来或许是一座生机盎然的小村子,但现在却满目疮痍,一片凄凉。走着走着,“我”在废墟之中碰到了一名“医生”模样的男子。他坐在地上,把自己的一条腿锯了下来。他的身旁放着一只黑包,包里很显然放着一根皮下注射针以及一些麻醉剂之类的医用品。

医生模样的人要给“我”一点吃的,“我”饿得发慌,就接受了。他说,只要“我”愿意提供下一顿,他很愿意与“我”分享,且向“我”保证他没有受到感染。他解释道,从脊柱的底部注射,什么疼痛的感觉都不会有。“我”拾来木材开始生火,他就在火上烤起肉来。

一个小女孩走上前来,他也给小女孩一些吃的,但告诉小女孩以后得偿还。他还说,有三个人在,存活相当长一段时间是没有问题的。但是,小女孩却哭了起来,喊着要找妈妈。

“坐下吧,”医生对她说。“我会照料你的。”(“Sit down,” the doctor told her. “I'll take care of you.”)

二、原作释读

这篇可谓“微型”小说,但具有一定的隐晦性,涉及少量医学方面的知识。全文读到最后才会有所理解。

---

① 参见克里斯廷·霍华德(Kristine Howard)创建并维护的网站“Roald Dahl Fans. com”,网址为:http://www. roalddahlfans. com/

In the Ruins[①]

Somewhere among the bricks and stones, I came across a man sitting on the ground in his underpants[②], sawing off his left leg. There was a black bag beside him, and the bag was open, and I could see a hypodermic[③] needle lying there among all the rest of the stuff.

"Do you want some?" he asked, looking up.

"Yes, please," I said. I was going crazy with hunger.

"I don't mind giving you a bit so long as you will promise to produce the next meal. I am quite uncontaminated."

"All right," I said. "Yes."

"Caudal[④] injection," he said. "Base of the spine. You don't feel a thing."

I found a few bits of wood, and I made a fire in the ruins, and started roasting a piece of the meat. The doctor sat on the ground doing things to the stump[⑤] of his leg.

A child came up, a girl of about four years old. She had probably seen the smoke from the fire or smelled the smell of cooking, I don't

---

① 本部小说的原文出自克里斯廷·霍华德(Kristine Howard)创建并维护的网站"Roald Dahl Fans. com",网址为:http://www. roalddahlfans. com/。

② underpants: *Plural Noun* an undergarment, especially for men or boys, covering the lower part of the body and having two holes for the legs(尤指男性的)内裤;衬裤

③ hypodermic: *Adjective* (of a needle or syringe) used to inject a drug or other substance beneath the skin(针,注射器)用于皮下注射的

④ caudal: *Adjective* near the tail or the posterior part of the body (近)尾部的;身躯后背部的

⑤ stump: *Noun* the small projecting remnant of something that has been cut or broken off or worn away(主体砍断、折断或磨损后的)残余部分

know which. She was very unsteady on her feet.

"Do you want some, too?" the doctor asked.

She nodded.

"You'll have to pay it back later," the doctor said.

The child stood there looking at the piece of meat that I was holding over the fire on the end of a bent curtain rod.

"You know something," the doctor said, "with all three of us here, we ought to be able to survive for quite a long time."

"I want my mummy," the child said, starting to cry.

"Sit down," the doctor told her. "I'll take care of you."

三、翻译探索

由于本篇篇幅极短，这里给出两个探索性的汉译版本。第一个为本书的第二著者王永胜所译，尽量保留原著"含而不露"的创作特色，但肯定有值得商榷之处；第二个是他的学生付莹[①]翻译的，有些地方做了增词处理，预先补足了作者"含而不露"的信息；有些句式"翻译腔"明显一点，但算是很不错的一个翻译探索。

探索之一

废墟之中

在残砖碎石之中的某个地方，我偶然碰到了一名男子，他穿着内裤坐在地上，锯掉了自己的左腿。他的旁边放着一个黑包，包敞开着，我可以看到包里面躺着一根皮下注射针，针的周围放置了一些其他物品。

"你想要些吗？"他问我，抬起了头。

---

① 付莹，渤海大学外国语学院英语系本科生，是本书第二著者王永胜所授《翻译理论与实践》课程班的学生——勤奋好学，翻译功底扎实

“好的,拜托了。”我回答。我饿得要发狂。

“只要你答应提供下一餐,我不介意给你一点。我一点也没有受到感染。”

“好吧,”我说。“我答应。”

“身躯背部注射,”他说。“从脊柱的底部注射,你什么感觉都不会有的。”

我找到几片木头,在废墟之中生起一堆火,开始烤其中一块肉。这位医生坐在地上,处理自己截肢后的残留部分。

一个小孩走上前来,是一个大约四岁的小女孩。她大概是看到了火堆冒出的烟,或者闻到了烹调的香味,但我不知道是哪个原因。她的双脚走起路来很不稳定。

“你也想要些吗?”医生问。

她点了点头。

“你以后必须得偿还,”医生说。

小女孩站在那儿,看着那块肉,那块肉被固定在一根弄弯了的窗帘杆末端,在火堆上方烘烤着。

“你要知道,”医生说,“有我们三个人在这儿,我们应该能够存活相当长一段时间了。”

“我想要妈咪,”小女孩说着,开始哭了起来。

“坐下吧,”医生对她说。“我会照料你的。”

探索之二

幸存者

在断砖乱石间的一个地方,我遇到一个穿着衬裤坐在地上的男子,正在往下锯自己的左腿。他的旁边放着一个黑色的包,从包敞开的口中,我可以看到在包里的东西中有一个皮下注射器针头。

“你想要一些肉么?”他抬眼问我。

“好啊。”我回答。我快要饿疯了。

“只要你答应,下一顿的肉从你身上出,我不介意分给你点儿。

我可是一点都没被污染过。”

“我答应，”我说。“就这么办吧。”

“对椎骨基部进行尾静脉注射，你就什么都感觉不到了。”他说。

我找到了些木材，在废墟上生起了火，开始烤腿肉。医生坐在地上处理自己的残腿。

这时，一个孩子跟跟跄跄地走到我跟前，是一个大约四岁的小女孩。她可能是看到了火堆升起的烟雾，也可能是闻到了食物的味道才过来的。我不确定是哪个原因。

“你也想要分一些吗？”医生问道。

她点点头。

“你以后必须得偿还。”医生说道。

小女孩站在那儿，看着我放在弯曲窗帘杆末端被火烤着的肉。

“你应该清楚，”医生说，“有我们三个人在，我们应该能活很长一段时间的。”

“我想找我妈妈。”小女孩哭着说道。

“坐下吧，”医生告诉小女孩。“我会照顾你的。”

第二节　《坠机余生》*Shot down over Libya*

罗尔德·达尔的《坠机余生》(Shot down over Libya)首次发表在《星期六晚邮报》(The Saturday Evening Post)杂志 1942 年 8 月 1 日发行的那一期上。估计本篇应该是达尔另一篇小说《小菜一碟》(A Piece of Cake)的“写实”版，而且本篇跟达尔另一篇具有个人传记色彩的故事《幸运开局》(Lucky Break)也有关联，只是情节有所不同罢了。

据说，这篇故事讲的就是作家罗尔德·达尔所驾驶的战机在利比亚沙漠上空坠毁的真实经历。但是，可能是达尔记忆力的原因，或者其他什么原因，关于坠机的原因，达尔的几部作品描述的都不太一样。

本篇故事中,达尔所驾驶的战机是被击落的,尽管本篇故事中的叙述者"我"是"隐性"的,但也不妨看作是达尔的化身;在1946年出版的《小菜一碟》(收录在《向你飞跃》"Over to You"一书)中,达尔则十分模糊地处理了坠机的原因——没有明说战机是被击落的;在后来的传记作品《独闯天下》(Going Solo)中,达尔则解释说,他所驾驶的飞机不是被击落的,"击落"的情节是《星期六晚邮报》的编辑后加的,《坠机余生》("Shot down over Libya",这个表达本身的意思是"在利比亚上空被击落")这个题目也是编辑后加上去的;在《幸运开局》中,则有这样的描述:"驾驶格斗士时,我自己曾被击落,飞机在利比亚沙漠深处、敌军的防线之间坠毁。当时,坠落后飞机起火,我则设法爬了出来,最终获救——被我们自己的战士安全地抬回,是在夜色的掩护下爬着穿越沙漠抬回去的。"(I myself was shot down in a Gladiator which crashed far out in the Libyan desert between the enemy lines. The plane burst into flames, but I managed to get out and was finally rescued and carried back to safety by our own soldiers who crawled out across the sand under cover of darkness);另外,还有一个完全不同的版本,那就是达尔所驾驶的飞机燃油耗尽,不得不在沙漠中迫降,结果酿成了坠机事件[①]。

一、原作导读

《坠机余生》从"我"躺在医院的病床开始讲起。躺在病床中的"我"想尽力去回忆事情发生的来龙去脉。没过多大工夫,"我"就慢慢记起了事情发生的经过。

飞行中队接到命令,说有大量意大利军队飞机集结在一起,要求中队飞机升空、前往轰炸。随即,"我"以及其他战友驾驶的六架"飓风"战机升空前往,要在黄昏时分发动攻击。接着,"我"用了大量篇

---

① 具体参见克里斯廷·霍华德(Kristine Howard)创建并维护的网站"Roald Dahl Fans. com",网址为:http://www. roalddahlfans. com/

幅来讲述驾机所做的一切(属于"专业性"炫耀)……突然,无线电对讲机里传来话音,说发现了敌机。所幸的是,我们这六架"飓风"没有与这群敌机发生正面冲突,而是继续向前直奔目标飞去。

最终,"我"和其他几名飞行员发现了地面上预定的目标,并开始俯冲扫射。"我"的战机被地面防空火力击中。"我"自认为能在飞机"负伤"的情况下,驾机逃离、返回基地,但事与愿违,"我"的战机不幸坠落沙漠之中。

"我"奋力爬出战机,卧在沙漠里等候救援。"我"身负重伤,鼻子也塌陷下去了,但最终被盟军其他成员救回,脱离了生命危险。迷糊之中,"我记不得更多,就记得我被推来晃去,有人不断地说:'放松。'我相信,有人一定带吗啡过来了。"(I don't remember much more, except that I was shoved about a lot, and someone kept saying "Take it easy." I believe someone had some morphia.)

小说的最后,作家引用了一份发自开罗的中东战报。战报是这样说的:"昨天双方几乎没有什么空中战事。我方一个战斗机编队在靠近西迪巴拉尼的地面上攻击了敌方的运输车,毁掉了很多车辆。我方一架战斗机失踪,但飞行员没有生命危险。"(There was little air activity yesterday on either side. A formation of our fighters attacked enemy transport on the ground near Sidi Barrani, damaging a number of vehicles. One of our planes is missing, but the pilot is safe.)

罗尔德·达尔在这篇小说中,以"纪实"的手法,描述了战争的惨烈和战场的残酷。

二、原作释读

这篇故事难以理解的地方就是驾驶飞机所做的各种操作,专业性很强。没有这方面的体验,恐怕理解不好。

Shot down over Libya[1]

"One of our planes is missing, but the pilot is safe," the communiqué[2] said. Here is that pilot's report.

They hung a label around my neck which said "Flying Officer—Possible fractured skull base. Concussion[3] and facial injuries. Church of England." I knew this because the medical orderly[4] read the label out loud to me at the base hospital.

I tried to remember just why that label was there, and why it said these things. I tried to ask someone, but no one heard, so I gave it up and just lay still. Then slowly it all came back; not clearly and brightly at first, but a little dimly, as though by moonlight. In the end, I got it all.

Operational order No.—from Fighter H. Q. Western Desert to No.—Squadron[5] STOP[6] Recco reports large number Italian vehicles

---

① 这部小说最初发表在《星期六晚邮报》(The Saturday Evening Post)杂志1942年8月1日发行的那一期上,这里的原文转引自克里斯廷·霍华德(Kristine Howard)创建并维护的网站"Roald Dahl Fans. com",网址为:http://www. roalddahlfans. com/。

② communiqué: Noun an official announcement 公报;官报

③ concussion: *Noun* [*Mass Noun*] temporary unconsciousness caused by a blow on the head. The term is also used loosely of the after-effects such as confusion or temporary incapacity(头部被击导致的)暂时知觉丧失;脑震荡

④ orderly: *Noun* an attendant in a hospital responsible for the non-medical care of patients and the maintenance of order and cleanliness(医院)护理员;勤杂工

⑤ squadron: *Noun* an operational unit in an air force consisting of two or more flights of aircraft and the personnel required to fly them(空军)中队

⑥ STOP: used in telegrams to indicate a full stop(电报中)句号的代字

parked close together 100 yards north of road 41 miles west of Sidi Barrani[1] STOP Six Hurricanes attack at dusk.

The C. O. wandered in with it in his hand while we were having late tea in the mess tent, and handed it to Shorty, who was in charge of B Flight.

There was nothing unusual about the order—we had had similar ones every day for the last month—except perhaps that the job looked a little easier than most.

Shorty carefully extracted[2] a fly from his tea and flicked it across the room. Then he read it a second time. "Hell's bells[3], what a piece of cake! Shall I take my flight, Sir? We'll have to start right away."

He handed it to Oofy, who stopped picking the sand out of his starboard[4] ear, read it slowly, then put it down and went on excavating his ear.

"I don't believe it," he said. "They never park them close together, but if they have, what a piece of cake!"

Outside, the Hurricanes were waiting, looking very dirty in their

---

① Sidi Barrani: Sidi Barrani is a town in Egypt, near the Mediterranean Sea, about 95 km (59 mi) east of the border with Libya, and around 240 km (150 mi) from Tobruk, Libya. 西迪巴拉尼(埃及的一座靠近地中海的城市,与利比亚东部边境相聚95公里,距离利比亚的托布鲁克港240公里)

② extract: *Verb* [with obj.] (usu. be extracted) remove or take out, especially by effort or force(用力)移开;取出;拔出

③ hell's bells: (informal) an exclamation of annoyance or anger(非正式)(表示恼怒或生气的感叹词)见鬼;讨厌

④ starboard: *Noun* the side of a ship or aircraft that is on the right when one is facing forward. The opposite of port(船舶、飞机的)右舷;右边(port的反义词)

desert camouflage①, which was just a coat of light-brown paint the color of sand. At a distance they merged into their surroundings. They looked a little thin and underfed, but very elegant.

Under the wings of each, in the shade, sat a fitter② and rigger③ playing naughts and crosses in the hot sand, waiting to help start up.

"All clear."

"All clear, sir." I pressed the button; she coughed once or twice, as though clearing the sand from her throat, and started. Check the oxygen, check the petrol brakes off, taxi into position behind Shorty, airscrew④ into fine pitch, mixture control to "rich," adjust tail trimmer; and now Shorty's holding his thumb up in the air. Yes, O. K. O. K. Thumb up, and everyone else does the same.

Six dusty left arms went out, six throttles were gently pushed forward and the six machines moved away, churning up⑤ the dust with their airscrews and creating a minor sandstorm in their wake⑥. Six people began to concentrate.

Shorty swung a bit to the right on take – off, but he always did that,

---

① camouflage: *Noun* [*Mass Noun*] the disguising of military personnel, equipment, and installations by painting or covering them to make them blend in with their surroundings 军事伪装

② fitter: *Noun* a person who puts together or installs machinery, engine parts, or other equipment 装配工;钳工

③ ringer: *Noun* a person who rigs or attends to the rigging of a sailing ship, aircraft, or parachute(帆船)索具操纵工;(飞机或降落伞)装配工

④ airscrew: *Noun* (Brit.) an aircraft propeller(英国英语)螺旋桨

⑤ churn up: [with obj.] break up the surface of (an area of ground) 打破(地的)表面

⑥ wake: *Noun* a trail of disturbed water or air left by the passage of a ship or aircraft(船)尾波;航迹;(飞机)尾流

and we all knew he always did it, so it didn't matter. Once air - borne, undercart up, adjust the revs, regulate the mixture and start looking.

This business of looking is the most important part of a fighter - pilot's job. You've got to have a rubber neck and you've got to keep it moving the whole time from the moment you get into the air to the moment you arrive back at your base. If you don't, you won't last long. You turn slowly from the extreme left to the extreme right, glancing at your instruments as you go past; and then, looking up high, you turn back again from right to left to start all over again.

Don't start gazing into your cockpit①, or, sure as eggs, you'll get jumped sooner or later; and don't start daydreaming or looking at the beautiful scenery—there's no future in it.

And so we started looking. We were flying straight into the sun, which was just beginning to touch the horizon. It looked like a blood orange. Shorty was leading, with two of us close in on either side in a V formation, with Oofy weaving about in the rear watching our tails. I was on the starboard side, next to Shorty and his wing - tip was only about twelve feet away.

I could see how the heat had blistered② the paint. It was flaking off and showing the shiny steel skin underneath.

It was getting hot in the cockpit. My shirt and pants were dark with sweat, and I smelt like hell. You can't take a bath in four pints of water a day when you've got to use it for drinking as well; at least I can't, because I'm pretty big. Wonder if Shorty could. But then he smelled, too, and so did the C. O. Jimmy smelt worst of all. He used to come into

---

① cockpit: *Noun* a compartment for the pilot, and sometimes also the crew, in an aircraft or spacecraft (飞机或航天器的)飞行员座舱(或机组人员座舱)

② blister: *Verb* [no obj.] form swellings filled with air or fluid on the surface of something 发气泡(或水疱)

breakfast every morning and say, "Hell, I smell good today," and nobody took any notice. When he'd eaten his first piece of bread, he'd look up and say it again, and nobody listened that time either. He told us once that he used to have a bath every day before the war, so I suppose he noticed the change more than most. I could see him there on the other side of Shorty every time my head traveled that way. He was smiling at something—heaven knows what. But then, Jimmy was especially good fond of ground strafes, and this looked like it was going to be a good one. It certainly ought to be, anyway, unless that Recco pilot was seeing things. Those boys don't often exaggerate. Anyway, there ought to be a lot of trucks about. Hope they're not all ambulances.

"Tallyho[①] three o'clock, tallyho three o'clock, tallyho three o'clock, over." I jumped a mile; I always did when someone tallyhoed. It's just a quick way of telling everyone that you've sighted enemy aircraft, and the clock code gives their exact position in relation to your line of flight. The nose of your aircraft is always twelve o'clock; three o'clock is sharp right; six o'clock is dead astern[②], and so on.

This time it was Oofy: I knew his voice over the R. T.[③] Everyone looked to the right, and sure enough, there, high above us, was a bunch of little black specks moving east along the coast in the opposite direction—Italian fighters on their evening patrol. They hadn't seen us because we were flying low over the land and our camouflage was good. Surprising how difficult it is to see aircraft flying low over the land when you're above them. They'd never see us.

---

① tallyho: *Interjection* 吠嗬

Verb 用吆喝声表示发现(狐狸)

② astern: *Adverb* behind or towards the rear of a ship or aircraft 在(或向)船(或飞机)的尾部

③ R. T.: Receiver-Transmitter 收发两用机

Then Oofy again, "Come on, Shorty, you slob[①]. What are you waiting for?"

And Shorty: "Leave them alone, leave them alone, leave them alone. We've got a job on. Keep your eye on them, keep your eye on them, over."

And so it went on. Shorty was right, of course. Oofy was just a blasted fool. He always wanted to do things like that. He'd buy it sooner or later. He was only nineteen and keen as blazes.

We ought to be there soon. We were skimming[②] along about fifty feet above the road at about 300 miles an hour, and I could see that Shorty had slid back the glass hood of his cockpit and was craning his neck and staring ahead of him. The road below seemed to slide under us and shoot past underneath while it was still a half a mile away, and it looked very black. You ought to see that desert road in Libya, the little narrow road that feeds two armies. It's not an ordinary dusty track; it's a modern black tar strip which runs slap[③] bang[④] across the desert from Alexandria to Bengasi[⑤]. It looks funny to see a tarmac highway out

---

① slob: *Noun* (informal) a lazy and slovenly person(非正式)懒汉;粗人;邋遢鬼

② skim: *Verb* [with obj.] pass over (a surface), nearly or lightly touching it in the process 掠过;擦过(表面)

③ slap: *Adverb* (informal) suddenly and directly, especially with great force (非正式)突然;猛然;直接地;径直地

④ bang: *Adverb* (informal, chiefly Brit.) exactly(非正式,主要在英式英语中)正;恰恰 completely 完全;彻底

⑤ Bengasi: Banghāzī, also spelled Benghazi, Italian Bengasi, city and major seaport of northeastern Libya, on the Gulf of Sidra 班加西(利比亚东北的一个城市,位于锡德拉海湾。自从古希腊、罗马时代即有居民,是主要港口,1951 年至 1972 年是利比亚首都。人口 367, 600。)

there.

And then suddenly, right out on the horizon, we saw a small black splodge, and Shorty came again over the R. T. "There they are, there they are, echelon[①] right, echelon right," and the two machines on the other side, together with Oofy moved over to the right, so that we were flying in one long line abreast.

Now quick: Trigger button from "Safe" over to "Fire," reflector sight on, throttle open, airscrew pitch a little finer, and nose down.

The place was stiff with lorries of all sorts, and as we came down I could see the soldiers running about all over the place. They had green uniforms, and I saw one stumble and pick himself up and go on running. I've never seen anyone pick himself up as quickly as that man. I saw another diving underneath a truck which had a large green tarpaulin[②] over it, and a lot of others fell flat on their faces and stayed there, very still.

I sighted about fifty yards in front of a large petrol lorry and pressed the button, and kept it pressed right on through it, so I couldn't miss. Four little sheets of flame burst from each wing, but with your helmet on you don't hear much—just a quick, muffled sort of rattle. You feel more than you hear. The plane seems to pause a little, shakes herself and then goes on. I kept it pressed for a couple of seconds for the benefit of the trucks on the other side of the tanker, and then up and around for another attack. Maybe the first one took five seconds, but I wouldn't know.

We'd all got split up now, and I could see someone already going in a second time. There was a lot of black smoke coming from two or three

---

① echelon: *Verb* [with obj.] (Military) arrange in an echelon formation(军)使列成梯队;使形成梯次配置

② tarpaulin: *Noun* [*Mass Noun*] heavy-duty waterproof cloth, originally of tarred canvas 防水油布

of the petrol wagons and the little green men were still running around between the trucks; and then, away on the left, I saw a lot of bright little flashes. They always were quick on their machine guns, these Italians. There were some more on the right. The flashes showed up quite clearly in the dusk. Better have a go at them; they always run when you come down. No, on second thought, lorries are more important. Must get some more lorries; nice fat petrol lorries; they burn so well.

Down once more, squirting lorries all along and watching the bullets making little flashes where they hit the metal, and throwing up little spurts of sand where they missed. Time to be going now, up and home. Hell's bells, what was that? Felt like she was hit somewhere. Blast this stick; it won't come back. They must have got my tail plane① and jammed my elevators②. Can't go up or down: engine seems O. K., though. Height? What is—Five hundred? Johnny tried to bale out from 500 over camp last week when he came back with his engine on fire, but he hit the ground before she opened. Funny what a big hole he made in the sand. Try the tail trimmer. That's stuck too. Probably be able to pancake③ down later by throttling back slowly. That ought to be easy. Yes, easy. Should be over our own lines again soon, but it's getting dark.

---

① tail plane or tailplane: A tailplane, also known as horizontal stabilizer (or horizontal stabiliser), is a small lifting surface located on the tail (empennage) behind the main lifting surfaces of a fixed-wing aircraft as well as other non-fixed-wing aircraft such as helicopters and gyroplanes 横尾翼;水平尾翼

② elevator: *Noun* a hinged flap on the tail plane of an aircraft, typically one of a pair, used to control the motion of the aircraft about its lateral axis(飞机的)升降舵

③ pancake: *Verb* [no obj.] (of an aircraft) make a pancake landing(飞机)平坠降落

And then Shorty's voice, "What's the matter with you? I'm just behind."

"Hello Shorty. Elevators jammed; otherwise O. K. Think I can make it."

"Good. I'll stay with you."

Then it happened. I don't know what it was that had jammed the elevators on my tail plane, but it had suddenly been shaken loose, and there they were, flapping in the slip stream[①], completely disconnected. The Hurricane dipped its nose and dived toward the ground, and there wasn't a thing I could do. Pulling the stick back made no difference, but I closed the throttle as soon as possible, in an effort to slow down the dive a little. I was doing about 250 miles an hour, so I suppose it took, roughly, two seconds to hit the deck, but it seemed a long two seconds. I remember looking down the nose of the machine at the ground and seeing a little clump of camel thorn[②] growing there all by itself, and my stomach felt as though someone were using it as a pincushion[③] for rusty hatpins.

And then I knew I was still alive, because I could feel the heat around my legs, but I couldn't see a thing. I remember trying to get out, and catching hold of my straps and pulling away at them, but they wouldn't come. I couldn't for the life of me remember where the quick - release pin was placed, and all the time the fire was roasting my legs and hands. Maybe that's what stimulated my brain, because suddenly I

---

① slipstream or slip stream: *Noun* a current of air or water driven back by a revolving propeller or jet engine (螺旋桨或喷气发动机的)滑流

② camel thorn: Alhagi camelorum (of the Middle East) and Acacia giraffae (of southern Africa), family Leguminosae(中东的)骆驼刺及(非洲南部的)吉腊夫氏相思树;豆科

③ pincushion: *Noun* a small pad for holding pins 针垫

remembered it. Of course, the pin was just down in front below the chest, holding all four straps together, and all one had to do was to pull it out. I released it and tried to get out again, but there was something else there weighting me down, and I couldn't move. Once more I sat still and thought, and I could see a lot of red circles going around inside my head, and once more it came back to me suddenly. The parachute. Twist the release and press it in, and now let's get out of this fire.

I didn't seem so strong as I used to be, and I couldn't see a thing, so it took some time to get out and tumble over the side.

Something still seemed to be burning, so I rolled about in the sand to put it out, crawled away from the fire on all fours and lay down.

My face hurt most. I slowly put a hand up to feel it. It was very sticky. My nose didn't seem to be there. I tried to feel my teeth to see if they were still there, but it seemed as though one or two were missing. And then the machine guns started off. I knew right away what it was. There were about fifty rounds of ammunition left in each of my eight guns and, without thinking, I had crawled away from the fire out in front of the machine, and they were going off in the heat.

I could hear them hitting the sand and stones all round, but I didn't feel like getting up and moving right then, so I dozed off.

Then, all of a sudden, there was Shorty, dancing around and yelling like a madman, and shaking my hand and saying, "I thought you were still inside! How did you get out? I couldn't land right by you, it was too bumpy, so I came down half a mile away and ran like hell. Are you all right?"

I said, "Shorty, where's my blasted nose?" and he said, "What d'you mean, where's your blasted nose?"

"It's not here," I said.

I heard him striking a match in the dark, and then he said, "Where's your blasted nose? What a mess! Does it hurt?"

"Don't be a damn fool. Of course it hurts."

And then he said he was going back to his machine to get some morphia[①] out of the emergency pack which we always carry in the fuselage[②], but he came back again soon and said he couldn't find the machine in the dark.

And then it started to get cold. It always gets cold at night in the desert, and Shorty lay down close alongside, so that we could both keep a little warmer. Every now and then he would say, "You'll look funny without a nose. I've never seen a man without a nose before. They'll laugh like hell." I kept spewing[③] a lot of blood, and every time I did it, Shorty lit a match. And then he gave me a cigarette, but it got wet, and I didn't want it anyway.

I don't know how long we stayed there maybe four or five hours. And then two or three British soldiers came up and wanted to know if we were Italians.

Shorty said, no, we damn well weren't and how far were we from Mersa Matruh[④]? I don't remember much more, except that I was shoved about a lot, and someone kept saying "Take it easy." I believe someone had some morphia.

Middle East war communiqué, Cairo: There was little air activity yesterday on either side. A formation of our fighters attacked enemy transport on the ground near Sidi Barrani, damaging a number of

---

① morphia: *Noun* old-fashioned term for "morphine" 吗啡

② fuselage: *Noun* the main body of an aircraft(飞机的)机身

③ spew: *Verb* [with obj.] expel large quantities of (something) rapidly and forcibly(大量)喷出;(快速)放出;涌出

④ Mersa Matruh: a town on the Mediterranean coast of Egypt, 250 km (156 miles) west of Alexandria; pop. 112,770 (1990) 马特鲁(埃及地中海滨海城镇,在亚历山大港以西250公里,即156英里处;1990年人口112,770。)

vehicles. One of our planes is missing, but the pilot is safe.

三、翻译探索

本篇翻译的难点是飞机操作方面的一些表达，专业性比较强，处理到位实属不易。另外，有些地名也要力求跟现有的译名保持一致。实在查找不到的，就只有根据读音来音译了。

坠机余生

他们将一枚标牌挂到我的脖子上，上面写着："飞行军官——颅骨基部可能碎裂、脑震荡、面部受伤，信奉英国国教。"这一点我清楚，因为在基地医院，医疗护理员把标牌上的内容给我朗读出来了。

我尽力要回忆起为什么会有这样一个标牌挂在脖子上，也要回忆起标牌上为什么要写上这样的内容。我尽量去问别人是怎么回事，但是，没人听见我说话。于是，我干脆不问了，只是一动不动地躺在那里。然后，慢慢地，一切都重现了：刚开始，不很清楚，也不很明亮，而是有一点儿暗淡，就好像是朦胧月光下看到的情景。最终，一切我都弄明白了。

军事行动命令下达了——从位于利比亚沙漠总部的战斗机编号到空军中队的编号都包括进去了——雷科报告说，有大量的意大利车辆紧密停靠在一起，位置就在西迪巴拉尼西部 65 公里处以北不到 90 米的公路上。黄昏时分，六架飓风战机要发起进攻。

我们大家待在军人食堂的帐篷里，吃着已经过了正点的午后茶点，这时指挥官手里拿着那道命令溜达了进来，把命令递给了矮个子肖迪，肖迪是第二趟飞行任务的负责人。

这道命令本身没有什么奇特之处——过去一个月时间里，每天我们都能接到多道类似的命令，只不过，这次的任务看起来要比多数任务简单一些。

肖迪仔细地将一只苍蝇从茶水中取出来，用手指将其弹过屋子，随后他又读了一遍命令。"见鬼，小菜一碟啊！我要起飞吗，长官？我们将立刻行动。"

他将那道命令递给了阔绰的奥菲,奥菲不再从其右舷侧的耳朵里往外掏沙子了,而是慢慢地读着命令上的内容,然后放下命令继续挖耳朵。

"我不相信这上面的内容,"他说。"他们从未在一起停靠过,但如果真是这样,可就是小菜一碟啦!"

外面,装扮了沙漠伪装物的飓风战机看起来脏兮兮的。那层伪装物其实就是一层沙子般淡棕色的油漆。从远处看去,飞机跟周围环境融合得很好——虽然看起来有点瘦弱,甚至营养不良,但很雅致。

每一只机翼下方的阴影里都坐着一位钳工和装配工,在热沙子上玩着"○×"井字棋游戏。

"一切就绪。"

"一切就绪,长官。"我按下了按钮,飞机喘息了一两声,就好像要将沙子从喉咙里清理出去似的,随即发动起来了。检查氧气量,松开油量闸,滑行到肖迪那架飞机的后方就位,螺旋桨调整到精确的螺距状态,燃油混合比调到"高燃"位置,调节好尾部配平器。现在,肖迪将大拇指竖起,举到空中。是的,OK,OK,拇指竖起,大家也都竖起了拇指。

六只布满尘土的左臂伸了出来,六个油门杆被轻轻地向前推去,六架飞机开始移动、起飞,螺旋桨卷起尘土,尾流形成一道微小的沙尘暴。六个人要开始全身心投入了。

起飞时,肖迪的机身稍微向右摇摆了一下。他总是这样做,我们大家都知道他总是这样做,所以,没有人在意。一旦飞到空中,收起起落架,调整好发动机的转数,调整好油量混合比,就要开始察看了。

对于战斗机驾驶员来说,察看这份工作尤为重要。你要长着一个橡胶脖子,从升空时刻起一直到返回基地那一刻止,你的脖子要一刻不停地转来转去。要是不旋转的话,你的命就不会长久。你要慢慢地从大左边转向大右边,边转边盯着各种仪表看,边转边向上面的高空看。然后,从右向左再来一遍,循环往复。

不要盯着驾驶舱内部看,也不要把握十足,那样你迟早得跳伞。

不要胡思乱想做白日梦，也不要欣赏机外的美景，那样没有任何前途。

因此呢，我们开始察看了。我们径直朝太阳方向飞去，太阳刚刚接触到地平线，看起来像一只红彤彤的橙子。肖迪打头阵，两边分别有我们的两架战机呈“V”字形跟进，奥菲跟在我们的尾部迂回穿行。我飞在右舷一侧，紧挨着肖迪飞，他的机翼尖部就在三米半以远的地方。

我能够看见，热量致使油漆起了泡，成片状脱落，显露出下面闪闪发亮的钢制外壳。

驾驶舱里开始热了起来。我的衬衫和短裤被汗水浸湿而变暗，闻起来恶臭无比。一天供应两升多的水，还包括饮用的，这点水是无法用来洗澡的，至少我不会拿来洗澡，因为我块头很大。寻思着，矮个子的肖迪或许会拿来洗澡吧。但是，他身上也发出臭味，指挥官也一样，但吉米闻起来最臭。每天早晨进去吃饭时，他常常说：“见鬼，今天我身上闻起来味道不错啊。”对此，没有谁会在意。吃完第一片面包后，他抬起头，又说了一遍。这一次，还是没有去听他的话。有一次，他告诉我们说，战争之前他常常是一天洗一次澡，因此，我想他比多数人更能注意到自己的变化。每一次我向那个方向看，我都能看到他。他在肖迪的另一侧，正对着什么东西微笑着——天知道他对着什么在微笑呢。可当时，吉米特别喜欢地面低空扫射，而这次任务看起来会是一个很好的低空扫射机会。不管怎么说，这次当然应该是一次低空扫射的好机会——如果那个叫雷科的飞行员当时看到的情况属实的话。那些小伙子不常夸大其词。无论如何，周围应该有不少卡车，希望那些不是救护车。

“呔嗬三点钟，呔嗬三点钟，呔嗬三点钟，完毕。”我惊恐不已。一听到有人发出“呔嗬”声，我总是会惊恐不已。这种声音旨在快速告诉大家：已经发现了敌机；时钟编码给出的是敌机的准确位置，这个位置与你的飞行线路相关。飞机前面的突出部分总是指向十二点，三点钟在正右方，六点钟正好指向飞机的尾部，以此类推。

这次喊话的是奥菲，通过对讲机我听出是他的声音。大家都朝右面看去。完全可以肯定的是,右方头顶上空有一串小黑点朝着相反方向沿着海岸线向东移动——意大利战斗机在进行傍晚巡逻。他们没有看见我们,因为我们贴着地面作低空飞行,而且我们伪装得很好。令人吃惊的是,要是你在上空,你就很难发现下方贴近地面低空飞行的飞机。他们永远都不会看见我们。

接着,奥菲又喊道:"快呀,肖迪,你这个邋遢鬼。你还等什么?"

肖迪回应:"别搭理他们,别搭理他们,别搭理他们。我们有任务在身。提防点儿他们,提防点儿他们,完毕。"

情况就这样继续下去。当然,肖迪说的没错。奥菲就是一个该死的傻蛋,总是像那样鲁莽行事,早晚会搭上性命。毕竟,他只有十八岁,热烈而火爆。

我们应该很快达到那个地点。我们从距离路面十五六米的空中掠过,速度大约是每小时480公里。我看见肖迪滑开了驾驶舱的玻璃罩,伸长脖子盯着前方。下方的公路离我们虽然有八百米的距离,却似乎从我们底下滑过,从我们下方一闪而过,看起来黑黑的。你应该来看看利比亚的沙漠公路——虽狭窄,却供两只军队使用。这不是一条普通的沙尘小径,而是一条现代的黑色柏油狭长带——从亚历山大港径直穿越沙漠,延伸至班加西。荒漠之中有这样一条柏油碎石铺就的公路,看起来很有意思。

突然之间,就在地平线处,我们看见一块小小的黑点。对讲机里又传来肖迪的声音:"看到他们啦,看到他们啦。向右列成梯队,向右列成梯队。"另一边的两架飞机连同奥菲的飞机一起向右移动,这样我们大家就呈一条长线并排飞行了。

现在,动作要快:射击按钮从"保险"状态切换到"开火"状态,扣上反射式瞄准镜,打开油门杆,螺旋桨调整到比较精确的螺距状态,飞机前端朝下。

下方那个地方满是各种运货卡车。向下俯冲时,我可以看见士兵在那里到处乱跑。他们都穿着绿色的制服。我看到其中一个跌倒在地,爬起来继续奔跑。我从未看到有哪一个人爬起的速度像他那样快。我还看见另一个士兵钻到一辆卡车的底下,那辆卡车上罩着一张防水帆布。其他很多人都脸朝下躺倒在地，一动也不动。

我将准星瞄在一辆运送汽油的卡车前方约四十五米的地方，按下了按钮，整个发射过程一直按着没有松开，于是，我知道目标肯定会被击中的。每只机翼喷射出四小片火焰，但是，你的脑袋扣着头盔，听不见太多的声音，只能听见快速而沉闷的那种"格格"声。更大的声音是你感觉到的，而不是你听到的。此时，飞机似乎暂停了一小下，机身摇晃着，然后继续飞行。出于对坦克另一边那几辆卡车的考虑，我将开火按钮多按住几秒钟，然后将之抬起，接着升空，转过身来进行另一番攻击。第一番攻击我或许用了五秒钟，但是，我不得而知。

现在，我们大家都分散开了。我能够看见，有人进行第二轮攻击了。两三辆运送汽油的卡车冒出大量的浓烟，小绿人仍然在卡车间慌乱地奔跑。紧接着，在左边以远的地方，我看见一些明亮的小点闪烁起来——这些意大利人用起机枪来动作就是快。右边也出现了更多的亮点。黄昏时分，这些亮点十分显眼。最好俯冲下去，打击他们一下。只要你俯冲下去，他们总是会四散奔逃。仔细再一想：不，卡车更为重要，一定要再击中一些卡车——笨重的运送汽油的卡车很不错，燃烧效果如此好啊。

再次俯冲下去，对着卡车一阵喷射，看见子弹在击中金属的地方闪出火花，在没有击中的地方溅起一小股、一小股的沙尘。现在是离开的时间了——向上拔起，往家飞行。真见鬼，那是什么？感觉飞机某处被击中了，击坏了就回不去了。他们一定是击中了我的水平尾翼，卡住了升降舵——无法升降了。尽管如此，引擎似乎还可以。高度呢？不会吧——150 米？上一周，约翰尼驾机返回时引擎着火，在营地上方 150 米高度时他尽力跳伞出舱，但是，没等伞打开，他就落了地。有意思的是，他在沙子上留下了好大一个坑。试试尾部配平器吧，也卡住了——或许随后慢慢调节油门减速时能够平坠降落吧。平坠降落应该容易做到，是的，容易做到。应该很快就会飞到我们的阵线上空，但是，天开始黑下来了。

接着传来肖迪的声音："你怎么啦？我就在你后面。"

"嘿,肖迪。升降舵卡住了,其他的没啥事儿。估计我能处理好。"

"好的。我不离开你。"

接下来,事故就发生了。我不知道是什么东西卡住了水平尾翼上的升降舵,但见水平尾翼突然间因为振动而松弛。这下坏了,升降舵在螺旋桨搅起的滑流中摇摆,完全散了架。飓风战机前端下沉,向地面俯冲下去,对此我无计可施。向后拉操纵杆,但拉与不拉没有什么区别。于是,我尽可能快地将油门关闭,力图放慢俯冲的速度。当时的速度是每小时400公里——我想大致就是这个速度。驾驶舱触地只需两秒的时间,但那似乎是漫长的两秒钟。我记得顺着飞机的前端往地面看去,看到那儿独自生长着一丛骆驼刺植物——感觉就像有人把那丛植物做成了针垫一样,针垫上插满了一根根布满沙尘的帽针。

紧接着,我知道我还活着,因为我能感觉到我双腿周围的热度,但是,我什么都看不见了。我记得我尽力要出去,抓住了固定带要拉开,但就是拉不开。我拼命地想,却怎么也想不起快速释放栓在什么位置,而大火自始至终烘烤着我的双腿和双手。或许这种烘烤刺激了我的大脑,因为突然之间我记起来了。当然,释放栓就在身前的下方胸部下面的位置上,它将四条固定带固定到了一起,只需将其拔出即可。我将释放栓拔出,再次要尽力出去,但还有其他什么东西将我往下压,令我无法移动。我再次静坐下来开始思考。我看到很多的红圈圈在我的大脑里萦绕,突然之间,我再一次记忆起来——降落伞。扭动释放钮,将其压进去。现在,让我们脱离火海吧。

我似乎没有以前那么强壮,两眼也什么都看不见,所以,费了些时间才出来,踉踉跄跄地跌到了一侧。

身上似乎还有什么东西在燃烧,于是,我在沙子里打滚将火熄灭,四肢着地爬离火源后,躺了下来。

我的脸烧得最重,我慢慢抬起一只手摸了摸,黏糊糊的。我的鼻子好像也不在那儿了。我尽力去摸了摸牙齿,想知道牙齿是否都在,但是,有一两颗牙齿似乎不见了。接着,机枪响了起来,我立刻明白是怎么回事儿了。我那架飞机上的八挺机枪中,每一挺里都剩下大约五十发子弹。于是，我不假思索爬离机枪前面的火海，任其在灼热中"格格嗒嗒"射击。

我能够听见那几挺机枪射击到周围的沙子和石头上发出的声音，但是就在当时，我不想起身，也不想移动。最终，我打起盹来，睡着了。

接着，突然之间肖迪出现了。他四处蹦跳，疯一般呼喊，摇晃着我的手说："我还以为你还在里面呢！你是怎么出来的？我无法在你旁边着陆——崎岖不平的，所以我在八百米以远的地方降落，猛劲跑了过来。你还好吧？"

我回答："肖迪，我毁掉的鼻子哪去了？"他回应道："你毁掉的鼻子哪去了？你说这话是什么意思？"

"鼻子不在了，"我说。

黑暗中，我听见他擦燃一根火柴，说道："你毁掉的鼻子哪去了？模糊一片啊！疼吗？"

"别犯傻了，当然疼了。"

然后，他说他要回到自己飞机那儿从急救箱里取些吗啡来，那只急救箱他总是随飞机携带。但是，他很快又折了回来，说在黑暗中无法找到自己的飞机。

接下来，天气就开始变冷了。沙漠的夜晚总是很冷的。肖迪紧挨着我躺下，以便我们能够保暖一点儿。他不时地说："没有鼻子，你看起来很滑稽。以前我看到过一个没有鼻子的人，没有鼻子的人笑起来很恐怖。"我不断吐血，吐了很多。每次一吐血，肖迪就点燃一根火柴。接着，他给了我一根烟，但烟弄湿了，再说，我也不想抽了。

我不知道我们在那儿呆了多长时间，或许四五个小时吧。然后，两三个英国士兵走上前来，想弄清楚我们是不是意大利人。

肖迪说，不，我们根本不是什么该死的意大利人，我们离玛特鲁多远？我记不得更多，就记得我被推来晃去，有人不断地说："放松。"我相信，有人一定带吗啡过来了。

发自开罗的中东战时公报是这样说的：昨天双方几乎没有什么空中战事。我方一个战斗机编队在靠近西迪巴拉尼的地面上攻击了敌方的运输车,毁掉了很多车辆。我方一架战斗机失踪,但飞行员没有生命危险。

第三节 《希腊孤女》*Katina*

罗尔德·达尔的《希腊孤女》(Katina)首次发表在《女士家庭杂志》(Ladies' Home Journal)1944年3月号上。后来,这篇故事又收录到《向你飞跃》(Over to You)、《罗尔德·达尔短篇故事集锦》(The Collected Short Stories of Roald Dahl)、《五部畅销书集》(5 Bestsellers)、《〈伟大写手〉及其他故事集》(The Great Automatic Grammatizator and Other Stories)、《〈卖伞男子〉及其他故事集》(The Umbrella Man and Other Stories)等书中。

《希腊孤女》选取的还是"隐姓埋名"的第一人称视角"我"——其实就是作家本人的化身,描述的是"第一场希腊之战中,英国皇家飞行员最后几天的事情(the last days of RAF fighters in the first Greek campaign)"。

一、原作导读

达尔这部小说里的故事发生在1941年4月初,地点在希腊的帕拉米西亚村。三名英国皇家空军飞行员暂时没有飞行任务,来到被德军轰炸后的帕拉米西亚村,看看能否帮上点什么忙。结果,他们发现了一个希腊小女孩一声不响地坐着,小女孩前额划出一道口子,鲜血直流。于是,他们三个人将小女孩抬回机场,让随队医生为她治疗。等到小女孩伤势好转的时候,他们得知,她的名字叫卡蒂娜,家人都死于轰炸中。

有一次,德军飞机轰炸小机场,士兵们都躲进了战壕,但卡蒂娜却站在场地里冲着敌军的轰炸机喊叫。就在那天晚上,她被正式列为他们飞行中队的队员。中队转移,她也跟着转移。每转移一次,就有更多的飞机遭受损失,战场情况也就变得越来越糟。

最终，他们中队转移到了一个叫迈加拉的小村庄，迫不得已使用了那里自修的狭窄跑道，最后将飞机藏到林子里。随后，队员接到命令，要飞机起飞去执行一次重要的护航任务，但没料到的是，德军早已作了打歼灭战的准备。第一架飞机甚至还没有飞离地面，就被敌机击中。德军的"梅塞施米特"战机"嗡嗡"飞过，将余下来的来不及起飞的战机一架架摧毁，大家急忙奔向掩体躲避。

就在这时，"我"探出头来，看见卡蒂娜向跑道中央奔去。她站在跑道中央，对着空中的敌机挥起了双拳。一架"梅塞施米特"向她射击，她跌倒在地。士兵纷纷向她跑去，但为时已晚，她已经死去。

"我"站在那儿，盯着熊熊燃烧的火焰，感到绝望和渺茫——"透过火焰，我看到的不是横七竖八、冒着黑烟的飞机残骸，而是希腊人民心中燃烧着的、难以抑制的怒火，那火愈烧愈炽热，愈烧愈强烈。"(I saw beyond it not a tangled mass of smoking wreckage, but the flames of a hotter and intenser fire which now burned and smouldered in the hearts of the people of Greece.)

"我"继续盯着火焰，盯着，盯着，眼前出现了幻觉——"透过这层亮光，我看到一个小女孩站在一个场地的中央，太阳光照亮了她的头发。就在一瞬间，她抬头仰望天空，天空蔚蓝而清澈，没有一丝云彩。紧接着，她转过身，看着我。就在她转身的时候，我看见她那件白色的印花衣服前面被浸得通红——鲜血一样的颜色。"(... and through it, beyond it, I saw a young child standing in the middle of a field with the sunlight shining in her hair. For a moment she stood looking up into the sky, which was clear and blue and without any clouds; then she turned and looked towards me, and as she turned I saw that the front of her white print dress was stained deep red, the colour of blood.)

这就是在第一场希腊战争中，作者在战场上亲眼目睹的几件事情。

二、原作释读

本篇难度适中，难点不多。有点纪实文学的色彩——真实，令人身临其境。

Katina[①]

Some brief notes about the last days of RAF fighters in the first Greek campaign.

Peter saw her first.

She was sitting on a stone, quite still, with her hands resting on her lap. She was staring vacantly ahead, seeing nothing, and all around, up and down the little street, people were running backward and forward with buckets of water, emptying them through the windows of the burning houses.

Across the street on the cobblestones, there was a dead boy. Someone had moved his body close in to the side so that it would not be in the way.

A little farther down an old man was working on a pile of stones and rubble. One by one he was carrying the stones away and dumping them to the side. Sometimes he would bend down and peer into the ruins, repeating a name over and over again.

All around there was shouting and running and fires and buckets of water and dust. And the girl sat quietly on the stone, staring ahead, not moving. There was blood running down the left side of her face. It ran down from her forehead and dropped from her chin on to the dirty print dress she was wearing.

Peter saw her and said, "Look at that little girl."

We went up to her and Fin put his hand on her shoulder, bending

---

① 本部小说原文出自"Roald Dahl. *The Collected Short Stories of Roald Dahl*[M]. England: Penguin Books Ltd., 1992"。

down to examine the cut. "Looks like a piece of shrapnel[①]," he said. "She ought to see the Doc."

Peter and I made a chair with our hands and Fin lifted her up on to it. We started back through the streets and out towards the aerodrome, the two of us walking a little awkwardly, bending down, facing our burden. I could feel Peter's fingers clasping tightly in mine and I could feel the buttocks of the little girl resting lightly on my wrists. I was on the left side and the blood was dripping down from her face on to the arm of my flying suit, running down the waterproof cloth on to the back of my hand. The girl never moved or said anything.

Fin said, "She's bleeding rather fast. We'd better walk a bit quicker."

I couldn't see much of her face because of the blood, but I could tell that she was lovely. She had high cheekbones and large round eyes, pale blue like an autumn sky, and her hair was short and fair. I guessed she was about nine years old.

This was in Greece in early April, 1941, at Paramythia[②]. Our fighter squadron was stationed on a muddy field near the village. We were in a deep valley and all around us were the mountains. The freezing winter had passed, and now, almost before anyone knew it, spring had come. It had come quietly and swiftly, melting the ice on the lakes and brushing the snow off the mountain tops; and all over the airfield we could see the pale green shoots of grass pushing up through the mud, making a carpet for our landings. In our valley there were warm winds

---

① shrapnel: *Noun* [*Mass Noun*] fragments of a bomb, shell, or other object thrown out by an explosion 炸弹碎片

② Paramythia: *Noun* Paramythia is a village and a former municipality in Thesprotia, Epirus, Greece. Since the 2011 local government reform it is part of the municipality Souli, of which it is the seat and a municipal unit 帕拉米西亚

and wild flowers.

The Germans, who had pushed in through Yugoslavia[①] a few days before, were now operating in force, and that afternoon they had come over very high with about thirty-five Dorniers and bombed the village. Peter and Fin and I were off duty for a while, and the three of us had gone down to see if there was anything we could do in the way of rescue work. We had spent a few hours digging around in the ruins and helping to put out fires, and we were on our way back when we saw the girl.

Now, as we approached the landing field, we could see the Hurricanes circling around coming in to land, and there was the Doc standing out in front of the dispersal tent, just as he should have been, waiting to see if anyone had been hurt. We walked towards him, carrying the child, and Fin, who was a few yards in front, said, "Doc, you lazy old devil, here's a job for you."

The Doc was young and kind and morose[②] except when he got drunk. When he got drunk he sang very well.

"Take her into the sick bay[③]," he said. Peter and I carried her in and put her down on a chair. Then we left her and wandered over to the dispersal tent to see how the boys had got along.

It was beginning to get dark. There was a sunset behind the ridge over in the west, and there was a full moon, a bombers' moon, climbing up into the sky. The moon shone upon the shoulders of the tents and

---

① Yugoslavia: a federation of states in SE Europe, in the Balkans 南斯拉夫(欧洲东南部巴尔干半岛的联邦国家。)

② morose: *Adjective* sullen and ill-tempered 闷闷不乐的;阴郁的(e. g. She was morose and silent when she got home. 回到家后,她闷闷不乐,一声不吭。)

③ sick bay or sickbay: *Noun* a room or building set aside for the treatment or accommodation of the sick, especially within a military base, ship, or school 军舰上的或驻地的医院或卫生所

made them white; small white pyramids, standing up straight, clustering in little orderly groups around the edges of the aerodrome. They had a scared-sheep look about them the way they clustered themselves together, and they had a human look about them the way they stood up close to one another, and it seemed almost as though they knew that there was going to be trouble, as though someone had warned them that they might be forgotten and left behind. Even as I looked, I thought I saw them move. I thought I saw them huddle just a fraction nearer together.

And then, silently, without a sound, the mountains crept a little closer into our valley.

For the next two days there was much flying. There was the getting up at dawn, there was the flying, the fighting and the sleeping; and there was the retreat of the army. That was about all there was or all there was time for. But on the third day the clouds dropped down over the mountains and slid into the valley. And it rained. So we sat around in the mess-tent drinking beer and resinato①, while the rain made a noise like a sewing machine on the roof. Then lunch. For the first time in days the whole squadron was present. Fifteen pilots at a long table with benches on either side and Monkey, the CO sitting at the head.

We were still in the middle of our fried corned beef when the flap of the tent opened and in came the Doc with an enormous dripping raincoat over his head. And with him, under the coat, was the little girl. She had a bandage round her head.

The Doc said, "Hello. I've brought a guest." We looked around and suddenly, automatically, we all stood up.

The Doc was taking off his raincoat and the little girl was standing

---

① resinato: (Italian) resinated (wine etc) 带有树脂香味的葡萄酒 resinate: *Verb* [with obj.] impregnate or flavour with resin 用树脂浸渍;使带树脂香味

there with her hands hanging loose by her sides looking at the men, and the men were all looking at her. With her fair hair and pale skin she looked less like a Greek than anyone I've ever seen. She was frightened by the fifteen scruffy[①]-looking foreigners who had suddenly stood up when she came in, and for a moment she half-turned as if she were going to run away out into the rain.

Monkey said, "Hallo. Hallo there. Come and sit down."

"Talk Greek," the Doc said. "She doesn't understand."

Fin and Peter and I looked at one another and Fin said, "Good God, it's our little girl. Nice work, Doc."

She recognized Fin and walked round to where he was standing. He took her by the hand and sat her down on the bench, and everyone else sat down too. We gave her some fried corned beef and she ate it slowly, looking down at her plate while she ate. Monkey said, "Get Pericles."

Pericles was the Greek interpreter attached to the squadron. He was a wonderful man we'd picked up at Yanina, where he had been the local school teacher. He had been out of work ever since the war started. "The children do not come to school," he said. "They are up in the mountains and fight. I cannot teach sums to the stones."

Pericles came in. He was old, with a beard, a long pointed nose and sad grey eyes. You couldn't see his mouth, but his beard had a way of smiling when he talked.

"Ask her her name," said Monkey.

He said something to her in Greek. She looked up and said, "Katina." That was all she said.

"Look, Pericles," Peter said, "ask her what she was doing sitting by that heap of ruins in the village."

① scruffy: *Adjective* shabby and untidy or dirty 破旧的;不整洁的

Fin said, "For God's sake leave her alone."

"Ask her, Pericles," said Peter.

"What should I ask?" said Pericles, frowning.

Peter said, "What she was doing sitting on that heap of stuff in the village when we found her."

Pericles sat down on the bench beside her and he talked to her again. He spoke gently and you could see that his beard was smiling a little as he spoke, helping her. She listened and it seemed a long time before she answered. When she spoke, it was only a few words, and the old man translated: "She says that her family were under the stones."

Outside the rain was coming down harder than ever. It beat upon the roof of the mess-tent so that the canvas shivered as the water bounced upon it. I got up and walked over and lifted the flap of the tent. The mountains were invisible behind the rain, but I knew they were around us on every side. I had a feeling that they were laughing at us, laughing at the smallness of our numbers and at the hopeless courage of the pilots. I felt that it was the mountains, not us, who were the clever ones. Had not the hills that very morning turned and looked northward towards Tepelene[①] where they had seen a thousand German aircraft gathered under the shadow of Olympus? Was it not true that the snow on the top of Dodona had melted away in a day, sending little rivers of water running down across our landing field? Had not Kataphidi buried his head in a cloud so that our pilots might be tempted to fly through the whiteness and crash against his rugged shoulders?

And as I stood there looking at the rain through the tent flap, I knew for certain that the mountains had turned against us. I could feel it in my

---

① Tepelene：此处的"Tepelene"，以及本段中的"Dodona""Kataphidi"都是指主人公驻地周围的希腊山脉的名字。

stomach.

I went back into the tent and there was Fin, sitting beside Katina, trying to teach her English words. I don't know whether he made much progress, but I do know that once he made her laugh and that was a wonderful thing for him to have done. I remember the sudden sound of her high laughter and how we all looked up and saw her face; how we saw how different it was to what it had been before. No one but Fin could have done it. He was so gay himself that it was difficult to be serious in his presence. He was gay and tall and black-haired, and he was sitting there on the bench, leaning forward, whispering and smiling, teaching Katina to speak English and teaching her how to laugh.

* * *

The next day the skies cleared and once again we saw the mountains. We did a patrol over the troops which were already retreating slowly towards Thermopylae①, and we met some Messerschmitts② and Ju-

---

① Thermopylae: *Noun* a pass between the mountains and the sea in Greece, about 200 km (120 miles) north-west of Athens, originally narrow but now much widened by the recession of the sea. In 480 B. C. it was the scene of the defence against the Persian army of Xerxes I by 6,000 Greeks; among them were 300 Spartans, all of whom, including their king Leonidas, were killed.

塞莫皮莱(又译温泉关,希腊山海间的一个山口,距雅典西北部约200公里,即120英里,原先窄小,现由于海的后退而渐宽,公元前480年6,000名希腊人在此处抗击薛西斯一世率领的波斯军队时全部牺牲,其中包括300名斯巴达人和他们的国王莱奥尼达斯),本文译作"温泉关"。)

② Messerschmitt: *Noun* aircraft in full Bayerische Flugzeugwerke 109, also called Me 109 Nazi Germany's most important fighter aircraft, both in operational importance and in numbers produced(第二次世界大战期间德国空军使用的)梅塞施米特式战斗机(尤指ME109型)

87s[①] dive-bombing the soldiers. I think we got a few of them, but they got Sandy. I saw him going down. I sat quite still for thirty seconds and watched his plane spiralling gently downward. I sat and waited for the parachute. I remember switching over my radio and saying quietly, "Sandy, you must jump now. You must jump; you're getting near the ground." But there was no parachute.

When we landed and taxied in, there was Katina, standing outside the dispersal tent with the Doc; a tiny shrimp of a girl in a dirty print dress, standing there watching the machines as they came in to land. To Fin, as he walked in, she said, "Tha girisis xana."

Fin said, "What does it mean, Pericles?"

"It just means 'you are back again'," and he smiled.

The child had counted the aircraft on her fingers as they took off, and now she noticed that there was one missing. We were standing around taking off our parachutes and she was trying to ask us about it, when suddenly someone said, "Look out. Here they come." They came through a gap in the hills, a mass of thin, black silhouettes[②], coming down upon the aerodrome.

---

① Ju or Junkers: It was a major German aircraft manufacturer. It produced some of the world's most innovative and best-known airplanes over the course of its fifty-plus year history in Dessau, Germany. "Ju"是"Junkers"的简写形式,原指德国的一家著名的飞机制造公司,本文中指的是德国的容克斯战机。它是第二次世界大战时纳粹德国空军(Luftwaffe)所使用的双活塞式引擎中型军用机,从1939年开始服役到1945年。于20世纪30年代中期由容克斯飞机与发动机制造厂的总设计师雨果·容克斯(Hugo Junkers)亲手设计出来。

② silhouette: *Noun* the dark shape and outline of someone or something visible against a lighter background, especially in dim light (尤指在暗淡光线中浅色背景下的)黑色轮廓像;剪影

There was a scramble for the slit trenches[①] and I remember seeing Fin catch Katina round the waist and carry her off with us, and I remember seeing her fight like a tiger the whole way to the trenches.

As soon as we got into the trench and Fin had let her go, she jumped out and ran over on to the airfield. Down came the Messerschmitts with their guns blazing, swooping so low that you could see the noses of the pilots sticking out under their goggles. Their bullets threw up spurts of dust all around and I saw one of our Hurricanes burst into flames. I saw Katina standing right in the middle of the field, standing firmly with her legs astride and her back to us, looking up at the Germans as they dived past. I have never seen anything smaller and more angry and more fierce in my life. She seemed to be shouting at them, but the noise was great and one could hear nothing at all except the engines and the guns of the aeroplanes.

Then it was over. It was over as quickly as it had begun, and no one said very much except Fin, who said, "I wouldn't have done that, ever; not even if I was crazy."

That evening Monkey got out the squadron records and added Katina's name to the list of members, and the equipment officer was ordered to provide a tent for her. So, on the eleventh of April, 1941, she became a member of the squadron.

In two days she knew the first name or nickname of every pilot and Fin had already taught her to say "Any luck?" and "Nice work."

But that was a time of much activity, and when I try to think of it hour by hour, the whole period becomes hazy in my mind. Mostly, I

① slit trench: *Noun* a narrow trench for a soldier or a small group of soldiers and their equipment 狭长掩壕

remember, it was escorting the Blenheims① to Valona②, and if it wasn't that, it was a ground - strafe of Italian trucks on the Albanian③ border or an SOS from the Northumberland④ Regiment saying they were having the hell bombed out of them by half the aircraft in Europe.

None of that can I remember. I can remember nothing of that time clearly, save for two things. The one was Katina and how she was with us all the time; how she was everywhere and how wherever she went the people were pleased to see her. The other thing that I remember was when the Bull came into the mess - tent one evening after a lone patrol. The Bull was an enormous man with massive, slightly hunched shoulders and his chest was like the top of an oak table. Before the war he had done many things, most of them things which one could not do unless one conceded beforehand that there was no difference between life and death. He was quiet and casual and when he came into a room or into a tent, he always looked as though he had made a mistake and hadn't really meant to come in at all. It was getting dark and we were sitting round in the tent

---

① Blenheim: *Noun* 布伦亨(德国西南滨多瑙河的一村落,1704年英军大胜法军于此),本文指的是布雷尼单翼轰炸机。

② Volona: *Noun* Also known as Vlore, one of the biggest towns and the second largest port city of Albania with a population of 79,948. It is the city where the Albanian Declaration of Independence was proclaimed on November 28, 1912. The city was for a short time the capital of Albania. 发罗拉(阿尔巴尼亚一城市)

③ Albanian: *Adjective* of or relating to Albania or its people or their language (与)阿尔巴尼亚(有关)的

④ Northumberland: *Noun* a county in NE England, on the Scottish border; county town, Morpeth 诺森伯兰郡(英格兰东北部的郡,与苏格兰相邻,首府莫珀斯。)

playing shove-halfpenny[①] when the Bull came in. We knew that he had just landed.

He glanced around a little apologetically, then he said, "Hello," and wandered over to the bar and began to get out a bottle of beer.

Someone said, "See anything, Bull?"

The Bull said, "Yes," and went on fiddling with the bottle of beer.

I suppose we were all very interested in our game of shove-halfpenny because no one said anything else for about five minutes. Then Peter said, "What did you see, Bull?"

The Bull was leaning against the bar, alternately sipping his beer and trying to make a hooting noise by blowing down the neck of the empty bottle.

Peter said, "What did you see?"

The Bull put down the bottle and looked up. "Five S – 79s," he said.

I remember hearing him say it, but I remember also that our game was exciting and that Fin had one more shove to win. We all watched him miss it and Peter said, "Fin, I think you're going to lose." And Fin said, "Go to hell."

We finished the game, then I looked up and saw the Bull still leaning against the bar making noises with his beer bottle.

He said, "This sounds like the old Mauretania coming into New York harbour," and he started blowing into the bottle again.

"What happened with the S – 79s?" I said.

He stopped his blowing and put down the bottle.

"I shot them down."

---

① shove-halfpenny: *Noun* [*Mass Noun*] a game in which coins are struck so that they slide across a marked board on a table 打硬币游戏(将放在桌面上的硬币打入标线区)

Everyone heard it. At that moment eleven pilots in that tent stopped what they were doing and eleven heads flicked around and looked at the Bull. He took another drink of his beer and said quietly, "At one time I counted eighteen parachutes in the air together."

A few days later he went on patrol and did not come back. Shortly afterwards Monkey got a message from Athens①. It said that the squadron was to move down to Elevsis② and from there do a defence of Athens itself and also cover the troops retreating through the Thermopylae Pass.

Katina was to go with the trucks and we told the Doc he was to see that she arrived safely. It would take them a day to make the journey. We flew over the mountains towards the south, fourteen of us, and at two-thirty we landed at Elevsis. It was a lovely aerodrome with runways and hangars; and best of all, Athens was only twenty-five minutes away by car.

That evening, as it was getting dark, I stood outside my tent. I stood with my hands in my pockets watching the sun go down and thinking of the work which we were to do. The more that I thought of it, the more impossible I knew it to be. I looked up, and once again I saw the mountains. They were closer to us here, crowding in upon us on all sides, standing shoulder to shoulder, tall and naked, with their heads in

---

① Athens: *Noun* the capital of Greece; pop. 3,096,775 (1991). Greek name athínai 雅典(希腊首都,1991 年人口 3,096,775,希腊语名"athínai"。)

② Elevsis: It should be correctly spelled as"Eleusis". Eleusis is a town and municipality in West Attica, Greece. It is situated about 18 km northwest from the centre of Athens 正确的拼写形式应该是"Eleusis",指的是希腊的埃莱夫西斯港,位于雅典市中心西北部 18 公里的地方。

the clouds, surrounding us everywhere save in the south, where lay Piraeus[①] and the open sea. I knew that each night, when it was very dark, when we were all tired and sleeping in our tents, those mountains would move forward, creeping a little closer, making no noise, until at last on the appointed day they would tumble forward with one great rush and push us into the sea.

Fin emerged from his tent.

"Have you seen the mountains?" I said.

"They're full of gods. They aren't any good," he answered.

"I wish they'd stand still," I said.

Fin looked up at the great crags of Panes and Pentelikon[②].

"They're full of gods," he said. "Sometimes, in the middle of the night, when there is a moon, you can see the gods sitting on the summits. There was one on Kataphidi when we were at Paramythia. He was huge, like a house but without any shape and quite black."

"You saw him?"

"Of course I saw him."

"When?" I said. "When did you see him, Fin?"

Fin said, "Let's go into Athens. Let's go and look at the women in Athens."

The next day the trucks carrying the ground staff and the equipment rumbled on to the aerodrome, and there was Katina sitting in the front seat of the leading vehicle with the Doc beside her. She waved to us as

① Piraeus: *Noun* the chief port of Athens, situated on the Saronic Gulf 8 km (5 miles) SW of the city; pop. 182,670 (1991). Greek name Piraiévs or Piraiéus 比雷埃夫斯港(雅典主要港口,位于雅典西南8公里〈5英里〉处萨罗尼克湾畔,1991年人口182,670。希腊语名 Piraiévs 或 Piraiéus。)

② Panes and Pentelikon: Two mountain in Greece 希腊的帕纳斯山和彭德利康山(古希腊雅典城邦的山脉。)

she jumped down, and she came running towards us, laughing and calling our names in a curious Greek way. She still had on the same dirty print dress and she still had a bandage round her forehead; but the sun was shining in her hair.

We showed her the tent which we had prepared for her and we showed her the small cotton nightdress which Fin had obtained in some mysterious way the night before in Athens. It was white with a lot of little blue birds embroidered on the front and we all thought that it was very beautiful. Katina wanted to put it on at once and it took a long time to persuade her that it was meant only for sleeping in. Six times Fin had to perform a complicated act which consisted of pretending to put on the nightdress, then jumping on to the bed and falling fast asleep. In the end she nodded vigorously and understood.

For the next two days nothing happened, except that the remnants of another squadron came down from the north and joined us. They brought six Hurricanes, so that altogether we had about twenty machines.

Then we waited.

On the third day German reconnaissance[1] aircraft appeared, circling high over Piraeus, and we chased after them but never got up in time to catch them. This was understandable, because our radar was of a very special type. It is obsolete now, and I doubt whether it will ever be used again. All over the country, in all the villages, up on the mountains and out on the islands, there were Greeks, all of whom were connected to our small operations room by field telephone.

We had no operations officer, so we took it in turns to be on duty for the day. My turn came on the fourth day, and I remember clearly what

① reconnaissance: *Noun* [*Mass Noun*] military observation of a region to locate an enemy or ascertain strategic features（军事）侦察

happened.

At six – thirty in the morning the phone buzzed.

"This is A – 7," said a very Greek voice. "This is A – 7. There are noises overhead."

I looked at the map. There was a little ring with "A – 7' written inside it just beside Yanina. I put a cross on the celluloid[①] which covered the map and wrote "Noises' beside it, as well as the time: "0631 hours."

Three minutes later the phone went again.

"This is A – 4. This is A – 4. There are many noises above me," said an old quavering voice, "but I cannot see because there are thick clouds."

I looked at the map. A – 4 was Mt Karava. I made another cross on the celluloid and wrote "Many noises—0634,' and then I drew a line between Yanina and Karava. It pointed towards Athens, so I signalled the "readiness' crew to scramble, and they took off and circled the city. Later they saw a Ju – 88 on reconnaissance high above them, but they never caught it. It was in such a way that one worked the radar.

That evening when I came off duty I could not help thinking of the old Greek, sitting all alone in a hut up at A – 4; sitting on the slope of Karava looking up into the whiteness and listening all day and all night for noises in the sky. I imagined the eagerness with which he seized the telephone when he heard something, and the joy he must have felt when the voice at the other end repeated his message and thanked him. I thought of his clothes and wondered if they were warm enough and I thought, for some reason, of his boots, which almost certainly had no

---

① celluloid: *Noun* [*Mass Noun*] a transparent flammable plastic made in sheets from camphor and nitrocellulose, formerly used for cinematographic film 赛璐珞(一种用樟脑和硝化纤维制成的透明易燃塑料片,旧时用于电影制作。)

soles left upon them and were stuffed with tree bark and paper.

That was April seventeenth. It was the evening when Monkey said, "They say the Germans are at Lamia, which means that we're within range of their fighters. Tomorrow the fun should start."

It did. At dawn the bombers came over, with the fighters circling around overhead, watching the bombers, waiting to pounce, but doing nothing unless someone interfered with the bombers.

I think we got eight Hurricanes into the air just before they arrived. It was not my turn to go up, so with Katina standing by my side I watched the battle from the ground. The child never said a word. Now and again she moved her head as she followed the little specks of silver dancing high above in the sky. I saw a plane coming down in a trail of black smoke and I looked at Katina. The hatred which was on the face of the child was the fierce burning hatred of an old woman who has hatred in her heart; it was an old woman's hatred and it was strange to see it.

In that battle we lost a sergeant called Donald.

At noon Monkey got another message from Athens. It said that morale was bad in the capital and that every available Hurricane was to fly in formation low over the city in order to show the inhabitants how strong we were and how many aircraft we had. Eighteen of us took off. We flew in tight formation up and down the main streets just above the roofs of the houses. I could see the people looking up, shielding their eyes from the sun, looking at us as we flew over, and in one street I saw an old woman who never looked up at all. None of them waved, and I knew then that they were resigned to their fate. None of them waved, and I knew, although I could not see their faces, that they were not even glad as we flew past.

Then we headed out towards Thermopylae, but on the way we

circled the Acropolis[①] twice. It was the first time I had seen it so close.

I saw a little hill—a mound almost, it seemed—and on the top of it I saw the white columns. There were a great number of them, grouped together in perfect order, not crowding one another, white in the sunshine, and I wondered, as I looked at them, how anyone could have put so much on top of so small a hill in such an elegant way.

Then we flew up the great Thermopylae Pass and I saw long lines of vehicles moving slowly southwards towards the sea. I saw occasional puffs of white smoke where a shell landed in the valley and I saw a direct hit on the road which made a gap in the line of trucks. But we saw no enemy aircraft.

When we landed Monkey said, "Refuel quickly and get in the air again; I think they're waiting to catch us on the ground."

But it was no use. They came down out of the sky five minutes after we had landed. I remember I was in the pilots' room in Number Two Hangar, talking to Fin and to a big tall man with rumpled hair called Paddy. We heard the bullets on the corrugated-iron roof of the hangar, then we heard explosions and the three of us dived under the little wooden table in the middle of the room. But the table upset. Paddy set it up again and crawled underneath. "There's something about being under a table," he said. "I don't feel safe unless I'm under a table."

Fin said, "I never feel safe." He was sitting on the floor watching the bullets making holes in the corrugated-iron wall of the room. There was a great clatter as the bullets hit the tin.

Then we became brave and got up and peeped outside the door. There were many Messerschmitt 109s circling the aerodrome, and one by

---

① the Acropolis: the ancient citadel at Athens, containing the Parthenon and other notable buildings, mostly dating from the 5th century B. C. 雅典卫城(包含帕台农神庙和其他有名建筑,大部分可追溯到公元前5世纪。)

one they straightened out and dived past the hangers, spraying the ground with their guns. But they did something else. They slid back their cockpit hoods and as they came past they threw out small bombs which exploded when they hit the ground and fiercely flung quantities of large lead balls in every direction. Those were the explosions which we had heard, and it was a great noise that the lead balls made as they hit the hangar.

Then I saw the men, the ground crews, standing up in their slit trenches firing at the Messerschmitts with rifles, reloading and firing as fast as they could, cursing and shouting as they shot, aiming ludicrously[①], hopelessly, aiming at an aeroplane with just a rifle. At Elevsis there were no other defences.

Suddenly the Messerschmitts all turned and headed for home, all except one, which glided down and made a smooth belly landing[②] on the aerodrome.

Then there was chaos. The Greeks around us raised a shout and jumped on to the fire tender[③] and headed out towards the crashed German aeroplane. At the same time more Greeks streamed out from every corner of the field, shouting and yelling and crying for the blood of the pilot. It was a mob intent upon vengeance and one could not blame them; but there were other considerations. We wanted the pilot for questioning, and we wanted him alive.

---

① ludicrous: *Adjective* so foolish, unreasonable, or out of place as to be amusing 滑稽有趣的;荒唐可笑的

② belly landing: *Noun* a crash-landing of an aircraft on the underside of the fuselage, without lowering the undercarriage(不使用起落架的)以机腹着陆

③ tender: *Noun* [with modifier] a vehicle used by a fire service for carrying specified supplies or equipment or fulfilling a specified role(装有特别设备的)辅助救火车

Monkey, who was standing on the tarmac[1], shouted to us, and Fin and Paddy and I raced with him towards the station wagon which was standing fifty yards away. Monkey was inside like a flash, started the engine and drove off just as the three of us jumped on the running board. The fire tender with the Greeks on it was not fast and it still had two hundred yards to go, and the other people had a long way to run. Monkey drove quickly and we beat them by about fifty yards.

We jumped up and ran over to the Messerschmitt, and there, sitting in the cockpit, was a fair-haired boy with pink cheeks and blue eyes. I have never seen anyone whose face showed so much fear.

He said to Monkey in English, "I am hit in the leg."

We pulled him out of the cockpit and got him into the car, while the Greeks stood around watching. The bullet had shattered the bone in his shin.

We drove him back and as we handed him over to the Doc, I saw Katina standing close, looking at the face of the German. This kid of nine was standing there looking at the German and she could not speak; she could not even move. She clutched the skin of her dress in her hands and stared at the man's face. "There is a mistake somewhere," she seemed to be saying. "There must be a mistake. This one has pink cheeks and fair hair and blue eyes. This cannot possibly be one of them. This is an ordinary boy." She watched him as they put him on a stretcher and carried him off, then she turned and ran across the grass to her tent.

In the evening at supper I ate my fried sardines, but I could not eat the bread or the cheese. For three days I had been conscious of my stomach, of a hollow feeling such as one gets just before an operation or

① the tarmac: a runway or other area surfaced with such material 柏油碎石铺的飞机跑道(或其他平面)

while waiting to have a tooth out in the dentist's house. I had had it all day for three days, from the moment I woke up to the time I fell asleep. Peter was sitting opposite me and I asked him about it.

"I've had it for a week," he said. "It's good for the bowels. It loosens them.

"German aircraft are like liver pills," said Fin from the bottom of the table. "They are very good for you, aren't they, Doc?"

The Doc said; "Maybe you've had an overdose."

"I have," said Fin, "I've had an overdose of German liver pills. I didn't read the instructions on the bottle. Take two before retiring."

Peter said, "I would love to retire."

After supper three of us walked down to the hangers with Monkey, who said, "I'm worried about this ground-strafing. They never attack the hangars because they know that we never put anything inside them. Tonight I think we'll collect four of the aircraft and put them into Number Two Hangar."

That was a good idea. Normally the Hurricanes were dispersed all over the edge of the aerodrome, but they were picked off one by one, because it was impossible to be in the air the whole time. The four of us took a machine each and taxied it into Number Two Hangar, and then we pulled the great sliding doors together and locked them.

The next morning, before the sun had risen from behind the mountains, a flock of Ju – 87s came over and blew Number Two Hangar right off the face of the earth. Their bombing was good and they did not even hit the hangars on either side of it.

That afternoon they got Peter. He went off towards a village called Khalkis, which was being bombed by Ju – 88s, and no one ever saw him again. Gay, laughing Peter, whose mother lived on a farm in Kent[1] and who used to write to him in long, pale-blue envelopes which he carried about in his pockets.

I had always shared a tent with Peter, ever since I came to the squadron, and that evening after I had gone to bed he came back to that tent. You need not believe me; I do not expect you to, but I am telling you what happened.

I always went to bed first, because there is not room in one of those tents for two people to be turning around at the same time. Peter usually came in two or three minutes afterwards. That evening I went to bed and I lay thinking that tonight he would not be coming. I wondered whether his body lay tangled in the wreckage of his aircraft on the side of some bleak mountain or whether it was at the bottom of the sea, and I hoped only that he had had a decent funeral.

Suddenly I heard a movement. The flap of the tent opened and it shut again. But there were no footsteps. Then I heard him sit down on his bed. It was a noise that I had heard every night for weeks past and always it had been the same. It was just a thump and a creaking of the wooden legs of the camp bed. One after the other the flying boots were pulled off and dropped upon the ground, and as always one of them took three times as long to get off as the other. After that there was the gentle rustle of a blanket being pulled back and then the creakings of the rickety bed as it took the weight of a man's body.

They were sounds I had heard every night, the same sounds in the same order, and now I sat up in bed and said, "Peter." It was dark in the tent. My voice sounded very loud.

---

① Kent: a county on the SE coast of England; county town, Maidstone 肯特(英格兰东南海岸一郡,首府梅德斯通。)

"Hallo, Peter. That was tough luck you had today." But there was no answer.

I did not feel uneasy or frightened, but I remember at the time touching the tip of my nose with my finger to make sure that I was there; then because I was very tired, I went to sleep.

In the morning I looked at the bed and saw it had been slept in. But I did not show it to anyone, not even to Fin. I put the blankets back in place myself and patted the pillow.

It was on that day, the twentieth of April, 1941, that we fought the Battle of Athens.

It was perhaps the last of the great dog-fighting air battles that will ever be fought, because nowadays the planes fly always in great formation of wings and squadrons, and attack is carried out methodically and scientifically upon the orders of the leader. Nowadays one does not dog-fight at all over the sky except upon very rare occasions. But the Battle of Athens was a long and beautiful dog-fight in which fifteen Hurricanes fought for half an hour with between one hundred and fifty and two hundred German bombers and fighters.

The bombers started coming over early in the afternoon. It was a lovely spring day and for the first time the sun had in it a trace of real summer warmth. The sky was blue, save for a few wispy clouds here and there and the mountains stood out black and clear against the blue of the sky.

Pentelikon no longer hid his head in the clouds. He stood over us, grim and forbidding, watching every move and knowing that each thing we did was of little purpose. Men were foolish and were made only so that they should die, while mountains and rivers went on for ever and did not notice the passing of time. Had not Pentelikon himself many years ago looked down upon Thermopylae and seen a handful of Spartans[①] defending the pass against the invaders; seen them fight until there was not one man left alive among them? Had he not seen the Persians[②] cut to pieces by Leonidas[③] at Marathon, and had he not looked down upon Salamis[④] and upon the sea when Themistocles and the Athenians drove the enemy from their shores, causing them to lose more than two hundred sails? All these things and many more he had seen, and now he looked down upon us, we were as nothing in his eyes. Almost there was a look of scorn upon the face of the mountain, and I thought for a moment that I could hear the laughter of the gods. They knew so well that we were not enough and that in the end we must lose.

The bombers came over just after lunch, and at once we saw that there were a great number of them. We looked up and saw that the sky was full of little silver specks and the sunlight danced and sparkled upon a hundred different pairs of wings.

There were fifteen Hurricanes in all and they fought like a storm in

---

① Spartan: *Noun* a citizen of Sparta 斯巴达市民

② Persian: *Noun* a native or national of ancient or modern Persia (or Iran), or a person of Persian descent 波斯(或伊朗)人

③ Leonidas: Leonidas is also known as Leonidas the Brave. He was a Greek hero-king of Sparta, the 17th of the Agiad line, third son of Anaxandridas II of Sparta, who was believed to be a descendant of Heracles, possessing much of the latter's strength and bravery 斯巴达国王列奥尼达斯

④ Salamis: *Noun* An island in the Saronic Gulf in Greece, to the west of Athens. The strait between the island and the mainland was the scene in 480 B. C. of a crushing defeat of the Persian fleet under Xerxes I by the Greeks under Themistocles 萨拉米斯(希腊萨罗尼克湾内一岛屿,位于雅典西,该岛与大陆之间的海峡为公元前480年薛西斯一世率领的波斯舰队惨败给塞米斯托克利斯率领的希腊舰队的战场。)

the sky. It is not easy to remember much about such a battle, but I remember looking up and seeing in the sky a mass of small black dots. I remember thinking to myself that those could not be aeroplanes; they simply could not be aeroplanes, because there were not so many aeroplanes in the world.

Then they were on us, and I remember that I applied a little flap so that I should be able to turn in tighter circles; then I remember only one or two small incidents which photographed themselves upon my mind. There were the spurts of flame from the guns of a Messerschmitt as he attacked from the frontal quarter of my starboard side. There was the German whose parachute was on fire as it opened. There was the German who flew up beside me and made rude signs at me with his fingers. There was the Hurricane which collided with a Messerschmitt. There was the aeroplane which collided with a man who was descending in a parachute, and which went into a crazy frightful spin towards the earth with the man and the parachute dangling from its port wing. There were the two bombers which collided while swerving to avoid a fighter, and I remember distinctly seeing a man being thrown clear out of the smoke and debris of the collision, hanging in mid - air with his arms outstretched and his legs apart. I tell you there was nothing that did not happen in that battle. There was the moment when I saw a single Hurricane doing tight turns around the summit of Mt Parnes with nine Messerschmitts on its tail and then I remember that suddenly the skies seemed to clear. There was no longer any aircraft in sight. The battle was over. I turned around and headed back towards Elevsis, and as I went I looked down and saw Athens and Piraeus and the rim of the sea as it curved around the gulf and travelled southward towards the Mediterranean. I saw the port of Piraeus where the bombs had fallen and I saw the smoke and fire rising above the docks. I saw the narrow coastal plain, and on it I saw tiny bonfires, thin columns of black smoke curling upward and drifting away to the east. They were the fires of aircraft which had been shot down, and I hoped only that none of them were Hurricanes.

Just then I ran straight into a Junkers 88; a straggler①, the last bomber returning from the raid. He was in trouble and there was black smoke streaming from one of his engines. Although I shot at him, I don't think that it made any difference. He was coming down anyway. We were over the sea and I could tell that he wouldn't make the land. He didn't. He came down smoothly on his belly in the blue Gulf of Piraeus, two miles from the shore. I followed him and circled, waiting to make sure that the crew got out safely into their dinghy②.

Slowly the machine began to sink, dipping its nose under the water and lifting its tail into the air. But there was no sign of the crew. Suddenly, without any warning, the rear gun started to fire. They opened up with their rear gun and the bullets made small jagged holes in my starboard wing. I swerved away and I remember shouting at them. I slid back the hood of the cockpit and shouted, "You lousy brave bastards. I hope you drown." The bomber sank soon backwards.

When I got back they were all standing around outside the hangars counting the score, and Katina was sitting on a box with tears rolling down her cheeks. But she was not crying, and Fin was kneeling down beside her, talking to her in English, quietly and gently, forgetting that she could not understand.

We lost one third of our Hurricanes in that battle, but the Germans lost more.

The Doc was dressing someone who had been burnt and he looked

① straggle: *Verb* [no obj., usu. with adverbial of direction] move along slowly, typically in a small irregular group, so as to remain some distance behind the person or people in front 掉队;落伍

② dinghy: *Noun* a small inflatable rubber boat (充气式)小橡皮筏

up and said, "You should have heard the Greeks on the aerodrome cheering as the bombers fell out of the sky."

As we stood around talking, a truck drove up and a Greek got out and said that he had some pieces of body inside. "This is the watch," he said, "that was on the arm." It was a silver wrist watch with a luminous dial, and on the back there were some initials. We did not look inside the truck.

Now we had, I think, nine Hurricanes left.

That evening a very senior RAF officer came out from Athens and said, "Tomorrow at dawn you will all fly to Megara①. It is about ten miles down the coast. There is a small field there on which you can land. The Army is working on it throughout the night. They have two big rollers there and they are rolling it smooth. The moment you land you must hide your aircraft in the olive grove which is on the south side of the field. The ground staff are going farther south to Argos② and you can join them later, but you may be able to operate from Megara for a day or two."

Fin said, "Where's Katina? Doc, you must find Katina and see that she gets to Argos safely."

The Doc said, "I will," and we knew that we could trust him.

……

At dawn the next morning, when it was still dark, we took off and flew to the little field at Megara, ten miles away. We landed and hid our

---

① Megara: Modern Megara sits on the southern slopes of two hills that served as the acropolises (citadels) of the ancient town 希腊一个定居点:迈加拉

② Argos: a city in the NE Peloponnese of Greece; pop. 20,702 (1981). One of the oldest cities of ancient Greece, it dominated the Peloponnese and the western Aegean in the 7th century B. C. 阿尔戈斯城(希腊伯罗奔尼撒半岛东北部一城市,1981 年人口20,702,古希腊最古老城市之一,公元前7 世纪时曾控制了伯罗奔尼撒半岛和爱琴海西部海域。)

Hurricanes in the olive grove and broke off branches of the trees and put them over the aircraft. Then we sat down on the slope of a small hill and waited for orders.

As the sun rose up over the mountains we looked across the field and saw a mass of Greek villagers coming down from the village of Megara, coming down towards our field. There were many hundreds of them, women and children mostly, and they all came down towards our field, hurrying as they came.

Fin said, "What the hell," and we sat up on our little hill and watched, wondering what they were going to do.

They dispersed all around the edge of the field and gathered armfuls of heather and bracken. They carried it out on to the field, and forming themselves into long lines, they began to scatter the heather and the bracken over the grass. They were camouflaging our landing field. The rollers, when they had rolled out the ground and made it flat for landing, had left marks which were easily visible from above, and so the Greeks came out of their village, every man, woman and child, and began to put matters right. To this day I do not know who told them to do it. They stretched in a long line across the field, walking forward slowly and scattering the heather, and Fin and I went out and walked among them.

They were old women and old men mostly, very small and very sad-looking, with dark, deeply wrinkled faces and they worked slowly scattering the heather. As we walked by, they would stop their work and smile, saying something in Greek which we could not understand. One of the children gave Fin a small pink flower and he did not know what to do with it, but walked around carrying it in his hand.

Then we went back to the slope of the hill and waited. Soon the field telephone buzzed. It was the very senior officer speaking. He said that someone must fly back to Elevsis at once and collect important messages and money. He said also that all of us must leave our little field at Megara and go to Argos that evening. The others said that they would wait until I came back with the money so that we could all fly to Argos together.

At the same time, someone had told the two Army men who were still rolling our field, to destroy their rollers so that the Germans would not get them. I remember, as I was getting into my Hurricane, seeing the two huge rollers charging towards each other across the field and I remember seeing the Army men jump aside just before they collided. There was a great crash and I saw all the Greeks who were scattering heather stop in their work and look up. For a moment they stood rock still, looking at the rollers. Then one of them started to run. It was an old woman and she started to run back to the village as fast as she could, shouting something as she went, and instantly every man, woman and child in the field seemed to take fright and ran after her. I wanted to get out and run beside them and explain to them; to say I was sorry but that there was nothing else we could do. I wanted to tell them that we would not forget them and that one day we would come back. But it was no use. Bewildered and frightened, they ran back to their homes, and they did not stop running until they were out of sight, not even the old men.

I took off and flew to Elevsis. I landed on a dead aerodrome. There was not a soul to be seen. I parked my Hurricane, and as I walked over to the hangars the bombers came over once again. I hid in a ditch until they had finished their work, then got up and walked over to the small operations room. The telephone was still on the table, so for some reason I picked up the receiver and said, "Hallo."

A rather German voice at the other end answered.

I said, "Can you hear me?" and the voice said: "Yes, yes, I can hear you."

"All right," I said, "listen carefully."

"Yes, continue please."

"This is the RAF speaking. And one day we will come back, do you understand. One day we will come back."

Then I tore the telephone from its socket and threw it through the glass of the closed window. When I went outside there was a small man in civilian clothes standing near the door. He had a revolver in one hand and a small bag in the other.

"Do you want anything?" he said in quite good English.

I said, "Yes, I want important messages and papers which I am to carry back to Argos."

"Here you are," he said, as he handed me the bag. "And good luck."

I flew back to Megara. There were two Greek destroyers standing offshore, burning and sinking. I circled our field and the others taxied out, took off and we all flew off towards Argos.

The landing ground at Argos was just a kind of small field. It was surrounded by thick olive groves into which we taxied our aircraft for hiding. I don't know how long the field was, but it was not easy to land upon it. You had to come in low hanging on the prop, and the moment you touched down you had to start putting on brake, jerking it on and jerking it off again the moment she started to nose over. But only one man overshot and crashed.

The ground staff had arrived already and as we got out of our aircraft Katina came running up with a basket of black olives, offering them to us and pointing to our stomachs, indicating that we must eat.

Fin bent down and ruffled her hair with his hand. He said, "Katina, one day we must go into town and buy you a new dress." She smiled at him but did not understand and we all started to eat black olives.

Then I looked around and saw that the wood was full of aircraft. Around every corner there was an aeroplane hidden in the trees, and when we asked about it we learned that the Greeks had brought the whole of their air force down to Argos and parked them in that little wood. They were peculiar ancient models, not one of them less than five years old, and I don't know how many dozen there were there.

That night we slept under the trees. We wrapped Katina up in a large flying suit and gave her a flying helmet for a pillow, and after she had gone to sleep we sat around eating black olives and drinking resinato out of an enormous cask①. But we were very tired, and soon we fell asleep.

All the next day we saw the truckloads of troops moving down the road towards the sea, and as often as we could we took off and flew above them.

The Germans kept coming over and bombing the road nearby, but they had not yet spotted our airfield.

Later in the day we were told that every available Hurricane was to take off at six p. m. to protect an important shipping move, and the nine machines, which were all that were now left, were refuelled and got ready. At three minutes to six we began to taxi out of the olive grove on to the field.

The first two machines took off, but just as they left the ground something black swept down out of the sky and shot them both down in flames. I looked around and saw at least fifty Messerschmitt 110s circling our field, and even as I looked some of them turned and came down upon the remaining seven Hurricanes which were waiting to take off.

There was no time to do anything. Each one of our aircraft was hit

① cask: *Noun* a large barrel-like container made of wood, metal, or plastic, used for storing liquids, typically alcoholic drinks(尤指装酒等液体的)大桶

in that first swoop[1], although funnily enough only one of the pilots was hurt. It was impossible now to take off, so we jumped out of our aircraft, hauled the wounded pilot out of his cockpit and ran with him back to the slit trenches, to the wonderful big, deep zig-zagging slit trenches which had been dug by the Greeks.

The Messerschmitts took their time. There was no opposition either from the ground or from the air, except that Fin was firing his revolver.

It is not a pleasant thing to be ground-strafed especially if they have cannon in their wings; and unless one has a deep slit trench in which to lie, there is no future in it. For some reason, perhaps because they thought it was a good joke, the German pilots went for the slit trenches before they bothered about the aircraft. The first ten minutes was spent rushing madly around the corners of the trenches so as not to be caught in a trench which ran parallel with the line of flight of the attacking aircraft. It was a hectic, dreadful ten minutes, with everyone shouting "Here comes another," and scrambling and rushing to get around the corner into the other section of the trench.

Then the Germans went for the Hurricanes and at the same time for the mass of old Greek aircraft parked all around the olive grove, and one by one, methodically and systematically, they set them on fire. The noise was terrific, and everywhere—in the trees, on the rocks and on the grass—the bullets splattered.

I remember peeping cautiously over the top of our trench and seeing a small white flower growing just a few inches away from my nose. It was pure white and it had three petals. I remember looking past it and seeing three of the Germans diving on my own Hurricane which was parked on

---

① swoop: *Noun* a swooping or snatching movement or action 飞扑;攫取;突袭

the other side of the field and I remember shouting at them, although I do not know what I said.

Then suddenly I saw Katina. She was running out from the far corner of the aerodrome, running right out into the middle of this mass of blazing guns and burning aircraft, running as fast as she could. Once she stumbled, but she scrambled to her feet again and went on running. Then she stopped and stood looking up, raising her fists at the planes as they flew past.

Now as she stood there, I remember seeing one of the Messerschmitts turning and coming in low straight towards her and I remember thinking that she was so small that she could not be hit. I remember seeing the spurts of flame from his guns as he came, and I remember seeing the child, for a split second, standing quite still, facing the machine. I remember that the wind was blowing in her hair.

Then she was down.

The next moment I shall never forget. On every side, as if by magic, men appeared out of the ground. They swarmed out of their trenches and like a crazy mob poured on to the aerodrome, running towards the tiny little bundle, which lay motionless in the middle of the field. They ran fast, crouching as they went, and I remember jumping up out of my slit trench and joining with them. I remember thinking of nothing at all and watching the boots of the man in front of me, noticing that he was a little bow - legged[1] and that his blue trousers were much too long.

I remember seeing Fin arrive first, followed closely by a sergeant called Wishful, and I remember seeing the two of them pick up Katina

---

① bow legs: *Plural Noun* legs that curve outwards at the knee; bandy legs 膝内翻;弓形腿

and start running with her back towards the trenches. I saw her leg, which was just a lot of blood and bones, and I saw her chest where the blood was spurting out on to her white print dress; I saw, for a moment, her face, which was white as the snow on top of Olympus.

I ran beside Fin, and as he ran, he kept saying, "The lousy bastards, the lousy, bloody bastards," and then as we got to our trench I remember looking round and finding that there was no longer any noise or shooting. The Germans had gone.

Fin said, "Where's the Doc?" and suddenly there he was, standing beside us, looking at Katina—looking at her face.

The Doc gently touched her wrist and without looking up he said, "She is not alive."

They put her down under a little tree, and when I turned away I saw on all sides the fires of countless burning aircraft. I saw my own Hurricane burning nearby and I stood staring hopelessly into the flames as they danced around the engine and licked against the metal of the wings.

I stood staring into the flames, and as I stared the fire became a deeper red and I saw beyond it not a tangled mass of smoking wreckage, but the flames of a hotter and intenser fire which now burned and smouldered in the hearts of the people of Greece.

Still I stared, and as I stared I saw in the centre of the fire, whence the red flames sprang, a bright, white heat, shining bright and without any colour.

As I stared, the brightness diffused[①] and became soft and yellow like sunlight, and through it, beyond it, I saw a young child standing in the middle of a field with the sunlight shining in her hair. For a moment

① diffuse: *Verb* spread or cause to spread over a wide area or between a large number of people 散播;传播

she stood looking up into the sky, which was clear and blue and without any clouds; then she turned and looked towards me, and as she turned I saw that the front of her white print dress was stained deep red, the colour of blood.

Then there was no longer any fire or any flames and I saw before me only the glowing twisted wreckage of a burned-out plane. I must have been standing there for quite a long time.

三、翻译探索

通篇文本翻译起来难度不大,棘手的还是一些专有名词,主要是地名类和山脉名称类的专有名词,需要一一查实。个别名不见经传的地名,查无结果,只能按照音译的原则来处理了。

希腊孤女

下面是一些简短的杂记,记录的是第一场希腊之战中,英国皇家飞行员最后几天的事情。

第一个看到她的人是彼得。

她当时坐在一块石头上,双手搭在膝盖上,整个人安静得很。她的双眼只是茫然地盯着前方,却没有看任何东西。在她的四周以及小小街道的上上下下,人们手里提着一桶桶水来回奔跑,通过窗户将水泼进着火的房子。

大街对面,铺着小圆石头的路面上躺着一具男孩的尸体,早已有人将其挪到靠近一边的地方,以免妨碍走路。

下方稍远一点的地方,一位老人正在扒拉一堆石头和瓦砾。只见他将石头一块、一块搬开,堆到旁边,有时候还蹲下身子往废墟里面观瞧,还一遍又一遍地反复念叨着着一个人的名字。

四周的喊叫声此起彼伏。人们拎着一桶桶水来回奔跑,火光四起,尘土飞扬。但是,这个小女孩只是安静地坐在石头上,眼睛盯着前方,整个人一动不动的。她的左脸有血液淌出,血液从前额流出,沿着下巴流淌到她身上穿的那件脏兮兮的印花衣服上面。

彼得看见了她,说道:“看那个小女孩啊。”

我们走近那个小女孩,芬恩将一只胳膊搭到她的肩膀上,弯腰查看她的伤口。“看起来像是一块弹片,”他说。“应该送她去看医生。”

我和彼得用手搭成一把椅子的形状,芬恩将她举到上面坐下。我们开始穿越大街往回赶,要赶回飞机场。我们两个走得有点笨手笨脚的——猫着腰,脸冲着手上坐着的小女孩。我可以感觉得到,彼得的手指跟我的手指交叉着,紧紧握在一起。我也可以感觉得到小女孩的屁股轻轻地坐在我的两只手腕上。我走在左边,血液从她的脸上滴落,滴到我的飞行服的袖子上,再沿着飞行服的防水布滴到我的手背上。小女孩始终没有动弹,也没有说一句话。

芬恩说:“她的血淌得够快了,我们最好再走快一点儿。”

她的脸部,我看不到多少,因为淌满了血,但是,我可以肯定,这个女孩很可爱:面颊骨高高的,双眼又圆又大,呈浅蓝色,就像秋日的天空一般的颜色,一头金发短短的。我猜想,她年龄大约有九岁。

时值1941年4月初,地点在希腊的帕拉米西亚村。我们的战斗机中队驻扎在靠近村子的一块泥地上。我们身处一条深谷之中,四周群山环绕。严寒的冬季已经过去,而目前,几乎就在不知不觉间,春天已经来到,来得悄无声息却又转瞬而至。湖泊里的冰融化了,山顶的积雪被风吹走。在整个机场上,我们可以看到一株株浅绿色的小草嫩芽破土而出,给着陆跑道盖上了一层地毯。我们驻扎的山谷中,和煦的风吹拂着,野花到处开放。

几天以前,德国兵经由南斯拉夫一路推进,现在已经展开了武力攻势。那天下午,他们驾驶着大约三十五架“道尼尔”战机在村子上空高高地盘旋,并轰炸了村子。我、彼得和芬恩暂时不执勤,于是,我们三个下到村子里去,看看能否帮忙做点援救工作。我们在废墟里挖来挖去,挖了好几个小时,还帮忙灭火。就在返回的路上,我们看到了这个小女孩。

现在,我们就要接近着陆场了,还看到了飓风战机在上空盘旋,纷纷着陆。医生就站在疏散帐篷前履行职责,看看是否有人受伤。

我们抬着受伤的女孩向他走去。芬恩走在我们前方几米远的地方，抢先说道：

“医生啊，你这个老家伙，这儿有你要干的活了。”

这位医生很年轻、很友善，但除了喝醉酒的时候，总是带着一副闷闷不乐的表情。喝醉酒的时候，他就一反常态，引吭高歌，歌声悠扬。

“把她带到医务所去，”医生说。我跟彼得将她抬进医务所，放到一把椅子上。然后，我们离开，往疏散帐篷里溜达，想看看伙计们那儿有什么情况发生。

天开始黑了下来。日落西山，一轮圆月爬了上来，挂在空中。这是一个适合战机轰炸的夜晚。月光洒在一座座帐篷的斜面上，染白了帐篷，使这些沿着机场边缘排列的帐篷看起来就像一座座小小的白色金字塔，一座座井然有序地笔直伫立在那儿。这些帐篷簇拥在那儿，活像受到惊吓的绵羊，而这些帐篷簇拥在一起的样子又活像一个个站立着的人。看起来，他们几乎好像知道要出麻烦事儿，就好像有人警告过他们，说他们或许会被遗忘、丢弃到身后不管。即便是我一眼看过去，我想，我看到他们在移动。我想，我看到他们向一起挤近了一点点。

接着，一言不发的群山悄悄地向我们所在的山谷爬近了一点点。

接下来的两天时间里，飞行战斗任务频繁。天刚亮就起床，接着起飞，然后战斗，最后睡觉。我们的大部队已经有了撤退的迹象。这两天就这些事情，做的也就这么多的事情。但是，到了第三天，云层高度降低，笼罩在群山之上，并向山谷滑落。紧接着，天下起了雨。于是，我们围坐在充当食堂的帐篷里，喝着啤酒和带有树脂香味的葡萄酒，而此时，雨滴拍打着帐篷顶部发出“啪啪啦啦”的声响，如同缝纫机缝纫时发出的声音。接下来，吃午饭。数天以来，这还是头一回，全飞行中队人都聚齐了。十五名飞行员围着长条桌子，坐在两边的长凳上，指挥官蒙凯坐在首席的位置上。

就在我们大家吃着煎咸牛肉的当儿，帐篷的门帘子“啪”的一声被掀开了，医生身穿雨衣走了进来，雨水从他头顶的雨衣帽子上“哗哗”往下淌。那个小女孩也跟他一起进来,躲在雨衣下面,头部缠了一圈绷带。

医生说:“嗨,大家好啊,我带来了一位客人。”我们大家张望起来,突然之间,大家自动自觉地全都站了起来。

医生往下脱雨衣,小女孩则站在那儿,两只胳膊松垮地垂在身体两侧,双眼看着这些大男人,而这些大男人则齐刷刷地看向她。她一头金黄的秀发,浅白的皮肤,令她看起来不怎么像我所见过的希腊人。一进门,十五名衣衫不整的老外突然间一下子站了起来,着实吓了她一跳。就在这一瞬间,她半转过身体,那架势好像是要跑出帐篷、躲进雨中似的。

蒙凯说:“哈喽,来了啊,你好啊。来呀,坐下。”

“说希腊语,”医生说。“英语她听不懂。”

我、芬恩还有彼得彼此看了一眼,芬恩说:“老天啊,是我们救回来的小女孩。医生,干得不错。”

小女孩认出了芬恩,绕到了芬恩跟前。芬恩抓起小女孩的手,让她坐到了长凳上,其余的人也都坐了下来。我们给了她一些煎咸牛肉,她慢慢吃了起来,一边吃一边低头看着自己的盘子。蒙凯说:“把佩里克莱斯叫来。”

佩里克莱斯是随队希腊语翻译员,是我们在亚尼纳吸纳的一位优秀人才。当时,他在亚尼纳当地教书,但是,战争一爆发,他就没有书可教了。“孩子们都不来学校了,”他当时说。“他们都上山战斗了。我总不能对着空空的桌椅板凳教算术吧。”

佩里克莱斯走了进来。他上了年纪,胡子长了出来,鼻子又长又尖,一对灰色的眼睛尽显忧伤之情。你看不见他的嘴,但是说话时,看他胡子的样子,就会知道他在笑。

“问她叫什么名字,”蒙凯吩咐道。

他用希腊语对小女孩说了一句,小女孩抬起头,说道:“卡蒂娜。”她就说了这三个字。

“听着,佩里克莱斯,”彼得说,“问问她,坐在村子里的那堆废墟上干什么。”

芬恩说:“看在上帝的分上,别再打扰她了。”

彼得说:“我们发现她时,她坐在村子里的那堆东西上干什么。”

佩里克莱斯在她身边的长凳上坐下,跟她说话。他轻柔地说着,帮着安慰她。你可以看得出来,他说话的时候,他的胡子上露出微笑的样子。小女孩听着,似乎过去了很长的时间,才开口讲话。讲话时,只不过几个字、几个字地往外蹦。随后,老人翻译道:“她说,她的家人被压到石头底下了。”

帐篷外面,雨下得更大了。雨滴拍打在食堂帐篷的顶部,“啪啪啦啦”地在帆布上弹跳,弄得帐篷跟着阵阵颤抖。我起身走到帐篷门边,掀起门帘子。外面烟雨迷蒙,隐没了远处的群山,但是,我清楚,群山就耸立在我们周围,四面八方无所不在。我有一种感觉,群山在嘲笑我们,嘲笑我们人少势微,嘲笑我们这些飞行员无能为力、有勇无为。我感到,群山才是智者,而不是我们。就在那天早晨,一千架德国战机在奥林匹斯山的阴影下集结,难道不是群山一转身,朝向北部的台佩莱纳时最先看到的吗?多多纳山顶的积雪一天内融化,雪水形成一条条小河奔流而下,冲毁了我们的着陆场地,这难道不是真实发生的吗?卡塔菲迪山将头部埋进一片云中,我们的飞行员毫不知情,意欲从白云中飞过,结果撞上了其遍布岩石的双肩,难道不是这样的吗?

我站在帐篷门口,透过掀起来的门帘子看着外面的雨。此时,我清清楚楚地知道,群山已经与我们势不两立。这一点,我从骨子里都能感觉得到。

我走回帐篷,发现芬恩坐在卡蒂娜身旁,尝试着教她英语单词。我不知道他的教学是否有进展,但是,我确确实实知道,只要让她欢笑起来,那么,他做得就相当出色了。我现在还记得,当时突然间听到她大声笑了起来,我们大家都抬起头,看着她的笑脸。那张小小的笑脸与以前的脸孔简直有天壤之别。这一点,除了芬恩之外,没人能够做得到。芬恩这个人欢快无比,在他面前你想严肃起来都很困难。他是个乐天派,高高的个子,黑黑的头发。只见他坐在那儿的长登上,面带微笑,身体前倾,轻声细语地教卡蒂娜说英语,教她如何学会欢笑。

第二天,天空清澈,我们又一次看到了周围的群山。大部队已经朝温泉关方向慢慢地撤退,我们则驾机在撤退的部队上空巡视了一圈。在这一过程中,我们遭遇了几架德军“梅塞施米特”式战机,还有几架“容克斯”87式战机,这些飞机正俯冲轰炸我们的士兵。我想,我击落了其中几架,但是,桑迪的飞机却不幸被击中,往下滑行。三十秒的时间里,我一动不动坐在驾驶位置上,眼看着他的飞机慢慢地向下盘旋。我坐在那儿,等待着,希望他跳伞。我记得,我打开无线电对讲机,轻轻地喊道:“桑迪,你现在必须跳伞了。你必须跳了,飞机快要着地了。”但是,他的飞机里并没有弹出降落伞。

飞机着陆、缓慢滑行一段距离之后,我们看到了卡蒂娜,她正跟医生一起站在疏散帐篷外面。一个如虾米般瘦弱的小姑娘穿着件脏兮兮的印花衣服站在那里,看着飞机一架架着陆。然后,她一边往帐篷里走,一边对芬恩说:“札格里西斯仙纳。”

芬恩问:“佩里克莱斯,这句话是什么意思?”

“那句话的意思只是‘你又回来了。’”回答完,佩里克莱斯微笑了一下。

飞机起飞时,小女孩已经拨拉手指数过飞机的数目,而现在,她却发现少了一架。我们围拢在一起,往下卸降落伞,她就趁机问少了一架飞机的事儿。突然之间,有人说:“注意,敌机来了。”一大群细小的、黑色的飞机剪影通过小山的间隙飞来,向机场俯冲下来。

人们一阵忙乱,奔向狭长的掩壕。我记得看见芬恩一把抓住卡蒂娜的腰部,抱起她跟我们一起奔跑。我记得,在奔往壕沟的途中,还看见卡蒂娜当时如同猛虎一般意欲挣脱。

一到壕沟,芬恩就将她放下,她就立刻跳了出来,跑到机场上。梅塞施米特式战斗机俯冲下来,机上的机关枪连续狂射。这些飞机俯冲得太低了,你都能够清楚地看到护目镜下面敌方飞行员那高高突起的鼻子。射出的子弹在四周的地面上激起阵阵尘烟。我看到我们的一架飓风战机突然起火,还看到卡蒂娜岔开双腿,背对着我们,就站在机场的正中央,眼睛看着德军飞机一架架俯冲而过。在我的一生中，从来没有见过任何比这位希腊孤女更渺小、更愤怒、更猛烈的。她似乎在冲着敌机喊叫，但敌机的噪音太强，除了引擎的轰鸣以及机上发出的枪声，什么都听不见。

接下来，一切都结束了。敌机来得快，去得也快。除了芬恩，大家都没有多说什么。分恩说道："我不会做那样的事情，永远也做不出来。就算是我发了疯，也不会做出那样的事情。"

那天晚上，蒙凯拿出中队的记录手册，将卡蒂娜的名字加了进去。负责设备的军官接到命令，发给她一座帐篷。于是，1941 年 4 月 11 日，她就成为中队的一员。

两天的时间里，她就熟悉了中队里所有飞行员的名字或者绰号，而且，芬恩已经教会她说"运气好吗?"以及"干得不错!"等句子。

但是，那段时期战斗飞行任务很繁重。尽力一小时、一小时地回想那段时期的事情时，一切都在心里变得朦胧模糊起来。我记得最多的事情就是，当时护卫"布雷尼"单翼轰炸机到发罗拉去。要是没有护卫任务的话，就飞到阿尔巴尼亚边境，向那里地面上的意大利卡车扫射，或者是去紧急救援诺森伯兰团，那个团发出紧急求救信号说，欧洲轴心国一半的飞机围住了他们，对他们狂轰滥炸。

那些事情我一样也无法记住，就算是记住了，也不是那么清楚，但是，有两件事情除外。其中一件是关于卡蒂娜以及她与我们形影不离的情景。她每到一处，都令那里看到她的人们兴高采烈、快乐无比。另一件事情与布尔有关。布尔是一个大块头的男子，宽厚的双肩稍微向上隆起，胸部就像是橡木的桌面。战争爆发前，他干过很多的事情，那些事情中的大部分其他人是无法做到的，除非在还没有开始干的时候，承认这样一个事实：生与死毫无差别。他这个人不善言谈、不拘小节。每进入一个房间，或者一座帐篷，他看起来总是一副做错了什么事情的样子：欲迈步进入，却又止步不前。我记得，有一天晚上布尔独自完成一次飞行巡逻任务后，走进食堂帐篷。当时，天渐渐黑了下来，他走进来的时候，我们大家正围坐在帐篷里，玩着掷硬币游戏。我们大家知道，他刚刚着陆。

他有点歉意地向四周瞥了一眼，然后说道："嗨，大家好。"随后就溜达到吧台那儿,拿出一瓶啤酒。

有人问:“布尔,看到什么没有呢?”

布尔回答:“看到了。”说完,他就不断地摆弄手中的啤酒瓶。

我想我们大家的兴趣都放在掷硬币游戏上面了,他回答完约摸五分钟的时间内没人说过什么话。接下来,彼得问:“布尔,你看到了什么?”

布尔身体靠在吧台上,一会儿小口喝着啤酒,一会儿往空啤酒瓶里吹气,酒瓶发出低沉的声响。然后,再喝啤酒,再吹响,就这样交替进行着。

彼得问:“你看到了什么呢?”

布尔放下酒瓶,抬起头来。“五架‘S-79’型轰炸机,”他说。

我记得听见他说过那事,但是,我也记得我们当时正玩到兴头上。况且,芬恩又要赢一把了。我们大家看着他,但他没有掷中,于是,彼得说:“芬恩,我想你赢不了啦。”芬恩说:“见鬼去吧。”

游戏结束,我抬起头,看见布尔仍然靠在吧台上,向啤酒瓶吹气,酒瓶发出声响。

他说:“这声音听起来就像老毛里塔尼亚号进入纽约港时发出的声音。”说完,他又接着往瓶里吹气。

“S-79怎么了?”我问。

他不再向瓶子里吹气,将瓶子放了下来。

“我将它们击落了。”

这话,大家都听到了。就在那一刻,帐篷里的十一名飞行员都停止了各自忙碌的事情,十一只脑袋“唰”的一下,转了过来,看着布尔。只见布尔又喝了一口啤酒,安静地说:“曾经有那么一次,我数了数,空中竟然总共漂浮着十八只降落伞。”

几天过后,他又接着执行巡逻任务,但却没有返回。不久以后,蒙凯收到一条来自雅典的消息,消息称:飞行中队要移动到埃莱夫西斯港,从那里保卫雅典,并掩护大部队通过温泉关撤退。

卡蒂娜要乘坐卡车走,于是,我们嘱咐医生要照看好她,确保她安全抵达,因为乘车的路程需要一天的时间。我们十四名飞行员则越过群山向南飞去,两点半的时候降落在埃莱夫西斯港。那里的机场真不错,有跑道,也有机库。再好不过的是,从那里到雅典,开车仅仅需要二十分钟的时间。

那天晚上天渐渐黑下来的时候,我双手插兜,站在帐篷外面,看着太阳落山,想着要去执行的任务。我越是想着要去执行的任务,我越是清楚:这个任务不可能完成。于是,我抬起头,又一次看到了群山。这里的群山高耸入云,山上光秃秃的。群山环绕在我们的四周,只有南部有一个缺口,那里通向开阔的大海,是比雷埃夫斯港的所在地。这里的群山肩并肩站立着,从四面八方向我们拥挤而来,离我们更近了。我知道,每天夜晚天黑下来之后,我们都精疲力竭地在帐篷里进入了梦乡,而那些山则会向前移动,蹑手蹑脚地、悄无声息地向前靠近一些,一点声响都没有发出来。到了最后的某一天,群山就会向前猛地一冲,随即将我们推入大海。

芬恩从他所在的帐篷里出来了。

"你看到群山了吗?"我问。

"山里面全是神仙,但并无善意可言,"他回应道。

"我真希望它们保持静止不动的状态,"我说。

芬恩抬头看了看帕纳斯山和彭德利康山的悬崖峭壁。

"山里面全是神仙,"他说。"半夜有的时候,趁着月色你能看见那些神仙坐在山巅。我们当初在帕拉米西亚村的时候,就看见了彭德利康山上的神仙,他的块头大得很,就像是一座房子,但却没有形状,颜色相当黑。"

"你看见他了吗?"

"当然,我看见了。"

"什么时候?"我问。"芬恩,你是什么时候看见他的?"

芬恩说:"我们进雅典城吧,去看看那里的女人。"

第二天,卡车载着地面人员和装备轰隆隆地奔着机场而来,卡蒂娜坐在领队那辆卡车的前排座位上,医生就坐在她的旁边。她跳下卡车,一边向我们挥手,一边向我们奔跑而来,边跑边笑,以希腊语的发音方式喊着我们的名字,显得很好笑。她仍然穿着那身脏兮兮的印花衣服,前额部位仍然围着一条绷带。太阳照亮了她的头发。

我们带着她进入了早已为她准备好的帐篷,也给她看了那件小棉睡衣,那件睡衣是前一天晚上,芬恩神秘兮兮地从雅典城搞到的。睡衣是白色的,前面绣了许多小蓝鸟。我们大家都认为睡衣很漂亮。卡蒂娜急于要穿上睡衣,于是,我们费了九牛二虎之力才向她解释清楚,那衣服是睡觉时穿的。芬恩不得不做出一连串复杂的动作来说服她,这些动作包括假装穿上睡衣、跳到床上、熟睡进入梦乡等。这些动作芬恩做了不下六个来回。最终,卡蒂娜使劲儿点了点头,表示明白了。

接下来的两天里,安然无事。只是,另一支中队的剩余人员从北部赶来,加入我们的中队。这些新加入的成员带来了六架飓风战机,这样,我们总共就有约二十架战机了。

然后,我们就原地待命。

第三天,德国侦察机露面了,在比雷埃夫斯港的高空盘旋。于是,我们起飞追逐,但一次也没有赶上时机逮住它们。这是情有可原的,因为我们的雷达型号很是特殊,现在已经老掉牙了,我甚至怀疑:我们的雷达是否还能起作用。希腊举国上下——每个村落里、每座山上、每个岛屿上,全民皆兵。他们都通过野战电话机跟我们这间小小的作战指挥室相连。

指挥室里没有指挥官,因此,我们大家白天轮流执勤。第四天轮到我在指挥室执勤,对于那天发生的事情我记忆犹新。

早晨六点三十分的时候,电话嗡嗡响起。

"这里是'A-7',"一个颇具希腊口音的声音说道。"这里是'A-7',头顶上空噪音阵阵。"

我看了看地图,发现亚尼纳旁边有一个小圈,里面标上了"A-7"的字样。地图表层是用明胶片覆盖着的,于是,我就在"A-7"旁边的明胶片上做了个叉形标记符号,写上"阵阵噪音",随便也标上了时间:"06:31"。

三分钟过后,电话又一次响起。

"这里是'A-4',这里是'A-4'。我上方噪音不断,"一个上了年纪的人用颤抖的声音说道，“但是，我却什么都看不见，因为云层很厚。”

我看了看地图，发现“A－4”地区是卡拉瓦山。于是，我又在明胶片上做了个叉形标记符号，写上“噪音不断——06:34”的字样。然后，我在亚尼纳和卡拉瓦之间画了一条直线，发现线条直指雅典方向。因此，我发出信号，示意“备战”状态的人员紧急起飞应战。这些人员起飞升空，在雅典城上空盘旋。后来，他们发现一架“容克斯”88型战机在他们飞机上方的高空搞侦察，但是，他们从未逮住这架敌机，因为他们的雷达运转起来就是这个样子。

那天晚上完成执勤任务时，我不禁想：那个年迈的希腊人独自一人住在“A－4”地区的小屋子里，坐在卡拉瓦山的山坡上，抬头仰望苍茫的天空，不分白天黑夜时刻听着天空里传来的飞机噪音。我想象得出他当时的迫切神态：听到天空里传来声响，一把抓起电话；电话另一端的声音重复着他报告的信息，并对他表示感谢；每每此时，他一定感到开心无比。我想到了他身上穿的衣服，想知道那身衣服是否足以保暖。不知为何，我想到了他脚上的靴子，几乎可以肯定，那双靴子的靴底磨得一点不剩，里面塞满了树皮和纸张。

当时的时间是 4 月 17 日，而蒙凯说下面这些话的时候，已经到了那天的晚上：“他们说德国兵到了拉米亚，那就意味着，我们处在他们战机的打击范围之内。好戏明天就要开场了。”

的确如此。拂晓时分，敌方轰炸机飞了过来，我方战机则在上空盘旋，观察着那些轰炸机，等待时机出击，但是，要是没有人对轰炸机实施干扰，我方战机则什么都做不了。

我想，在敌方轰炸机到来之前，我方有八架飓风战机已经升空。这次没有轮到我升空应战，于是，我就从地面观看这场空战，而卡蒂娜就站在我的身旁。这个女孩一句话都不说，但脑袋却不时地随着空中上下升降的银色小斑点移动着。我看见一架飞机拖着一股黑烟下落，随后又看了眼卡蒂娜。这个女孩子脸上露出的憎恨之情，如同一位胸中有恨的年迈妇女脸上所燃烧着的强烈的憎恨之情。她的恨分明就是一位年迈妇女的恨，看着就令人觉得不可思议。

这场空战中,我方失去了一名中士,他的名字叫唐纳德。

中午的时候,蒙凯收到了雅典发来的另一条信息,信息说首都的士气低沉,还要求每架可用的飓风战机都到城市上空编队飞行,目的就是向民众表明我们的强大程度和飞机数量之多。于是,我们中的十八人随即起飞升空,在主大街居民屋顶上方呈密集队形上下飞行。我可以看见下方的人们手搭凉棚、向上观看,看着我们从头顶飞过。在其中一条大街上,我还看见一位老妇人,从未抬头看我们一眼。下方没有一个人挥手致意,于是我知道,他们听任命运的安排了;下方没有一个人挥手致意,于是我知道,尽管我看不到他们的脸,但我们从上空飞过并不令他们面露喜色。

然后,我们转头飞向温泉关,沿途在雅典卫城上空转了两圈。这是我第一次如此近距离地观看到雅典卫城。

我看见了一座小山——看起来近乎一个小土丘,看见山顶立着一些白色的柱子,柱子数量众多,秩序完美地排列在一起,但并没有挤到一起。在阳光的照耀下,这些柱子色泽亮白。当时看着这些柱子的时候,我不禁纳闷儿起来:在这样一座小山的顶部,谁会以如此优雅的方式放置这么多柱子,又是如何放置的呢?

接下来,我们飞到了温泉关的上空,我看见一长串、一长串的汽车慢慢地向南行驶,驶向大海的方向。我偶尔看见一缕缕白色的烟雾,那是炮弹落到山谷里爆炸时发出的。我还看见其中的一枚直接击中了道路,将一长串卡车一分为二,但是,我们却看不见敌人的飞机。

着陆后,蒙凯说:"赶快再加满油,然后再起飞升空。我想,敌机正等着要将我们消灭在地面上。"

但为时已晚。我们着陆五分钟后,敌机就从天空俯冲而来。我记得,当时我在二号机库的飞行员室,正跟芬恩和一名高个子的大块头男子交谈,他的名字叫帕迪,头发乱蓬蓬的。谈着谈着,我们就听到子弹在机库的波纹状铁皮屋顶上扫射的声音,紧接着传来了阵阵爆炸声。于是,我们三个人就往屋子中间的小木桌子底下钻。但是,桌子翻倒了,于是,帕迪将其放好,爬到了下面。"藏在桌子底下有一种说不清的感觉，"他说，"感觉藏在桌子底下比较安全。"

芬恩说："我从来都没有什么安全感。"他坐在地板上，看着子弹在屋子波纹状铁皮的墙壁上射出一个个洞来。子弹击中铁皮时，发出噼里啪啦的响声。

接下来，我们便勇敢起来，站起身向门外张望，看到外面有很多梅塞施米特 109 式战机在机场上空盘旋。这些战机一个接一个拉起，然后俯冲飞过机库，同时用机关枪向地面狂扫。更有甚者，他们一边扫射，还一边滑开驾驶舱盖，随手向外甩小型炸弹。这些小炸弹一落地就炸开，释放出数不清的大块铅弹，猛烈地四下飞散。我们刚刚听到的就是这样的爆炸声，还有铅弹击中机库时发出的极大噪音。

接下来，我看到那些地勤人员从狭长的壕沟里站起身，用步枪朝梅塞施米特敌机射击，射完再装弹，然后再尽可能快地射击，边射击边咒骂、喊叫。他们只是用步枪瞄准飞机射击，显得既胜算渺茫，又可笑荒唐。在埃莱夫西斯，唯有如此防御了。

突然之间，梅塞施米特飞机都转头朝老窝飞去，但是，只有一架没有往回飞，却向下滑落，没有放下起落架就以腹部着地，平稳地落到机场上。

接下来就是一阵阵的喧嚣和骚动。我们周围的希腊人提高嗓门喊叫起来，跳上辅助救火车，朝坠落的德军飞机奔去。与此同时，更多的希腊人从机场的各个角落奔涌而出，喊着、叫着，要求敌方飞行员血债血还。这属于复仇行为，也无法多加指责。但是，还有其它方面的问题需要考虑的：我们想审讯一下敌方飞行员，得留活口。

站在柏油、碎石铺就的飞机跑道上的蒙凯冲着我们大喊，于是，我、芬恩以及帕迪三人就跟着他一起跑向一辆客货两用车，那辆车停放在离我们不到五十米的地方。蒙凯跳上车，快如闪电，随后发动引擎将车开走，而车开走的瞬间，我们三个人刚好跳到了车的踏板上。乘坐辅助救火车的那些希腊人由于车速不快，离坠落的敌机还有一百八十米远，而其他那些奔涌而来的希腊人则离得更远。蒙凯开得很快，把那些人甩到了四十五米开外。

我们三个踩着踏板跳上车，奔向梅塞施米特飞机。那架飞机的驾驶舱里坐着一名金发男孩,脸颊粉红,眼睛蓝蓝。我还从来没有看见过谁的脸,像他的脸那样,恐惧不堪。

他对蒙凯说:“我的腿中弹了。”

我们将他从驾驶舱里拖出来,放入车中,而那些希腊人则站在四周观瞧着。子弹击碎了他小腿前部的骨头。

我们开车将他载回去,交给了医生。这时,我看见卡蒂娜站在近旁,看着那个德国人的脸。这名九岁的希腊小女孩站在那儿,看着那名德国男孩,但讲不出话来,甚至无法移动。只见她的双手紧紧攥住衣服的下摆,眼睛盯着那名男孩的脸。“什么地方出错了,”她似乎这样说道。“一定是搞错了。这个德国人脸颊粉红、头发金色、眼睛蓝蓝,不可能是那帮家伙中的一员。他就是一个普普通通的男孩子嘛。”她看着他被放到担架上抬走后,转过身,穿过草地,向自己住的帐篷跑去。

晚上吃饭的时候,我只吃了点煎沙丁鱼,面包或者奶酪什么的就吃不下去了。三天以来,我一直感觉自己的胃不太对劲儿,有一种空落落的感觉,就像一个人被手术前所具有的那种感觉,或者被拔牙前在牙医室等待时所产生的那种感觉。三天之中,每天一整天的时间里都有这种感觉——从早晨醒来那一刻起,到晚上入睡那一刻止。彼得就坐在我的对面,于是,我就问他这种感觉是怎么回事。

“这种感觉,我已经有一周了,”他说。“对肠胃有好处,可以让肠胃松弛下来。”

“德军战机就像是利肝药片,”芬恩坐在桌腿的位置,说道。“对你有很大的好处,难道不是吗,医生?”

医生回答:“或许你服用的过量了。”

“我是服药过量了,”芬恩说。“德国利肝药片,我服过量了,都怨我服前没有阅读瓶子上的说明:退役前服两片。”

彼得说:“我很想退役。”

晚饭后,我们三人跟蒙凯一道向机库走去。途中,蒙凯说:“对这种低空扫射,我很是担心。敌方从不攻击机库的,因为他们知道,我们从不往机库里放什么东西的。我想,今晚我们将四架战机集中起来,放入二号机库。”

那个主意不错。通常情况下,飓风战机分散放在机场的四周,但是,却被一个个摧毁,因为作战时,它们不可能同时升空的。于是,我们四个人一人开出一架,慢慢地滑进二号机库,然后我们齐心协力将滑动式机库大门关上、锁好。

第二天早晨太阳还没有从群山后面升起的时候,一群容克斯 87 式敌机就奔了过来,将二号机库从地球表面炸得踪影全无。他们的轰炸技术很不错,都直击目标,甚至没有一次偏离到机库的两边。

那天下午,敌人夺走了彼得的生命。当时,他飞向一个名叫哈尔基斯的村子,那个村子当时正遭受容克斯 88 式敌机的轰炸,但没有人再看到他。欢快、爱笑的彼得啊,他的母亲住在肯特郡的一座农场上。母亲常常给他写信,用的是长长的、淡蓝色的信封,他将信装在衣兜里,随身携带。

自从我来到这个飞行中队起,就始终跟彼得同住一个帐篷。那天晚上我躺下后,他又回到了帐篷。你没有必要相信我,我也不期望你相信我,但是,我给你讲的都是当时实际发生的事情。

我总是先上床,因为在那样的帐篷里,没有供两个人同时转身的空间,而彼得通常在我上床两三分钟后回来。那天晚上,我上床躺下,心里想:今晚他不会回来了。我想象着,飞机也许在某个荒凉的山坡坠毁,或者坠落海底,他的尸体躺在飞机里,跟飞机残骸纠缠到一块儿。我只希望,他的葬礼会举行得体面一些。

突然间,我听到有东西移动的声音,只见帐篷的门帘打开,又合上,但是听不见脚步声。接着,我听到他坐到自己床上的声音,这种声音在过去的数周里,我每天晚上都能听得见,而且他每次发出的声音都是一样的:“嘭”的一声坐下,行军床的木头腿随即发出“嘎吱嘎吱”的声响。两只飞行靴先后脱下,扔到地面,而且,其中一只脱下来所用的时间总是另一只的三倍。然后,一条毯子被轻轻地拉到身上,发出窸窣的声音,随即一张摇摇晃晃的床由于一个男子的体重而被压得咔嚓作响。

这些声音我每天晚上都能听得见,不仅声音一样,而且发出的顺序也是一样的。现在,我从床上坐起来说道:“彼得。”帐篷里很黑,我的声音格外响亮。

“哈喽,彼得,你今天运气不佳,很倒霉吧。”但是,没有回应。

尽管如此,我却没有感到心神不安,或者恐惧不堪,但我记得当时我用手指触摸了一下自己的鼻尖,以肯定我当时不是在做梦。接下来,由于我很困乏,就睡着了。

早晨醒来,我看了眼那张床,发现的确有人在上面睡过了,但是,我没有让任何人来看,哪怕是芬恩。我只是把毯子放回原位,然后拍了拍枕头。

就在那一天,也就是1941年4月20日,雅典之战爆发,我们参战了。这场战役也许是有史以来最后一场大混战,因为现如今,飞机和人员都是编队作战,只要指挥官一声令下,进攻起来都是井然有序、有条不紊的。现如今,除非在极个别场合,空中不再进行那样的大混战了。然而,雅典之战耗时很长,是一场漂亮的空中大混战。在长达半个小时的时间里,我方十五架飓风战机应战众多的德国轰炸机和战斗机,其数量在一百五十到二百架之间吧。

下午的时候,敌方的轰炸机早先一步飞了过来。当时是和煦春日里的一天,太阳第一次发出一丝只有夏日才有的温暖的光线。天空蔚蓝,只是有几缕淡淡的云彩在这儿点缀一下、在那儿装饰几点。在蔚蓝天空的映衬下,群山轮廓清晰地凸显出来,显得黑压压的。

彭德利康山的头部已不再被云层覆盖,只见它俯身我们上方,面目狰狞,令人生畏。它观察着下方的每一个举动,清清楚楚地知道我们所做的每一件事儿都意义不大。人很傻,人一出世,就意味着最终会死亡,而山脉和江河则永世存在,全然不会注意到时间的流逝。多年以前,屈指可数的几个斯巴达勇士守卫着温泉关,浴血奋战来抵抗入侵者,最后没有一个活下来,这个场面难道不是彭德利康山它自己当时居高临下、亲眼所见吗?列奥尼达斯在马拉松将波斯人打得七零八落,难道不是它亲眼所见吗?塞米斯托克利斯跟雅典人一道,将敌人从自己国家的海岸赶走,使敌人损失掉二百多艘帆船,这难道不是它俯视萨拉米斯、面临大海、亲眼所见吗?它亲眼见到所有这些事情，还亲眼见到许多其他方面的事情，而现在，它在我们上方俯视着。在它眼中，我们等同于不存在。这座山脸上的表情几乎等于是对我们的轻蔑和不屑一顾。我想，有那么片刻时间，我能够听到山中诸神的嘲笑声。那些神仙清楚得很，我们人少势微、寡不敌众，最终一定损失惨重。

午饭刚过，轰炸机就奔了过来，而且数量众多。我们抬起头，看见天空满是小小的银色斑点。阳光照在一百对翅膀上，光线跳跃着，闪烁着光芒。

我们一共有十五架飓风战机，它们在空中暴风雨般地奋勇应战。对于这样一场战役，要记住其中的很多内容不太容易。但是，我记得我抬头仰望，看见天空中有一大片黑压压的小点点。我记得我当时独自思忖：那些小点点不可能是飞机，之所以不可能就是因为世界上没有那么多的飞机。

接着，他们对我们发起了进攻。我记得我当时轻轻翻转了一下机翼，以便可以急速转圈。随后，我只记得一两个细小事件，如同照片一般印在我的心里。一架梅塞施米特敌机从我的右舷正后部发起进攻，敌机的机关枪喷出阵阵火焰；一个德国飞行员跳伞，伞打开的时候起火了；有一个德国飞行员从我旁边拉升飞机，冲着我伸出手指，做出粗俗无礼的动作；飓风战机与梅塞施米特飞机相撞；一架飞机把一名飞行员扯住了，当时这名飞行员正乘降落伞下降，但他的伞却朝地面疯狂地旋转，很是吓人，结果，人跟伞都从飞机的左舷悬吊下来；两架轰炸机突然转弯要避开一架战斗机，却彼此相撞，我清清楚楚地记得一名飞行员从碰撞产生的烟雾和碎片中被一下子甩了出来，双臂伸开、双腿岔开悬吊在半空中。我告诉你，那场战役中没有什么事情不会发生。有那么一会儿，我看到孤零零一架飓风战机绕着帕纳斯山峰紧急转弯，后面跟着九架梅塞施米特飞机。紧接着，我记得，突然之间，天空晴朗起来。此时，视野之中看不见任何飞机了，战斗一下子结束了。我调转机头，朝着埃莱夫西斯方向往回飞。途中，我向下看去，看到雅典城、比雷埃夫斯港，还有大海的边缘，大海沿着海湾弯弯曲曲地延伸，一直向南延伸至地中海。我看到了比雷埃夫斯港,那里还有炸弹纷纷落下,烟雾和大火从码头上方升起。我看到了狭窄的大海沿岸平原,上面有一小堆、一小堆的火燃烧着,细细的烟柱和黑黑的烟雾盘旋升起,往东飘散。那些火堆是飞机被击落后燃烧引起的,我只希望那当中一架飓风战机都没有。

就在那时,我遭遇到一架容克斯88型战机,是一架掉队的敌机,就是刚才实施轰炸任务时最后一个返回的。这架飞机遇到了麻烦,其中一只引擎往外汩汩地冒着黑烟。我朝它开了枪,但是,我认为开不开枪意义不大,因为它本身就在不断下降。当时我们都在大海之上,我看得出,对方不准备着陆,也没去着陆。那架飞机腹部朝下平稳地落向蓝色的比雷埃夫斯湾,落在离海岸三公里多一点的海域。我尾随着、盘旋着,以便确定其机组人员安全出舱、登上紧急救生筏。

那架飞机开始慢慢地下沉,机头浸没到海水里,机尾则翘起,指向空中。没有任何迹象表明,其机组成员还有存活下来的。突然之间,在毫无防备的情况下,其尾部机关枪开火了。这帮家伙用机尾机关枪开火射击,子弹在我的飞机右舷凿出参差不齐的孔洞。我立即调转机头。记得我当时冲他们大骂。我滑开驾驶舱罩盖,大喊:"你们这些该死的、胆大妄为的杂种,希望你们都淹死。"那架轰炸机很快地就从机尾沉入了大海。

我返回的时候,大家都围拢在机库外面站着,清点伤亡情况。卡蒂娜坐在一只箱子上,眼泪顺着面颊流淌,但却没有哭出声来。芬恩跪在她身旁,用英语跟她静静地、轻柔地说着,全然忘记她不懂英语这个事实。

那场战役中,我们损失掉三分之一的飓风战机,但德方损失得更惨重。

医生正在给一个烧伤的包扎伤口,抬起头说:"轰炸机从空中跌落下来时,你真应该听听机场上希腊人的欢呼声。"

我们聚拢在一起站着,交谈着。这时候,一辆卡车驶到近前,一个希腊人下了车,说车里装了些尸体碎块。"这块手表,"他说,"是戴在那只胳膊上的。"他说的是一块银色的腕表,表盘闪闪发光,表的背面写了几个词的首字母,但我们并没有向车内看去。

我想，现在我们只剩下九架飓风战机了。

那天傍晚，一位级别很高的皇家空军军官从雅典赶来，说道："明天拂晓时分，你们都得飞到迈加拉——海岸线以下大约十六公里的地方。那里有一个小机场供你们降落，陆军会连夜抢修那个机场。那里有两台大型压路机，会把场地压得很平整的。你们一着陆，就要将飞机藏到橄榄树林中，那片树林位于机场的南端。地面人员会继续往南移动，到阿尔戈斯城去，你们随后加入到他们的行列中。在此之前，你们可能会在迈加拉展开一两天的军事行动。

芬恩说："卡蒂娜哪里去了？医生，你一定得找到她，确保她安全抵达阿耳戈斯城。"

医生说："我会的。"我们清楚，他是可以信赖的。

第二天拂晓时分，天还没怎么亮，我们就起飞，飞往十六公里外迈加拉的那个小机场。着陆后，我们将飞机藏进橄榄树林，折断一些橄榄枝覆盖在飞机上。然后，我们坐在一座小山的山坡上，等待下达命令。

太阳从群山顶部升起的时候，我们看到机场对面有一大批来自迈加拉村的希腊村民朝我们机场方向走来。他们有好几百人，多数是妇女和儿童，都朝我们机场方向走来，一边走一边加快了步伐。

芬恩说："搞什么名堂？"于是，我们大家都从小山坡上站起来，观察着，想知道他们要做些什么。

他们分散到机场的四周，捡来一抱抱灌木和蕨类植物，抱到机场上，然后自动排成长排，将捡来的灌木和蕨类植物分撒到草坪上。原来，他们是在帮助我们伪装着陆场地。压路机当时将地面压平以供我们着陆的同时，也留下了痕迹，这些痕迹从空中很容易发现。所以呢，希腊人纷纷走出村子，不管是男人、女人，还是孩子，都帮忙摆平这件事儿。直到今天，我也不知道是谁告诉他们这样做的。他们拉开距离形成一大长排，走过机场，边慢慢向前走，边分撒灌木。我和芬恩走过去，走到了他们的行列当中。

他们之中，多数是年迈的妇女和上了年纪的男子，都很瘦小，面带忧伤之情，黝黑的脸上布满了深深的皱纹。他们慢慢地行走，边走边分撒灌木。我俩走过他们的时候,他们就停下来,微笑着,用希腊语说着一些我们听不懂的话语。其中一个孩子递给芬恩一朵粉红色的小花,但芬恩不知道该拿那朵花做什么,于是,他就手里拿着那朵花,走来走去。

然后,我俩走回小山坡那儿待命。很快,野战电话机嗡嗡响了起来,讲话的正是那位级别很高的军官。他说,一定得有人立刻飞回埃莱夫西斯一趟,取回重要消息,并把钱带回来。他还说,我们大家当晚必须离开迈加拉的小机场,赶往阿耳戈斯城。其他人则说,他们要等到我带着钱飞回来,然后再一起飞往阿耳戈斯城。

与此同时,有人告知那两个仍然在机场压路面的陆军人员,要把压路机毁掉,以免被德军弄到手。就在我往我驾驶的那架飓风战机驾驶舱钻的当儿,我记得,我看见两辆大型压路机穿过机场向彼此冲了过去。就在两辆车要碰撞到一起的瞬间,我记得,我看见那两名陆军人员向旁边跳了下去。紧接着,"轰"的一声巨响。我看见正在分撒灌木的希腊人都停止了动作,抬起了头。一瞬间,他们如岩石般静止不动,看着两辆撞到一起的压路机。接着,其中一名希腊人跑了起来,跑起来的是位年迈的妇女,她拔起双腿就往村子里跑,尽力奔跑。刹那之间,在场地里的所有男子、妇女、儿童似乎都惊慌失措起来,跟着她恐惧地奔跑。我想奔过去,跟在他们旁边奔跑,以便跟他们解释一下,对他们说:我很抱歉,但是别无他法。我想对他们说,我们不会忘记他们的,总有一天我们会回来的。但是,那样做一点作用也起不到。在迷惑不解和极度恐惧的情况之下,他们跑回家中。他们都不停地奔跑,哪怕年事已高,直至在我们的视线里消失。

我起飞了,飞回埃莱夫西斯,在一个废弃的机场降落,将飓风停好。那里一个人影都没有。走向机库的时候,轰炸机又奔了过来。于是,我躲进一条沟里面,直到他们轰炸完事才站起身,走向那间小小的指挥室。指挥室里,那部电话还放在桌子上,出于某种考虑,我拿起话筒,说道:"哈喽。"

另一端,一个很具德国口音的声音作了回应。

我说:"能听见我说话吗?"对方说:

“是的，能，能听见你说话。”

“好的，”我说，“仔细听好了。”

“是的，请继续。”

“这里是英国皇家空军。总有一天，我们会回来的，你明白吗？总有一天，我们会回来的。”

接着，我将电话线从插座上一把扯下来，将话机从紧闭着窗户的玻璃甩了出去。走到外面的时候，我看见一名小个子男子穿着老百姓的衣服，站在门口附近，他一只手握着一支左轮手枪，另一只手拿着一个小包。

“你想要什么东西吗？”他用纯正的英语问道。

我回答：“是的，我想要重要消息和文件，带回阿耳戈斯。”

“给你，”他说完，将小包递给我。“祝你好运。”

我飞回迈加拉。途中，我看见两艘希腊驱逐舰在近海区域一边燃烧，一边下沉。我盘旋在机场上空，等着别的飞机都滑行出来、起飞后，我们才一起飞向阿耳戈斯。

阿耳戈斯的降落地点就类似于一小块平坦的地面，四周被浓密的橄榄树林包围着。我们将飞机缓缓地滑入其中，隐藏起来。我不清楚这块场地有多长，但是，在上面着陆着实困难。你必须靠螺旋桨控制飞机，使其处于低空悬浮状态，飞机触地那一刻，你必须紧急制动，猛地将其拉住，然后在机头着地、机身意欲仰翻的同时，再释放制动将其拉回。最后，只有一架飞机滑出跑道坠毁。

地面人员早已达到。我们下飞机的时候，卡蒂娜跑上前来迎接。她手里拎着一篮子黑色橄榄果，每人给了些，然后指着我们的肚子，那意思是说，我们必须得吃下去。

芬恩弯下腰，用手挠乱了她的头发，说道：“卡蒂娜，等以后找一天时间，我们进城去，给你买一套新衣服。”卡蒂娜冲他笑了笑，但不明白他说的是什么意思。随后，我们大家开始吃起黑橄榄。

接下来，我向四周看了看，发现林子里到处都是飞机，林子的每一个角落都隐藏着一架飞机。问及此事后，我们才得知，希腊人将其整个空军所有飞机都运到阿耳戈斯，停放在那片小树林里。那都是些使用了很多年的飞机型号,没有一架的服役时间少于五年,我也不清楚究竟有多少架藏匿其中。

那天晚上,我们就睡在树下。我们给卡蒂娜裹上大大的飞行服,用飞行头盔给她当枕头。等她睡着后,我们围坐在一起吃黑橄榄,从大桶里往外倒带有树脂香味的葡萄酒喝,但是,我们疲乏得很,没有多久都进入了梦乡。

第二天一整天的时间里,我们看到一卡车、一卡车的军队沿着公路向大海方向移动,我们也尽可能多地起飞升空,在军队上方巡视。

德军不间断奔来,轰炸附近的道路,但是,他们还没有发现我们的新机场。

当天晚些时候,我们接到通知,要求每一架可用的飓风战机都要在傍晚六点起飞,以便为一次重要的海上运输保驾护航。于是,现在所剩的九架都加满了油,严阵以待。差三分钟六点的时候,我们开始将飞机缓缓滑出橄榄树林,停在场地上。

其中两架飓风首先起飞,可是,就在这两架飞机刚一离开地面,天空之中有某种黑乎乎的东西横扫过来,击中这两架飞机,当即着火。我向周围一看,发现至少有五十架梅塞施米特110型敌方战机在场地上方盘旋。甚至就在我看的当儿,有些敌机转头,向等待起飞的其余七架飓风俯冲而来。

做什么都来不及了。在第一轮突袭中,我们这几架战机无一幸免,都被击中,但是一个滑稽的事实是,只有一名飞行员受伤。现在,起飞是不可能的,因而我们跳出飞机,将受伤的飞行员从驾驶舱拽出来,一起跑向狭长的壕沟,壕沟很棒——大大的、深深的、弯弯曲曲的,是希腊人挖掘出来的。

梅塞施米特战机可以不慌不忙地进攻了,因为不管是从地面,还是从空中,都没有抵抗的力量存在,除了芬恩之外——他正用自己的左轮手枪射击呢。

特别是在敌机的机翼上装有加农机关炮的情况下,遭遇其低空扫射可不是一件令人愉快的事情。要是没有狭长的深壕沟躲避的话,简直就没有生存的希望可言。出于某种考虑,或许德军飞行员认为这个玩笑比较好开，于是，他们在攻击飞机前，先扫射狭长的壕沟。前十分钟时间里，我方人员绕着壕沟的拐角疯狂奔跑、疲于逃命，一面被困在壕沟的某处，因为来袭的敌机飞行方向与壕沟呈平行状态。这十分钟是在忙乱和恐惧中度过的，不时地有人喊“又有一架飞来了”，喊完后，就是一阵忙乱和奔跑，大家绕过拐角冲进壕沟的另一部分。

接着，德国飞机攻击飓风战机，同时，扫射一大片停放在橄榄树林各处的希腊老战机。敌机将这些飞机一个接一个击中，燃起了大火，而且，击中、引燃的过程井然有序、有条不紊。到处都发出巨大的噪音，到处都有子弹在喷射——树林里、岩石上、草地里。

我记得，当时我谨慎地透过壕沟的顶部向外窥探，看见一朵小白花就生长在离我鼻子几厘米远的地方。那朵花是纯白色的，长有三个花瓣。我记得，透过那朵小花看过去，我看见三架德军战机向我的那架停在机场另一端的飓风战机俯冲。我记得，当时我冲着它们大喊，尽管连我都不知道自己喊的是什么。

接着，突然之间，我看见卡蒂娜。她正从机场远端的一个角落全力奔跑起来，跑向火力交织、烟雾蒸腾的中心区域，机关枪在她的周围吐着火舌，飞机在她的周围熊熊燃烧。奔跑途中，她跌倒过一次，但是又飞速爬了起来，继续奔跑。最后停下，站在那儿，抬起了头，冲着一架架呼啸而过的敌机举起了双拳。

现在，她站在那儿，我记得，当时我看见其中一架梅塞施米特战机调转机头，低空直奔她而来。我记得，当时我想，这个小女孩太瘦小，敌机就是射击的话，也打不中的。我记得，当时那架飞机一边奔着她俯冲过来，机关枪一边喷射出阵阵火焰。我记得，当时我看见这位希腊小女孩在极其短暂的时间里，直视着飞机，身体一动不动。我记得，风吹起了她的头发。

接着，她倒下了。

接下来的那一刻，我永生难以忘怀。如同变魔术一般，人们从四面八方的地面蜂拥而出——从各自的壕沟里蜂拥而出，就像一群愤怒的狂人，涌向机场，奔向那位渺小、瘦弱的希腊孤女。她躺在机场的中央,一动不动。他们快速奔跑,奔跑中不时地蹲伏下来。我记得,当时我从自己躲避的狭长壕沟里跳了出来,加入到他们的行列。我记得,当时我什么都没有想,只是边奔跑边看着前面那名男子穿的靴子。我注意到,他的腿有点罗圈形,他穿的那条蓝裤子太长了。

我记得,当时我看见芬恩首先到场,紧随其后的是一位叫威如意的中士。他们两个抱起卡蒂娜就开始往回跑,跑向壕沟。我看到她的一条腿满是鲜血,骨瘦如柴,我还看见她的胸部涌出鲜血,染红了那件白色的印花衣服。就在一瞬间,我看见了她的那张脸,白得如同奥林匹斯山顶的积雪。

我在芬恩旁边奔跑着,芬恩边跑边不断地骂道:"这帮该死的杂种,该死的、残忍的杂种。"到达壕沟的时候,我记得我当时向四周看了看,发现周围既听不到噪音,也看不见扫射,敌机一下子都飞走了。

芬恩喊道:"医生呢?"突然之间,医生出现了,站在我们旁边,看着卡蒂娜,看着她的脸。

医生轻轻地摸了摸她的手腕,然后,头也不抬地说:"她已经死了。"

他们将她放到一棵小树下。我转过身去,看见四周全是数不清的飞机在熊熊燃烧,也看见自己的那架飓风战机在附近燃烧着。我站在那儿,目不转睛盯着自己那架飞机燃烧的火焰,火焰在引擎周围上下跳跃着,火舌舔舐着机翼的金属。这时,我感到绝望、渺茫。

我站在那儿,呆呆地盯着那火焰。看着,看着,火焰变得越来越红,透过火焰,我看到的不是横七竖八、冒着黑烟的飞机残骸,而是希腊人民心中燃烧着的、难以抑制的怒火,那火愈烧愈炽热,愈烧愈强烈。

我仍然盯着那火焰。看着,看着,我发现,在火焰的中心,也就是红色火焰燃起的地方,一股明亮的、白色的热浪升腾起来,那股热浪闪闪发亮,没有颜色。

看着,看着,那火焰的明亮的部分弥漫、扩散开来,开始泛黄,散射力增强,就像太阳的光芒。透过这层亮光,我看到一个小女孩站在一个场地的中央,太阳光照亮了她的头发。就在一瞬间,她抬头仰望天空,天空蔚蓝而清澈,没有一丝云彩。紧接着,她转过身,看着我。

就在她转身的时候，我看见她那件白色的印花衣服的前面被浸得通红——鲜血一样的颜色。

接下来，火焰消失了，大火也不再熊熊燃烧。在眼前，我只看到一架燃烧过后变得热烘烘的、扭曲变形飞机的残骸。在那里，我一定是站了很长的时间。

参考文献

[1] DAHL, R. The Wonderful Story of Henry Sugar and Six More [M]. England: Penguin Books Ltd., 2002. 2.

[2] DAHLl R. The Best of Roald Dahl [M]. England: Penguin Books Ltd., 2006. 2.

[3] DAHL, R. The Collected Short Stories of Roald Dahl [M]. England: Penguin Books Ltd., 1992.

[4] Dictionary. com LLC's. Dictionary. com [DB/OL]. Oakland, CA: Dictionary. com LLC's Online, http://dictionary. reference. com/.

[5] Farlex, Inc. The Free Online Dictionary [DB/OL]. Huntingdon Valley, PA: The Free Online Dictionary by Farlex, Inc. http://www. thefreedictionary. com/.

[6] HOWARD, K. Roald Dahl Fans [Z/OL]. Australia: http://www. roalddahlfans. com/ (1996 – 2013).

[7] Merriam – Webster, Incorporated. Merriam – Webster [DB/OL]. Springfield, MA: Merriam – Webster Online, http://www. merriam – webster. com/.

[8] Oxford University Press. Oxford Dictionaries [DB/OL]. Oxford: Oxford Dictionaries Online, http://www. oxforddictionaries. com/.

[9] Wikimedia Foundation, Inc. Wikipedia [DB/OL]. http://en. wikipedia. org/.

［10］ 陈钰. 畸形精神世界的工笔画家——谈罗·达尔的小说创作特色［J］. 武汉：外国文学研究，1985(4).66－69.
［11］ 金山软件. 金山词霸2009牛津版［CP］. 北京：北京金山软件有限公司，2008.
［12］ 施议对. 人间词话译注(增订本)［M］. 长沙：岳麓书社，2008.
［13］ 新华社译名室. 世界人名翻译大辞典［M］. 北京：中国对外翻译出版公司，2007.
［14］ 周定国. 世界地名翻译大辞典［M］. 北京：中国出版集团、中国对外翻译出版公司，2008.

后 记

我们对罗尔德·达尔“非儿童类”短篇故事(小说)进行研究和翻译已经持续三个多年头了。其间,因教学和其他科研的缘由,有所间断,但多数时间是在研读和翻译达尔的这部分短篇小说中度过的。研读、翻译达尔的这部分短篇作品共计六十篇。

在研究和翻译罗尔德·达尔的这部分作品的过程中,历尽了艰辛,特别是在翻译过程中,不时会遇到这样或那样的“坎坷”。达尔在写作过程中,时常会“卖弄”自己所掌握的某些专业方面的知识,如葡萄酒、收藏、音乐、医学等,这就逼着译者硬着头皮去熟悉相应的知识。另外,达尔还偶尔会“显摆”一下自己英语之外的词汇,如法语、拉丁语等,这对于译者来说,未免有些“捉襟见肘”了——有的词,任凭怎么查也不得结果。达尔原文中的某一段有时会罗列出若干的专有名词,本着一丝不苟的研究态度,翻译过程中对它们均一一查证——哪怕对其中某些表达已经相当熟悉了。对于这样的“坎坷”,下笔前会来回踱步、反复思量、仔细斟酌,正如鲁迅先生在译完《死魂灵》谈到翻译时所言:“我向来总以为翻译比创作容易,因为至少是无须构想。但到真的一译,就会遇着难关,譬如一个名词或动词,写不出,创作时候可以回避,翻译上却不成,也还得想,一直弄到头昏眼花,好像在脑子里面摸一个急于要开箱子的钥匙,却没有。”(鲁迅《“题未定”草·且介亭杂文二集》)

在研究和翻译罗尔德·达尔的这部分作品过程中,还会遇到语言及文化差异方面的“绊脚石”,处理起来颇费工夫,正如严复在谈《天演论》翻译的《译例言》中所言:“新理踵出,名目纷繁,索之中文,渺不可得，即有牵合，终嫌参差，译者遇此，独有自具衡量，即义定名。”另外，对于查询无果的地方，也得认真加以思考，甚至经过了很长时间才“创造性”地下笔定论，可谓“一名之立，旬月踟蹰。我罪我知，是存明哲”（严复《译例言》）。由此可见，译事之难，不亚于李太白笔下的“蜀道之难，难于上青天”了！

幸运的是，在对罗尔德·达尔这些“非儿童类”短篇小说进行研究和翻译过程中，我们得到了许多朋友和同事热情的帮助和有力的支持，感激之情无以言表。

对罗尔德·达尔短篇小说的研究和翻译源于英国朋友马礼（他的英文原名叫“Jonathan Rackham”，时任渤海大学外籍英语教师）2009年赠送给著者的一本书，书名叫《罗尔德·达尔小说精品集》（The Best of Roald Dahl）。在阅读这本书的过程中，得到了启发，萌生了要研究并翻译作家罗尔德·达尔“非儿童类”短篇小说的念头。我们2010年9月开始动笔，从此一发而不可收。在对原文理解过程中所遇到的难题，得到了马礼耐心而细致的解答，甚至在他回到英国后，还继续通过电子邮件、越洋电话等方式给予我们热情的解答。在此，衷心感谢好友兼同行的马礼，感谢他热情相助！

译文从初稿到成稿，虽经数次校正修改，仍然存在不少问题。此时，我们的学长兼兄长又兼同事的刘恩东先生及时伸出了援助之手，对最终的成稿在“忠实”的基础上进行了“通顺”方面的梳理。刘恩东先生虽身为渤海大学英语教师，但是，其汉语功力不可小觑，令吾等外语研究者难以望其项背，特别是他古汉语的功力，甚至超出很多古汉语的专业研究者。有了我们兄长的梳理和理顺，毛坯一样的成稿方焕发出光彩。兄长的修改，虽然有时只是增填一个字，或者是删除一个词，但却救译文于“水火”之中。可以说，没有兄长的理顺，名为“成稿”的译文只能如同一个咿呀学语、走路不稳的婴儿。在此，衷心感谢兄长刘恩东先生，感谢他辛苦的付出！

研究伊始，一个偶然的机会，我们搜索到克里斯廷·霍华德（Kristine Howard）创建并维护的网站“罗尔德·达尔粉丝网”（Roald Dahl Fans. com），并就罗尔德·达尔有关问题联系过霍华德女士，收到了她及时的回复。整个研究也因霍华德女士的网站而受益匪浅。在此,衷心感谢克里斯廷·霍华德女士,感谢她在网站里所提供的全面而翔实的资料!

同时,我们十分感谢渤海大学国际交流学院领导和教师给予我们的有力支持!十分感谢渤海大学外国语学院领导和教师给予我们的有力支持!十分感谢哈尔滨工业大学出版社田新华主任在出版方面提供的有力支持!十分感谢为本书的出版而忙碌的所有编辑人员和工作人员!同时,我们十分感谢为本研究提供帮助的所有朋友和同仁!

当然,由于时间和能力所限,错误在所难免,还望读者赐教、斧正,并多提宝贵意见。

对罗尔德·达尔"非儿童类"短篇故事(小说)研究、翻译所成之书,难免泛泛而论,甚至是流于平庸,但是,我们本着扎实做学问、做学问如做人的思想,从起点出发,稳扎稳打,力戒浮躁之风,勿求好高骛远。记得《礼记·中庸》里有言:"君子之道,譬如行远,必自迩,譬如登高,必自卑。"愿以此语共勉。

著者

于本凤　王永胜

2014 年早春于渤海大学